A SINNER AT THE HIGHLAND COURT

THE HIGHLAND LADIES BOOK EIGHT

CELESTE BARCLAY

OLIVER
HEBER
BOOKS
GNARLY WOOL PUBLISHING
EST. 2011

0 9 8 7 6 5 4 3 2 1

Published by Oliver Heber Books

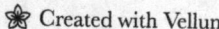 Created with Vellum

"Hell is yourself and the only redemption is when a person puts himself aside to feel deeply for another person."
~Tennessee Williams

It's not easy to forgive and forget when you must forgive yourself. We're all flawed, but in our flaws we can find our greatest opportunities.

Happy reading, y'all,
Celeste

SUBSCRIBE TO CELESTE'S NEWSLETTER

Subscribe to Celeste's bimonthly newsletter to receive exclusive insider perks.

Have you read *Their Highland Beginning, The Clan Sinclair Prequel?* Learn how the saga begins! This FREE novella is available to all new subscribers to Celeste's monthly newsletter. Subscribe on her website.

Subscribe Now

Have you chatted with Celeste's hunky heroes? Are you new to Celeste's books or want insider exclusives before anyone else? Subscribe for free to chat with the men of Celeste's *The Highland Ladies* series.

Chat Now

THE HIGHLAND LADIES

A Spinster at the Highland Court
A Spy at the Highland Court
A Wallflower at the Highland Court
A Rogue at the Highland Court
A Rake at the Highland Court
An Enemy at the Highland Court
A Saint at the Highland Court
A Beauty at the Highland Court
A Sinner at the Highland Court
A Hellion at the Highland Court
An Angel at the Highland Court
A Harlot at the Highland Court

PREFACE

The Highland Ladies follows the lives and loves of the ladies-in-waiting at King Robert the Bruce's court. If you are a fan of Highlander romances, then you've surely encountered the time period that spans the Wars of Scottish Independence, along with the rise and reign of Robert the Bruce. I have taken creative license in a number of areas, especially the creation of characters such as our hero and heroine, but the events in the early portion of this story are true to history.

Christianity was the only accepted religion in Medieval Europe, and the faith dominated people's everyday lives. If you follow the series, you'll notice that faith plays a part in many of our characters' experiences. I've incorporated this element not as a personal statement or advocation of any beliefs, rather because it would have been a realistic and integral part of their lives.

In this story, Madeline MacLeod was banished from Robert the Bruce's court by her brother Kieran during *A Wallflower at the Highland Court* and has made a home for herself at Inchcailleoch Priory. There is no definitive historical proof that this particular priory existed, but the name "island of the old women" leads historians to believe that one may have existed during the Middle Ages. There is an Inchcailleoch Island, and a priory does exist nearby on the mainland.

Since Madeline lived among and trained with the nuns, prayer would have consumed much of her day. She and her fellow postulants, novices, and nuns would have attended prayer services known as the Liturgy of Hours throughout the day and night. The worship schedule is sometimes referred to as the Divine Office, the Work of God (*opus dei*), or canonical hours.

I have incorporated several traditional prayers that would have been recited in Latin during this time period. All Masses and prayer services were conducted in Latin, so in reality, very few people understood what was said. But they would have known the routines and been able to recite the prayers by memory.

While the prayers are true to their Medieval form, I have used a little creative license to make some exist decades before their time. The "Lord's Prayer" appears in the Gospels of Matthew and Luke, so it would have been part of the Masses and prayer services during the early 14th century when our story takes place. If you'd like to read the prayer in its more antiquated form, Ewan Grant recites it in *A Rogue at the Highland Court*.

The "Apostle's Creed" first appeared in a letter dated as far back as 309 AD. Much like other prayers, there have been variations and alterations over the centuries, especially the 6th and 7th centuries AD.

The "Hail Mary" has been a cornerstone prayer in the Catholic Church for centuries, but its 13th century version would have been a simple "Hail Mary, full of grace, the Lord is with thee." I opted for the full prayer because of the point our heroine, Madeline, makes when she recites it.

Prayer beads have been a tradition in the Catholic Church since its early inception. Pious tradition states that the idea of the rosary was given to a saint during a dream where an apparition of the Virgin Mary appeared. Meditation while praying the rosary dates back to the late 1300s-early 1400s. Pope Pious, in the late 1300s, established the standard fifteen mysteries that Madeline says she must deeply meditate upon.

Praying the rosary generally takes about twenty minutes, but for Madeline's needs, I made it sound like it was much longer. The reference I make of how many times she recites it each day is purely a work of my imagination.

The other shorter prayers that are included in praying the rosary in this story were also common in the Middle Ages, but I don't think they necessitate quite the same explanation as the rosary, the "Lord's Prayer," the "Apostle's Creed," and the "Hail Mary." The verses of the hymn I included would have been familiar to many churchgoers.

Hopefully, this historical context makes it clear why I included these professions of faith primarily by our heroine Madeline but, at times, also our hero Fingal.

As always, the geography and the majority of the clan dynamics are true to the time period. But the specific actions of our characters is my imagination come to life.

I hope you enjoy *A Sinner at the Highland Court* and come to love Madeline MacLeod and Fingal Grant as much as I have.

Happy reading,
Celeste

PROLOGUE

I hate him. I hate him. I hate him. How can he do this to me? How could he pick her over me? That fat sow. Kieran will regret this till the day he dies. He and she both. This is her fault. All her fault. I hate her too.

Madeline MacLeod felt the four walls of her tiny convent cell closing in upon her. Her brother, Kieran, had dragged her from Robert the Bruce's royal court at Stirling Castle and dumped her at Inchcailleoch Priory earlier that week. She refused to accept that any of her words or actions had caused her fall from grace. She'd only spoken the truth each time she told Maude Sutherland how unconventionally curvaceous she was. Why her brother wanted to marry a woman who looked more like a tavern wench than a lady was beyond Madeline.

He just wants a good rut. He'll realize what a dreadful mistake he's made when he takes her home to Stornoway. He will realize that tupping her won't be worth the humiliation of having such a plain-faced, round as a barrel, heifer for a wife. He could have had Laurel Ross!

As Madeline listened to the bells toll for yet another Mass, she grimaced. All she seemed to do was pray these days, but God certainly wasn't listening because she remained at the priory despite her fervent appeals. She kneeled among the other novices, postulants, and nuns eight times throughout the day and night as they followed the Liturgy of Hours. The bells in the background signaled Prime, so she knew it was still very early. She'd already attended Matins in the middle of the night and Lauds at sunrise.

Madeline glanced out the narrow window set high in the wall, thinking that the masons must have designed it so the women couldn't escape. The sunlight, weak and dismal, matched Madeline's mood. When she lived at court, six o'clock in the morning was an hour she'd never seen. Now that she lived at the convent, she'd already been awake for an hour and a half.

Madeline dragged herself from her cot and her introspection. She could feel her anger simmering below the surface, and if she wanted to avoid another outburst—which would result in two days of wearing a hair shirt for penance — she would do well to calm herself. She splashed freezing water from the washbasin onto her face. It was refreshing, but it only reminded her of the austerity she now faced daily. Already dressed in her postulant's dark gray gown, she'd tucked her roughly shorn hair beneath her wimple, and a large wooden cross hung around her neck. The undyed wool of the dress made her skin itch, and it chafed the open cuts upon her back. But it was far better than the hair shirt they forced her to wear the third day she arrived. She'd lashed out at another postulant who bumped into her as they entered their pew. The postulant was formerly a lesser noble, and Madeline reminded her that she, Madeline, was the sister of a laird and a former lady-in-waiting to Queen Elizabeth de Burgh. Madeline's voice carried, but the other woman was more discreet in her own set-down, as she pointed out that

Madeline's brother was the one to banish her from court.

When she spewed her spleen at her fellow postulant, Madeline earned herself an hour of self-flagellation in the misericord, the room where nuns were punished. This was followed by two days of wearing the penitent's hair shirt. She'd been in agony for those two days, and was convinced she would surely die. It was a severe and successful lesson, and now she knew to keep her foul temper to herself. "Once bitten, twice shy" was now her mantra. She had no intention of ever earning such a punishment again.

If I must bite my tongue all the way through, I won't say a dicky-bird. None of these eejits are worth being flayed alive.

Madeline made her way into the chapel, but the Mother Abbess pulled her aside. The older nun's expression was stern, but there was a kindness in her eyes that made Madeline narrow her own. She didn't trust the woman. No one human had as much patience and forgiveness as the Abbess.

"Madeline," Mother Abbess greeted her. Madeline fought to keep her expression neutral. While she was relieved that they didn't call her "sister," the stripping of her title as a lady chafed. She was in limbo, and the form of address only added to the hurt and anger. "How do you fare this morn?" the older woman asked.

The kindness and concern in the woman's tone took Madeline aback. The Mother Abbess had expressed her disappointment when Madeline appeared before the prioress for her punishment. She hadn't expected the nun to ask about her welfare.

"Madeline, you made your penance. The Lord has forgiven you." Mother Abbess smiled softly. "While it may take Mary longer to forgive you, God already has. If your contrition was genuine, then your sin is like a grain of sand, and God's grace is a

3

wave. Once you've begged forgiveness, the wave washes it away. It no longer remains."

Madeline sucked in her breath. She hadn't once asked for forgiveness. She'd railed against the injustice as she silently fumed. She'd cursed those around her and blamed anyone in sight for her plight.

"Ah," Mother Abbess filled the silence. "Perhaps your sin remains more like a pebble than the grain of sand. It is caught in your shoe and will pierce your sole until you remove it." Madeline's lips pursed at the woman's play on words. She understood the wisdom in the nun's metaphor, but she wasn't ready to relinquish her bitterness. It was all she had, a lifeline to her past.

"Yes, Mother Abbess," Madeline demurred.

"Madeline, you know you will live out your days within the walls of this priory. You have a choice; only you can make that choice. You can accept that this is your home and your future. Or you can continue to resent being here, everyone in your presence, and your brother and his future wife."

It struck Madeline as odd that the woman's voice could sound both benevolent and chastising at the same time. She had to admit that the nun spoke the truth. Madeline swept her gaze around the filling chapel. The nuns, novices, and postulants, along with several friars from the nearby monastery, had their heads bowed in prayer as they waited for the liturgy to begin. Sunlight filtered through the stained-glass window above the altar and shone upon the hanging crucifix. If she weren't filled with such anger and resentment, she would have admitted that the light, with dust motes floating around the cross, was beautiful. It appeared to give the replica of Christ an aura.

She'd never been devout in her beliefs, even after Queen Elizabeth forced all of her attendants into hours of prayer on bent knees. Arriving at court and learning that most didn't attend Mass until Terce had been a relief. The nine o'clock service still felt terribly early, since most courtiers didn't retire until the wee hours of the morning, but Terce was still better than the expectations at her family's home on the Isle of Lewis. The MacLeods began their day with Prime, the Mass she now attended. Unlike at home or at court, Madeline now attended a church service nearly every three hours.

As the long years stretched out ahead of her, Madeline felt a different weight settle upon her shoulders. She stared once more at the crucifix as she considered her choices. She could spend the rest of her life railing against being a nun, or she could accept her fate. The weight of exhaustion replaced that of injustice. She'd barely eaten or slept since she arrived, her fury being the only sustenance she needed. But she didn't want to live out her years being miserable.

Madeline turned back to the Mother Abbess, but the woman had walked away, taking her place near the altar. The priest spoke the opening collect, and Madeline hurried to take a place in the nearest pew. As she settled on her knees, the beam of sunlight shifted, now engulfing the crucifix in gold, orange, and red. It appeared to glow. Even though she was expected to have her eyes closed and head bowed, Madeline couldn't look away. She blinked rapidly, but the figure continued to gleam.

Is that truly God's light shining not upon, but from, Christ's body? It can't be. That's ridiculous. The figure is naught but wood, and the light is from the sun. But God created the sun, the moon, and the earth. If He created the sun, then it must be His will where it shines. I know that crucifix hasn't looked like that before, in all the days I've been here.

God, are you telling me something? What am I supposed to hear?

Madeline closed her eyes, but kept her head raised. She swallowed and strained to hear anything but her own voice within her head.

God, I don't hear You. But perhaps that isn't how You speak to Your lambs. I'm not Abraham or Isaac, or Moses or Jonah. Mayhap I won't hear Your voice. But my soul feels lighter than it has since I arrived at court. It feels clean. Are You the wave that Mother Abbess said to seek? Have You sent Your Holy Spirit to wash away my sins? I don't ken the answer to that, but that's how it feels. Mayhap Your presence is here in all things, just like the nuns say. My choice is to believe You reside here and that You have placed me on the path to being a bride of Christ.

For the first time in her life, Madeline lowered her head and listened to the service with an open heart and open mind. The sight of the crucifix had moved her in the most unexpected and inexplicable way. The prayer service passed more quickly than it ever had. Madeline was unprepared to file out of the chapel and walk to the refectory. She received the bowl of porridge with a slight smile and nod of thanks. The surrounding nuns stared at her in disbelief before they remembered themselves. Unlike her previous reactions, she bowed her head and clasped her hands in a prayer of thanksgiving for both the food and her new opportunity.

CHAPTER ONE

F our Years Later

Madeline wiped the sweat from her brow as she prepared to tug at the tenacious weed once again. She was determined that the third time would yield success. Perspiration trickled between her shoulder blades beneath her undyed tunic and black scapular. The nuns wore the "yoke of Christ" as an apron when they worked. While it protected their tunics, it was also a reminder that the burden of toiling within the Lord's house was much like the burden Christ carried for their redemption. While the garden was Madeline's favorite place to work, she sweltered that day. Her wimple stuck to her forehead, and she could feel the fabric clinging to the back of her neck.

The weed came loose, and as it did, Madeline barely caught herself before tumbling backwards. She dumped the weed in her basket and brushed her hands together to knock the soil from them. She surveyed the rows of vegetables around her, pleased with what she'd accomplished that day. While she enjoyed working in the herb gardens, Madeline preferred to spend time in the vegetable patches. It filled her with a sense of worthiness and fulfillment to know that her toils helped nourish the women she lived, worked, and prayed beside.

As she stood to dispose of the weeds, Madeline caught sight of the Mother Abbess approaching. The years had been kind to the older woman; she looked no different than she had nearly five years ago when Madeline arrived. She still exuded the same kindness and patience, and Madeline had discovered soon after she accepted her life at the convent that the prioress had a dry sense of humor and a tendency to curse.

Madeline had stumbled upon the nun kneeling on the cobbled path within the cloister a month after she arrived. Mother Abbess had smiled ruefully and explained she'd been begging God's forgiveness for the oath she'd sworn when she stubbed her toe. Madeline eventually stopped noticing when she would come across the prioress praying in the most unpredictable places.

"Sister Madeline," Mother Abbess greeted as she approached. Madeline bowed her head and kissed the woman's ring, after which the abbess tucked her hands into the opposite sleeves of her habit and continued speaking. "Please join me in my solar."

Madeline had learned many lessons about herself during her postulancy and novitiate, among them that deference to the senior nun came more easily than it had to the queen. While Queen Elizabeth de Burgh's regal status and power awed Madeline, she disliked the queen's position and wealth. She'd mocked Queen Elizabeth's piety, and balked at the hours the ladies-in-waiting were required to spend in prayer.

But Madeline was gentler and more accepting now, and she understood much of that came from the prioress's tutelage. Mother Abbess was an amiable woman, and while she, too, wielded power, Madeline never resented it once she accepted her future. Learning that the prioress was a Highlander had helped. Mother Abbess's dry humor resonated with Madeline, who'd grown up in the Hebrides. Their backgrounds made them more similar than they were to the Lowland nuns. Inchcailleoch Priory lay a day's ride west from Stirling, but while many considered Stirling the bridge between the Highlands and Lowlands, the priory felt distinctly part of the Lowlands.

As more and more of the habits she'd developed both at home and at court fell away, she realized that her mind and her body felt lighter. In the beginning, she thought often of her mother and younger sister Abigail. The three women used to run roughshod over first her father, then her brother. They demanded the best candles, the finest linens and fabrics, and the coin to do as they pleased. Her father indulged the trio so they would leave him alone. Once her older brother Kieran became laird, he was less apt to give in, but he did on occasion. And Madeline's life at court had only exacerbated her vanity and selfishness. When she reflected upon all those years of narcissism—and even, in some cases, cruelty—her stomach soured, and her chest ached.

In her relative isolation, Madeline had done as much as she could to make amends. At the start of the previous winter, Arabella Johnstone—now Arabella Sutherland—had turned up at the convent. Madeline knew that her fellow lady-in-waiting had barely recognized her appearance or her attitude. She'd aided Arabella in escaping the priory with Lachlan Sutherland, the man who was now her husband. Though pride was a sin, Madeline couldn't help but be pleased with the woman she'd become.

As her novitiate drew closer to its end, she looked forward to taking her final vows. The only two regrets she held were that she'd never apologized in person to Maude for all the cruel things she'd done and said to her sister-by-marriage. And she wished she'd had an opportunity to find love and build a family like Maude and Kieran had. Before arriving at Inchcailleoch, she'd always assumed she would marry and have children. She'd looked forward to having a little girl she could dress up with ribbons, or a son who would become a fine warrior worthy of her boasting. The lost opportunity still pained her.

After arriving at the prioress' solar, both women genuflected to the crucifix hanging on the wall before kissing the feet of the Christ figure on the crucifix. Mother Abbess took her seat behind her desk while Madeline stood, avoiding the chair reserved for guests. Madeline waited expectantly as Mother Abbess passed an assessing gaze over Madeline.

"Sister, you have nearly completed your time as a novice. You've sworn your preliminary vows and become a valuable member of our community. You pray with fervor and you're a hard worker." Madeline wanted to shift her feet. Something about the unexpected compliments made her wary. "But I'm not convinced that God has called you to the offices of a nun."

Mother Abbess held up a hand before Madeline could speak, staying any objection the novice might make. She offered a benevolent smile before glancing at the chair in the corner.

"Bring that chair over, my child. I believe we shall be here for a while. Sister, we both know why you came to the priory. You are a very different woman from the wrathful and shallow girl who arrived. I cannot say that I know what brought about your conversion so soon after you arrived, but it was impos-

10

sible to ignore. Mayhap our merciful Lord spoke to you, but I do not believe your life was meant to be spent cloistered away from the world. You have a way with children that I couldn't have anticipated. You're patient and gentle with them when you go into the village to minister to their bodies and souls."

Madeline's tension eased with the prioress's compliment, but she still wondered why she'd been summoned.

"Plainly put, I see the longing in your eyes, Madeline," the prioress said with a wistful smile. "You wish your life would have taken you in a direction that led to a husband and children. Prayer and faith alone do not make a calling."

Madeline sat in stunned silence. Everything the abbess said was true, but it was disconcerting to hear it from the head of the priory. Her wariness slid into fear as she waited to hear what the nun had to say next.

"Sister, let me share a story that only a handful of nuns here know. They are the ones still alive from when I arrived. I haven't spoken of this in almost forty years. I was the youngest sister of the Gunn's former laird. Thomas was not a kind man; rather, he was a vain and greedy one. He raided the Sinclairs and Mackays often, and he frequently made it look like other clans were to blame. He fueled animosity among the three clans, then sat back and watched what happened."

Madeline tried to remember what she knew of the Highland clans, but she was most familiar with the politics across the Hebridean islands.

"My next older brother, James, was duplicitous and conniving. He had coveted Siùsan Mackenzie—now Siùsan Sinclair—since she was a young girl. My sister Elizabeth married Siùsan's father within days of his first wife's death. Siùsan was born moments before her mother passed, and Elizabeth had naught but scorn for her infant stepdaughter. While there was no issue of consanguinity, it felt unholy for James to desire his niece-by-marriage. Farlane was the last of my brothers, and he was no better than Thomas or James. He died during a fight a few years ago, when he and his son, Arlan, were challenged by the Gordon twins, who discovered Arlan had assaulted Cairstine Grant."

Madeline gasped. She and Cairstine had been friends while they both served at court; they had bonded over their nastiness toward the other women. If Cairstine had been attacked before she become a lady-in-waiting, Madeline could understand why Cairstine was angry at the world and why she pushed people away. Madeline wondered which of the Gordon twins she married. She'd had no word from court since she arrived and only a handful of missives from Kieran, Abigail, and her mother. She'd received one missive from Maude not long after she married Kieran. Maude had offered her forgiveness and wished Madeline well. It was that missive that made Madeline sob for hours, for it was the first genuine contrition she'd ever felt. When Madeline realized that Mother Abbess was silent, she drew herself out of her thoughts and turned her attention back to the woman's story.

"When I was six-and-ten, I often slipped away from Clyth to escape my brothers and sister. I wandered all over, usually without a guard. There was a loch close to our border with the Sinclairs, and I would ride out early in the morning and not return until just before the evening meal. I fished, swam, and just watched the waves lap against the shore. I enjoyed the solitude and peace. I would think aboot the wonders of God's creation, of all things great and small. I marveled at the awe-inspiring world around me, and I was happy."

The prioress paused as if to collect her thoughts. Madeline noticed the far-away gaze and the mistiness that gathered in the corners of her eyes. She wondered what brought such sadness to the woman who had just recalled her own happiness.

"It was during one of those trips to the loch that I stripped bare and went for a swim. I'd been going there for years and seen naught more than a deer or rabbit. As I was aboot to climb out of the water, I heard hooves galloping toward the loch, and I had few places to hide, with no time to dress. It terrified me that whoever approached would accost or kidnap me. The first mon through the trees was enormous. Ma brothers were tall and broad shouldered, but this mon was a veritable mountain galloping toward me. He had dark brown hair that wafted behind him in time with his horse's gait, and even from a distance, I could see the cleft in his chin. He was the brawest mon I've ever laid eyes on."

The corners around the nun's eyes crinkled as she smiled. Madeline suspected the older woman hadn't noticed a burr slipping into her speech. She and Madeline had used Gaelic when Arabella and her father arrived at the priory. Laird Johnstone intended to abandon Arabella there to keep her from marrying Lachlan, and Madeline and the abbess had used their mother tongue to discuss the laird's plans, knowing that neither he nor Arabella could understand the language. It was but one moment in the years Madeline spent at the convent, but it was the closest she'd felt to anyone since she arrived.

"He ordered his men to remain in the trees," the abbess continued. "He looked around, his hand already on the hilt of his sword as he dismounted. The loch was so close to the border that the Gunns and

Sinclairs often argued over whose land it lay on. I can still remember the timber of his voice as he asked me who I was. With nay clothes on and nay arisaid with me because of the summer heat, there was naught nearby to distinguish me. But it was clear from his *breacan feile* that he was a Sinclair. I stuttered ma given name, Ceana." She paused and shook her head. "I havenae said that in five-and-thirty years. Not since I took my final vows."

Keh-na. Fair one. It suits her. Madeline didn't hide her smile as the prioress continued.

"When he asked me what I was doing there, I could only blink. Then I blurted out, 'I would think it's a wee bit obvious what I am doing here. The better question, is what the bluidy hell are ye doing here?'" The Mother Abbess didn't stifle her chuckle.

"I shall pray on that one later," Mother Abbess winked, and Madeline choked on a giggle. "The mon reached into his saddlebag and drew out a spare plaid. When he shook it open, I was certain it was long enough to cover the table on Clyth's dais. It was certainly longer than ma brothers' plaids, and theirs were longer than average. He approached as I sank deeper into the water, so it hid everything up to ma mouth. He swung the plaid around his back and stretched out his arms before spinning on his heels. He held the plaid as a shield, so his men couldnae see me as I left the water and while I dressed. He didna make a peep."

Madeline listened to the lilting brogue of the abbess, and she felt at home in a way she hadn't since before she left for the royal court. She'd adopted a pretentious courtly accent within minutes of arriving at Stirling Castle. As she did so, she looked down her nose at Maude, whose burr sometimes slipped into her speech. Madeline had abandoned her own courtly accent the day she accepted her fate, and her islander's brogue surprised many. But by using it she felt authentic for the first time in years. Now the sound was like a lullaby, familiar and comforting.

"Once I dressed, he turned around. But he kept his extra *breacan feile* stretched across his back, keeping me out of his men's sight. He was aghast that I didna have at least one guard with me. Anger, fear, and something akin to sadness passed through his eyes. With a sigh, he declared me a Gunn and explained that while being a lass is why he wouldnae let his men see me in the skin, it was being a Gunn that kept him from allowing them to see me as we talked. My horse grazed nearby, and I could ride around the far side of the loch to return home. As I mounted, he asked if I would ever see him again. I answered only if he told me his name. Dugan Sinclair. He was the laird's younger son. We both recognized one another's position, and we both knew it was reckless to even consider seeing one another again. But we did. Often."

A light pink blush entered the woman's cheeks, but her fond memories further deepened the creases around her eyes, which crinkled as she smiled wistfully. Even so, her sigh was one of missed opportunity and regret.

"We met along the border whenever we could. He would stand on his side, and I would stand on mine. We'd keep several feet apart and talk. Neither of us dared cross onto the other's land, but we enjoyed our conversations. We met at least once a sennight for three moons before I smuggled a blanket and picnic lunch with me. We estimated where the border was and spread the blanket over it. We sat on our own sides while we ate, then laid back and watched the clouds. We continued meeting like that for two more moons before Thomas called me before him. He railed against me for meeting with a—well,

I canna go so far as to say what kind of Sinclair he said, but it wasna vera nice. He told me that his patrols often saw me, but when Dugan kissed me, they reported it to Thomas. From what I gathered, they hadnae shared how many moons I'd been meeting Dugan. I'd feared they would tell Thomas since I knew we had to have been seen, but when I wasna called before ma brother, I kept testing ma luck. I kenned from what Dugan told me that his father took a more sympathetic view, saying that I was a lass and didna deserve to be caught in the middle of clan fights."

Madeline realized she was leaning forward in her seat as she listened to the tale with rapt attention. She never dreamed that the nun sitting before her could have been involved in an illicit affair. It was as though Madeline's world had been turned upside down and inside out. She studied the woman more closely, taking in the impish twinkle that had entered her hazel eyes. She assumed the woman's hair was gray or white beneath her wimple, but she wondered about its original color. For some reason, Madeline envisioned fiery red locks.

"Being threatened with imprisonment in ma chamber wasna enough to keep me from continuing to see Dugan. We'd fallen deeply in love, and neither of us regretted the passion we shared. Both Sinclair and Gunn territories reach the coast of the North Sea. Rather than meeting in a meadow near our border, we met on the beach. We assumed it was less likely that a Gunn patrol would spot me. I kenned the Sinclair patrols turned a blind eye to us since Laird Sinclair didna object. I willna say much beyond we anticipated the wedding we believed we would have."

Mother Abbess's cheeks turned from their previous pink to a deep red, but she maintained her eye contact with Madeline. "I was three moons along before I realized ma condition. It was ma sister Elizabeth who pointed it out. She announced it at the evening meal the day before she left to marry Laird Mackenzie. I feared Thomas would have an apoplexy. I have never seen a mon turn that shade of red. It almost looked blue. He had guards drag me to ma chambers, so I didna ken he led a raid that night on the Sinclairs."

The tears tumbled from the nun's eyes, and she did nothing to wipe them away. Madeline already knew how this story would end. She could imagine what happened next, and she suspected she knew why the Mother Abbess came to the priory. But she listened nonetheless.

"It was a sennight before Thomas let me leave ma chamber. He made me stand before the dais as the clan gathered at the tables behind me. I was unprepared when he threw something at me. Dugan's brooch landed at ma feet." The older woman paused as she pulled a drawer open. She retrieved an intricately carved brooch with a ruby gem in the center. She'd worn the stone smooth, and Madeline knew she must have passed her thumb over it countless times, just as she did now. It shocked Madeline that the abbess possessed such a fine, worldly good.

"I confess I hid it when I came here," the prioress nearly whispered. "I ken it's likely a sin that I still keep it, and I've prayed for forgiveness many a time. But I canna part with it. It's all that I have in this world that keeps me connected to Dugan. When I picked it up from among the rushes, I kenned that moment that I would never see Dugan again. I couldnae even go to his burial. Even kenning ma condition, Thomas lashed me in the bailey the next day. He made certain the entire clan watched ma disgrace. But I felt nae a lick of remorse for ma choices.

At the time, I had ma beloved's bairn growing within me."

Madeline didn't dare ask what happened to the child, despite being eager to know. She glanced down and found her hands clasped so tightly in her lap that her knuckles were white.

"The lashing wasna enough for Thomas because I wouldnae repent. He beat me until I feared I would lose the bairn. It was ma brother's captain of the guard and the captain's wife who smuggled me out of Clyth and took me to Dunbeath. I showed up on the Sinclairs' doorstep, beaten and with child. They took me in without questions and allowed me to stay until I healed."

The prioress paused, and Madeline could tell the older woman was envisioning these memories.

"Lady Kyla Sinclair had the gentlest touch I've even felt. The auld laird and lady were still alive, but it was Lady Sinclair who tended to me. She'd been a Sutherland, just as Maude was. In fact, she was their aunt. She'd survived her father's abuse before marrying the current laird, Liam. I believe she saw herself in ma injuries.

"They offered to let me stay, to become part of their clan, but I couldnae. Everywhere I looked, something reminded me that I was in Dugan's home. I even slept in the bed that I thought I would one day share with him. I begged to retire to a convent where I could have the bairn and live as a secular member of the community. Inchcailleoch was the furthest convent that I could think of; I thought Thomas would never suspect I was here. The current Laird Sinclair and Lady Sinclair escorted me here. While she had an angel's touch, she had the devil's stubbornness."

Mother Abbess grinned and shook her head. She watched Madeline as the younger woman absorbed the story. The tale enthralled Madeline, but she couldn't figure out why the prioress shared such a deeply personal story with her. "I had always been strong in ma faith, and joining our community here was easy. I imagined that I would live here with ma child and work alongside the sisters. Or mayhap, I would find a cottage in the village but continue to serve the nuns. But those grand plans changed when ma bairn was stillborn. He was the perfect image of Dugan. I was certain ma grief would kill me. But once I could move past ma tears and anger, I realized the Lord brought me here for a reason"

"Nay one suggested a convent, so nay one ever suggested I come here," the abbess smiled as her story came to an end. "When I was six-and-ten, I assumed ma life would lead me to be a wife and mother one day. But as I told ye in the beginning, before I met Dugan, I spent hours in meditation aboot God's wonders. When ma babe didna survive, I realized I was already where I belonged. God had called me here. Madeline, ye and I both arrived in disgrace. But I was meant to serve the Lord nae a laird. Ye are meant to be a mother and a wife one day."

"What?" Madeline jerked out of her seat. "Nay, Mother Abbess. I'm to take ma final vows in a fortnight. I canna be a wife and mother if I'm a bride of Christ."

"Ma child, the agreement with yer brother was that ye would remain here indefinitely. But there was always the chance that after yer novitiate, ye might be allowed to return to Lewis. Respectful behavior might have released ye early, but ye seemed to have a calling to the sisterhood. But as the time for yer terminal vows approaches, I canna ignore the restlessness I see in yer spirit. Ye have accepted our way of life here, but I see ye looking toward the village. I see the eagerness to leave the cloister and visit the secular world. I've watched ye with the weans and bairns. Madeline, ye were meant to have a family of yer own. It isnae a sin to nae belong here as a nun. But it would be a sin to ignore His will. Ye arenae called to be a nun, ma child."

"That's it?" Madeline choked. "Five years, and ye're forcing me out?"

"Ye ken I would never do that. But ye canna remain a novice forever." The prioress walked around her desk and wrapped her arms around Madeline. The younger woman remained rigid for a moment before giving in to her tears.

"But where will I go? I dinna ken if Kieran would allow me to return." Madeline's body shook with the force of her tears, but the abbess kept her in the warm cocoon of her embrace until Madeline could control her breathing. "Mother Abbess, I'm scared."

"I ken, lass," the nun murmured as she straightened Madeline's wimple. "It's frightening to suddenly leave what ye've kenned for years. Ye've done it twice before, when ye left yer clan and when ye left court. But ye arenae the same person as ye were back then. Ye have more fortitude than ye give yerself credit for."

"But where will ye send me?" Madeline whispered. "Can I go home?"

"Aye, Madeline. Laird MacLeod offered to escort ye back to Stornoway when I wrote to him of ma concerns."

"Ye already wrote to him? Ye didna tell me that ye believed I dinna belong here, but ye told Kieran?" Madeline asked.

"I did. I wanted to explain to him ma observations aboot ye over the years and how ye would be a valuable member to yer clan, to any clan really. He and I have been in touch throughout the years, and he kens how different ye are from when ye arrived. He's the one who suggested ye return to Stornoway."

"He wants me to come home?" Madeline's emotions threatened to consume her.

"He and Lady MacLeod both do," Mother Abbess reassured. "But Madeline, yer presence has been requested at court first."

Madeline had noticed that the abbess had stopped calling her sister, and now she was stunned to find that she expected her to return to the same court where she'd humiliated and disgraced herself and her clan.

"I—I canna. I have naught appropriate to wear if I'm nae a nun. Why would anyone want me there?" Madeline wondered aloud.

"I canna say, ma child. But once I kenned Laird MacLeod wanted ye to come home, I had to inform the queen. She, too, has taken an interest in yer progress over the years."

"The queen kens aboot me here?" Madeline was surprised. "I mean, I ken she's aware I wound up here. But I mean, she kens what I'm like here?"

"Aye. I dinna ken that she wishes to reinstate ye, but she has ordered ye to appear."

Ordered. That was more accurate than requested. From a member of the royal family, a request was as good as a summons at knifepoint.

"When do I leave?" Madeline asked.

"The start of next sennight," Mother Abbess answered. There was nothing for Madeline to do but nod. The women prayed together before the prioress offered Madeline a blessing, and the former novice slipped from the solar.

CHAPTER TWO

Madeline swallowed her trepidation as she dismounted from her horse in Stirling Castle's bailey. She glanced at her brother's men, who had appeared at the priory to escort her to the royal court. Since she entered the priory, she hadn't been further than the village across the narrow span of Loch Lomond that separated the isle on which the priory sat from the village of *Bealach Mo-Cha*, or Balmaha. Madeline had found it difficult to leave what many called the "island of auld women."

Many had come out of their cottages in Balmaha to wave goodbye, but Madeline forced herself not to look back once they were on the road to Stirling. She felt strangely foreign in a world she'd once inhabited. The bailey was bustling with people and animals, and the fetid air made her choke. Noise reverberated from the walls of the outbuildings. She wondered how she'd ever belonged in such a place. She recalled how eager she'd been when she first arrived in Stirling as a lady-in-waiting-to-be. Unlike before, she dreaded stepping foot within the keep. She wanted nothing more than to mount her horse again and ride north, putting half of Scotland between her and the courtiers who awaited her inside.

"Lady Madeline?" One of her guards cleared his throat. She'd only been away from the priory for a day, so being addressed by her title felt odd and uncomfortable. It reminded her of who she had once been. She tried not to flinch each time the men addressed her as "Lady Madeline."

"Aye." She nodded and inhaled deeply. She couldn't avoid the inevitable by lingering in the bailey. She took her first step, and it was as though she went back in time. But this time she came as a spectator rather than a participant. She watched as people rushed to the Great Hall, where Madeline knew the men and women would enjoy a lavish evening meal before spending the rest of the night twirling to music. She wanted to seek a chamber and hide. She forced her hands at her side when she wanted to self-consciously run them over her hair. Her shoulder-length ebony tresses would stand out compared to the intricate coiffures of the matrons and the waist-length locks most of the ladies-in-waiting adorned with ribbons.

Madeline took the steps that led to a side door of the castle, glad she already knew her way around the keep. But she wouldn't be able to remain invisible for long. She would have to make her presence known to the mistress of the bedchamber, or she would have nowhere to sleep that night. She prayed she could wait until the following morning before appearing before the queen. Even though she no longer wore a wimple, she still wore the gray tunic from the abbey. They had given her gown to Kieran before he left the priory, so she had no formal attire, even if it would have been five years outdated. She had a spare tunic, and she was desperate to get clean and don the fresh gown before being seen in her wrinkled and dusty one.

Madeline tiptoed along the passageways as she

made her way toward where she suspected the mistress of the bedchamber would be given the hour. The woman oversaw all things to do with the ladies-in-waiting. Madeline's mind compared the courtier and Mother Abbess. The two women were nothing alike, but both were in charge of the women who served beneath them. Madeline rounded the corner and stumbled to a stop. Laurel Ross stood before her, blinking rapidly as Madeline's mouth hung open, and her eyes widened.

"Madeline?" Laurel whispered.

"Aye," Madeline answered in an equally soft tone.

"What are you doing here?" Laurel asked as she peered around Madeline, only to find they were alone in the passageway. Madeline considered her answer, but there was little reason to be evasive. Why she was there was still unknown, so there was nothing to hide. In fact, it surprised her to find Laurel still at court. She assumed she would have married and left years before. She wondered if there was anyone else she knew among the ladies.

"I am on my way home to Stornoway, but I was summoned here first," Madeline explained.

"Home? Summoned?" Laurel once again glanced over Madeline's shoulder. "Come with me. We need to get you out of sight before the others come to dress for the evening meal."

"Nay. I need to find the mistress and be assigned a chamber," Madeline argued.

"Madeline, I don't have a roommate at the moment. You can spend at least tonight in my chamber. After all, you know what the others will be like. Is this how you want to make your first appearance?"

Madeline's spine straightened and her chin rose, a posture she hadn't held since her first week at Inchcailleoch. It was that of a laird's sister and a queen's lady-in-waiting. "I have naught to be ashamed of

25

when it comes to my appearance. I am a servant of the Lord."

"Aye, and you will be a servant to the queen, most likely. You may not mind your appearance, but would you like to be on the receiving end of what you used to dole out to Maude? Because you've been replaced, and your successor is a bitch." Laurel grabbed Madeline's wrist and dragged her down the passageway. Madeline had no chance to argue, and Laurel's words stunned her. While she knew Mother Abbess swore to herself, she had heard no one use anything close to profanity in five years. They entered Laurel's chamber, and Madeline paused just inside the doorway. Little had changed in the chamber since she left. Laurel shut the door behind her and turned to the young woman brushing out a velvet gown.

"Ina, fetch the tub and hot water. Sharp's the word, quick's the action," Laurel commanded but added a softer "please" at the end. Laurel strode across her room and opened her wardrobe. She rifled through her gowns before settling on a dove-gray kirtle. It was nearly the same color as Madeline's tunic, but it was made of velvet and satin. Laurel marched toward Madeline and held the kirtle beneath Madeline's chin. "This shall work. You're thinner than you were, but we used to be the same size. My maid can launder your tunic."

Madeline stood dazed as she listened to Laurel speak. It surprised her that Laurel didn't threaten to burn the tunic, and her expression must have reflected her thoughts. Laurel offered what had once been an uncharacteristically warm smile. Her hand patted Madeline's upper arm before she laid the dress aside.

"I ken I'm rushing you, but we were once friends. For better or for worse, we were allies against the rest of the world. I can tell you're different. Everything

26

aboot you. Not just your appearance, but your demeanor and the way you carry yourself. There's a calm and grace I haven't seen before. I don't doubt your mind is as keen as it ever was, but the ladies will devour you alive if they see you dress this plainly. If you've changed as much as I suspect, then you don't deserve that kind of welcome."

Before Madeline could respond, a rap at the door signaled the servants with the tub and bathwater. Neither Madeline nor Laurel spoke while the servants prepared the bath. While she'd developed a greater sense of modesty while at the convent, she'd lost all modesty about her body before other women. She'd been sick more than once, and in her third winter at the priory she had developed such a high fever that she required ice baths in the infirmary. After that, she no longer cared whether any of the women saw her undressed, as plenty had during her illness.

Madeline couldn't get past how much Laurel had changed, as well. While Madeline had a mean streak that instigated more than one occasion of bullying, Laurel was known to have a viperous tongue. During her novitiate, Madeline had thought about her friendship with Laurel many times. She'd forced Laurel to befriend her, manipulating her and threatening to destroy both the young woman's reputation and that of her family and clan. She'd often suspected that Laurel hadn't been a shrew before arriving at court, but her association with Madeline had driven her to cruelty. This made Madeline question why Laurel was being so accommodating.

"I ken you're wondering why I'm being nice to you. I mean, after everything that happened," Laurel smiled dubiously. "Much has happened in the time you've been away. Not only have Elizabeth Fraser and Maude married, but so have Cairren Kennedy,

27

Allyson Elliot, Cairstine Grant, Blair Sutherland, and Arabella Johnstone."

"There's no one left but you," Madeline murmured.

"Aye. I am the last of the auld guard." Madeline didn't miss the sadness in Laurel's tone and her eyes. She regretted pointing out that Laurel was still unmarried. Laurel's Highland roots slipped out momentarily when she smiled and said, "Dinna fash."

Madeline grinned. "I've already slipped back into my courtly accent, and I didn't realize it. But it sounds good to hear a Highlander after all these years."

"Slipped back into? Did you not keep speaking like these bluidy Lowlanders we're around all day and night?"

"Nay," Madeline shook her head before pulling her tunic over her head and peeling down her stockings. "I quit sounding like them and went back to how I spoke most of my life. The Mother Abbess was a Highlander herself many moons ago, but besides her, were no other women from up north or the islands."

"I fear that it's become too much a part of me after all these years, even if I cannot stand the sound of Scots. I'd prefer Gaelic any day of the sennight and twice on feast days." Laurel and Madeline chuckled, and by silent agreement, they lapsed into Gaelic as Madeline stepped into the tub. Laurel's Highland accent and Madeline's Hebridean one sounded richer to Madeline's ear than what she would hear at court, or even what she heard at the priory.

"Laurel, why are ye doing this? Helping me. I was wretched to ye. I deserve yer loathing, nae yer generosity."

"Because we both erred for many years, but

28

we've both changed," Laurel responded. "I admit that yer departure made it easier for me, but it was Cairren's ordeal that really changed me." When Madeline raised an eyebrow in invitation, Laurel continued. "Ye ken she was ma roommate. The king and her father betrothed her to Padraig Munro."

"Munro? Wasna he the mon yer sister Myrna planned to wed?"

"Aye. I kenned before she left that the Munros wouldnae welcome her. I kenned Myrna would make her life miserable. And I kenned that Padraig would give in to ma sister at every turn. The best I could do was warn Cairren of what awaited her. But it was so much worse than I could have ever imagined. They ostracized Cairren for her dark olive skin and for being a quarter Saracen. Padraig lusted for her, but he was convinced he still loved Myrna. So he and Cairren were both enemies and lovers

"Long story short, Myrna wasna what anyone believed. At least anyone but me. I've kenned all her secrets for years. I kenned she was the reason ma parents sent me here. She's now married to an auld mon who belches and passes gas from sun-up to sun-down, but is as randy as an auld goat. Cairren and Padraig fell in love, and now they have a family of their own. But that changed me. Ma heart broke for Cairren before she left, and it shattered all over again when she returned to court for a brief time before she finally found happiness."

"Blessed Lord," Madeline made the sign of the cross. "How long ago was that?"

"Nae vera long after Maude and yer brother married. They have been to court a few times over the years, and Maude is nae longer the wallflower she once was. I even think yer brother is a wee less protective each time they come."

"He had every right to want to shield Maude

from ma hatefulness and the seeds I sowed here. Ma mother and sister werenae any better than me when she first arrived at Stornoway. But they have reconciled since then." Madeline lathered soap onto a piece of linen and began scrubbing. "Tell me of Cairstine and Allyson. I heard that Cairstine married one of the Gordons."

"They both did. Or rather Allyson married Ewan, and Cairstine married Eoin." Laurel grinned. The Gordon brothers had been known for their devilish good looks and charm. Women fell under their spell with little more than a glance. No one could have predicted how deeply in love they would fall with their wives, or how devoted they would be to their marriages. "Allyson ran away."

"Pardon?" Madeline froze.

"Aye. She'd had some run-in with the twins when she and Cairren were on their way to the queen's solar. Later that day, she discovered she was to marry the roguish Ewan. She bolted. She rode out to Culcreuch first, hoping to seek shelter with Elizabeth and Edward. But Edward couldnae go against his adopted brother, especially when the mon is the king. Allyson fled from there and traveled all the way to the border. She wound up kidnapped and taken to Chillingham." At Madeline's confused expression, Laurel explained. "It's a castle of horrors. King Edward's favorite torturer once lived there. Longshanks had given the mon free rein to terrorize the Scots just across the border. Allyson would have likely died had Ewan and Eoin nae rescued her. I dinna ken all that happened while they were away from court, but they came back married and vera clearly in love."

"And Cairstine? I thought she didna want to marry. I thought that was part of her nastiness," Madeline mused.

"It was. She didna want to marry, but her father

began forcing her hand. She thought to become a nun. When that didna work out, she begged Eoin to pretend to be her betrothed long enough for her younger sister to marry the mon she loved. Eoin originally refused, but there was already a bond between them. I dinna ken the whole of that story either. But Cairstine was being pushed toward marrying her cousin a few times removed. She didna want Fingal. From what she said, he isnae a bad mon, and they were vera close; she simply didna want to marry him. But I suppose one thing led to another, and Eoin became a reformed rake. So Allyson and Cairstine now live at Huntly Castle with their husbands and children."

"Oh, ma!" Madeline tried to digest all that she'd been told. She slipped beneath the water, enjoying the first bath she'd had in nearly five years. She knew she was dawdling, but the steaming water felt magnificent after so many years of just a basin and unscented soap. She knew the evening meal would start soon, if it hadn't already, but she longed to remain in what felt like sinful decadence. "What aboot Blair and Arabella?"

"Blair ran into a childhood friend here. Laird Hardwin Cameron came to court to pay his clan's taxes, but there was some sort of problem. He became laird when six people ahead of him died. Can ye believe that? He was untrained for the position, since he was the second son and nephew to the last laird. He'd fostered with the Sutherlands, but they never trained him to be laird. Nay one ever expected it. That's how Blair and Laird Cameron kenned each other; they practically grew up together. I dinna ken if it was love at first—or would that be second— sight. It didna take long to see Blair and Laird Cameron were besotted with one another. She arrived at Tor Castle to find members of the clan plotting against Laird Cameron, and an attack from the Mackintoshes soon followed. The Sutherlands and their army, and yer brother along with Maude, their weans, and his army showed up just as the Cameron and Blair foiled the attack. Something aboot a hidden tunnel and burying men alive."

"That doesnae surprise me. Maude, Blair, and Lachlan are exceptionally close. If something happened to Blair, I doubt Kieran could have kept Maude at home. For all ma taunts, I always kenned Maude had a backbone of steel. I think that's why I wanted to see if I could make it bend." Madeline lathered soap into her short hair, then waited for Laurel to pour the bucket of fresh water over her head. She had no excuse to remain in the bath, so she hurried to towel herself dry as Laurel recounted Arabella's tale.

"Did ye ever suspect that Arabella and Lachlan carried a flame for one another?" Laurel asked. Madeline shook her head before pulling a comb from the small sack that held only the comb, her spare tunic, and a withered shard of soap. "Aye, well, they didna do aught because they feared what would happen to Arabella's friendships with Maude and Blair. Once they married and left, there seemed like little standing in their way. But Lachlan waited too long. Laird Johnstone was ready to sign a betrothal between Arabella and Laird Gunn."

"Laird Gunn?" Madeline's mind jumped to the story the Mother Abbess had told her only a week earlier. She wondered if the man was as horrible as the other men in his family.

"Aye. From what I ken through ma own family, the Gunns are naught but a nuisance to the Sutherlands, Sinclairs, and Mackays. The last laird's son, Arlan, was the one who attacked Cairstine all those years ago. He and his father Farlane ended up fighting Ewan and Eoin. They both died, so the lairdship passed to Beathan. From what I hear, he was a better laird to his clan, but just as bad to women as his brother."

"Was?"

"Och, aye. I suppose he's the previous laird now. He stole Arabella away from Lachlan. Twice, from the rumors I heard."

"Arabella came to the priory. She ran away with Lachlan," Madeline whispered.

"She did?" Laurel mused. "Aye. Her father brought her there after forcing her away from here. I just didna hear what happened afterwards."

"Did he covet her for her beauty or for her dowry?" Madeline wondered, but Laurel only shrugged.

"There was a battle that involved the Mackays, the Sinclairs, and the Sutherlands. But it was Arabella who killed the mon. Do ye ken why she left court?" Laurel's unexpected question startled Madeline. She could only shake her head. "I heard she was into the drink. She was hiding whisky in her chamber and having a nip or six every day. But the story is that Lachlan helped her past whatever plagued her enough to drink, and they married and live at Dunrobin."

"That is quite a lot to take in all at once." Madeline turned her back to allow Laurel to pull the kirtle's laces snug. She hovered her hands over the fine material, remembering the gowns she'd once worn. It felt odd, almost uncomfortable, after so many years of the simple wool garments. She was no longer used to the confining feel or the weight of courtly attire.

"There's naught to do aboot yer hair, but ye can use ma combs or ribbons. Mayhap that'll help." Laurel pointed to the table where her oils and hair accoutrements sat. Madeline struggled with her self-consciousness about her uncommonly short hair, but she glanced in the looking glass. She knew her hair curled after she washed it, but she'd never seen it before. In fact, it was the first time in almost five years that she had seen her own reflection.

She stepped toward the table and leaned forward. She brushed her fingertips over her cheeks and nose before feathering them over her hair. She recognized the woman she'd once been, but there was something she couldn't pinpoint that was different, and it wasn't her hair. "Ye're less pinched," Laurel offered.

"Pinched?" Madeline straightened and looked back at Laurel.

"Aye. Ye—well, I suppose we both—used to look like we'd eaten year-auld pickled herring. Our faces looked pinched," Laurel explained. Madeline mulled over her former friend's words. She wasn't certain if she and Laurel were friends once more, and if they were, what would become of the relationship, but she appreciated the woman's generosity.

"I suppose I dinna feel so pinched anymore. I confess, I'm nervous to be here, but ma life has been calm since I left," Madeline admitted.

"Then why have ye returned?" Laurel prodded gently.

"Ma time at Inchcailleoch is through. The Mother Abbess recognized that while I came to appreciate ma life at the priory, entering the sisterhood isnae ma calling. They released me on good behavior," Madeline smiled ruefully. "Kieran and Maude wish for me to return home, and that's where I thought I would go. But Mother Abbess informed me that the king and queen summoned me here. I dinna ken aught more than that."

Laurel glanced warily at Madeline as she held the chamber door open. They both surmised that Madeline was likely to discover an arranged marriage was in the works. However, Madeline refused to worry about that until she knew what was happening. Until then, she focused all her attention on surviving her first evening meal at court.

CHAPTER THREE

Fingal Grant stood against a wall in the Great Hall, watching couples dance past him as his narrowed eyes assessed each unmarried woman. The past fortnight had been excruciating. He'd danced with nearly all the ladies-in-waiting and several widows, but each of them had grated on his nerves. Whether it was the sound of their voices, their incessant chattiness, their doleful eyes when he barely responded, their cloying perfume, or their conspicuous finagling to learn if he was looking for a bride, it all irritated him. If he wasn't looking for a wife, he would have fled.

Fingal's piercing gray eyes swept the crowd once more. There were delegates from clans he recognized, but no one that he wished to speak to. He preferred conversing with the men while they trained in the lists during the day. His goal in the evenings was to find a bride. So far, he'd had no luck. He was wondering if there was anyone at court who would meet his needs. He didn't need to fall in love with the woman. He just had to tolerate her enough to bed her often enough to have at least an heir and a spare, and he needed to be confident she could run the keep once his cousin passed away. He didn't believe he was asking for much, but it was turning out to be a Herculean trial.

Fingal sighed once more before glancing at the dais. King Robert had invited him to attend court to aid his search, knowing Fingal and his distant cousin, Laird Edward Grant, had found no appealing candidates from the surrounding clans. There seemed to be a shortage of eligible, marriageable women in the Highlands. Most were either already wed or too young for him to cast even a first glance. He wasn't interested in a child bride. While he felt no compulsion to remain faithful, he was also disinclined to wait years to bed his wife.

He'd noticed a stir toward the beginning of the meal, when two women arrived after the first course. He hadn't been close enough to hear, but they both appeared to be ladies-in-waiting. He thought one of them was Laurel Ross, but he didn't recognize the other woman. Laurel was attractive, but he knew she was practically a pauper. Fingal canted his head as he admitted that was a bit of an exaggeration as he considered the woman. Her father was the Earl of Ross, but she was the fourth out of five daughters. Even the youngest had married, so the clan had paid a fortune in dowries to other clans. As the last unmarried daughter, it was well-known that Laurel's dowry would be a pittance. Fingal might not have objected to finding her in his bed from time to time, but he would not feed and clothe a woman for the rest of her life if she brought nothing but her womb to the marriage.

The other woman, however, caught his attention. She appeared reserved and out of place. Her short, cropped hair stood out; while she was beautiful in the gray gown, the muted colors made the contrast between her appearance and the other ladies even more marked. She entered with a regal bearing that could only come from years of training, so he assumed she was a laird's daughter or sister. Had she not looked so different from the other attendants, he would have been certain she was a lady-in-waiting, but something told him she wasn't, or at least she wasn't anymore. He supposed she could be a young widow, given her kirtle's color. She was a mystery to him, but not a puzzle he intended to solve. If she was still in mourning, it would be pointless to pursue her. They couldn't have the banns read and marry before he left.

He was abandoning his place against the wall, ready to retire for the night, when Laurel and the stranger caught his attention once more. He'd seen Laurel partner with several men, but he realized as he stared that the unnamed lady hadn't passed him once. The two women stood together near the opposite wall, leaning their heads together and whispering in heated conversation. Fingal watched Laurel purse her lips as the short-haired woman shook her head. Her ebony locks brushed her shoulders as candlelight caressed them. Fingal felt a momentary temptation to run his hands through them. He was curious what hair so short would feel like. He'd never seen a woman whose hair wasn't at least nearly to her waist. He caught himself staring, and sighed yet again before retreating to his chamber.

"Laurel, the queen has shown no interest in me, so there is no reason for me to remain. I'm not accustomed to being up so late, and I spent all day riding here. I'm exhausted. There will be other nights for me to meet potential suitors. Please, I'd like to retire." Madeline's head pounded as she forced herself not to rub her temples. She'd forgotten how stuffy the Great

Hall grew in summer. She'd fought bouts of light-headedness since she walked in. She suspected the temperature was only partly to blame.

While Laurel was the only lady-in-waiting remaining at court from her time there, Madeline's reputation preceded her. It took only a moment for a buzz to pass through the group of attendants and to make its way to other tables. People shifted to stare at her. Some did nothing to hide their disdain, while others wore expressions of shock and disbelief. But most people cast her mocking glares. She'd kept her head down and remained silent except for when someone spoke to her. When she wasn't answering prying questions, she silently prayed. She took solace in meditation, even with the periodic interruptions.

"I didn't think of that. I'm sorry. It was insensitive of me not to think about how long your day must have been. I'll go back with you," Laurel offered.

"I haven't forgotten my way around. I don't want you to leave early on my account, but thank you for the offer," Madeline said as she squeezed Laurel's hand. She inched her way along the wall until she could escape through the large wooden doors. She drew in a deep breath as clean, cool air wafted over her.

Madeline hurried to Laurel's chamber, fearful of who she might encounter if she lingered in the passageways. Her tainted reputation would be a beacon to the less-scrupulous men. She understood how their minds worked. If she was already ruined, bedding her without marriage could do little more harm. She wasn't interested in any such offer.

Ina helped Madeline out of her borrowed gown and into one of Laurel's chemises. Madeline felt guilty for being so indebted to Laurel. One of her brother's guards had given her a pouch of coin, so she knew she had enough money to commission at least one gown and chemise, but it would take several days for them to be ready. Until then, she would return to wearing her tunic. She'd made her obligatory appearance at the evening meal. She conceded that she might need to borrow one more gown when she presented herself to the queen, but other than that, she saw little reason to go out in public. If the king was arranging a marriage for her, her attendance would be inconsequential. And she certainly wasn't in search of a husband.

Madeline's eyes drifted shut as she pulled the bedcovers over her shoulder. She was in a deep sleep within moments, and slept through Laurel's return. However, when her eyes snapped open in the pitch-black chamber, she knew there was little chance she would fall back to sleep. It was time for Matins. Madeline shifted but could see nothing in the dark. She considered lying in bed until she finally fell back to sleep, but her conscience niggled at her. It took only a minute before she rose from her bed and shuffled around in the dark. She found her sack and pulled her fresh tunic from within. She pulled it over her head before tying the rope belt around her waist. She'd removed her large wooden cross as she entered the bailey the day before, but she'd felt bare without it. She tucked her chin before slipping it around her neck. She glanced in Laurel's direction as she crept out of the chamber.

The passageway was silent, but lit torches in sconces lined the walls. She hurried through the keep until she came to the chapel. She paused and listened, but she heard nothing around her or from inside. She had a moment of doubt, wondering whether they held the middle of the night service at the royal court. Even if they didn't, she reasoned, the altar candles would still be lit. She could recite the liturgy to herself. She opened the door a crack and spied within. Two elderly monks stood at the altar preparing for the prayer service.

Madeline eased open the door enough for her to enter. With her palms together and fingers pointing toward Heaven, Madeline bowed her head and made her way to the third pew on the left. She'd sat in the same third pew on the Gospel side of the chapel every day at Inchcailleoch. She'd discovered the pews on the right, or Epistle side, were draughty at Inchcailleoch. At Stirling, she took this seat out of habit.

Madeline noted the surprise on the priests' faces as she knelt, but they continued the liturgy from memory. She experienced the same tranquility she always felt during services, and she wondered how it was possible that she wasn't called to be a nun. It felt natural and right. But as Madeline gave it more thought, she wondered if it was more a sense of familiarity than anything else. She had, after all, attended eight Masses a day for the better part of half a decade. She continued to reason through her feelings when she returned at sunrise for Lauds and an hour later for Prime. Laurel did not stir when Madeline came and went from the earlier services, but she opened one eye as Madeline returned from the mid-morning Terce.

"Did ye go to Mass?" Laurel yawned when Madeline returned to their chamber for the fourth time since she retired.

"Aye," Madeline replied as she clutched her cross in her hand. She expected Laurel to mock her, but Laurel just shrugged, stretched, and threw back the covers with a groan.

"I've never liked mornings, and I dinna think I ever will," Laurel bemoaned. She padded across the chamber to her washstand and splashed water onto her face before scrubbing it along with her neck. Once she was dry, she looked at Madeline, tilting her head to study her. Without a word, she nodded and went to her wardrobe. She glanced back at Madeline once before lifting out a lavender gown with a deep purple trim. The material was lighter than the gown she lent Madeline the night before. "This will suite ye."

"Laurel, thank ye. But ye dinna need to loan me yer wardrobe. I have ma clean tunic on. I'm presentable as I am," Madeline demurred.

"Presentable, aye. Acceptable, nay. Madeline, ye're asking for naught but trouble if ye insist upon the tunic. For a nun, ye seem to want to draw a lot of attention to yerself," Laurel mused, an eyebrow cocked to make her point.

"I'm nae a nun. I was a novice," Madeline clarified. "I'm nae looking to draw attention to maself, but these gowns arenae who I am anymore. It feels wrong to me."

Laurel nodded, but looked unconvinced. "Madeline, when ye return to Stornoway, ye can wear yer tunic or whatever else a novice wore. But at court, ye do yerself nay favors by nae conforming. At least where yer clothes are concerned. I'm nae saying go back to how ye were to fit in. Just dinna stand out. Ye ken this gown and the one from last eve are modest by all accounts. Ye dinna need aught ostentatious, but ye do need to meet the queen's expectations. She willna be pleased to see ye before her, looking like a threadbare pauper compared to the rest of us."

Madeline knew Laurel spoke the truth. She wanted nothing more than to learn why Queen Elizabeth sent for her and to be on her way. If blending in made her time easier, then she would blend in. Her clothing wouldn't change who she'd become or how her faith mattered to her. She reached out for the gown; as she took it, she couldn't help but return Laurel's infectious smile. It wasn't long before Madeline and Laurel left their chambers in search of the morning meal. When a trio of ladies-in-waiting intercepted their route to the Great Hall, Madeline realized Laurel had offered sage advice. The women cast disdainful looks at her hair but remained quiet.

The queen didn't attend the morning meal, so Madeline left the other women and returned to Laurel's chamber. She was uncertain what to do with herself until it was time for Sext, the midday prayer, so she meditated on God's will for her future. The same two monks from the early morning services officiated at Sext. By her fourth appearance, the men seemed to have accepted her presence, though they did not notice her more ornate clothing. Madeline, however, was distinctly uncomfortable with such extravagance in the Lord's house. She exchanged the lavender gown for her tunic before returning midafternoon for None. Laurel opted not to say anything when she passed Madeline in the passageway before Vespers at sundown, but she gave Madeline a speaking look when Madeline returned to their shared chamber after Compline with little time to change into yet another borrowed gown. The deep russet-colored fabric contrasted with Madeline's robin's egg–blue eyes. Madeline recalled how, once upon a time, she would have preened before the looking glass and expected Laurel to compliment her appearance. Now, when Laurel gave her heartfelt appreciation unprompted, Madeline grew embarrassed, the attention unnerving.

Together, Laurel and Madeline made their way to the evening meal. Unlike the previous night, there was less tittering at Madeline's arrival, but she couldn't help but see the nudges, smirks, and looks in her direction. She ate in silence for much of the meal, and once again retreated into meditation to keep from panicking and fleeing.

"Lady Madeline?" A page stood behind Madeline's right shoulder. The boy couldn't have been more than eleven summers. "The queen expects you in her solar before you join Her Grace for her morning constitutional."

Madeline nodded before her eyes darted to Laurel, who could only stare back at Madeline. The rest of the evening passed at a snail's pace for Madeline. She was relieved when she could escape, her eyelids sagging from being awake far past the time when she usually retired. She spent her late night and early morning prayer services in contemplation and prayer as she prepared to face the queen for the first time in five years.

CHAPTER FOUR

F ingal was once more standing against the wall as he watched people move around the Great Hall. He'd spent most of the day in the lists, and he'd taken a blunted sword across his ribs. The impact from the flat side of the blade nearly knocked him off his feet, and now his side ached with each breath he took. But he realized he was in a better mood than he had been the previous evenings, when he'd only spent the morning training. At home at Freuchie Castle, Fingal was responsible for training the clan's warriors along with assisting the laird with clan business. He'd been trained to be his cousin's tánaiste since he was a young boy, when it was clear Lady Grant wouldn't bear Laird Grant a son.

When Fingal grew old enough to understand the significance of being the laird's heir, he threw himself into his training. He pushed himself to be among the finest warriors in his clan, and while he despised being indoors for his studies, he excelled at learning to read, write, and speak Gaelic, Scots, French, and Latin. He was even better with numbers. His relationship to the laird was just distant enough that Fingal carried an ever-present worry that someone might question or even deny his inheritance. He challenged himself to prove his worth to his clan, even though no one had ever given him cause to worry. He was the grandson of the current laird's uncle, and there were no other blood-related males to stand between him and the lairdship. But it was always possible that the clan council could vote someone else in as the new laird when the time came. Edward Grant assured Fingal no such thing would happen, but Fingal wouldn't be completely certain until the day he made his pledge to his clan.

Fingal arrived at the evening meal later than usual, having taken the time to bind his aching ribs. His men found a table closer to the ladies-in-waiting, which turned out to be a mixed blessing. While several of the more brazen women offered him suggestive glances that he ignored—no woman would force him into marriage by a scandal—his seat allowed him to watch the group. He assessed those who spoke the least. He was uninterested in marrying a shrew; he desired a woman who would understand her place as his wife, and that place didn't require much talking.

His gaze returned more than once to the woman with the shorn ebony hair. Their gazes met once before her eyes darted away. Their hue, a bright blue that made them her dominant feature, struck him as unique. He noticed that she rarely spoke and kept her head bowed as she ate. She appeared docile, even submissive. His mind flashed to his docile wolfhound that awaited his return to Freuchie. He dismissed the comparison, since the woman was far better looking than his hound.

Fingal continued to watch the dark-haired woman even after servants cleared the tables and moved them aside. The music began, and couples came together to dance. The young lady remained a wallflower for a second night in a row. He shrugged and pushed himself away from the wall. He was there to find a wife, not gawk at the newcomer. He forced himself to dance with one woman after another. During his dance with a beautiful widow, his partner offered him directions to her quarters.

Fingal was tempted, and his bollocks tightened. He'd been without a woman for more than a moon, between his fortnight-long journey to Stirling and his self-imposed celibacy during his time at court. It was by sheer willpower that he declined his partner's offer with regret. He wouldn't have time to woo a woman before he needed to marry her, but he had the common sense not to begin a dalliance weeks before his wedding. However, a night of carousing with his men would solve the hardened rod in his leggings. He signaled for his men and left, finding distraction and an ease to his discomfort at the Merry Widow, a notorious tavern in town.

Madeline noticed the lion-colored hair before she saw the appraising gray eyes. She saw him staring at her from her peripheral vision several times, and he met her gaze and held it the one time she dared look at him directly. His face had been impassive, but their eyes locked, and neither looked away for several heartbeats. Eventually, Madeline shifted her eyes to her food, and his attention moved elsewhere.

Once she had looked away, Madeline could admit to herself that the man was attractive, with thick hair just a little shorter than her own. He was broad shouldered, with the build of a trained warrior. His leine stretched tight around his biceps as he ate. His thick-corded neck was bronze from hours of training outdoors. But it was his eyes that held her attention. They were dove gray, much like the gown she'd worn the day before. She felt all too seen, and it made her want to squirm.

Madeline couldn't help but notice the man again as he danced with several of the young women, as well as a notorious widow she recognized from her time at court. The widow had been a matron during Madeline's tenure, but she and her husband had both conducted their affairs in the open. When Madeline noticed the widow's enticing glances toward her dancing partner, she was certain the couple would leave together. It surprised her to see that the man left with his men instead. From the guards' jovial expression, she assumed they would find their amusement in town.

A few men looked in her direction, but none asked her to dance. Her emotions vacillated between feeling hurt and rejected and feeling relieved. She knew she remembered the steps to every dance, but she feared she would embarrass herself by being rusty. She tucked her hair behind her ears several times, self-conscious of its shortness, and feeling exposed without her wimple.

Fewer people looked in her direction than the previous night, but it unnerved her when several unabashedly pointed at her. It seemed her past would follow her for however long she remained at court, alienating her from men and women alike. However, she was uncertain if it was her notorious behavior during her service to the queen or the fact that she was supposed to become a nun that made her an oddity. She assumed most people believed that she had been banished from the convent, just as she had been from court. She overheard two women wondering how Madeline had the audacity to return to the place of her past crimes.

Even though she longed to escape, the unwanted attention only made Madeline more resolved to remain in the Great Hall. She refused to appear as though she was fleeing from the attention. Though she fervently wished it would cease, a spark of the old Madeline's pride grew into a toasty fire in her belly. While she'd kept her head down during the meal, she refused to allow her status as a wallflower to cow her. The irony that she'd become the pariah she'd turned Maude into didn't escape her. She supposed it was God's way of tempering her pride.

Despite her exhaustion from staying awake hours later than her norm, Madeline plastered on the serene smile she'd mastered upon her first arrival at court. She nodded to those who glanced at her and defiantly met the eyes of those who stared. But when she noticed people beginning to retire, she didn't dawdle. She made a hasty retreat to her chamber for a few hours of sleep before Matins.

CHAPTER FIVE

Fingal's head bobbed as his eyes drooped shut. He hadn't been so intoxicated in years. He and his men encountered members of Clan Fraser of Lavat, allies and friends of Clan Grant. The men began the evening wagering on which wench they would tup, but the wagers soon turned away from women to a competition of who could consume the most ale and whisky without heaving.

Fiercely competitive, Fingal refused to back down. He'd won at the expense of his entire body. He'd jarred his shoulder against a building as he stumbled back to the castle, stubbed his foot as he climbed the steps to the keep, and banged his head when his blurry vision made him turn a corner too soon. Even though he was barely conscious, he still knew he would rue his choices the next day. He longed for his bed, where he could collapse into oblivion.

I should be there by now. Where the bluidy hell did ma chamber go? I'll pish ma bleeding breeks if I dinna get to a chamber pot. What's that moving? Are there two? Wait, nay. Just one. What is that?

Fingal struggled to put one foot in front of the other; as the moving figure grew closer, he reached out a hand to brace himself against the wall. He reached for his sword, only to vaguely remember relinquishing it when he returned to the keep. His hand fumbled for his dirk. As he made to draw it and prepare to ward off whatever wraith approached, a woman's voice permeated his fog.

"Yer oot yer tree," came the feminine voice. Fingal scowled when a chuckle followed the comment about his inebriation. He blinked several times to clear his vision when he realized only a Highlander or an islander would use such a phrase. "Canna see me?" she continued. "Or should I ask how many of me do ye see?

Madeline canted her head and leaned forward as bleary, bloodshot eyes struggled to focus. She was tempted to sway and confuse the man further, but she feared he would vomit if she did. She'd seen her brother in his cups more than once and had played the same game with him—until he once cast up his accounts on her feet.

"Lass," Fingal warned. He strained to his full height, then wobbled. Madeline's hands shot out to support him before she realized what she was doing. They both looked at where her hand rested on his upper arm before she dropped them. "Thank ye," he muttered.

Fingal reached out as if to see if there was more than one figure before him. When his hand found Madeline's cheek, he cupped her jaw and leaned forward to kiss her. Madeline's hands came up to his chest and gave him a forceful push. Fingal tilted to the side before falling backwards on to his arse.

"Lass," Fingal warned again. He squinted and saw the woman fold her arms. A large wooden cross draped over them. "Shite. I mean, I'm sorry, sister. I never would have if I'd kenned ye were one of them."

"One of them, *lad*?" Madeline stressed the last word but expressed confusion with the others. When Fingal's eyes drooped, Madeline knew she wouldn't get much more out of him, even if she was enjoying their exchange. She leaned forward to help him to his feet when his eyes snapped open. They appeared clearer than they had only moments ago.

"Did ye call me a *lad*? I'm a *mon*," Fingal snapped. This only earned him another chuckle from Madeline. When he growled, Madeline giggled.

"Ye sound like ma brother when he was ten summers and trying to convince Father to let him into the lists," Madeline smirked. "Dinna get in a tiswas. Ye're as much a lad as I am a lass."

"Aye. Ye're a nun," Fingal grumbled.

"Nay, I'm nae."

"Ye look like one."

"Ye canna see yer own hand in front of yer eyes. How can ye see what I may or may nae be?" Madeline retorted.

"Yer cross. It's big enough for Christ to see."

"Ye had best hope He sees ye. Ye could use divine intervention right now. I should leave ye where ye lie," Madeline huffed.

"That wouldnae be vera Christian of ye, ye bride of Christ."

"I told ye, I amnae a nun."

"Then what are ye doing wandering the keep at this hour? Did ye come from the chapel? Or do ye wear the cross to hide being a whore?" Fingal winced as soon as the words were out of his mouth. He'd gone too far. As air hissed from the woman's mouth, he struggled to his feet. When hands wrapped around his arm, he wasn't certain if he was about to be helped up or knocked back down.

"If ye werenae in such a sad state, I might take offense. I will say a rosary for yer soul at Lauds. In the meantime, ye should retire before someone sees us." Madeline helped Fingal to his feet and made sure he was steady before she let go. She pointed toward the opposite end of the passageway. "Go to the end and up the stairs. Ye'll be in the bachelor quarters. Good luck to ye."

"Thank ye. Wait," Fingal murmured as he caught her wrist. His vision had cleared, and blessedly his head didn't feel like there was cotton wool between his ears. He realized the woman standing before him was the same woman he'd stared at during the evening meal. "I dinna ken yer name. I'm Fingal Grant."

"Cairstine's Fingal?" Madeline blurted, then winced when Fingal froze. "I'm sorry. That sounded different from what I meant. I recognized yer name from a story aboot Cairstine. We were friends once. I'm Madeline. Madeline MacLeod." She waited for him to recoil in disgust.

"I've been wondering who ye are. Thank ye." Fingal leaned in and bussed a quick kiss to her cheek before turning away. He threw over his shoulder, "Until next time. *Lass*."

Madeline crossed her arms and watched the man walk away, unsure if she continued to watch him to assure herself that he wouldn't pass out drunk or because he had the most perfect backside she'd ever seen on a man. She'd let him get the last word because she wouldn't caterwaul down the passageway. Her days of making scenes were over. Instead, she returned to her chamber, but she found it difficult to settle back into sleep when a certain tawny-haired warrior kept appearing every time she closed her eyes.

Fingal felt as though he were swimming through porridge as he made his way up the stairs and to his chamber. Finally, he crashed onto his bed as his world once again spun. Face down on the cover, Fingal's eyes drifted closed, and he felt drool trickle from his lips.

But even so close to sleep, his mind kept replaying his encounter near the chapel. Something about the woman's Hebridean accent put him at ease, even before he knew who she was. Her voice was soft and lilting, and its teasing edge made her laughter tinkle. When his vision cleared enough to recognize her as the woman from the Great Hall, it surprised him to discover that she was stunning up close. Even in the dim light from the torches, her eyes shone brilliant blue. Her even teeth had bitten into her bottom lip more than once as she struggled not to laugh at him. His mind and his rod both jumped to the idea of his teeth being the ones nipping at her lip.

He'd known from the start that she was neither a whore nor a woman slipping through the halls after a tryst. He'd regretted his accusation the moment the words left his mouth. Even now, he couldn't believe he'd said something so uncouth to her. A twinge of guilt tried to take hold as he struggled to piece together why she was in the passageway at such an hour. He'd made out the soft gray tunic and large cross that made him think she was a nun, though she denied it. But he couldn't reconcile that with the gowns he'd seen her wear the past two nights. He assumed she'd come from the chapel because of where they stood, but he knew few people outside of clergy who attended Matins.

Once Fingal decided that she wasn't a nun but a strangely devout woman, he remembered that she'd called him a lad. No one had called him that since he was three-and-ten, when he grew eight inches in one summer and put on a stone of muscle. He knew she'd said it in response to being called a lass, but even old women were called "lass." He hadn't meant it to be an insult. Then again, he'd asked if she was a whore, labeled her as "one of them" when he believed she was a nun, and then called her a girl. He cringed as he turned his head to wipe the moisture dribbling down his chin. He supposed he should look for her the next day—or the day after that—and make a proper apology. He intended to sleep away the alcohol for the next several hours, then he expected to be miserable with a pounding head and a queasy belly.

Why did I drink that much again? Fingal caught himself snoring and twitched before falling into a deep sleep.

CHAPTER SIX

Madeline was unprepared for the queen and her attendants to arrive just before Terce. She recalled her days as a lady-in-waiting accompanying Queen Elizabeth to the early morning service. This morning, she kept her head bowed as the queen floated by and the young women filled the pews. Everyone but Laurel studiously avoided her row.

She'd glanced at Laurel from the corner of her eye to see her exhausted roommate attempting to remain upright and awake. Madeline had done just that countless times during her first experience at court. Late nights of dancing and gossiping left her with little sleep before the nine o'clock service. Before joining the convent, Madeline believed Terce was the perfect time to catch up on her sleep. Now she listened to the monks as they intoned the liturgy, and her mind recited the prayers along with them.

After the service, the women broke their fast. Once the morning meal ended, she struggled not to fidget as she filed out of the Great Hall with the ladies-in-waiting, who trailed after the queen. When they reached the doors to the royal solar, Madeline swiped her damp palms on her skirts. She once again wore the dove-gray gown. She'd told herself that she preferred it, since it was closer to the color of the tunic she had worn as a novice, and it was the demurest of her options. But a small sliver of her knew she'd chosen it because it reminded her of Fingal's eyes. Their conversation occupied her mind during the early morning services, despite how she tried to remain attentive. But she'd recited the prayers so many times that they were rote, whereas Fingal was a brand-new experience. Her mind couldn't shake the feel of his warm lips brushing against her cheeks. The gesture was unexpected and, in her mind, unwarranted. But the spot tingled each time she thought about it. Each unwanted recollection led to a prayer of forgiveness for her wayward and wanton thoughts.

When the doors swung open, Madeline noticed the queen already seated in her chair, a cooing baby cradled in her arms. She realized that she was looking at Prince David, the future king of Scotland. Queen Elizabeth had married Robert the Bruce more than a decade ago, but her captivity and house arrest under the English King, Edward Longshanks, had forced them apart. She knew Queen Elizabeth had longed for a child of her own for many years, even though she helped raise Marjorie, King Robert's daughter from his first marriage. Prince David was only a few months old, and he reminded Madeline of the children from Balmaha, who she'd told stories about wild sea creatures that inhabited the Hebrides. They were the same stories she'd heard as a child, and she discovered an unexpected joy in being around the children and entertaining them.

"Lady Madeline," Queen Elizabeth beckoned. Madeline approached and dipped into a deep curtsy, relieved that she didn't wobble from being out of practice. When she rose, she felt, more than saw, the queen's assessing gaze sweep over her. When she raised her eyes, the queen was looking directly at her.

"Good morn, Your Grace," Madeline spoke softly, but when the baby gurgled as though he were accepting the greeting for himself, Madeline didn't think to repress her smile. When she realized what she'd done, she made her expression impassive before looking back at the queen.

"I hear you have a way with children, Lady Madeline," Queen Elizabeth remarked. Madeline fought to hide her surprise. It disconcerted her to know the queen was that well informed about her time away from Stirling. "You're wondering how I know that. Your abrupt departure along with your brother's marriage soon after made me curious aboot how you fared. Maude is your sister now, and she is my goddaughter, after all."

Madeline swallowed and her stomach formed a knot, the news that the victim of her scorn was the queen's goddaughter leaving her nauseous. Maude's relationship with the royal couple was a well-guarded secret. She, her sister Blair, and her brother Lachlan were all the king and queen's godchildren, along with their Sinclair cousins. Not inclined to abuse their familial connections, none ever mentioned their personal ties to the monarchs. Madeline realized just how much more egregious her sins had been.

"I suppose you know," the queen continued, "that Maude and Kieran have three children now. It wouldn't surprise me if a fourth, fifth, and sixth follow. Your sister Abigail is now handfasted to Laird Lathan Chisholm, so she'll surely be a mother soon as well. What aboot you, Lady Madeline?" Queen Elizabeth spoke her question as she rose from her chair and offered the young prince to Madeline to hold.

Touched, Madeline cradled the bairn in her

arms, inhaling the soft scent that was unique to infants. His blue eyes stared into hers, and he gurgled when she wiggled her eyebrows at him. When she adjusted the blanket away from his face, his tiny hand grasped her pinky. But before she could answer, the door swung open, and King Robert and Fingal Grant entered the chamber.

Madeline gaped at the Highlander, who looked like he'd been chewed up and spat out. His bloodshot eyes barely drew her attention from his wet but disheveled hair. She was certain she could see spots where he'd missed shaving. He was also wearing his plaid. Madeline's eyes drank in the sight of the man she encountered the previous night, finding she much preferred him in his Highland garb than attempting to fit in at court with leggings and a doublet.

"My dear," the Bruce greeted his wife as he kissed the back of her hand. "I thought to visit our son before taking root in the Privy Council chamber for the rest of the day. Grant and I are meeting, but I stopped here first."

Madeline wasn't sure if the king wanted to hold his son or if they expected her to continue rocking the babe while the king peered at him. She glanced at Fingal, who wore a bemused expression. It was as though he approved of seeing her holding Prince David, but wasn't quite sure what to make of the scene—not that Madeline understood why it mattered. When the king made no move to lift the infant from her arms, she shifted his position to make it easier for the king to see his son.

"Lady Madeline, you are quite adept at holding a bairn. But your sister is not that much younger than you, and was unwed last you saw her," King Robert observed.

"Thank you, Your Majesty. I spent quite a lot of

time over the past five years in the neighboring village with the children," Madeline explained.

"You seem comfortable with them. A natural, wouldn't you say, Grant?" King Robert asked Fingal, who remained near the door. The king had turned his back to him, but Madeline noticed the shock register on Fingal's face.

"I suppose so, Your Majesty. But I know naught aboot bairns," Fingal said, an uncomfortable expression taking over his face. Madeline pressed her lips together and sucked in her cheeks, as if to keep herself from laughing. It earned her a scowl from Fingal, which only made her want to grin that much more.

When the baby whimpered, Madeline shifted her hold once again, putting the baby against her shoulder as she bounced him. She patted Prince David's back, which elicited a loud belch than made many of the ladies-in-waiting titter. Fingal cast an annoyed glance at them before returning his gaze to Madeline. He admitted to himself that the woman looked wholly at ease with the babe in her arms.

Uncertain of what led him to do it, Fingal drew close enough to hear Madeline humming. The king and queen were conversing, but Fingal noticed how their eyes darted between Madeline and himself. He recognized the tune as one his mother had sung to him when he was a child, before she passed away. His grandmother had been a Mackinnon from the Isle of Skye, so Fingal knew it was a Hebridean lullaby.

"You do look at ease, my lady," Fingal whispered as he drew closer. "Do you wish for your own bairns one day?"

Madeline's eyes widened, and her mouth dropped open. She didn't know how to answer the question because she wasn't sure how she felt. She found herself nodding her head before turning to look at the baby, who now snored softly in her arms.

"You are a mystery to me, lass," Fingal confessed in hushed tones. "How can you appear like a nun in the middle of the night, dress like a lady-in-waiting during the day, and have a mother's touch?"

"And you are a mystery to me as well. How can you drink like a fish and stumble about the keep in the middle of the night, pleat your plaid with straight creases, and look pale as a ghost?"

It was Fingal's turn for his mouth to drop open. He shook his head before grinning. "I asked you first."

"And you still sound like my brother when he was ten," Madeline countered. She shifted to see who watched them. Many darted glances at them, but only a few women were brazen enough to stare. She caught sight of Laurel, who sat in the window embrasure embroidering. Her friend continued her precise stitching even as she grinned at Madeline's situation. She'd confessed to Laurel that she'd run into Fingal, and while she didn't relay all the details, she'd admitted that he was three sheets to the wind when she found him wandering.

"Mayhap, but that doesn't answer my question," Fingal pressed.

"Persistent, are you? I will answer your question if you answer mine." Madeline waited until Fingal begrudgingly nodded. "I served the queen as one of her ladies several years ago. Lack of discretion and a mean streak landed me at Inchcailleoch Priory. I was to take my final vows in a fortnight, but it wasn't my calling to become a nun. I was summoned here before I make my way back to Lewis."

Fingal was silent as Madeline gave an honest explanation of who she had been and how she'd gotten to where she was now. But he wondered what she meant by "lack of discretion." Was she sent there because she ruined her reputation with a man, perhaps even gotten pregnant?

"Dinna look so flummoxed," Madeline whispered. "I was sent away because I was a bully, not because I was loose."

"Were you sent away from the convent for the same reason?" Fingal pressed, but when Madeline's eyes shuttered, he wished once again that he hadn't gone so far.

"Mother Abbess believes the Lord has a calling for me outside the priory." Madeline shifted Prince David, wishing she could hand him back to his mother and flee the solar. She didn't want to share her secrets with a stranger, even if she felt oddly at ease with him. "I've answered more than your original question. It's your turn."

"I entered far too many wagers last night on who could drink the most. I won, but I am paying for my pride today. I can pleat my plaid in my sleep, and I may very well have done so. And I'm pale as a ghost because I'm struggling not to keel over." Fingal swiped his hand over his brow, wiping away small beads of perspiration.

"Why are you not still abed?" Madeline wondered.

"The king summoned me, so I had no choice but to drag my carcass from my chamber," Fingal sighed.

"And he bid you to accompany him here," Madeline stated.

"He kens I'm looking for a wife, so I suppose he thought to bring the rooster to the henhouse," Fingal grinned.

Madeline turned her nose up, but looked at him from the corner of her eye. "And you suppose that you're the cockerel we'll all want?"

Fingal hadn't expected Madeline's blunt reply or

the innuendo. "Perhaps God didn't intend you to be a nun."

"Or perhaps I've been around animals enough to understand them," Madeline raised an eyebrow.

"And would you prefer a gelding or a stallion?" Fingal narrowed his eyes, thinking he'd backed her into a corner and would make her blush.

"Either would be better than an ass," Madeline retorted. Fingal had nothing to say. At least nothing he could say to a lady, and not where the king and the queen might hear.

"I shall bear that in mind, my lady." Fingal dipped his head just as the Bruce turned back to them. Fingal didn't miss the monarch's speculative gaze, but he didn't dare look back at Madeline, who'd stepped forward to give the babe to his wet nurse. Fingal followed King Robert from the chamber, but as he passed through the doorway, he glanced over his shoulder to find Madeline seated in the window embrasure with Laurel. She appeared to be looking at Laurel's stitching until her bright blue eyes met his. Something passed between them, but he couldn't identify what it might be.

CHAPTER SEVEN

"What was that all aboot?" Laurel queried.

"I don't ken," Madeline replied. "One moment the queen is telling me that she kens I'm good with the weans, then the next I'm holding the prince. Before I can make heads or tails of that, King Robert and Fingal Grant are standing there."

"And what did Fingal have to say? He appeared keen on talking to you."

"He wondered how I ended up here," Madeline shrugged.

"And?" Laurel waited for Madeline to reply, but when she only received a blank stare, she huffed. "Don't play daft with me. I ken your mind far too well for that. What did you tell him?"

"That I was sent to Inchcailleoch because I was a bully, but I wasn't called to be a nun. I mentioned that I was summoned here before I return home."

"You told him all of that?" Laurel stammered.

"I don't lie anymore, Laurel. I'm neither proud of the woman I was nor will I boast aboot the one I've become. But I won't shy away from the consequences of my past. I am who I am, flaws and all. Besides, he's looking for a wife. He will have already forgotten what I said."

"And do you ken that he looked at you longer than he has any of the rest of us?" Laurel pointed out.

"Impossible. He's been here since before I arrived," Madeline furrowed her brow.

"And in the fortnight he's been here, he spoke more to you than he has all the rest of us combined," Laurel reported. "We all believed him to be surly, but I saw him grin at you."

"That means naught. I basically asked him how he's not hanging his head over a chamber pot. That's the only reason I ken he's looking for a wife. The king brought him here for him to see the others."

"And the only person he saw was you, Madeline. The king didn't give him time to speak with anyone else."

Madeline glanced at the door that Fingal passed through only minutes ago and wondered if there was any truth in what Laurel said. She wasn't certain what to make of the Highlander. The idea that such a virile man might look in her direction for a wife made her want to squirm more than waiting for the queen's attention.

"Madeline," Laurel broke into her thoughts. "Queen Elizabeth wishes to speak to you."

Madeline held in her sigh as she handed the embroidery back to Laurel. She returned to where she'd been standing, clasped her hands before her, and offered the queen a submissive mien. She'd hoped that Elizabeth de Burgh had lost interest in her, but she realized the king and Fingal's visit was only a brief intermission from her interview.

"Lady Madeline, you and Fingal appear familiar with one another. I wasn't aware that you'd met when last you were here."

"We hadn't, Your Grace. I mentioned Cairstine," Madeline offered, but she didn't clarify that she'd

68

done that in the passageway the night before. "And I think he appreciated a familiar accent."

Queen Elizabeth's astute mind seemed to hear everything Madeline didn't say. "I imagine you know why the king and I requested your attendance at court." When the queen said no more, Madeline realized that the statement actually begged a question.

"I'm uncertain, Your Grace. But I imagine it is for me to make amends for my past transgressions," Madeline offered.

"I suppose you can do that. But there is no one here to apologize to other than Laurel. And you two seem to have picked up your friendship where you left off," Queen Elizabeth observed. Madeline couldn't keep from flinching. She and Laurel had fallen back into an easy friendship, but it was as different from what it had been as chalk and cheese. There was no manipulation or threats. They were no longer allied against the other ladies. Instead, Madeline and Laurel had both changed for the better, and this had fostered a genuine relationship between them. The queen continued, "No, Lady Madeline, that was not why you are here. You are to be wed."

"Wed?" Madeline repeated.

"Aye. My correspondence with the Mother Abbess at Inchcailleoch has kept me abreast of how you've changed. And as I said, I'm aware you have a way with children. Since you are not to become a nun, you will become a wife."

"Yes, Your Grace. Uh—" Madeline stuttered. "To whom?"

"That has yet to be decided."

"Does my brother ken?" Madeline wondered if Kieran was a party to this arrangement.

"He's been informed. The king will sign the betrothal documents in his place," Queen Elizabeth explained.

"So I won't see my family again before I marry," Madeline whispered as she fought down her rising gorge.

"Likely not, unless your husband allows you a visit."

Allows me. And if he doesnae? I'll never see ma mother, brother, and sister again. I'll never apologize to Maude in person, and I'll never meet ma nieces and nephew. But ye'd already accepted that once. Aye, but it was different when I thought I gave that up to serve the Lord. Ye likely will serve a laird. Nae the same, and ye ken it. What if ma husband is a cruel mon and willna even allow me to write, let alone visit? Oh, dear Lord in Heaven, he'll expect to bed me. I ken that God ordained marriage for the begetting of weans, but—it's so —so base. And once upon a time, ye found that intriguing. That was a sin. Coupling isnae for pleasure. It's for bearing bairns, which I ken I want. But lust will get me nay where but Hell, and I will face naught but damnation.

"Lady Madeline?" Queen Elizabeth's voice permeated the rapid thoughts firing through Madeline's mind. "I see this is a lot for you to take in. Did you not guess that a marriage awaits you?"

"I suppose I did, Your Grace. But now that it's been spoken aloud, it's—um—rather—uh—daunting. I haven't considered becoming a wife in many years. I shall have to adjust."

"And you will, Madeline," Queen Elizabeth softened her tone. It surprised the younger woman that the queen dropped Madeline's honorific and just used her given name. "You've been at court all of two days, and it's plain to see how you've changed. If your face weren't the same, I would think you a stranger. I don't think any of us have reason to fear a return to your auld ways. I think you're happier now than you were."

Happier? I wouldnae say happier, but I was content, until they sent away me from where I believed I would live out ma last days. I dinna ken how happy or content I am now. I want to curl up and cry. I dinna ken that I can be a wife if it means a mon coming to ma bed. Mayhap it willna be often, and mayhap he willna expect much more than for me to lie there. Now that it's before me, I dinna think I want love and a family if it means naught but more sin.

"Madeline, do you fear who the king will choose?" Queen Elizabeth prodded.

"Aye," Madeline blurted.

"Neither the king nor I harbor any animosity toward you for the past. You are like a new person to us. Your marriage will not be a punishment. Hopefully, you will find fulfillment, and even happiness."

"Aye, Your Grace. Thank you."

"The king will likely decide within the next day or two. You'll be informed of who the mon is within a sennight. The king may waive the required three sennights of posting the banns. I doubt anyone could devise a reason that you couldn't marry. You've been in a convent for years."

"Aye, Your Grace. Thank you," Madeline repeated the only thing she could think to say. She prayed the queen would dismiss her soon. Madeline guessed it was close to time for the midday meal, which meant she needed to make her way to the chapel for Sext. She curtsied again and backed away. She clung to her faith as the only tether she had to keep from falling into a well of despair and panic.

Dinna panic until there is a reason to. Mayhap the mon will be auld with twelve children and have nay need for me beyond running his keep and minding his children. Then I could have the family I wish for.

In her heart, Madeline knew that wasn't what fate had in store for her.

CHAPTER EIGHT

F ingal fought the urge to huff as he waited for the chamberlain to bid him entry into the Privy Chamber. He'd followed the king there and then was made to wait in the passageway until it was his turn to have an audience, remaining until it was time for the noon meal. He discreetly looked around for Madeline, but she was nowhere in sight. He wondered if she was fasting her day away in the chapel now that the queen was in the Great Hall.

When the meal concluded, Fingal found himself once again standing in the passageway outside the Privy Council chamber, wanting to bash in the chamberlain's smug face. Fingal understood the short man's haughtiness came from his disdain for Highlanders. As the afternoon passed, the chamberlain graciously invited various Lowlanders in to speak to the Bruce while keeping the Highlanders waiting.

The mon doesnae seem to realize that each of us Highlanders could snap him like a twig in winter. He enjoys antagonizing us because he thinks his position protects him. Ye would think he'd learned his lesson when Lachlan Sutherland picked him up by the collar and dropped him inside the chamber after trying to block the mon's way. People are still clishmaclavering over that, and it happened how many moons ago? Bluidy eejit.

"Grant," the chamberlain's nasal tones echoed in the brick corridor. Fingal pushed away from the wall and walked toward the man. He flexed his chest to make his muscles stand out. The chamberlain backed into one of the guards. Fingal jerked his head forward as if to signal he would lunge at the court official, but he only looked down his nose as he entered the chamber.

"Making friends, I see," King Robert mused. Fingal glanced around the room, noticing the courtiers gathered in small groups while several men sat together with parchment before them. One held a quill. The Bruce gestured to a chair at the large table in the center of the chamber. "Join me."

Fingal waited until the monarch took his seat before sliding into his. He'd been awaiting this audience since he arrived. He wondered if King Robert had any suggestions as to whom he should marry. He still held doubts that he would find anyone suitable at court, though an image of Madeline MacLeod once again flashed before his eyes. Their banter amused him, and it surprised him to find he liked her sharp mind. He supposed he'd spoken to her more than he had any other woman, barring Cairstine and her sister Fenella. He usually kept his conversations with women short and purposeful: ordering food and drink and accepting offers to their beds.

"Do you have anyone in mind?" the king asked, without preamble.

"Nay, Your Majesty. I hoped I might find a recommendation or two," Fingal responded.

"What type of woman do you desire?"

"The kind that doesn't make for a laird's wife," Fingal grinned. He relaxed when the king guffawed. Fingal grew serious as he considered what kind of woman would make an ideal wife. "I wish for a wife who can run Freuchie Castle once my cousin-by-marriage passes. I'd prefer a comely woman, but her looks won't matter in the dark. One who comes from a mother who bore plenty of healthy bairns is preferable."

"You describe a serving woman, not a lady, Fingal," King Robert pointed out archly.

"She will have a great deal of work to do as Lady Grant. I don't want a vain woman who will drain our coffers and inhale our food. A healthy dowry would make up for a homely woman."

King Robert sat silently for so long that Fingal feared he'd been too straightforward about his expectations. When the king finally spoke again, he leaned back and steepled his fingers in front of his chin. "And have you found such a woman?"

"Among the ladies-in-waiting and widows, I can't say that I have," Fingal admitted.

"The ladies and widows? Have you found a serving wench you prefer? She won't come with a dowry," King Robert teased.

"Nay. There are plenty who are comely enough, but as you noted, no dowry. I simply wish for a woman who won't drive me barmy with incessant and inane chatter, or bleed my clan dry with her vanity and demands," Fingal explained.

"And you came to court, a place filled with Lowlanders who know naught of the Highland way of life, to find a wife," the king stated rather than asked.

"Aye. There don't seem to be very many eligible women in the north," Fingal sighed.

"And since Cairstine married Eoin Gordon, you lost your broodmare," King Robert said sardonically.

"I assumed Cairstine and I would wed ever since we were very young, but she's happy with Eoin. The mon loves her unconditionally, and she loves him just as much. Besides, she's far too outspoken. She would have driven me around the bend. I prefer a quieter woman."

King Robert watched Fingal over his fingertips before nodding. He leaned forward and rested his hands on the table as his jaw moved from side to side, as though he considered what he would do to Fingal rather than just what he would say. Fingal sat as the king's gaze bore into him. When the monarch narrowed his eyes, Fingal felt sweat trickle down his back.

"Very well. Continue looking, and I will ask the queen for her recommendations. Good luck to you," King Robert nodded before flicking his fingers over his shoulders. One of his courtiers scrambled to his side with a sheaf of parchment. Fingal understood that he was dismissed. Even though the king no longer looked at him, Fingal bowed deeply and backed away until he could turn and exit the chamber.

Fingal took a seat at a table he and his men shared with the Frasers of Lovat. He felt surly after wasting a day waiting for the king, who offered no suggestions or solutions. He was also still suffering the aftereffects of imbibing far too much the night before. He hadn't trained in the lists, and his restless energy made his patience short. When the ladies-in-waiting arrived for the meal, the high pitch of their voices put him further on edge. But he found himself calming when Madeline walked past. She didn't look at him, and he wondered if she'd even noticed that he sat one table away from her. But her presence seemed to be a balm to his irritation.

"I dinna ken a single woman with hair so short. If her breasts weren't enough to feast upon, I would think her a mon," one of the Fraser men snorted. Fingal looked at the speaker, and a sudden urge to plow his fist into the man's face swept over him. It wasn't as though he hadn't said similar things about other women countless times, but Madeline seemed too gentle and reserved for such a comment. Her piety struck him as a little extreme now that she no longer lived and toiled among the nuns, but she was a devout woman, and the comment chafed. "All those years locked away may have made her skinnier, but her tits are still divine," the Fraser man chortled.

The men at the table found the comment uproarious, knowing that she'd nearly become a nun. Fingal looked around the table, realizing the Fraser men knew Madeline from before she left court years earlier. He was curious about her, and he sensed he would learn more from the men than he would trying to overhear gossip.

"Why was she locked away?" Fingal asked around a mouthful of steaming pottage.

"Ye wouldnae ken it from the looks of her now, but she was a right bitch back in the day. Her list of sins wasna vera long, but she had more than one venial on there," one of the Fraser guards, called Jamie, explained. "Pride, jealousy, sloth, gluttony. She was once the queen bee among the ladies-in-waiting. She wasna the bonniest of them all, but men flocked to her when she arrived. She was flirtatious back then, and the attention from the men made her feel superior to the other women. She used that to push her way into becoming their leader. She was a right piece of work to Maude Sutherland."

"They were as different as wine and water," another Fraser man picked up the story. "Funny how the Lord hands down his justice. The vera woman Lady Madeline tormented to nay end, persecuted really, married Lady Madeline's brother and is now

Lady MacLeod. Maude was a bonnie enough lass, but a wee broad across the beam. Lady Madeline, Lady Cairstine—begging yer pardon—and Lady Laurel made Lady MacLeod's life miserable. Lady Madeline was incensed to discover Laird MacLeod's interest in the bonnie wallflower. From what I ken, she and her brother argued, and the queen overheard."

Jamie picked the story back up. "The queen likely sentenced her to extra hours of prayer, and Lady Madeline went berserk. She launched an angry tirade at Lady MacLeod without realizing who could overhear. Laird MacLeod practically lifted her off her feet as he pulled her away from the table where Lady MacLeod sat with her sister, Lady Cameron. The laird dragged her from the table and next anyone kenned she was on a horse bound for the 'isle of auld women.'" Jamie finished with a shiver as he stuck a chunk of bread in his mouth.

Fingal glanced in Madeline's direction and found her with her head lowered and her food untouched. When she raised her head and reached for the bread in front of her, he realized she'd been praying. He noticed she avoided rich foods with thick sauces, preferring the bread and plain dishes. When she wasn't chewing, she kept her eyes downcast, nodding periodically when someone spoke to her.

The woman Fingal observed was a stark opposite from the woman he'd heard described. He wondered if Madeline continued to manipulate those around her, and if her docile appearance was a charade performed to keep people at a distance. But something the woman across from her said made her jerk her head upward, and even from a distance Fingal could see the deep red staining her cheeks and the tears she struggled to hold back.

As though she sensed him, Madeline turned to

look in his direction. No one could fake the fear Fingal saw in her eyes before she looked away. She nodded her head at the same woman. Fingal watched her reach toward her chest, but catching herself, Madeline appeared to pull a piece of lint or thread from her gown. Fingal knew she was reaching for the cross he'd seen hanging around her neck the night before.

"The queen is surely trying to marry her off," theorized Simon, one of the Grant guards. With that comment, Fingal's attention returned to the men sitting around him.

"If she's so changed, then these women will eat her alive like a pack of she-wolves," Fingal reasoned. "And if she isnae so different, then the queen doesnae need her pishing vinegar in their cups."

"Perhaps ye should marry her, Fingal," Harry Grant, the most senior of the guards, suggested. Fingal grunted as he took a bite of lamb. The thought had already crossed his mind. Madeline might be exactly the woman he needed. She was unassuming, amusing, and would come with a good dowry.

The only barrier to their marriage Fingal could think of was her piety. He didn't need a love match, and he did not want a wife harping at him about keeping a leman. If Madeline wanted to lie in bed like a dead fish while they coupled, Fingal couldn't care less. But he wouldn't allow the devout would-be nun to stand in the way of his pleasure. Marrying her would be convenient, and that's what he wanted most out of the arrangement. Perhaps Madeline was just who he was looking for.

Madeline's ears rang as she hurried along the passageways to Matins. Despite excusing herself early from the evening meal, she hadn't slept once she returned to the chamber she shared with Laurel. The mistress of the bedchamber had granted them permission to be roommates until Madeline left. She'd already asked God to forgive her deceitfulness when she pretended to be asleep as Laurel returned to their room hours after Madeline retired.

She'd nearly fallen off the bench backwards when Blythe Dunbar informed her that the most likely groom for her, given her past, was Edwin Douglas. He was a lesser chieftain and an experienced warrior known for his cruelty in battle. She remembered stories about him from years earlier. His name was the one the ladies-in-waiting would threaten one another with. He'd already outlived three wives, each of whom died giving birth to enormous sons.

Blythe recounted the man's last visit to court only a sennight before Madeline arrived. Edwin slayed a guard in the lists when the much younger man challenged him to spar. Everyone claimed it was an accident, but Blythe pointed out that accidents happened frequently around Edwin, an observation that terrified Madeline.

Blythe's sister Emelie pointed out that the much older Edwin would likely die long before Madeline, if no accidents befell her first. She could then marry one of the chieftain's adult sons or wait for the king to marry her off to someone else. The suggestions horrified Madeline, who still wasn't certain if she could serve as any man's wife, let alone a father and son combination. It felt sacrilegious and incestuous to even consider such a notion.

Madeline once again eased into the third pew on the Gospel side for Matins. She lowered herself to her knees and made the sign of the cross before bowing her head.

Holy Father, please dinna send me such a mon as Edwin Douglas. Have I nae shown Ye genuine contrition over the years? Dinna I repent when I realize I've sinned? Please Lord, dinna make him the one the king chooses. There must be someone else who willna terrify me. I need nae love him, and he need nae love me. Just a mon who willna abuse me or whose bairn I willna die trying to bring into this world.

I suppose if I can fear dying in childbirth, I must be able to accept lying with a mon. I dinna have to enjoy it. But I can tolerate it, and mayhap it willna be so insufferable if the mon can be gentle. Mayhap I'll even get with child easily and quickly, then he willna have to bed me that often. He can do as he pleases while I run the keep and tend the children.

Can I really turn a blind eye to an unfaithful mon? Do I really have a choice? I never assumed I'd marry for love. In fact, I assumed the mon I would marry would keep a leman and that I might even take a lover once I did ma duty and bred him an heir. But what aboot now? I wouldnae be unfaithful, and I dinna covet the sins of the flesh. Ma husband will be ma laird and master. If he wishes to lie with other women, there is naught I can say. What he does will be between him and the Lord. I can only control what I do. I dinna want to try to control anyone else ever again. That's what led me down the path to sin the last time. I dinna need love. I need convenience.

Madeline realized the Matins prayer service was over, and the monks who officiated had already retreated to the sacristy. She made her way back to her chamber and slipped off her tunic. She'd felt bare earlier that night when she'd reached for her cross; now, she wrapped her palm around it and fell asleep with it pressing against her skin, a comfort amidst her swirling thoughts.

CHAPTER NINE

"I believe I have a few candidates for you to consider," King Robert announced to Fingal as the hunting party rode out of the bailey with the early morning sunlight at their backs.

It had surprised Fingal to find the queen and several women, including Madeline, mounting horses as he entered the bailey. He'd planned to go to the lists, but as he left his chamber, a page informed him that the king requested his company on the hunt.

"Thank you, Your Majesty. Who do you have in mind?" Fingal responded.

"The Dunbar sisters both come with a healthy dowry. Caitlyn Kennedy can be a wee talkative, but she has a good head on her shoulders, and likely a significant dowry. Laurel Ross won't bring much of a dowry, but marrying her will make you the son-by-marriage to the Earl of Ross." King Robert watched Fingal's face as he named four of the most obvious candidates.

"They would all make an advantageous match to the right mon. Your Majesty, you ken the Grants aren't on good terms with the Camerons. If I marry Lady Laurel, I would ally the Grants with the Rosses and, indirectly, the Sutherlands, since Lady Blair

Sutherland is now Lady Cameron. The Rosses wouldn't make good bedfellows for the Grants. Ladies Blythe and Emelie come from a prosperous clan, but their—uh—um—father's uh—" Fingal stammered as he tried to choose his words wisely. Laird Dunbar only came around to Robert's side toward the end of the Wars of Scottish Independence. The man's fealty was officially to Scotland, but he hadn't cut all ties across the border. The Grants were staunch supporters of the Bruce, and the thought of marrying a woman from a treasonous clan made Fingal furious.

"Aye, Grant. I ken what you can't seem to spit out. Perhaps the Dunbars aren't such a wonderful choice. What aboot Caitlyn Kennedy?" the king asked. Fingal made his face a blank, unsure how to admit that the gregarious young woman would likely drive him barmy if he had to spend the next two or three score years listening to her prattle. King Robert looked at Fingal's attempt at a neutral expression. "Hmm. Mayhap not."

"What aboot Lady Madeline MacLeod?" Fingal attempted to keep his voice light. "I need a wife, and she is here because she needs a husband."

"But her sister handfasted with Lathan Chisholm. If you objected to Lady Laurel on the grounds of a thready connection to the Camerons, then I cannot imagine you'd marry a woman whose sister is in a handfast with the laird of a clan you can't get along with. You would have sisters choose sides against one another?"

Fingal hadn't considered that. He'd used the spiderweb of alliances to disqualify Laurel simply because he didn't want an impoverished bride. "Mayhap Lady Madeline is the right bride if our marriage brought aboot a truce with the Chisholms. As much as I despise the ruddy bastard, even Lathan wouldn't wage war on his wife's sister."

As he spoke the words aloud, Fingal found the notion of marrying Madeline more palatable by the moment. Convenience was what he was truly looking for. The prospect of a truce with his clan's most obnoxious rival while gaining a wife who would likely look the other way when he did what he pleased seemed a nearly perfect solution. King Robert was about to speak when an arrow flew past Fingal's right shoulder. It appeared to be aimed at nothing until an angry snort and a thud sounded just ahead of them. Madeline rode past him, her bow in her hands with an arrow knocked but lowered. She reined in and released the arrow into the now visible—and writhing—boar's neck. The animal twitched once more, then ceased moving.

"Well done," Fingal said as he reined in beside Madeline. She looked at him in disbelief.

"Well done? 'Thank you' would be more appropriate," Madeline retorted.

"What do I have to be thankful for?" Fingal looked at her as if she was daft, her tone surprising him.

"While you were chewing the fat with the king, neither of you was paying attention to the boar stomping and swiping his hoof on the ground. The beast was ready to charge, and it's your mount it would have reached first. Your horse could be dead right now; instead, we are having roasted boar for the evening meal." Madeline shook her head as she threw her leg over her horse's rump and climbed down. She moved closer to the slain animal, but maintained a safe distance. Her first arrow protruded from the wild pig's chest, while the second still vibrated from its position in the animal's neck.

Fingal looked at the disturbed dirt near the swine

and realized Madeline was right. He was so intent upon his conversation that he hadn't noticed the wild beast preparing to attack. His pride rankled as he realized his finely honed warrior skills were not so attune to danger as he wanted to believe. It embarrassed him to be shown up in front of the woman he was considering for a betrothal, but Fingal realized it was concern and irritation in Madeline's eyes, not pride or mockery.

"Ye're right, lass. I owe ye an apology. And I thank ye for being alert and a fine shot," Fingal dropped his voice as he spoke close to Madeline's ear, his burr warming Madeline's insides. When she turned her head and looked up at him, he watched the cords in her neck strain as she swallowed. They stood close enough that Fingal could have easily kissed her. The thought was strangely tempting, but a high, pierced squeal shattered the moment.

Fingal drew his dirk and hurled it in the direction of the sound. A short bleat sounded as the dirk embedded itself in a juvenile boar's forehead. He'd thrown it hard enough to pierce through the animal's thick skull. He supposed Madeline slew the young boar's mother, and it was squawking for justice. Its tusks were already long enough to do serious damage if it speared someone. It was too close to Madeline for Fingal's comfort; Madeline's pale face indicated that she felt the same way.

"Thank ye," Madeline murmured.

"Ye can thank me with a kiss, lass," Fingal whispered in her ear. Madeline's eyes widened in shock before her gaze swept the trees, searching for anyone in their hunting party who might have heard Fingal's suggestion.

"Why would I do that?" Madeline hissed.

"Cause ye might enjoy it," Fingal suggested. He

watched Madeline's stunned expression turn into an icy glare as she took a step back from him.

"I can imagine the women ye are used to, Fingal. But I amnae one of them. There is naught to be enjoyed aboot sinning," Madeline said before she turned away, but Fingal caught her arm.

"I didna mean to offend ye, Madeline. I was teasing," Fingal explained.

"I dinna think so. I think ye believe I would kiss ye and that I would enjoy it. Ye're too arrogant a mon for me, Fingal. I didna realize it before." Madeline shook her head as disappointment filled her. Fingal would expect more from her than she could offer a husband, and she suspected she would wind up with little more than a broken heart.

"Madeline, we've jested a few times and now saved one another's lives, but that doesnae mean we ken each other that well. I can be arrogant, and I ken that. But I really meant ma comment in jest. I'm sorry if it didna come across that way," Fingal released her arm and offered her a remorseful smile.

"Nay harm done, I suppose. I may be a touch too sensitive. I amnae used to speaking to men anymore. Sometimes it's like I never forgot, and at others, it's rather overwhelming," Madeline confessed.

"Madeline, which men have ye been speaking to? Ye dinna dance in the evening, and I never see ye during the day. Who could overwhelm ye?" Fingal asked.

"Ye." Madeline turned away and walked back to her horse. She mounted and wheeled the animal around. She spurred her horse forward, her MacLeod guards encircling her as they rode back to the castle.

"Still wish to marry her?" King Robert's voice came from behind Fingal.

"I do." Fingal realized it wasn't just convenience

that made him affirm his choice. Madeline intrigued him in a way no other woman ever had. He'd never imagined wishing for a woman's council once he became laird, but he suspected Madeline would offer sound advice. She was comely, would come with a substantial dowry, looked to be healthy enough to give him several children, was intelligent and didn't chatter mindlessly, and wasn't interested in forming an attachment. He would have a wife who bore him an heir, ran his keep, gave excellent advice, and stayed out of his way.

"Then the better question is whether you think she'll marry you," King Robert mused.

"She's reasonable. She'll see that a marriage of convenience is what we both need," Fingal shrugged.

"Is that how you intend to woo her? I think your courtship skills need some work," the king chuckled.

"Why woo her when you will be the one signing her betrothal contract in her brother's place?" Fingal pointed out.

"Because you don't want your bonnie bride to murder you in your sleep," King Robert replied as he clapped Fingal on the shoulder. "Do yourself a favor and keep your opinion that she's the perfect broodmare to yourself. Even in an arranged marriage, no woman wants reminding she's little more than chattel. At least not before you say the vows."

Fingal stared in the castle's direction, even though Madeline and her guards were nowhere in sight. He turned to look at the king. "I will keep that advice in mind, but I don't have time to woo anyone. I've been here a fortnight and on the road for a fortnight before that. If I must wait three sennights for the banns, then I'll be away from Freuchie for nearly three moons."

"Is there a reason you need to return in such a rush?" the monarch wondered. "I imagine Edward expected this to take several sennights, if not at least a moon, to arrange. He kens the time to travel to and from Stirling."

"My laird bade me to remember that it might take time to find a wife, so he is not in a rush for me to return. But that doesn't change my duties to my clan. While I am away, someone else is responsible for training the men. Someone else is taking my patrols. Someone else is standing watch for me," Fingal pointed out.

"When will you accept that your inheritance is secure, Fingal? You don't have aught to prove to your clan. Or to me," King Robert reassured.

"Yes, Your Majesty," Fingal nodded, unprepared for the king's paternal tone. It was easy to forget that, even though the Bruce only had two legitimate children, he had several born on the wrong side of the blanket. He'd spent little time with most of them over the years while he'd fought one campaign after another across Scotland and northern England. But he was still a father, and his oldest natural son, Robert Bruce, was the Lord of Liddesdale and guardian of Hermitage Castle, an honor bestowed after he fought alongside the king.

"Come to my Council chamber after the midday meal, and we will draft and sign the contracts. She'll ken of the arrangement before the evening meal, where I will announce your betrothal." King Robert sounded as relieved as Fingal felt, knowing the search for a bride was over. Fingal murmured his thanks and followed the rest of the party back to the keep.

CHAPTER TEN

Madeline made the sign of the cross as she rose from her pew, the midday prayer service over. It had surprised her to receive an invitation from the queen to join the hunt that morning; she hadn't participated in one since her days on Lewis. She hadn't expected to enjoy tracking an animal and then successfully bringing it down. She'd had a twinge of guilt for killing one of God's creatures, but it disappeared as quickly as it came when she reminded herself that the boar would feed the castle, and she'd likely saved Fingal's life.

Madeline had said a prayer of thanksgiving and contrition for her actions during the service, and she felt more at peace after her disappointing conversation with Fingal. She was grateful that she'd spied the irate animal before it charged Fingal, and she was glad her aim was still true despite not having held a bow in years. But she'd felt conflicted while riding back to the keep, curious about Fingal's suggestion that she might enjoy kissing him. She feared she was slipping back into the Madeline who once enjoyed flirting and kissing men, who'd taken pleasure in the attention. She fought the lust that she felt whenever she saw—or even thought about—Fingal.

"Lady Madeline."

Madeline turned to find Queen Elizabeth approaching her. She'd seen the queen enter the chapel alone, seeking silent contemplation, just after she'd slipped into her own pew. But now they were face-to-face, and Madeline felt more apprehensive than she had earlier that morning when she greeted Queen Elizabeth in the bailey.

"I am pleased to find you here. I would have a word," Queen Elizabeth said.

"Yes, Your Grace," Madeline replied as she dipped into a curtsy.

"The king has decided," Queen Elizabeth announced.

"Already?" Madeline gasped. She fought to compose herself as her heart beat a rapid staccato behind her ribs.

"Yes. King Robert will sign the contracts this afternoon, and he will announce the betrothal at the evening meal. You will wed in a sennight."

"That's it?" Madeline whispered. She steeled herself for the name of her betrothed, fearing it would be Edwin Douglas. "Who am I to marry?"

"Fingal Grant."

Madeline stood in stunned silence. Only that morning she'd told the man he wasn't right for her. Now she would marry him in a matter of days. Her heart raced, but for an entirely different reason. An image of him kissing her flashed before her eyes, and the temptation she felt for him scared her.

"Does he know?" Madeline wondered.

"He was the one to suggest you," Queen Elizabeth mused. "You've made an impression upon him."

Madeline nodded as she tried to digest the news. She suspected she looked like the village fool standing before the queen, saying nothing, only blinking. Her mouth grew dry as she tried to think of something, anything, to say.

"Thank you, Your Grace." Madeline forced the words from between her lips. She glanced at the pew, her instinct to return to prayer. But for the first time in years, prayer didn't bring its usual solace.

"Madeline," Queen Elizabeth murmured, for once forgoing formality. "You look petrified. I assumed from your time at court that you knew what happens between a mon and woman, but your mother isn't here to explain. Perhaps I should be the one to do so."

"Thank you, Your Grace, but I do know. My mother explained many years ago, and I heard far more than I ever should have while I was in your service."

"Then you fear marrying a mon you don't ken," Queen Elizabeth surmised, and Madeline nodded her head. "When I married the king, I was little more than a girl. I knew who he was. Who didn't? But I didn't know *him*. He was a mon with vast experience of the world that I knew naught aboot. He'd sired several children and had already been married. I couldn't imagine how we would get along, and eight years of separation complicated our lives. But my husband is a good mon, as is Fingal Grant. He will treat you well and provide for you. You will learn to get on together."

Madeline noted that the queen empathized with her, but she had little to say about Madeline's future groom. Queen Elizabeth didn't suggest that either King Robert or Fingal valued fidelity or even fondness between husband and wife. At least at the convent, Madeline felt valued among the sisters. She'd found warmth and fulfillment in her friendships with the other nuns. Even among the senior nuns, they had all been equals. Madeline suspected Fingal expected her to be seen and not heard, more like a child than an equal. It somehow hurt her to know that Fingal would likely never see her as more than another responsibility.

"Thank you for the kind words. I will bear them in mind," Madeline replied, forcing a smile. When the queen excused her, she sought her chamber. Too drained from the morning to even pray, she slept through the late afternoon until Laurel returned to their chamber and woke her. It was the most she'd slept at one time, besides being ill, since she left court for the priory.

"Lady Madeline's dowry includes lands in Assynt. While that isn't close enough for your clan to use as pastureland, it will bring you revenue from crops, trade, and rents. It is Lady Madeline's dower land should you die before her. Otherwise, it will pass to any daughters she bears you. Laird MacLeod promises one hundred merks, along with forty heads of cattle, a horse for Lady Madeline, and a silver set of plates and chalices. He has provided her a purse to arrange a suitable wardrobe for her time at court, but I doubt you intend to remain long enough for a seamstress to complete it. Laird MacLeod also includes an adequate allowance to clothe your bride once you arrive at Freuchie Castle. There are several pieces of jewelry that will pass to Lady Madeline from her mother. What say you?"

Fingal was speechless. He knew the MacLeods of Lewis were prosperous, and he'd expected Madeline to have a healthy dowry that included land, but the number of livestock surprised him. He hadn't given thought to Madeline's attire, but he supposed he would be responsible for such things. It gave him pause to wonder where she'd gotten the gray, lavender, and russet-colored gowns she'd worn in public. He suspected she borrowed them from Laurel, which made him wonder what she would wear when they arrived at his—their—home. After a sennight in the saddle, her tunic would be threadbare, and she would arrive looking more like an urchin than the future Lady Grant.

"That is a generous dowry that exceeds what I anticipated," Fingal admitted. "Laird MacLeod is generous. I accept those terms and the others we discussed. I am prepared to sign the contracts."

"Very good. Lady Madeline may sign this evening, though her mark isn't necessary to execute the contracts. I will announce the betrothal at the meal, and you may marry in a sennight."

"Will there be no posting of the banns, Your Majesty?" Fingal asked.

"Since my excommunication, I can make such decisions as I see best for Scotland. Your bride has lived a secluded life in a convent for five years. I cannot imagine an impediment on her side. Do you have another wife of which I should be aware? I'm certain there are no concerns about consanguinity."

"No wives or children, Your Majesty," Fingal replied.

"Then let us sign and make your marriage official," King Robert proclaimed.

Fingal stared at the documents laying on the table before him. Marriage brought him to court, but now that he was betrothed, reality felt vastly different from what it had an hour earlier. He picked up the quill and scrawled his signature at the bottom of the agreement. The king quickly followed suit. And like that, Fingal was for all intents and purposes married to Madeline MacLeod. Legally, he could bed her that night without the benefit of a wedding service.

A cold sweat broke out across his brow as the weight of his additional duty settled on his shoulders. He'd been responsible for other people since he assumed the position of tánaiste, but he'd never been so accountable for a single person's life before this moment. He wondered if he'd acted too impetuously.

The Bruce seemed to read his mind. "Every groom has a moment of worry. You have assumed a new responsibility unlike any you've had before. It's normal to have a moment of doubt. For what it's worth, I think you will find you've made a wise choice with Lady Madeline. I think what the future holds in store for you both will pleasantly surprise you."

Fingal could only nod his head, his eyes still looking at the documents. He suddenly thought about Madeline the woman rather than Madeline the dowry. "Does she ken?"

"By now she will. Queen Elizabeth will have informed her."

"Should I see her, speak to her, before the announcement?" Fingal wondered.

"That might be wise. I will ensure she meets you in my antechamber before the evening meal. You may enter the Great Hall as a couple and dine together," King Robert decreed.

"Thank you, Your Majesty," Fingal replied before taking his leave.

CHAPTER ELEVEN

Madeline inhaled deeply as she glanced down at her gown once more. She knew there were no wrinkles, not a thread out of place on the kirtle. It was a deep sky blue that matched her eyes. The gown clung to her shapely body and accentuated her ample bust while cinching tight around her narrow ribcage and waist. It flared out over her hips before hanging loosely around her legs. While Laurel had lent Madeline the other three gowns she'd worn at court, her friend insisted Madeline keep this one. She argued that it was far more suited to Madeline than to Laurel herself. When Madeline attempted to refuse, Laurel proclaimed it was her wedding gift to Madeline, ending the discussion.

Now Madeline stood at the doors to the antechamber, butterflies fluttering within her belly as she shook out the skirts. A guard opened the door for her, and she glided into the antechamber. She employed every bit of grace her mother drilled into her as she presented herself to her future husband. The door closed behind her, and Madeline looked around the empty room. She had a moment's trepidation that she'd imagined the entire afternoon, or that even worse, Fingal rejected her. She walked to the fireplace, appreciating the cheery blaze despite the summer heat outside. Doubt reached out its chilling tentacles and began to coil around her.

Madeline jumped when she felt the air move as someone stepped behind her. She spun around to find Fingal. She hadn't heard him enter. A gleam entered his eyes; it was lust, and he directed it at her. An ache low in her belly made her core tighten. She glanced past Fingal's shoulders and realized they were alone.

"Madeline, you look stunning," Fingal whispered. Fingal had never seen fabric such an exact shade as someone's eyes, but Madeline's eyes shone brightly as pink infused her cheeks. "Madeline?"

Fingal grew worried when Madeline didn't move but to blink and breathe. She barely acknowledged his arrival after her initial surprise. She stood as still as a statue, her eyes meeting his, but her expression was inscrutable. He reached out his hand and took one of hers, finding it icy. As he ran his thumb over her palm, he felt the calluses that had developed from her years of working in the gardens and around the convent. She attempted to snatch her hand back, her pink cheeks turning red, but Fingal held it tightly. He turned her palm over before lifting her other hand.

"There is naught to hide, Madeline. These hands are earned. They tell me you aren't afraid of hard work, which is important for life in the Highlands. I don't expect you to toil among the servants, but it confirms what I already suspected. You are not a vain or selfish woman," Fingal said.

"How can you ken that from my hands?" Madeline whispered. Her emotions were in turmoil as she tried to make sense of what he said, while her body continued to react to his presence and his touch. Her breasts felt heavy, and the ache low in her belly intensified with each sweep of his thumb. She recognized the reaction as lust, but she grappled with the guilt that went along with it.

"I am certain no lady here has hands that bear the proof of hard work and humility. Fashion and gossip will have no place at our home in the Highlands. I imagine it is much the same on the islands. Life can be harsh, and it takes the work of all clan members to survive the winters and the tribulations we face."

Madeline's guilt shifted from her desire to her past. She felt compelled to confess that she had experienced no difficulty or deprivation while she lived on Lewis. "Fingal, fashion and gossip were all I cared aboot when I was still on Lewis. I never took an interest in running the keep or what the servants had to do. I was frivolous, selfish, materialistic, and prideful."

"Are you still those things, Maddy?" Fingal asked as he brought her hands to his mouth. He placed a kiss on each upturned hand where her fingers met her palms. "I don't think so."

"How can you? You don't know me," Madeline responded as she tugged her hands away. Fingal released them, and they fell to her sides.

"You may have been changed while you were at Inchcailleoch, but I don't think you want to revert to who you were before that. I think you prefer the woman I see before me; she is a woman who would thrive in the Highlands or the Hebrides. Mayhap my cousin will have to teach you how to run a keep, but I believe you'll be a diligent pupil."

"But how can you be so sure?" Madeline demanded.

"I don't ken. I just am," Fingal murmured before his hand cupped her jaw, and he lowered his mouth to hers. He paused for a breath, and when she didn't pull away, he pressed his lips to hers. He went slowly, unsure of how she might react. When her lips parted, he slipped his tongue into her mouth. He felt her hands come to rest upon his chest as her body leaned toward his, proving her interest. A soft moan signaled her capitulation as her tongued twirled with his. Fingal realized he was kissing a woman who knew what she was doing. He had a flash of jealousy; he'd assumed she would be inexperienced, relying on him to teach her. But he knew that whatever experience she had took place years ago, before she joined the convent.

Madeline's hand crept up his chest until it tunneled into his hair at the base of his neck. As the kiss drew on, and her body relaxed against Fingal's, he wrapped his arm around her waist, his hand still gently cupping her jaw. Madeline felt Fingal's hardened cock pressing against the juncture of her thighs, his leggings doing nothing to hide his arousal. A restlessness set in as Madeline's body demanded more. Sensing what she needed, Fingal's hand slid over her lower back to rest at the top of her backside. Another inch further, and he would be cupping it.

When they pulled apart, breathless, Madeline rested her forehead against Fingal's chest. He felt her tremble, and a moment of pride made him think his prowess had overwhelmed her. But when her hand fisted his doublet as if she needed something to keep her from falling apart, he grew concerned.

"Maddy?" Fingal pressed her shoulders back until there was space between their bodies. His heart seized as he saw the stricken look on Madeline's face. "Maddy, what's wrong? Didn't you like that? Are you worried because I can tell you've been kissed before? I'm not angry," Fingal tried to reassure her, but when her eyes widened, he realized she hadn't been thinking about that. "Maddy?"

"I—I need to go," Madeline whispered.

"Where? The king's going to announce our betrothal soon."

Madeline pulled away and frantically looked around the room. When she spotted a crucifix hanging on a wall, she brushed past Fingal and went to kneel before it. She made the sign of the cross and bowed her head as she murmured the Lord's prayer to herself, stressing the verse with "lead me not into temptation." She begged forgiveness for her wanton behavior and the lust she experienced, the lust she knew she still felt for Fingal. One kiss hadn't satisfied it. Instead, it had sparked and turned it into a wildfire.

Fingal watched Madeline, uncertain what to do. He'd worried that he'd frightened her, then he'd been confused. Now he shifted between anger and humiliation. He raised his chin and marched toward Madeline. He would not have a wife who ran from him at a mere kiss. How would he ever get her with child if a kiss sent her into a spiritual crisis? He laid his hand on her shoulder as Madeline made the sign of the cross again, and helped her to her feet

"I'm sorry, Fingal," Madeline blurted. "I—I—can't do this. It's wrong."

"Madeline, you are making no sense. What can't you do? What is it that's wrong? We're to be married soon. The contracts are signed, and we are betrothed."

"You were right. I did enjoy that, and I shouldn't have," Madeline replied.

"Why not? I would think it's a good thing that a husband and wife are attracted to one another."

"Because we kissed for the pure pleasure of it. It should have only happened if it was a prelude to you trying to get me with child," Madeline stated as though it made perfect sense.

"You wish to couple right now?" Fingal asked, astonished.

"You would be within your rights," Madeline said as she lowered her head.

"I might be, but that wasn't what I asked. You have a habit of avoiding what I ask you, Maddy."

"Why do you call me that?" Madeline wondered.

"Call you what?" Fingal's irritation showed in his voice. He was growing frustrated by her evasiveness, and the rejection still smarted.

"Maddy. Why do you call me that? No one ever has."

"No one?" Fingal's brow creased. "Even when you were a child? I don't know why I do. It just fits. And you shall drive me mad if you don't explain yourself more clearly. So you don't wish to couple?"

"I do," Madeline sobbed. "And that's the problem. I shouldn't. Lust and covetousness are sins. The Bibles teaches us that God ordained marriage and the marriage bed for the begetting of children. I shouldn't have kissed you if we're not married and if we're not trying to get me with child."

"That's what you believe," Fingal couldn't keep the shock from his voice. "So it's your intention to never enjoy aught physical between us. And if I should like to enjoy the woman I'm bedding?"

Madeline didn't have an answer to that. At least not one that wouldn't leave her conflicted and heartbroken. Her shoulders curled as she struggled not to cry. She swallowed and waited for what Fingal would say next. She knew what was coming, but she didn't want to hear it and she did not want him to see the pain it brought her.

"Madeline, I am still a young mon. I do not intend to go through life only bedding a woman who doesn't want me there. If you refuse to make it enjoyable, then I will find someone who will," Fingal threatened. "You can just lie there while I spill my seed into you, or you can sleep through it for all that it matters, as long as it takes root. I'm not short of options."

Fingal felt hollow as he said exactly what he'd planned to do all along. It was among the strongest reasons he had for marrying Madeline. But after their kiss, after the passion he'd tasted, the thought of another woman left him disgusted with himself and frustrated with Madeline.

"That is your right as my husband. I cannot stop you," Madeline whispered.

"But this is your wish?" Fingal pressed. Madeline opened her watery eyes, and Fingal knew the answer. But he knew she was too conflicted, too mired in guilt, to admit it.

"I can be the wife that you want. I can bear your children and run your keep. But I can't be the woman you want."

"How convenient," Fingal growled.

"Isn't that what you wanted? A marriage of convenience. One where your wife would leave you in peace to do as you please. I thought it would relieve you to know that I won't stand in your way," Madeline hurled at him. She was growing angry in addition to feeling guilty. "You can't have everything, Fin. It might be convenient to have a wife who wants you to rut on her, but you can't have it all."

Fingal looked at Madeline's despondent face and realized whatever emotions she held—ones he didn't understand—were deeply entrenched in who she was. He wasn't sure if he wanted to change her, or if he even wanted to make the effort. He nodded his head and held out his arm. She looked at it for a moment before placing her hand on his forearm. Fingal escorted Madeline to the Great Hall, where the king announced their betrothal as they stood before the dais. While everyone else made merry, with their impending marriage as an excuse to indulge, Madeline and Fingal sat in near silence, morose as they ate the boar Madeline killed to protect Fingal.

CHAPTER TWELVE

Sleep eluded Madeline, so she abandoned the pretense when the time came for Matins. She went through the ritual of the service, but once it concluded, she remained in her pew. She prayed that Fingal would respect her enough not to parade his lemans before her, and that he wouldn't humiliate her in front of her new clan. She feared meeting the women Fingal bedded.

Madeline's chest ached at the idea of turning Fingal away from her, but she knew she had to. He might accept his sins with no remorse, but she couldn't do that. She didn't want to return to the woman she'd worked so hard to leave behind. If she accepted pleasures of the flesh so easily, any lesser vice would come far too easily. She would do her duty to Fingal and to the Grants, and she would continue along the path to redemption. It was her only choice.

She spent the hours between Matins and Lauds in meditation in the chapel trying to discern God's will for her, but the more she prayed, the less she felt she heard. No peace or grace settled over her like it usually did. She feared her transgressions that night had been enough to turn God from her. But she reasoned that wasn't how God or faith worked. She reminded herself that it was in the hours of her greatest sins and deepest doubt that she would find her resolve and conviction. She continued to pray, even past the end of the Prime prayer service, and only left the chapel when her stomach growled loudly enough to echo.

Madeline made her way to the Great Hall, refusing anything but bread and watered ale. She'd decided a day of fasting and prayer would help her resolve her turmoil. She would remind herself that if God could sacrifice His only son, and Jesus could sacrifice His life, then Madeline could sacrifice her desires. Hunger would be a powerful reminder of her purpose.

She broke away from the group of ladies-in-waiting as they went to join the queen for her morning walk. Madeline hadn't been reinstated as an attendant, so she assumed she was not required to join the others throughout the day. When she turned the corner to the passageway to the chapel, she ran into Fingal. Her nose landed in the divot of his breastbone. She looked into the gray eyes that seemed to see too much of her, that felt as though they stripped her bare even though her layers of clothing remained.

"I thought I would find you here," Fingal explained.

Fingal had spent a restless night tossing and turning, regretting how his first kiss with Madeline devolved into such a disaster. He'd given up on sleep when the earliest rays of sun peeked through his chamber window, so he dressed and went for a walk. He was returning from his stroll when he spied Madeline leaving the chapel for the Great Hall. She seemed lost in thought, her face pale and drawn. He picked up his pace, thinking to catch her and apologize for the night before, but his rebellious streak kept him from doing so. He figured she was free to make herself miserable if she so wished. But when she only accepted the heel of bread and a tankard of watered ale, he decided to intervene.

Madeline was punishing herself for something that he was just as much a part of. He'd lashed out to hurt her, to cover his own hurt feelings. Her comment that he reminded her of her brother at age ten came back to him, and he'd chafed at the comparison. But throughout the night he thought about it again, and he realized she was right. He acted like a petulant child at times. He was approaching thirty summers, and he still grew churlish when he didn't get what he wanted. While he wished things with Madeline had ended on a better note, their conversation did give him reason for introspection. He realized there were several qualities he didn't care for when he thought of himself in the laird's seat. They wouldn't make him the leader his clan deserved. As he sought out Madeline, he felt compelled to confess that to her.

"You've found me," Madeline replied softly.

"Will you walk with me? I'd like to talk," Fingal offered. Madeline nodded, and they turned away from the chapel. "I owe you an apology, Maddy. I said hurtful things for the sake of being hurtful. I was being mardy rather than mature."

"I didn't think you were being petulant. At least not that time. I figured you'd spoken like any mon would," Madeline shrugged. But Fingal didn't want absolution.

"Regardless, I shouldn't have been so crass and insensitive. You didn't deserve that when you were being honest with me aboot how you feel," Fingal admitted. They stepped into the brilliant sunlight, making them shade their eyes. They turned their heads toward the sound of voices, both recognizing the queen's entourage on their morning constitutional. In silent agreement, they turned the other way, Madeline leading Fingal away from the flower garden to where the produce was grown. She sighed as she saw the rows of vegetables, which reminded her of her work at Inchcailleoch. She missed the feel of dirt between her fingers. Fingal noticed as her whole demeanor changed. "Do you enjoy gardening?"

Fingal's question took Madeline aback. She'd nearly forgotten he was there. "I do. I tended the gardens at the priory and discovered I had a green thumb. It was peaceful and purposeful work." She turned to face Fingal, grateful that his height and broad frame blocked the sun from her eyes.

"Maddy, I dinna want to change ye," Fingal said as he lapsed into his brogue. They'd both maintained their courtly accents since they'd spoken on the hunt. Allowing his natural cadence into his speech made their conversation feel more intimate.

"I dinna want to change. I'm a better person as I am now, but that may nae make me the woman ye want." Madeline sighed as she gathered her courage. "Please dinna flaunt yer lemans in front of me, or humiliate me in front of yer clan. I will do naught to stand in yer way. I willna be a harpy or make demands, Fin."

Fingal stood speechless as he looked at Madeline. He'd hoped to ease her into enjoying intimacy with him. Instead, she was giving him permission to be unfaithful. He supposed nothing had changed about his intentions, but he'd hoped to at least make Madeline warm to him enough so their times together wouldn't be miserable. Pride alone made him want to ensure he satisfied her.

He looked around and found a shady spot near the undercroft. He led Madeline to it, looking back to ensure no one watched them. He tried to collect himself as she stood looking at him, the innocence in her eyes belying the experience she'd shown during their kiss. She was a dichotomy that Fingal wondered if he would ever understand.

"I still regret what I said, Maddy. I dinna want ye to just lie there, or even sleep through our coupling. I would like to ken ye are satisfied when we are done," Fingal stated.

"I imagine being a mother will be vera satisfying." Madeline offered a soft smile, but it fell when Fingal stared at her. She realized she'd misunderstood. Her cheeks flamed as she thought about the physical satisfaction she had heard men and women boast about when she'd been at court. She shook her head. "I dinna need that, Fin. I will always welcome ye in ma bed, and I will bear as many children as we are blessed with. But as ye said, ye will find pleasure elsewhere. I just ask that ye treat me with respect."

"Maddy," Fingal said in exasperation.

"Fin," Madeline responded with a cocked eyebrow.

"Why do you call me Fin? Only ma mother did." Fingal kept his tone light, but the color leeched from Madeline's face.

"I'm sorry," Madeline whispered. "That was far too presumptuous of me. I shouldnae have intruded upon that memory."

Fingal eased his hand onto her waist, and when she didn't shy away, he took a step closer. "Ye judge yerself harsher than even God would. It wasna presumptuous. I—I like it. I miss it." Fingal thought he would happily drown in the depths of her blue eyes.

They stood close enough that Madeline had to tilt her head back to look him in the eye. A charged silence passed between them.

Fingal lowered his chin and placed a soft kiss on her forehead. It was much like the kiss on her cheek the night they'd met outside the chapel. She didn't reject him, so he dropped a kiss on each cheek. He felt her tense, but she didn't pull away. She continued to watch him as he lowered his mouth to hers. Her eyelids drooped closed as he pressed his mouth to hers. The desire from the night before flooded them both, but while Fingal's instincts pushed him to deepen the kiss, Madeline's deigned that she should run. She pushed away from Fingal and shook her head before dashing toward the keep.

"Madeline," Fingal called after her. "Maddy!" Madeline appeared to miss a step, but she continued to run toward the doors of the keep. The moment they were both inside, he pulled her to a stop. His grasp was light, and he released her when she pushed him away. But she stood there, breathless and shaken. She didn't run again or even turn away from him.

"What do ye want from me?" Madeline pleaded. "I canna do this."

"Why? Ye havenae given me a straightforward answer. Mayhap if ye would explain it, I can understand."

Madeline scrubbed her hands over her face as she nodded. "Fin, if I give into this...*lust*, then it will be only a matter of time before I fall back on ma old habits and return to being naught but a sinner."

"Maddy, we're all sinners," Fingal responded in frustration.

"But ye are more than that. Ye are a warrior. Ye're yer clan's tánaiste. I'm certain ye must train yer men. Ye likely uphold justice among yer people. Mayhap ye oversee some of the accounts. But what am I? Naught. I'm neither a nun nor a wife. Even once I'm a wife, I willna be chatelaine, and I willna become a mother right away. What will I have but ma old ways to fall back on if I give in to temptation?" Madeline couldn't meet Fingal's eyes as she confessed her worst fear.

"Maddy, what did they do to ye?" Fingal murmured as he brushed hair away from her temple.

"What did who do?" Madeline asked.

"The nuns. What did they do to make ye believe such?" Fingal tried to tuck hair behind Madeline's ear, but she swatted his hand away. She narrowed her eyes, and Fingal realized the woman he'd assumed would never argue with him had a temper. And he had just unleashed it.

"They did naught to me but welcome me into their community. They housed me, fed me, clothed me. They made me one of them, even when I hissed and scratched and acted more like a feral animal than aught else. They didna do this to me. Do ye really think we discussed such things? What nun believes she'll one day shoulder the burden of being a wife? What nun fears damnation for lusting after her husband? Ye arrogant arse. Do ye nae believe I'm capable of figuring things out on ma own? That I can only think and believe what I'm told?"

Fingal sucked in a whistling breath through his nose, his eyes narrowing as he latched onto a single word. "I will endeavor to make yer life as ma wife less of a burden. Fear nae. I willna bother ye often once ye bear me an heir. And while I wait, I shall endeavor to keep our time together brief."

Madeline staggered backwards as though he'd struck her. She nodded as she stumbled away. When she could, she turned and fled to the chapel for sanctuary. Fingal watched her go. His temper flared, keeping him from chasing her a second time. Every time he opened his mouth, he insulted her. And every time she spoke, she made marriage to him sound like a sentence of hard labor. They'd been betrothed less than a day, and Fingal was finding having a bride far from convenient.

CHAPTER THIRTEEN

The next five days passed in a blur for Madeline. She'd ventured into town with her guards to see if there were any seamstresses or haberdashers that carried ready-made gowns, or if she could convince them to sell any incomplete ones that other women had commissioned. She left every shop empty handed. When three trips into Stirling resulted in nothing, Laurel insisted that Madeline take four of her kirtles.

"I can't do that, Laurel. I can't take from you when I know you need them more than I do," Madeline argued.

"That's ridiculous. You need clothes because you have none! I don't need them anymore than I do most of the ones hanging in my wardrobe," Laurel retorted.

"But you gave me the blue gown as a wedding gift. I can't take more from you," Madeline said emphatically, even as she looked with longing at the intricate embroidery on each gown. She pursed her lips, thinking, then went to her small satchel. She retrieved the pouch of coins and offered it to Laurel. "I won't take the kirtles, but I will buy them. You embroider better than any seamstress in town, and your sense of style exceeds anyone else at court." When Laurel resisted, Madeline insisted. "Don't think of it as me paying for your services, but leaving you with coin to replace the fabric."

Madeline waited and knew Laurel's practical side would win out if she remained quiet long enough. Laurel eventually nodded her head, but teasingly scowled at Madeline.

"What will you do for a wedding gown?" Laurel asked, to which Madeline responded with a shrug. "You need something, Madeline. You can't show up in your chemise."

"I suppose the blue one," Madeline pointed to the kirtle laid out on her bed. A chest Fingal had delivered sat open on the floor beside the bed. She was preparing to pack, since she and Fingal would marry the next afternoon, and she would leave with the Grants the following morning.

Madeline couldn't admit that she wished to wear the blue gown because Fingal said she looked stunning in it. She chose to remember that rather than the argument and despair she'd felt at the end of that same night. She'd barely spoken to Fingal all week. They avoided one another during the day and exchanged pleasantries when they sat together at the evening meal. They danced together twice, then retreated to opposite walls and slipping out before the music ended.

"That's a good choice," Laurel smiled. "Madeline?"

"Aye?" Madeline looked up as she folded the other gowns to place in the trunk. Laurel suggested Ina do Madeline's packing, but Madeline declined. She was still uncomfortable having someone serve her. She only accepted the maid's help when she couldn't lace a gown on her own.

"If you don't want to go through with this, I'm

certain Kieran wouldn't force you. He could buy your release from the betrothal contract, and then you wouldn't have to marry Fingal, or anyone at all," Laurel suggested.

Madeline offered her friend a sad smile and shook her head. "Nay. I will have to marry someone at some point." Madeline shrugged as she returned to folding. "We may not get along all the time, but I ken I'm safe with him. He won't mistreat me, I'll have a safe home with people who will treat me well enough."

"You're not a bluidy dog, Madeline. But that's exactly how you've just described yourself. What? He won't beat you? He won't leave you out in the rain? He'll do more than throw you scraps? His clan members won't kick you? Madeline," Laurel pleaded.

"You're making a mountain out of a molehill. With time, we will likely grow used to one another. One day, we will be Laird and Lady Grant, and I will run his keep and be the mother to his children. He will lead our clan and provide for us. That's a far sight better than many women in our position." Madeline spoke only a partial truth. She wouldn't admit that she wished she had more to look forward to. She suspected that even if she could bring herself to enjoy sharing intimacies with Fingal, he was not a man interested in falling in love with his wife. Despite his openly stated intention to bed other women, Madeline sensed he was a man that she could love. That made knowing about his plans to share his bed with a leman all the more painful.

Madeline had received a letter from Kieran and Maude. She knew they'd sent it before she left the priory, but it wished her happiness with her future husband. They reminded her that she was always welcome at Stornoway, and they hoped she could visit one day. They'd shared news of their children, and Madeline could picture her brother and sister-by-marriage together with their young family. She'd never seen them married, but she could imagine the love they shared. It was envy that made her hateful—even more hateful—after she discovered Kieran had fallen in love with Maude. Now she struggled with envy again. At least this time it didn't come with a vicious desire for retribution.

"Madeline, I understand why and how you've changed, but I wish a smidge of the old Madeline would poke through. She wouldn't accept a future she doesn't want quite so meekly," Laurel asserted.

"And where did that get the old Madeline? In a convent, lashing herself for an hour only to wear a hair shirt for two days. Och, aye. I was a great joy to be around when I arrived at Inchcailleoch. That version of me found naught but trouble."

"You wore a hair shirt? What they say aboot the 'isle of auld women' is true?" Laurel was aghast.

"Once. That's all it took. And it's on the rarest of occasions that any of the sisters earn themselves such a punishment. I deserved it," Madeline stated earnestly. "Laurel, I never expected to marry a mon of my choice. I've accepted that I'll never be a nun. And I'm all right with that because, God willing, I'll become a mother one day. I could do far worse than Fingal Grant." Finally, Laurel sighed and nodded, resignation in her eyes.

"The blue gown it is," Madeline grinned, to lighten the mood. She had a moment of eagerness, hoping Fingal liked how she looked on their wedding day. She finished packing the chest, and the two women walked to the Great Hall together for Madeline's last evening meal as an unmarried woman.

Fingal watched Madeline enter the Great Hall with Laurel as he swirled the whisky in his mug. His eyes narrowed as Madeline gave Laurel's arm a reassuring pat before she straightened her spine and turned toward him. He hated that his bride had to gather her resolve to face him, but his days-long foul mood did little to make Madeline look forward to sharing a meal with him.

He'd dined and danced with Madeline each night before escaping to his chamber to change in plainer clothes and slip into town. He tried the most popular taverns, The Picked Over Plum, The Merry Widow, and The Wolf and Sheep. He'd been unable to bring himself to even consider any of the older, hardened whores at The Picked Over Plum. He'd had three rounds of whisky to try to wash away Madeline's face and the feel of her in his arms, but still she lingered in his mind. The wenches with their foul breath and rotted teeth turned his stomach, and he wondered how he'd ever frequented the tavern before.

He found more than one merry widow when he ventured to the tavern by that name, which earned its moniker from the courtly women who conducted their affairs there. He'd approached a woman the first night he went, but her blond hair looked like faded straw compared to the shine of Madeline's raven-colored locks. The next night two women approached him together, their invitation obvious. He'd felt his cock stir until Madeline's voice echoed in his ears asking him to respect her. If he dallied with either or both women, word would fly through court, and Madeline would undoubtedly hear about it. Disillusioned as he was about his impending marriage, he couldn't intentionally humiliate Madeline.

His visit to the Wolf and Sheep ended before it began. A comely serving wench approached him when he arrived. Her hand found his crotch, and his rod twitched on its own. Fingal thought he'd finally found a potential bed partner, but he caught her wrist when she tried to slide his coin pouch from his waist. He'd glowered at the would-be thief until she ran away. He wasn't interested in being swindled just for a night between a woman's thighs.

So he sat in Stirling Castle's Great Hall, gulping down his whisky for another night in a row, knowing that he wouldn't leave the castle after his last supper. His cheek twitched at his own humor. He nearly smiled when he considered how offended Madeline would be if he shared that quip aloud. Each night, she sat beside him, appearing unmoved by their approaching wedding day. She was the model of civility and etiquette, while he simmered silently. His only consolation had been seeing her drawn and exhausted face as he hid each night and watched her slip into the chapel for Matins.

He discovered her schedule by accident the first night he ventured out, but then he timed his return so he could watch her. His conscious niggled at him for the deviousness, but for some reason he didn't want to examine, he took solace in seeing the private moments where Madeline let her guard down. She looked as weary as he felt each time she slipped along the silent passageways. He wondered if she slept at all. He knew he hadn't slept well since the night he kissed her for the first time.

"Good eve," Madeline greeted the men at the table. She glanced down at Fingal, but his face barely registered her arrival. She turned a serene smile to the other Grant men, pretending that Fingal's surliness didn't hurt.

"Good eve, Lady Madeline," Harry replied. The man was Fingal's best friend and his second. They'd known each other since they were children, and they had few secrets from one another. Fingal sensed Harry waited for him to address Madeline, but he kept his eyes down as he drained his third mug of whisky before the meal began. "Ye look well, ma lady."

Fingal glared at Harry, knowing his friend was trying to goad him into jealousy. He glanced at Madeline, whose bright blue eyes were fixed on Harry. Seeing the movement from the corner of her eye, she turned to Fingal. Her smile slipped a little when his blank expression didn't change.

"Good evening, Fingal, Harry." Madeline nodded to the other men who'd traveled with Fingal. She leaned forward to greet the MacLeod guards as well. She felt as though she should say something to Fingal, since the previous evenings had been nearly unbearable. But she didn't know what to say. She didn't want to remonstrate him for his callous behavior, to confess that it hurt her. She didn't want to beg him to pay attention to her after she'd give him carte blanche to ignore her.

Madeline lowered her voice so only Fingal could hear. "Thank you for sending the chest. I hadn't aught to put in it until Laurel gave me one of her gowns as a wedding present. I was able to purchase a few more. I won't embarrass you in front of your people, Fingal. I promise. I'll figure out how to hide my short hair until it grows longer."

Fingal slowly turned his head to look at Madeline, who'd leaned close to keep her voice from carrying. "You think I care how you look?"

As the words left his mouth, Fingal wanted to bash his own face in as he watched the stunned expression on Madeline's face. She swallowed several times and blinked to keep her tears at bay as she looked down at her trencher. He noticed her clenched hands in her lap, one thumb running over the back of the other as she struggled to sooth herself. He knew from watching her dine with the ladies-in-waiting that she was either praying or slipping away to the place in her mind that she occupied when she wanted to disappear. Fingal grunted when the toe of a boot landed against his shin. He watched Madeline close her eyes, and he knew she understood Harry had kicked him under the table. Fingal glanced up at his friend, whose scathing glare made Fingal feel worse.

"I'm sorry, Maddy," Fingal whispered. Her head whipped around as she narrowed her eyes. He sensed she was about to tell him that he had no right to use the diminutive. "I meant that your appearance doesnae matter to me, so it willna embarrass me. I never thought that it would." Fingal glanced up when he noticed Harry's hands fisted on the table. His friend looked at him as though Fingal was a simpleton. As he attempted to dig himself out of the hole he'd landed in, along with the whisky he'd drunk, his brogue slipped back into his words. "I meant ye're lovely nay matter what ye wear, Maddy. I ken ye willna embarrass me because ye will do yer best to make a good impression."

"Thank ye," Madeline croaked. Despite Fingal's foul mood each night, sitting among her fellow Hebrideans and the Highlanders allowed her to speak naturally. She didn't say much, but when she did, she didn't have to worry about modulating her accent.

"Would ye care for wine, ma lady?" Harry intervened.

"Nay, thank ye," Madeline offered another soft smile to Harry, and Fingal wanted to drive his fist into his friend's face. He was angry at himself, but it was easier to direct it at someone else than admit that Harry was stepping up to welcome Madeline since Fingal himself was failing.

Fingal appeared to focus on his food, but he observed Madeline from his peripheral vision. As a betrothed couple, they shared a trencher. He watched as she discreetly pushed most of the food onto his side. He noticed which foods she avoided, mostly the ones with the heavy sauces. She appeared to enjoy the fish and leeks, but barely touched the beef or lamb. She ate the chunk of bread he handed her before she ate her half of the meat pie. He noticed that she savored the cheese and apples served at the end of the meal.

He resolved to ask his cousin's wife, Lady Davina Grant, to have the kitchens prepare only foods Madeline liked during her first week at Freuchie. They would spend a sennight on the road, and her favorite foods would be a welcome luxury after the long trip. After the week he'd spent being an arse to her, he swore to himself that he would make Madeline feel welcome when they reached their home.

When he looked up at Harry, his friend quickly shifted his attention away from Madeline. Their eyes met, and Fingal recognized the challenge in Harry's gaze. Harry's eyes darted back to Madeline before he sent Fingal a warning glare. Fingal sensed Madeline wasn't the only one fighting temptation.

"Maddy, will ye walk with me after the meal?" Fingal whispered. She turned doleful eyes toward him and nodded. He was making her miserable, and he knew it. When the music began, Fingal led her to the other dancers. He'd recognized the piece the musicians played, and he knew it would keep them partnered throughout the dance. He held Madeline a little closer than necessary, but within the bounds of decorum. They moved around the floor together, both graceful and well-trained dancers. Fingal had wondered on several occasions if they would move that well in bed together. The idea would make his cock lengthen, then he would become angry at Madeline for his own thoughts. As the music slowed as the song ended, Fingal steered them toward doors that opened onto a terrace.

Fingal wrapped Madeline's arm around his as he guided them toward the steps that would take them along the path to the vegetable garden. The moon and stars shone on the leafy plants, and the night air had a light loamy scent. He eased Madeline around until they faced one another. He sensed her unease, and once more, he knew he was to blame for it.

"I owe ye an apology, Madeline. I've been foul-tempered for days, and ye've borne the brunt of it. I'm sorry," Fingal spoke clearly. He wanted Madeline to understand that he was sincere. He needed her, for reasons he didn't recognize, to accept that his sentiment was genuine.

"I accept yer apology, and I offer one of ma own. I ken I've disappointed ye, and I'm sorry. I'll do what I can, so ye nay longer regret asking for me," Madeline said.

"Madeline, I'm nae disappointed in ye. I never have been. I'm disappointed that ye keep rejecting me, but I'm nae disappointed in ye."

"Isnae that the same thing? And I dinna mean to reject ye, Fingal. It's the temptation to sin that I reject," Madeline tried to explain.

"It's nae the same thing. Ye are a fine woman, one to be admired, so I'm nae disappointed in ye. I'm disappointed that I find maself so attracted to ye, but ye dinna feel the same, or at least ye willna admit to it," Fingal clarified.

"Why are ye being so honest with me?" Madeline wondered.

"Because we're marrying tomorrow. I willna keep secrets from ye, and I want ye to ken that I respect ye."

"I can think of a secret or two that I would ask ye to keep to yerself. I dinna want to ken," Madeline sighed.

"Perhaps we can get through tomorrow night and the journey home before we worry aboot that," Fingal suggested.

"Will we stop at any inns, or will we be under the stars each night?"

Fingal's brow furrowed at the question. He wasn't prepared for the change in the conversation. "There may be a night or two at an inn," Fingal answered.

"Then I think now is as good a time as any to ask ye to keep those secrets where I dinna need to find out," Madeline replied. Fingal's head fell forward in disbelief.

"Ye believe that I would take ye to an inn just to bed some wench under the same roof as ye?" Fingal said incredulously.

"I dinna see how it's any different from ye bedding yer leman under the roof we'll share at Freuchie. And Fingal, ye arenae as stealthy as ye think. I've seen ye each night as I go to Matins. The whisky practically pours off ye. It doesnae take much to understand what ye've been doing each night." Madeline turned her head away and closed her eyes.

"I willna deny I've tried. Tried every damn night for the past five days, but it doesnae work," Fingal growled as he ran a hand through his hair. He watched as Madeline looked at his groin before looking up at him in shock. His chuckle had no mirth. "That's nae what I meant. It works just fine. But it seems to only want ye. Or at least ma conscience has discovered its voice."

Madeline's mouth dropped into a wide o, and Fingal groaned. He knew Madeline didn't understand how her expression affected him, but his cock ached nonetheless. As he watched Madeline's eyes

123

lower to his midsection again, he noticed her curiosity.

Mayhap seducing ma bonnie bride will warm the ice in her veins. At least it could make her blood tepid, so I can enjoy maself tomorrow eve. I will do ma duty by her and ma clan, then I will sort this mess out once I return to Freuchie. I wish I had a leman to look forward to.

"Maddy, I may be a hard mon to marry, but I dinna mean to be cruel," Fingal said.

"I ken, Fin. Ye dinna realize what ye do until afterward," Maddy stood on her toes and kissed his cheek. "Ye can be a wee thoughtless with yer words, but mostly, ye dinna do it to be malicious. I ken because I used to be cruel to others on purpose. I can spot the difference. Thank ye for bringing me out here and talking to me. I ken that ye're trying, and I will do the same. I promise."

"Thank ye, lass," Fingal smiled, and Madeline's heart turned over. She'd been fighting the ache within her belly the entire time they stood together, just as she did every evening that they sat side by side. She'd nearly given in to her lust and kissed his mouth rather than his cheek, but her iron will came in handy as she battled the lust that grew stronger each time she was near Fingal. It was tempting to give in to her desire for Fingal, and it was tempting to give up her convictions for the sake of an easier life. But she knew her conscience would never let her be at peace.

Fingal left her at her chamber door, knowing that it was likely that the next time he saw Madeline would be on the steps of the castle's kirk. He wondered what she would wear. He smirked to himself as he recalled telling Madeline that what she wore didn't matter to him.

It may nae matter, but I can still be curious.

CHAPTER FOURTEEN

The day passed in a rush as Madeline hurried to prepare for her wedding and her departure from Stirling. She and Laurel spent the morning with the other ladies-in-waiting before slipping back to their chamber for Madeline to rest while Ina pressed out her gown. Laurel oversaw her maid's work, wanting everything to be perfect for Madeline. That included the sense of satisfaction that it was one of her secret creations that Madeline would wear and amaze all of those in attendance. Laurel had rarely worn the blue gown, and it had been at least a year since the last time she had. She knew it flattered Madeline far more than it did her. Laurel was confident that, by wearing the dress with the jewelry the queen had lent for the wedding, Madeline would be a breathtaking bride.

As Madeline soaked in a steaming bath, she tilted her head back and closed her eyes. She allowed her mind to go blank for the first time in ages. She didn't think about Fingal or marriage. She didn't meditate on Jesus's divinity or God's ubiquitous power. She didn't pray for guidance. She just rested, and it gave her soul a boost that her faith had not provided. She supposed she could reason out God's role in that serenity and rejuvenation, but she didn't want to. She just wanted to let her mind rest.

Once she finished her bath, she sat still as Ina curled various strands of her hair while pinning up others. When the maid finished, the coiffure amazed both Madeline and Laurel. With the ribbon woven into the style, it was impossible to tell that Madeline's hair was shorter than that of most courtiers. Laurel and Ina worked together to lower the kirtle over Madeline's perfectly fashioned hair, then Ina laced her into her gown. Madeline looked around the chamber before she left it for the last time. She'd been there little more than a sennight, but her time with Laurel had made it comfortable and homey. Servants had retrieved Madeline's chest earlier that afternoon, taking it to the chamber she would spend the night in with Fingal. There was nothing left of hers in the lady's-in-waiting chamber when Laurel pulled the door closed behind them.

Fingal adjusted his belt and sporran for at least the fourth time, as Harry shot him a bemused look. He'd taken out his frustration with his friend while they trained that morning. Harry had baited him with banal comments about Madeline to the point where he became reckless. He now sported a bruise to the other set of ribs. He wondered what Madeline would think of the fresh black and blue bruises on one side and the green and yellow remnants of the old bruises on the other.

As he waited for Madeline, he couldn't discern whether he looked forward to her arrival because he wanted to be done with the wedding or because he actually wanted to see her. He supposed it was a combination of both. He was tugging at his leine yet again when the crowd in the bailey suddenly went silent. Fingal looked around for a threat as he reached back for his sword. But as his arm lowered when he didn't spot any danger, the crowd had opened and let Madeline pass through. The soft rays from the setting sun made her raven hair shimmer as she approached. He immediately recognized the gown she wore, and he wondered if she'd thought of him and their first kiss when she chose it as her wedding gown. As she passed a group of women, he was certain no other woman could hold a candle to Madeline's beauty.

As she approached, Fingal broke with custom and walked down to meet her at the base of the steps. He lifted her hands to his lips and brushed kisses across her knuckles. Madeline blushed, but her smile was more dazzling than the afternoon sun on the brightest day.

"Maddy, ye take ma breath away," Fingal whispered. "I didna think ye could look lovelier than the first time I saw ye in this gown, but ye're the bonniest lass I've ever seen." Fingal meant every word, and as something akin to trust entered Madeline's eyes, he realized that the first step in seducing Madeline was as simple as being charming.

"Thank ye, Fin. Ye look mighty fine. I havenae seen ye in yer laird's family plaid before. The other day was yer hunting one. It's good to see ye looking like a Highlander, a braw Highlander," Madeline finished in a hushed tone. Her cheeks felt as though heat radiated from them, but she felt his honesty deserved hers in return. It cost her nothing to offer him the compliments, and his smile in return made her less self-conscious.

They walked up the steps together until they reached the priest, who bound their wrists with a ribbon and draped a swath of Grant plaid over their joined hands. If asked later what she'd promised, Madeline could not have answered. She only remembered the way she felt as she locked gazes with Fingal. The rest of the world fell away, and she suddenly felt as though she was where she belonged. She wondered if the Mother Abbess had foreseen Madeline's future, and her last doubts that she was meant to be a wife rather than a nun fell away.

Fingal returned Madeline's gaze as he listened to the murmur of their voices repeating what the priest said, but his mind was marveling at the unprecedented calm he felt as he pledged himself to Madeline. He wondered if she felt the same way he did, and he found himself praying that she did to at least make their coming night easier.

After they exchanged their vows, they moved inside the kirk for the wedding Mass. Fingal watched as Madeline moved through the service as if she were an automaton. She lowered herself to her knees before anyone else. She led the congregation each time they needed to stand. She recited each prayer perfectly in sync with the priest. The reality of Madeline's existence for the past five years finally registered with Fingal as he watched how naturally each moment of the liturgy and Eucharist came to her. If she'd been a man, she could have led the Mass. The reverence on her face and in her voice was genuine, but it made Fingal sigh when he realized that if he wished to seduce Madeline, he would have to compete with God. He felt he was admitting defeat before he fully entered the challenge.

When the Mass concluded, and the priest presented them to the congregation as a married couple, Fingal eased his hands around Madeline's waist. He was certain the softness of her mien came from the spiritual fulfillment she gained from the service, not from knowing they were now husband and wife. But he would never forget the faith he saw in her eyes, and he decided to believe it was toward him as he dipped his head to kiss her. He kept the kiss light and brief, but it was Madeline's lips that parted and silently invited him to lengthen and deepen the exchange. It was only a moment more, but when they pulled away, they both knew they'd wanted that kiss to last longer. He waited for Madeline to recoil, for the guilt and regret to overcome her, but she only offered him a smile.

They led the way to the Great Hall, where they took their seats as honored guests on the dais. It was Fingal who moved the food around in their trencher, offering her what he believed she would prefer. He offered her the chalice of wine each time she reached for it, and she sliced an apple with her eating knife, giving him half. If they didn't know better, and if they were watching themselves as though they were someone else, Fingal and Madeline might have believed themselves a happily married couple, one who shared a genuine fondness for each another. But the bubble burst when the king announced it was time for the newlyweds to retire, claiming they would have an early start in the morning.

Raunchy comments about how they would start their morning made Madeline flinch. Fingal feared she would bolt as she trembled beside him, her panic rising as people clamored for a bedding ceremony. When she looked at him, desperate for him to protect her, Fingal put a stop to the demands. He'd been witness to several bedding ceremonies, had been one of the men to offer lewd pieces of advice. But as his bride seemed to shrink before his eyes, he was resolved that no man would ever see her naked but him. He could only imagine the discomfort she would feel once they were alone. He wouldn't let courtiers with nothing better to do than to traumatize his wife enter their chamber.

"No," Fingal said with force but without raising his voice.

"No?" King Robert repeated.

"There will be no bedding ceremony," Fingal stated, giving the king a pointed look. "My wife arrived here from a convent. There is no doubting her innocence."

The Bruce understood, and offered an apologetic nod to Madeline. But the rest of the courtiers were not so easily dissuaded. They pounded mugs and fists on tables as they offered suggestions to them both. Madeline drew in a shaky voice as she rose to stand beside Fingal. The back of her hand brushed against his before he wrapped his pinky around hers. Madeline looked out over the crowd as she dredged up the confidence to speak.

"If you wish to join us in our chamber, then you must also wish to join me afterward in the kirk when I pray for God to forgive you for your sins of lust, envy, and gluttony," Madeline projected her voice so everyone could hear her. As she spoke, a stunned silence fell over the crowd. She forced herself not to cross her arms when she finished, but she swept an imperious gaze around the gathering hall. When no one made a sound, Madeline turned to Fingal. "Husband, if it is your wish to retire, I am ready."

Fingal shook himself out of his stupor as he lifted his hand and offered it to her. She laid her palm on his, and a spark blazed up each of their arms. Fingal was careful not to squeeze the fine bones as he wrapped his fingers around her hand. He'd noticed the first time that he held them that while her palms showed evidence of manual labor, they seemed tiny and fragile compared to his much larger ones.

He led his new wife from the dais, and Madeline

carried herself with the same posture that she'd shown when she entered the Great Hall the first night he saw her. She was the daughter of a laird, the sister of a laird, and the wife of a future laird. She glided across the floor with the poise and dignity that could only come from years of training and her nobility. Still, Fingal didn't miss how her hand trembled in his. He'd never been so proud of anyone as he was of his wife as she walked past hundreds of staring and judging eyes, having set all of them in their place. When the doors shut behind them, Fingal swept her into his arms and carried her to their chamber.

CHAPTER FIFTEEN

Madeline stood behind the screen and pulled the pins and ribbons loose from her hair as Ina unlaced her kirtle. When she was left in only her chemise, Ina bobbed a curtsy and hurried from the chamber. Madeline steeled herself for what would happen now that she and Fingal were alone. She knew she couldn't dawdle, or she would only make it more awkward between them.

When she stepped around the screen, she was unprepared to find Fingal sitting on the end of the bed with only his plaid wrapped loosely around his waist. Her eyes traveled from his long feet over the muscular calves and thighs that poked out from beneath the patterned wool to the ridges and grooves of his abdomen. Her eyes lingered as she watched Fingal's muscles twitch under her perusal. She surveyed the defined muscles of his chest, thinking how much harder the planes of his body were compared to hers. She suspected his arms were as wide around as her thighs. She noticed his Adam's apple bobbed several times as she looked him over. When her eyes landed on a wide and jagged scar on his right shoulder, her eyes jumped to his.

"It was a long time ago, Maddy. It's been healed

for ages, and I dinna notice it anymore," Fingal reassured her as he stood. When she made no move to draw closer to him, Fingal walked over to her. She couldn't understand why, but she found watching his feet fascinating. It felt deeply intimate. "Do ye ken what will happen, Maddy?

She nodded, then looked up at him. Fingal moved slowly, giving her an opportunity to predict what he would do with each movement. He tucked a lock of hair behind her ear before tunneling his hand beneath her locks. He flexed his fingers and ran them through her hair, surprised when the ends slipped through his fingers. He did it twice more before resting his hand on the nape of her neck.

When Madeline didn't startle or balk, Fingal rubbed the muscles of her neck and shoulders. Her eyes drooped as she lowered her head and sighed. Fingal slipped his other hand around her waist and drew her against him. She rested her forehead against his chest as she welcomed his ministrations. They eased the tension from between her shoulder blades and made her accustomed to his touch. He didn't hurry, keeping his movement slow and his touch gentle.

"Are ye frightened?" Fingal whispered. Madeline nodded again. "I will go slowly and do aught that I can to keep from hurting ye."

Madeline looked up at Fingal, drawing her lips into a line before responding. "I trust ye, Fin. If ye lead, I will follow."

Fingal led her to the bed where the covers were already drawn back. Madeline slid onto the bed, and Fingal realized she intended to keep her chemise on. He stifled a groan as she crushed his eager anticipation at finally seeing her bare. He reminded himself that less than a moon ago, the woman thought she'd be taking her final vows as a nun in a sennight. He had plenty of time to warm her to the idea of letting him see her. Fingal slipped into bed beside her and eased her onto her side, so they could look at one another. He trailed the back of his hand over her arm. He'd been burning to ask her a question all evening, and he knew he was risking ruining their night, but he had to know.

"Maddy, the kiss we shared in the kirk. Ye didna object to that. Was it because we're married now?"

Madeline's brow creased. "That's part of it. But I kenned that the kiss was the beginning of this."

"This?" Fingal wondered if Madeline could speak out loud what they were about to do.

"Our first attempt at conceiving a child. Ye claiming me as yer wife, making our marriage lawful," Madeline explained.

There was nothing intimate in her comment. Instead, it was reasonable and direct. And it saddened Fingal. He propped himself up on his elbow as he leaned forward and initiated their kiss. Madeline lay still for a moment before she opened to him. As Fingal shifted to bring his upper body over hers, she laid back, her hands gliding over his bronzed chest. He kept the kiss light until Madeline sighed. The soft sound triggered Fingal's need, and he swiped his tongue against hers, enticing her tongue to duel with his. He felt Madeline's heart race as his hand trailed down her shoulder to her breast. When he cupped the supple mound, he groaned as he imagined slipping inside her.

Madeline froze. She'd drifted away on a cloud of pleasure and need. But the sound of Fingal's masculine groan brought reality crashing back down. She turned her head away as Fingal looked at her with confusion. She'd felt his rod lengthen against her leg, but her mind hadn't registered the sensation even if her core had. Now she glanced down at Fingal's plaid.

"I—I believe ye're ready," Madeline's voice rasped. She closed her eyes as she inched her chemise higher. Fingal stared as she revealed each tantalizing inch of her legs. When the juncture of her legs became visible, Fingal brushed his fingertips over the thatch of black curls before pressing between Madeline's closed thighs. With her eyes still closed, she nodded and opened her legs. She expected to feel pain as Fingal forced his way inside her. Rather than agony, a jolt of pleasure shot all the way to her toes. Madeline's eyes flew open as she grasped Fingal's wrist, trying to keep his fingers from gliding along her seam again. "What're ye doing? That willna get me with child."

Fingal shut his eyes for a moment while he gathered his patience. "Madeline, I'm nae going to force ma way inside ye and injure ye just so ye can hurry and be done with me."

He failed to hide the edge in his tone, and Madeline stared at him, dumbfounded. "Ye dinna have to force me. I'm willing. I didna mean to rush ye. I just didna want to make ye wait on ma account."

"Och, Maddy. Mayhap ye dinna ken as much as we both thought. Will ye trust me enough to give me yer hand?" Madeline assented, and Fingal guided it to her sheath. The moment her fingertips brushed the heated flesh, she ripped it away.

"I canna do that. It's wrong," Madeline gasped.

"Madeline, I didna mean for ye to pleasure yerself. That is a conversation for another time. I just meant for ye to feel that yer body isnae as ready for me as ye think."

"It is. I told ye, I'm ready," Madeline insisted.

"Madeline, ye ken how a mon's body changes when it's ready to couple with a woman." Fingal guided her hand to cup his rod. Unlike when she touched herself, Madeline didn't reel away in disgust. He released her hand and pulled his plaid from his waist before continuing. "A woman's body changes, too. If a woman's body isnae ready to receive a mon's and he forces his way, then he'll hurt her. I dinna ever want to do that to ye, Maddy. I ken what ye believe, but to spare ye more pain than is inevitable, ye must be aroused to make it easier for me to join with ye."

"I am aroused," Madeline asserted. "I want to do this."

"Mayhap," Fingal said doubtfully. "But that's yer mind. Yer body hasnae caught up. Yer sheath will grow moist just as ma sword grows hard. Both make it easier for our bodies to join. The only way to make yer body do that is to touch ye, lass."

"Are ye certain? Mayhap that's only the case with the women ye prefer. Have ye every tried to with a— uh—more chaste woman?" Madeline wanted to sink into the floor.

"This isnae a matter of how chaste a woman is. It's how yer body is made. If a woman's body isnae ready but a mon insists, then he's forcing her. I dinna rape women, Madeline. I willna start with ma wife."

"It's nae rape if I'm yer wife, and I've said aye," Madeline argued, confused by his logic, since she was now as much his possession to do with as he wished as was his horse.

"I dinna care if ye're ma wife or nae. If I have to force ma way into yer body, it's because ye dinna understand what's happening or ye dinna really want to. That's rape, Madeline." Fingal hissed his last words. Madeline's eyes grew glassy as she nodded her head. She let him guide her fingers to her entrance, and she noticed there was little of the moisture he mentioned.

"I told ye, I trust ye. Ye lead, and I will follow," Madeline murmured. She laid back against the covers and closed her eyes. She jumped when Fingal's finger dipped within her sheath. As he moved the digit inside her, she felt her legs relax and fall open once again. When he pressed a second finger into her sheath, her body grew restless, as though it knew it needed to move in rhythm to Fingal's strokes.

Fingal watched as Madeline's body came alive beneath his hand. He watched as she shifted and squirmed before her back arched. He cupped her breast as his thumb rubbed a slow circle around her nub. He trailed kisses along her jaw and down her neck before nipping at her bottom lip until he flicked his tongue between her lips. Madeline couldn't stifle her moan as her arms reached up to wrap around Fingal's neck. She would be a liar if she tried to deny enjoying his kisses. As the kiss carried on, Madeline's body ached with a need she didn't understand. Her hips lifted as she tried to draw more of Fingal's hand into her entrance.

"Maddy, feel," Fingal whispered as he brought the tips of her fingers to her swollen flesh. She felt the dew gathering between her legs, drenching her nether lips. "This is what it means to be aroused. Ye're ready for us now."

Madeline nodded, drawing her chemise higher as Fingal settled between her thighs. He continued to kiss her as the tip of his cock pressed against her seam. As Fingal rocked forward, Madeline's legs bent, and her knees clasped his hips. Her body knew what it wanted, and it moved on its own as her hips tilted to receive Fingal's rod. Her conscience remained silent as her need to be with Fingal grew. Fingal drew her legs around his hips as he surged forward, breaking through her barrier.

Madeline's back bowed off the bed as pain tore

through her. She clenched the sheets beside her as she tried not to scream. Her whimpers tore at Fingal's heart as he watched Madeline retreat into her shell. She laid still, her arms and legs spread on the bed. He feared she'd passed out when she went limp.

"Is—is that…" Madeline trailed off.

"Nay, wee one. That isnae it. I swear it will never hurt like that again. And this will feel better now that I've breached yer maidenhead."

"I'm yer wife now in truth?" Madeline asked.

"Aye, Maddy." Fingal rocked his hips with a gentleness that belied how badly he wanted to thrust into her. Madeline nodded, but kept her eyes closed and lay still. Fingal's own need for relief gained control, and while he wanted Madeline to experience pleasure, to believe what they could share wasn't sinful, the urge to thrust and spill took over. He surged into her over and over, her sheath so tight that he was certain he would make an end quickly. He dropped onto his forearms, once more pressing kisses along Madeline's neck. He closed his eyes, shutting out her disinterest, allowing his imagination to believe she enjoyed their joining as much as he did.

Madeline was lost in her thoughts. *The pain is ma punishment. It is to remind me of mon's original sin. God makes it so that way a woman remembers how she caused mon's fall from grace, his expulsion from the Garden. But Lord, why does it now feel so good? Is this Yer way of testing ma devotion to Ye, Lord? Why are Ye testing me? Do Ye believe me weak? I willna succumb to the temptation that is ma husband's body. I willna sin. I willna.*

Madeline fought against the need to move beneath Fingal. She cursed her weakness as her body could no longer remain still.

This isnae what I mean to do, God. It's as though something or someone else controls ma body. Ma will says nae, but

139

ma body craves this closeness, this connection with Fingal. It isnae just aboot lust. I dinna understand any of this.

Madeline's conscience lost the battle, and she wrapped her arm under Fingal's as her other hand turned his head back toward hers. Their mouths met as Madeline's heels pressed into the bed. She lifted to her hips to meet each of his thrusts.

"Maddy, God bless. Ye dinna ken what ye're doing to me. I'm trying nae to be rough with ye, but ye're sapping the last dregs of ma control." Fingal thrust harder while he watched Madeline's face. Her eyes remained closed, but she no longer looked conflicted. Fingal shifted his weight, circling his hips, changing the rhythm of his thrusts. He did anything he could think of to bring Madeline to release, but her body didn't respond. She continued to move against him, but he couldn't bring her to climax, and suddenly he could no longer hold back. He felt his seed shoot from him in jets as he slowed his thrusts to a rocking motion. When he feared he would crush Madeline beneath his much larger frame, he rolled to his side. He watched as Madeline pushed her chemise down to cover herself. Once the cotton gown covered most of her legs, she bit her lower lip and turned her head toward Fingal.

Madeline was unprepared for the tender kiss he pressed to her lips, and the half-smile he offered her. His fingers slipped around her nape as his thumb brushed away a dried tear on her cheek. She hadn't realized that any had fallen. She waited for Fingal to speak, unsure of what she could say that wouldn't sound ridiculous.

"Are ye all right, Maddy?" Fingal asked softly. She returned his smile as she nodded. He kissed the tip of her nose before rolling away and wrapping his plaid around his waist. He left the bed and went to wet a linen square in the basin on the side table. He squeezed out the excess water and turned toward Madeline. She'd rolled onto her side, away from where he'd laid, and drawn the cover over her shoulder. Fingal's shoulders slumped as he watched the slow rise and fall of Madeline's chest. He glanced down at his softening cock, the evidence of her innocence clearly marking him. He supposed she was exhausted and overwhelmed from the day.

He cleaned himself before moving to the chair beside the fire where he'd laid his clothes. They'd been given a chamber in the wing for married couples and families. He sighed as he resigned himself to leaving his wife's bed to seek his own. He figured he would grow accustomed to this, since he doubted Madeline would ever allow them to couple more than once in a night. He slipped his leine over his head and didn't bother to pleat his *breacan feile*, rather throwing the extra yards of material over his shoulder. He gathered his stockings and boots before walking toward the door.

Madeline listened to Fingal moving around the chamber as she squeezed her eyes shut to hold back the tears. She thought he would stay with her for at least a few minutes before taking his leave. But he'd barely rolled off her before he got out of bed. She wondered whose chamber he would go to next. Her chest tightened with a pain she never expected. She didn't want her husband to go to another woman's bed, not that night or any other. She fought the sense of betrayal as she waited for the sound of the door to open and close. When she didn't hear the door or Fingal moving, she sat up. She found Fingal staring at her, his boots in one hand while the other rested on the door handle.

As much as Madeline had fought to keep from indulging in carnal sin, she was desperate to keep her husband from seeking pleasure elsewhere. She threw back the covers and eased her legs over the side. An ache of a different sort settled between her legs as she rose, but she pushed it aside as she looked at Fingal. Her husband didn't move but continued to watch her. She gathered her courage and reached for the hem of her chemise. Before she could think better of it, she drew the cotton gown over her head and dropped it to the floor beside her.

"Dinna go," Madeline whispered. She held her breath as Fingal stood beside the door, his fingers opening and closing around the handle. As he stood there watching her, humiliation engulfed her, followed by a tsunami of guilt that threatened to drag her under. She turned her head away, then bent to pick up her gown, feeling foolish and disgraced. Before her fingers found the material, she heard the thunk of Fingal's boots on the floor. He crossed the room and lifted her into his arms. His arms encircled her middle as her hands rested on his shoulders, bringing them eye-to-eye.

"Maddy," Fingal breathed just before their lips came together. It was the comfort after the storm that they both needed, but thought the other rejected. He laid her on the bed as though she were so fragile she would shatter. He followed her onto the bed, but moved to her other side.

"I thought ye were leaving," Madeline confessed.

"I thought ye wanted me to," Fingal replied.

"When ye got up...I thought ye had other plans for tonight," Madeline couldn't look at him as she admitted her suspicions.

"Madeline, ye believe I would leave ye in the bed where we coupled to go to another woman? On our wedding night?" Madeline's assumption deeply hurt him. Even if he took a leman once they arrived at Freuchie, he would never leave Madeline's bed only to fall into another woman's arms moments later.

"I didna ken," Madeline shrugged her shoulder. "I dinna ken how this works."

"I told ye that I would respect ye and never humiliate ye in front of our people. I would never leave yer bed to go to another woman's the same night." Fingal didn't understand why Madeline flinched, but she nodded.

"Thank ye." Madeline twisted to look over her shoulder at the door. "Then why did ye get up if ye werenae leaving?"

"Och, Maddy. I thought to offer ye a kindness. I was fetching a cool wet cloth for yer—to clean—" Fingal was rarely embarrassed about discussing what passed between a man and a woman, but despite the proof on the sheet upon which they laid, Madeline was still so very innocent. Her naivete showed in her expression and her question. "I feared ye might still be in pain and thought the cool compress would ease it."

"Ye were trying to take care of me?" Madeline looked down at her bare body and felt foolish again, but for a different reason. She didn't understand these parts of a relationship with a man. She never imagined that any husband would tend his wife in such an intimate manner.

"This hasnae been an easy night for ye in many ways. I would do what I can to make it better," Fingal offered.

"It's nae been bad, Fin. Just vera confusing."

"Is there aught that I can say or do to help it make sense?" Fingal asked with sincerity. He worried about what was going on in Madeline's mind. He hoped to set her straight before any of her misguided and dogmatic notions took hold.

"I understood what ye explained aboot ma body needing to be ready. I could feel it changing. I was certain I could withstand the temptations, and I did.

143

But I still couldnae keep ma body from moving with yers." Madeline shrugged again. "I suppose that is what a wife is supposed to do to ensure her husband can—mmm—finish."

Fingal knew he trod dangerous ground with a fine line between correcting Madeline's way of thinking and pushing her into a downward spiral of guilt and remorse. "Maddy, I canna explain what it means to me that ye wanted to ensure I enjoyed being with ye. And I did. Vera much. Ma body would have finished even if ye hadnae moved, but it was exquisite when ye did." He wanted to pull back his words when he realized how Madeline would interpret them. "Ye didna lead either of us to commit a mortal sin, Madeline. It showed me how much of a giving person ye are. Ye were willing to try something ye werenae comfortable with, that ye even feared, because ye wished to make our time together better for me. Ye are a selfless woman, Madeline. There is nay sin in that."

"Thank ye, Fin," Madeline said before drawing in a deep breath. "I fear I willna always have such resolve to fight the temptation of original sin. I find ma mind is weak, ma resolve easily shaken when we're together. But I dinna want to push ye away or fail ye, Fin."

"Fail me? Madeline, we've been married a few hours. How could ye fail me? Ye havenae refused to let me come to yer bed. Ye havenae stabbed me, strangled me, suffocated me, or poisoned me. I dinna think ye could fail when there has been so little time to do aught." Fingal grinned, and Madeline chuckled at his exaggerated reasoning. She felt her mood lighten between his reassurance and his jests. Madeline bit her top lip as she considered what she was about to say. She hadn't found herself in the fiery pits of hell, so she figured her transgression hadn't been that grave.

"May I kiss ye?" Madeline asked.

Fingal slid his arm beneath her neck and drew her closer before resting his hand on her hip. "Ye never need to ask, lass."

He'd given the same answer to many other women when they asked him for a kiss. But he'd always been teasing when he responded. He knew he'd spoken the truth as Madeline eased her lips against his, tentative at first but growing braver as her tongue passed between his lips. He enjoyed Madeline's exploration as she flicked her tongue against his before swiping the smooth interiors of his cheek. Her hand rested lightly on his waist before sliding over his back, her fingertips feathering over his skin. When she felt his cock spring back to life, she moaned and shuffled closer. She made to wrap her leg over his hip, but she froze as she realized she'd allowed herself to get lost in the sensations Fingal's body elicited from hers.

"Maddy, nae again so soon. Ye will be sore in the morn, and we have a long way to ride," Fingal kissed her cheek before brushing his thumb over her cheekbone. "I dinna want to turn ye down, but it is the right thing to do. Though it may vera well kill me."

Madeline sighed, but agreed that he was right. She tried not to groan when she shifted away from him, the soreness from their coupling already setting in. Fingal drew the covers over Madeline before kissing her forehead. He rolled to his side of the bed and stood. When he looked back at Madeline, he registered her confusion and hurt.

"Madeline, ye need to sleep. We will set a grueling pace every day. Enjoy a night of sound rest in a comfortable bed while it's available to ye. I shall do the same. I'm nae going anywhere but to ma chamber. Alone," Fingal explained.

Madeline fought back the tears yet again as she nodded. She didn't make a sound or roll over to watch Fingal leave. She thought he would stay once he climbed back onto the bed with her. She thought he'd want to couple with her again once he saw her naked. But she supposed that once he'd sated his needs and spilled his seed, he saw no reason to remain with her. She had assumed she would welcome the privacy and not think twice about him going to his chamber. She never assumed being left alone would hurt so much. She closed her eyes and drifted to sleep, Fingal's scent on the pillow beneath her head.

CHAPTER SIXTEEN

"Where the devil is ma wife?" Fingal fumed as he stalked toward the chapel. "I swear, if she thinks we'll wait for her through Prime, I'll throttle her and ask for redemption later."

Harry walked beside him in silence. They'd already checked the chamber Madeline slept in, but it was empty. Fingal had slammed the door shut. Memories from the night before flashed before his eyes, but he pushed them aside as his anger grew. He yanked the door open to the chapel, making the monks officiating the prayer service look up. They were the only two inside.

"Where is—"

"Fingal!"

Fingal and Harry turned around to find a MacLeod guard rushing toward them. Fingal narrowed his eyes at the man, preparing for whatever excuse he had on Madeline's behalf.

"Lady Madeline is waiting in the bailey, wondering where ye were. She's apologizing over and over for rousing us so early, but she thought ye wished to leave at sunrise."

"She's in the bailey already?" Fingal snapped.

"She's been there at least a quarter hour. She's

growing anxious that ye—erm—arenae coming or that ye—uh—already left," the guard shifted uncomfortably. Fingal scowled at the man as he pushed past him, the guard and Harry trailing in his wake. When they reached the bailey, Fingal found Madeline already in the saddle. He jerked to a stop when he noticed what she was wearing. His brow furrowed into deep ridges as he approached. He looked over the familiar undyed tunic, then the MacLeod *breacan feile* wrapped around her waist, with the opening in the back. The long plaid covered her legs where her stocking would have shown while she rode astride. The MacLeod guard whispered, "She did that when she rode here from the priory."

Fingal half expected her to pull a wimple from her sack, but he noticed that the large cross she often wore was not around her neck. Fingal grunted as he took two bannocks from one of his men and offered them to Madeline.

"Thank ye, but nay. I'm all right," Madeline replied.

"We arenae stopping for a midday meal, and I dinna need yer collapsing from hunger. The bread of Christ isnae a meal." Fingal barked. Madeline's smile vanished as she sat up straight. She inhaled so deeply that Fingal saw her chest expand, and the look of disgust on her face took Fingal aback.

"Dinna fash aboot me, Fingal. And ye ken Lauds is a prayer service with nay Eucharist. I went to the chapel for Matins and Lauds, and I dinna want yer bannocks because Stuart," she jutted her chin toward one of her guards, "already gave me bannocks and dried beef while we waited for ye. Ye'd ken I rise before the sun is up, if ye had—" Madeline snapped her mouth shut before she admitted aloud what everyone already knew: that Fingal hadn't spent the night with her. She looked at the MacLeods and nodded before squeezing her horse's flanks and urging it to move.

"Ye are a bluidy arse," Harry growled. Fingal ignored him as he mounted his horse, and the Grants followed the MacLeods beneath the portcullis. "Ye're angry at her, but she's the one humiliated. Mayhap ye could try to go one day without making the lass feel worthless. Ye would have kenned she'd already gone to the chapel if ye'd bothered to spend the night with yer bride. Ye abandoned a woman who was likely terrified last night. She probably stayed up all night praying for her salvation."

Harry urged his horse forward, leaving Fingal to stew in his own anger and guilt. He had abandoned Madeline. He could have just as easily remained beside her and slept, but he'd chosen to return to his chamber because he didn't plan to couple with her again. He hadn't seen the point in remaining. It never even crossed his mind how she would feel when she was alone. He figured she would fall asleep and that he would have to wake her. He'd even thought to give her a good morning kiss. He thought he was angry because she slowed their start that morning, but instead, she waited for him, fearing he'd abandoned her that morning just as he had the night before. She'd been trying to prove her worth by being early, and his foul mood rejected her all over again.

I dinna ken if I'm made to be a husband.

As the day wore on, Fingal felt more and more confused by Madeline. The Grants led the party since they headed to his home. He could hear Madeline's voice behind him as she chattered with the MacLeods. Fingal knew she hadn't seen the men in

149

more than five years before they escorted her to Stirling, but she carried on an easy and convivial conversation with them. Each time they stopped to rest and water the horses, Madeline slipped from her saddle and made her way behind a bush. She was always standing beside her horse when they were ready to mount. She asked for nothing, but was polite when Harry offered her an apple at midday. Fingal could have kicked himself as he looked at the strip of dried beef he was about to eat. He hadn't thought to offer Madeline anything. He supposed he assumed one of the MacLeods would give her something like that morning.

It was Madeline who built the fire when they stopped for the night. She'd looked at Fingal when it was time to eat, confused by where she should sit. He waited too long to offer her a seat, so she moved to sit with her men. Harry shook his head at him and sighed as though Fingal was hopeless. As they prepared to bed down, Fingal drew the line at Harry offering Madeline one of his extra plaids. Even though Madeline was now a Grant, she'd been one for only a day. It was inappropriate for her to wear another man's plaid when he was from a different clan.

"Maddy," Fingal murmured as he stepped beside her. "It'll grow cold tonight, and I dinna want ye to be chilled." Fingal offered her his spare plaid. He'd watched her lay out the MacLeod plaid she'd been wearing, and he knew she intended to wrap herself in a cocoon, but it wouldn't be enough.

"Thank ye, Fin. I appreciate it. I admit it is rather cool." Madeline smiled as she turned away.

"Maddy."

Madeline turned back toward Fingal and raised her eyebrows. "Aye?"

"I'd like ye to keep it. At least until we arrive at

Freuchie, and Davina can get ye one the right length for an arisaid," Fingal suggested. He held his breath.

"Thank ye. I'd like to wear the Grant colors now, but I will be sure to return it to ye without delay." Madeline forced a tight smile. Fingal realized that yet again, he'd put his foot in his mouth. He'd made his offer sound conditional when he'd thought it would make Madeline less uncomfortable accepting it.

"Actually, Maddy, I'd like ye to keep it even once ye have an arisaid," Fingal admitted.

"Because it's yers?" Madeline's shoulders slumped. "Fin, everyone will already ken I'm yer wife. Ye dinna have to give me yer plaid to make others ken."

Fingal blinked several times as he realized she thought he was using it as his personal brand to mark her as his. He grasped her elbow and led her away.

"That isnae why I want ye to have it. I just want ye to have something of mine. Something personal," Fingal confessed. "It's nae much of a wedding gift, but it's something from me."

"Fin," Madeline breathed before she went on her toes and kissed him. It wasn't a peck. Madeline pressed her body against his, and Fingal wasted no time wrapping his arms around her and holding her tight. The kiss was languid and gentle. Fingal tramped down his desire to carry Madeline into the trees and wrap her legs around his waist before thrusting into her. He knew in that moment that he'd desired Madeline more than he had any other woman, and he knew he was a glutton for punishment, since she would never return his feelings.

When they broke apart, Fingal waited for the tears and regret that would surely come from Madeline. He loosened his hold on her, expecting her to run away. But she stood there, her hands on his arms, his plaid draped over one of hers. She looked dazed, but she didn't fall to her knees to beg forgiveness. Fingal counted that as a small success. He was the one who took a step back, but Madeline squeezed his arms and pulled him back toward her. She cupped his skull and pressed his head down to hers. She met his kiss, and it was her desire that sparked a fire between them. Their kiss was filled with passion and need, and it shocked Fingal that Madeline was the one to initiate and prolong it.

"Fin, I'll sort things out with God later, but I wanted to do that," Madeline said. "The plaid means a great deal to me. More than I expected." She pulled away and wrapped Fingal's plaid around her shoulders before he led her to her place beside the fire. Knowing that it was his plaid wrapped closest to Madeline's body, rather than one of the MacLeod's, was deeply satisfying.

CHAPTER SEVENTEEN

Fingal's eyes opened as the scent of fresh bannocks and eggs wafted over to him. He couldn't reason why he smelled eggs when he recalled that they were on the road to Freuchie. He sat up and spotted Madeline leaning over the fire as she fried the batter for bannocks, and to his disbelief, he saw eggs beside them.

Madeline looked over and smiled at him. "Are ye hungry?"

"Aye. But how did ye get eggs?" Fingal approached and realized they were quail eggs. There were ten eggs in the pan enough for each member of the party to have one.

"When I sought some privacy this morn, I noticed the nest on the ground. I looked around but realized that because it had fallen from the tree, the mother bird wouldnae return. I thought to put them back into the branches, but I couldnae reach. I shook one and knew they werenae close to hatching. I brought them back for everyone to break their fast."

"Madeline, the sun isnae even up. How'd ye have enough light to even see aught?"

"I told ye, I rise before the sun is up. I have for

153

five years because I had to. I didna go far from the camp since it was hard to see. The firelight helped."

Fingal nodded as he watched Madeline prepare the food. It surprised him to see how easily she maneuvered cooking over an open flame. She had little trouble sliding the eggs on top of bannocks before handing them out. She offered two to Fingal.

"Maddy, we arenae stopping for a midday meal today. Ye should eat. I amnae taking yers."

Madeline shook her head. "I canna eat quail or their eggs. It makes me ill these days. I tried at Stirling—twice—and both times it left me miserable. I have bannocks and dried beef, so I will be fine."

Fingal stared at her before nodding and offering his thanks. She'd known she couldn't eat what she prepared, so instead of only making nine, she'd offered her portion to Fingal. He suspected it was in deference to his senior position within their party and his position as her husband, but her thoughtfulness touched him.

When the men finished eating, they broke camp. Once more, Madeline stood by her horse, ready to leave when the men finished. Fingal had assumed she would need help mounting and dismounting, but she was always in the saddle before he could offer. She wasn't exceptionally tall, but she was strong after years of toiling at the convent.

Madeline grasped the saddle to keep herself upright. She waited for her knees to stop shaking and for her legs to bear her weight before she let go. She was stiff and sore from their second day on the road. She swallowed her moan as she took her first steps, and her thighs chafed together. She'd discreetly tried to arrange her skirts and Fingal's plaid to keep her legs from rubbing against the leather saddle, but the plaid's wool wasn't as soft as her worn tunic and it only made the chafing worse.

Madeline swept her eyes over the camp until she spotted Fingal. She tilted her head toward the stream and held up her sliver of soap. When Fingal finally nodded after scanning the area, Madeline slipped down to the cool water. She pulled the plaid loose and rushed to strip off her boots and stockings. She waded in, pulling her tunic high enough to keep the hem from soaking as she lowered herself to her knees. The chilly water was a balm to her raw skin. When she feared her legs would grow numb, she hurried back to the shore and rushed through her ablutions, knowing the men would want to wash soon too.

"Lady Madeline," Harry approached her as she returned to camp. He held out a small jar to her. "The salve should help."

Madeline's cheeks flushed, but she nodded her thanks as Harry smiled kindly. He said nothing else, and Madeline felt grateful for the salve. When he turned back to the men, she slipped behind a bush and slathered it onto her thighs. It stung, then burned, then felt cool and soothing. She reapplied a thick coat the next morning before they set off. It helped in the beginning, but as the day wore on, the effects wore off. Each time they stopped briefly to rest the horses, she gritted her teeth and forced herself not to hobble when she sought privacy.

"Fingal, ye need to slow the pace," Harry muttered. The guard looked over his shoulder for a fourth time that afternoon. "Yer wife is ready to fall off her horse."

"What?" Fingal looked back to where Madeline rode in the middle, the Grants in front of her, and the MacLeods behind her. "She's hale."

"Nay, she isnae," Harry argued. "She's ready to collapse. She hasnae spent years in the saddle like we have. Aye, she's a strong lass, but the only animal she's likely ridden in years is an ass or a mule." Harry pressed his lips together to keep from laughing when both men realized the double entendre. He shook his head and raised a hand in surrender when Fingal looked ready to murder him. Neither missed what it insinuated about Madeline's past, and Fingal didn't like it.

Fingal looked back again and watched Madeline, finally noticing what Harry said was obvious. There were deep furrows between her brows, and more perspiration fell from her brow than the weather warranted. She swayed a few times before jerking herself upright.

Fingal looked past Madeline and saw four angry MacLeod faces glaring at him. He glanced at his men, who shrugged. Everyone had noticed his wife's condition but him. He'd assumed she would speak up if she needed to rest. Cairstine and Fenella never complained when they used to travel with him, but they'd tell him when they needed privacy or were growing too tired to carry on.

He called the riders to a stop after steering them toward a clearing. He dismounted and threw his reins to one of his men before turning toward Madeline. Harry was already reaching up to her, and she leaned so far over that she nearly toppled from the saddle. Fingal watched as his best friend kept his hands on Madeline's waist as she steadied herself. Harry said something to her that he couldn't hear. Madeline smiled and nodded before looking at Fingal. Her smile slipped before she lowered her head. Fingal was ready to glare at Harry when he saw his friend's look of disgust and disappointment, directed at him.

"Maddy," Fingal turned toward her when he heard her emerge from the bush she'd used for privacy. He noticed the shadows under her eyes, and the tight skin over her cheekbones. "If ye need a rest, ye must tell me."

"Aye, Fingal. Thank ye." Madeline agreed, knowing she had no intention of speaking up. She would do nothing that would make Fingal regret having her along with him, and she would do nothing that would inconvenience the other men. She reminded herself that she'd once lashed herself for an hour, then worn a hair shirt for two days over the open cuts. If she could survive that, then a few days in the saddle wasn't unbearable. She reasoned she would grow used to their pace, and her body would adjust to the demands being placed upon it.

They remained in the clearing for an hour, and even Fingal appreciated the unexpected break from the hours of being jostled on horseback. It wasn't that he never grew saddle sore. He'd just grown so used to it over the years that he rarely thought about the aches and pains that were a part of his life when he rode patrol or traveled. When they could no longer delay returning to the road, he looked for Madeline and found Harry's hands once more wrapped around her waist as he lifted her into the saddle. He held her reins as she adjusted her tunic and plaid.

As his senior guard, Fingal expected Harry to join him as they led the party. But when they started riding again, Harry hung back and talked to Madeline. Fingal seethed as he felt Harry usurping his role as Madeline's protector. When they stopped for the night, he watched Madeline and Harry as they continued to talk as one of the MacLeod men took their horses' reins and led the animals away. Their conversation seemed natural, as though they'd been friends for years. But just as the last time, when Madeline looked over at Fingal, her smile dropped, and she wouldn't look him in the eye.

Good. Feel guilty for yer shameless flirting. Do ye really think I wouldnae notice? And with ma best friend.

When Madeline walked away, Fingal stalked over to Harry. He pushed his friend towards the trees where no one could overhear them or see them. Fingal grasped the front of Harry's leine and tugged. "She's already married. To me. I swear to ye, Harry, if ye try to bed ma wife, I will kill ye."

"I dinna want yer wife, and she wouldnae have me if I did. Ye're an eejit, and ye dinna care aboot her, so dinna pretend. Ye dinna want anyone else sniffing around her, but ye dinna bother with her unless ye think someone else is," Harry snarled. He pushed Fingal hard enough that he took a step back. But Fingal still had a hold of Harry's leine.

"Ye're in love with her already," Fingal accused. Harry's expression told Fingal everything he needed to know. His best friend coveted his wife.

"Even if I was, I wouldnae betray ye, Fingal. And I certainly wouldnae disgrace Lady Madeline by doing aught. But the lass needs someone to protect her since ye clearly willna. She is in pain, but she'll never admit it. She's exhausted, but she willna tell anyone."

"Then she is prideful, and she can pray for forgiveness for her sins," Fingal spat.

"And when will ye pray for yers? She isnae prideful. She's terrified ye'll leave her behind," Harry reasoned.

"Did she tell ye that?"

"Nay—"

"Then ye're just guessing," Fingal accused.

"It doesnae take much to reason it out. Fingal, she may have wanted to be a lady-in-waiting, but her brother had to agree. From all accounts, he was likely glad to have her gone from Stornoway. Then she was dragged away from court and left at a convent for five years. And once she finally believed she belonged there, she was dumped out of there, too. With the way ye act, what's to make her think she's any more wanted now than she ever was before? She didna have a choice whether she married or who she married. Ye did. And now ye must live with what comes along with that."

"Ye think ye ken ma wife so bluidy well from what? One conversation?"

"I ken her better than ye," Harry taunted. He ducked before Fingal's fist landed against his jaw.

"She willna have ye any more than she'll have me. Then again, I already have," Fingal sneered. A feminine gasp made both men release each other. They looked toward the sound and found Madeline staring at them. Fingal had never seen anyone's face change color so drastically so fast. The color leeched from it, and he feared she would faint. Then she grew bright red. She spun on her heels and dashed toward the river.

"Now ye've done it," Harry muttered as he pulled his leine back into place. Fingal gave his friend's chest one last shove before he rushed to follow Madeline. He found her kneeling on the bank, splashing water on her face.

"Maddy?" Fingal placed his hand on her shoulder, but she jerked away. "What did ye hear?"

Madeline cast a scathing look at him. "What does it matter? I heard enough to ken ye dinna trust me or yer friend. I ken ye left me as soon as ye did what ye needed, but ye'd boast to yer friend aboot it. Leave me alone, Fingal."

"Maddy—"

Madeline lurched to her feet. "Dinna ever call

me that again, Fingal. Ye dinna care aboot me. Ye canna, so dinna pretend with yer words. Yer actions prove everything. I told ye, I'll have yer children and run the keep when the time comes. I will be civil and respectful to ye always, but there's naught between us but duty. So dinna fash yerself over me. I will bed ye when ye wish, so rest assured I willna shirk ma responsibilities. And I amnae going to any mon's bed. It's bad enough ye'll be coming to mine."

Madeline's shoulder rammed into his with more force than Fingal expected as she walked past him. He stood stunned as he watched her walk away. She'd once told him that she feared disappointing him, but it was clear that the only disappointment was him. As angry as he'd been at Harry, he knew it stemmed from guilt because he'd been too self-involved and dimwitted to think about Madeline's needs. But now she faced him with pure loathing. He tilted his head back and closed his eyes as he inhaled deeply. It had only been a few days earlier that she was holding him close as she kissed him passionately. Now he feared she would sleep through their next coupling just so she wouldn't have to look at him.

CHAPTER EIGHTEEN

Madeline's MacLeod guards separated from the party as they turned northwest, and the Grants turned northeast toward the Cairngorm Mountains. Madeline watched as her last link to her old clan rode away, leaving only a cloud of dust in their wake. They'd been on the road for five days and were nearing the Cairngorms. She'd only heard of the mountains, but she was eager to see if they were as majestic as she'd heard.

Despite the constant discomfort of riding, Madeline enjoyed the crisp fresh air with the scent of Highland summer flowers. It reminded her of her childhood on Lewis. The only thing missing was the smell of the sea in the air. It had taken her a few days at Inchcailleoch to realize that part of what made it easier to adjust was that she once more lived on an island. Even though Loch Lomond was freshwater—with the familiar scent of salt water missing—knowing she was near water was calming and reassuring.

Now she was alone with just the Grants. It had been two days since her argument with Fingal along the riverbank. He'd been courteous to her, stopping more frequently and for longer stretches. They made camp earlier than before, and she knew it was only for her benefit. But when Fingal barely looked in her direction and never spoke to her, she tried to convince Harry that she didn't need to delay their travels. He was still kind to her, but he wasn't as open with her as before. She was left with men she didn't know and with whom she didn't even share a common clan history. Her only friend kept his distance, and her husband wanted nothing to do with her.

She prayed for forgiveness for the way she'd spoken to Fingal, knowing the respect she'd promised him as his wife was absent when she hurled angry words at him. She'd thought to ask Fingal for his forgiveness, but every time she looked, he was avoiding her. She decided it would be better to leave him alone than poke an angry bear.

She gripped the saddle tightly between her thighs, wincing from the pain that had grown more excruciating by the day. She'd continued to use the salve Harry gave her until it ran out. She didn't dare admit that her condition was worse, or Harry might insist that Fingal let them stop. She feared Fingal wouldn't forgive her for that. She turned her head into her shoulder as she wiped away the sweat that had dripped from the tip of her nose onto her upper lip. She wished for nothing more than a bed, even her old cot in her cell, and days of uninterrupted sleep. She'd had no appetite as their journey wore on, but she forced herself to eat. She knew if she didn't, she would collapse.

As the sun beat down on her head, Madeline knew she was truly unwell. There was no other reason to explain the chills that swept over her between the bouts of profuse sweating. Her hands shook as she held the reins, and she was grateful that she had a reliable horse who was unfazed by her trembling. Each time they stopped to rest, she hurried to dismount before anyone came close enough to look at her. She kept to herself even more than usual because she was too miserable to force a smile.

"Fingal, she's ill," Harry whispered as he approached his friend that evening. The men hadn't spoken to one another for two days, but eventually their tempers settled, and they fell back into their normal dynamic. But Fingal bristled when Harry commented on Madeline, proving the man was still watching his wife.

"Harry," Fingal warned.

"I'm serious, Fingal. She's really ill. I gave her a jar of salve when we first started out, but I suspect she's used it all. She can barely walk. Ye need to speak to her, see what's wrong. I'm warning ye, if ye dinna, I will. And I willna ask yer permission to do whatever she needs to care for her."

"Ye are in love with ma wife," Fingal accused.

"Someone should be," Harry muttered, guilt written across his face. "But how I feel is irrelevant. I'm telling ye she's sick. Please. Go see to her." Fingal saw the earnestness in his friend's eyes, and Fingal knew Harry would never beg him to do anything if he wasn't truly serious. Fingal looked over his horse's back and watched as Madeline wrapped her arm around her waist as the other hand held her plaid and tunic out of the way.

Madeline hobbled several steps before she seemed to catch herself. He watched her try to walk without a limp, but she failed. Even from a distance, he could see the sweat pouring down her forehead and her damp hair. Fingal glanced back at Harry and nodded. Madeline looked terrible. He wondered how he could have missed such obvious signs, but he'd been ignoring her as he licked his wounds. Then it seemed as if she'd given up on him, so he kept his distance.

Fingal followed her to the river and watched as she sagged against a boulder before sliding down to the ground. She sobbed silently, and Fingal's heart broke as he watched tears streamed down his stalwart wife's face. He could see her biting her lip as she bent her legs to pull off her boots and stockings. With her legs stretched out in front of her, she rested her head against the rock with her eyes closed, exhausted from the effort. Fingal could see her labored breathing, and his heart raced as he realized Harry hadn't exaggerated. Madeline was desperately ill.

"Maddy," Fingal whispered as he squatted beside her. Her eyes barely opened, and her head didn't move when she looked at him. He used her plaid to wipe away the sweat from her face, as gentle with her as though she were a newborn babe. When he placed the back of his hand against her brow, her skin scalded his. "Dear God, Madeline. Ye're burning with fever. I need to get ye cool. Can ye get yer clothes off? I'll help ye into the water."

Madeline's head lolled from one side to the other. "I'm fine, Fingal. Dinna fash. I can take care of ma-self," her dry throat croaked. She tried to lift her hand to push him away, but she hadn't the energy to move it from her lap.

"Madeline, I need to see yer legs," Fingal whispered. When she made no effort to stop him, he feared he was too late to help her. Her eyes were closed, and her lips were chapped, even though sweat poured down her face to her neck. He pushed her tunic up to her waist and gasped when he saw the condition her legs were in. He suspected she hadn't been able to see how severe her injuries were if she bathed without taking her clothes off.

The skin at the top of her inner thighs was raw in

places, with scabs in others. He could see the yellowy-green pus around the scabs and across the open wounds. Her legs were more than chafed; they were infected. Fingal had to look away as his upper arm covered his mouth. He'd seen worse wounds, but seeing Madeline's injuries made him want to cry for the first time in decades. He collected himself before turning back to her.

"Maddy, lass. Can ye hear me?" Fingal cupped her jaw. She tried to nod and licked her lips, but her eyes didn't open. "How long have they been like this?"

"Started first day but got worse. Been like this for three days," Madeline rasped. Madeline cleared her throat and forced her eyes open, even though the dim evening light made them burn. "Help me to ma feet so I can take care of them."

"Maddy, nay. Ye canna do what must be done. I beg yer forgiveness now because I'm going to have to cause ye far more pain before these will heal." He dropped a soft kiss on Madeline's forehead before he went back to inspecting Madeline's legs. As he looked closer, he realized it was even worse than he initially thought. The raw skin wrapped from the front to the back of her legs, and even the skin at the juncture of her thighs was bruised. He couldn't imagine how she'd managed through the pain with nothing to help but a brief soak in cold water each night.

"Harry!" Fingal bellowed. "Bring me the salve, bandages, and whisky. No one comes near us nay matter what ye hear. Only if ye hear ma voice." Fingal glanced down at Madeline before pulling her tunic down to her knees. She hissed as the fabric touched her skin, but he would protect her modesty when Harry approached. He met Harry before he got close enough to see Madeline.

"Is it bad?" Harry murmured.

"Far worse than either of us could have imagined. We have to go to an inn. She canna travel like this. If I push her any harder, I think I may kill her." Fingal looked back over his shoulder in Madeline's direction before turning back to Harry. "I'm sorry for the things I've said and how I acted. If ye hadnae been watching over her—Thank ye."

Harry looked at his distraught friend, fear and guilt twisting Fingal's features. He watched as his friend kept looking back toward Madeline, and sighed in acceptance. "If ye dinna already love her yerself, Fingal, ye soon will."

Fingal's eyes locked with Harry's as he nodded. "I already ken."

Harry turned away, and Fingal rushed back to Madeline's side. He eased her tunic back up her legs, trying not to shudder as he saw the evidence of his selfishness all over again. The last thing Madeline needed was him falling apart. He rushed to strip off his boots, stockings, and leine. He rested his sword behind him where it would be within his reach once they were in the water. Then he eased her limp body onto her feet as he inched the tunic up her body.

"Fin, dinna leave me again," Madeline mumbled as she sagged against him.

"Never, wee one." Fingal braced her against him as he lifted the tunic over her head. He cautiously lifted her into his arms, trying to keep from pressing her legs together. He'd noticed that she still clutched her soap and linen square in her hand from when he approached, so he pried them from her. Once she let go, her head lolled back, as though the last dregs of her strength were gone. Just before he entered the water, he pulled his plaid from his waist and waded in until he could sit with Madeline in his lap and the water came to her waist. He didn't care about the pebbles and grit that bit into his backside.

Fingal cradled Madeline's head as he eased her body backwards until her hair and shoulders dipped into the water, and it washed over her breasts. He did nothing but let her soak, praying her fever would go down, even if only a little. As the minutes crept by, Fingal feared keeping her in the water too long. He fumbled, but did the best he could to lather soap onto the linen. He wiped Madeline's brow and cheeks, washing away the remnants of tears that had left streaks on her cheeks where dust from the road covered them. As he moved the cloth lower to wash her neck and collarbones, he felt Madeline's hand graze his hip beneath the water before her arm wrapped around his waist. She turned her head toward him and opened her eyes a crack.

"Fin, I dinna feel so well," Madeline admitted. Fingal smiled at her understatement, knowing what this confession was costing her. He finally understood that it wasn't pride that kept Madeline from admitting that she couldn't keep up. It was her sense of duty to the group. It was due to her concern for others that demanded she not delay them or be a burden upon them. He was certain she'd heard his men discussing what they looked forward to most when they returned home after being away for most of the summer. And he knew she'd been trying to earn his respect.

He wanted to think he already respected her, but he knew he hadn't. If he'd respected her, he would have ensured her comfort and wellbeing, and he wouldn't silently mock her faith and fears. He knew the blame lay solely on his shoulders. He was the one with more life experience, or at least experience traveling. He'd pledged to love, honor, and cherish her for better or for worse, in sickness and in health. He'd made it worse, and he'd caused her sickness.

"Dinna blame yerself," Madeline rasped. "I

should have listened to ye. Ye told me I would have to ask ye for rests. I did this to maself, and now ye must clean up the mess that I've made. Someone is always having to do that for me." Tears leaked from her eyes.

"Shh, Maddy. If ye insist on shouldering blame, then it can only be partial. I'm as much at fault, if nae more, as ye. I willna make the same mistakes twice. I willna ever put ye in this position again. I dinna want ye ever to fear telling me something. And Madeline, before ye assume I'm doing this out of duty or because I want to get us back on the road, I need ye to ken that I want to tend to ye. It's nae guilt either. I care aboot ye, Madeline."

Madeline's eyes fluttered open as she looked up at Fingal. Her eyes searched his. She saw sincerity in his concern and heard it in his words. She was seeing the true Fingal, the one she'd only seen hints of until now. The arm that she'd coiled around his waist tightened as she struggled to lift her hand to his face. She cupped his cheek as he turned to kiss her palm.

"Fin, I'm scared," Madeline whispered. "When I've been this ill before, I had an infirmary to go to. I wasna on the open road."

"I'm scared too, Maddy," Fingal admitted. "I canna get ye to an inn by tomorrow eve, but I can the next day. I need ye to manage another day and a half."

Madeline whimpered and looked away. "I dinna think I can. I canna ride, Fin."

"I wouldnae let ye. Ye'll be with me. Ye'll be in ma lap, so both legs can hang over the side. I'll hold ye. I willna let aught happen to ye," Fingal swore.

"Thank ye. I'm just so tired. Can I sleep now?" Madeline asked.

"Soon, wee one. I need to finish bathing ye, and we need to treat yer injuries. It will be painful, so I

168

doubt ye will sleep through it. I apologize now for what I must do to keep the infection from getting worse. All I seem to do is cause ye pain, Madeline. I swear I will try harder from today on to never do that again."

"I believe ye," Madeline's voice trailed off as her eyes drooped again. Fingal realized she'd fallen asleep despite her efforts not to. He hurried to wash her hair and the rest of her body before shifting so he could see what he was doing as he washed her wounds. He was careful not to rub away any of the scabs, but he had to scrub harder than he wished to clean away the pus.

Madeline flinched and moaned, but she didn't wake. That frightened him as much as the state of her legs. He wrapped her in his plaid when they left the water, and he rubbed her arms and back to dry her. Her skin was much cooler, but he knew she still ran a fever.

Fingal laid Madeline flat before retrieving the jug of whisky. He hated what he had to do, but he wasn't convinced the soap had been enough. He'd seen plenty of wounds go putrid, even after being scrubbed with soap and doused in whisky. He wouldn't risk Madeline getting worse because he'd only used soap. He gritted his teeth and would have closed his eyes, but he needed to see what he was doing. He took a deep breath before pouring the whisky over her wounds. Much like she'd reacted to the pain on their wedding night, Madeline's back bowed off the plaid, and her eyes flew open. She released a blood-curdling scream before whimpering as she looked at Fingal in confusion and distrust.

"I'm so sorry, but I told ye, I have to make it worse before I can make it better." Fingal turned his head as he heard movement approaching. "Stay back! I told ye nay to come unless ye heard ma voice." Fingal shifted his naked body to block anyone's view if his men drew too close.

"Fingal," Harry's voice carried from a distance. "Do ye need aught else?"

"Nay. Just privacy," Fingal called back.

"Willow bark," Madeline struggled to speak. "For tea. For ma fever." She tried to prop herself up on her elbows, but they gave way under her weight.

"Find some willow bark and fetch water from further down," Fingal called back to his men, uncaring who followed his order. He eased one leg then the other off the plaid as he examined the wounds. The light was nearly too dim to see, but he could tell that while the wounds were still angry and weeping, they were clean. He let the air evaporate the whisky before he pulled a glob of salve from the jar. "Ye ken this will burn and sting before it soothes."

Madeline nodded. She scrunched her eyes closed as she anticipated this pain. She released a hissing breath as Fingal smeared the ointment on her legs. Her breathing quickened as she worked through the second round of searing pain.

"Ye are such a brave lass. I'm so proud of ye." Fingal dropped a butterfly soft kiss on her lips. "And before ye remind me that pride is a sin, I dinna care. I amnae pleased aboot yer stubbornness that got ye into this mess, but I'm proud of ye for trying to put the others before yerself."

Fingal looked around and realized that Madeline had brought no fresh clothes with her to the riverbank. He assumed she hadn't planned to undress. He knew she'd washed her spare tunic and laid it out to dry the other night, but he feared even the tunic would be too form-fitting and force her legs too close together. He considered how long his leine was on him, so he knew she would swim in his.

"Harry, bring me ma spare leine," Fingal called.

"And an extra plaid." His own nakedness didn't bother him, but he knew it would mortify Madeline if any of his men saw her when she wasn't fully covered. If she'd worn his plaid to hide her stocking from showing, she would be beside herself if she thought she'd been immodest. He would dress her in his leine since it would come to at least her mid-calf, then wrap her in the plaid he'd given her and the one she lay on now. He wanted her to sweat out her fever, knowing he would likely have to bathe her again in the morning, if not in the middle of the night. He met Harry in the trees again, far enough away that his friend couldn't spy Madeline.

"Did ye pour the whisky on without giving her any?" Harry asked.

"Aye. I dinna ken if it would be good for her to have it with such a fever. She's so tiny compared to us. I feared it would be too much for her," Fingal explained. "I dinna ken if we can ride tomorrow after all. We may need to stay here for a day, even though I wish to get her to an inn as soon as we can. I'm scared to move her."

"It's really that bad?" Harry asked.

"The skin is more than just chafed. It's raw. Some parts have scabbed over, but I could see where rubbing against the saddle wore them away. Both legs are infected. That's why her fever is so high. She was scalding when I found her. The soak helped, but I could already feel her growing hot again. I shall see if I can sweat the fever from her by keeping her bundled up all night. I'll decide whether we push on in the morn after I see how tonight goes."

"Just tell me and the others what ye need. None of us want to see Lady Madeline suffer."

"I ken. I canna thank ye enough for forcing me to see what was under ma nose. I'm ashamed of how I failed her. And I'm sorry for the position ye're in, for

171

the one I've put ye in. But ye are right. I do care for ma wife vera much. I hate that it took this to make me realize."

"Do ye realize that she cares aboot ye too?" Harry asked. At Fingal's look of disbelief, Harry nodded his head. "Then ye dinna ken that she always asked what she could do for ye. Each time we stopped, she asked if ye needed aught, or if there was aught ye would want her to do. At first, she tried to be vague when she asked how ye fared, but eventually, she gave up and just asked me outright. Fingal, despite how big an arse ye were to her, and for reasons I canna figure out, yer wife cares aboot ye. I think most of the time she even likes ye. Mayhap nae the last few days, but at times."

"I dinna ken how ye can believe that," Fingal muttered as he looked back in Madeline's direction.

"Because as much as it pains me, she only has eyes for ye, ye daft mon," Harry huffed. Fingal looked back at him and frowned, but he could tell his friend meant what he said.

"I ken that canna be easy for ye," Fingal muttered.

"I'll get over it. Naught but puppy love. Go tend to yer wife," Harry jutted his chin in Madeline's direction and clapped his hand on Fingal's shoulder. "But dinna muck this up again. Or I will be the shoulder yer wife cries on."

Fingal nodded before returning to Madeline. Her eyes were open, and she watched his approach. He hastened to wrap the spare plaid around his waist, not wanting to embarrass her any more than he had to. When he squatted beside her, he realized she was clear-eyed and alert.

"What did ye hear?" Fingal asked.

Madeline sighed. "Enough to ken Harry canna keep a secret."

"Did ye hear what I said before that?" Fingal knew to what she was referring. She nodded her head, but remained quiet. She watched him as though he were an unpredictable animal, and she was unsure of what he would do next. He eased her into a sitting position before he twisted and sat facing her, his arm awkwardly wrapped around her shoulder to help support her weight. "I wasna lying, Maddy. I care aboot ye. I'm ashamed of how I've treated ye since our betrothal and especially since we married. Part of it I can only blame on self-centeredness. But part of it was each time it felt like rejection, I lashed out at ye."

"I never rejected ye, Fin. Well, mayhap except for the nasty things I said the last time I overheard ye and Harry."

"I understand that now. I let ma physical desire for ye overshadow ma emotions. And I put ma wants ahead of yer needs." Fingal relied upon the light from the rising moon and the sparse stars to see Madeline's face. She was more coherent than she had been, but he could see the strength she'd mustered was waning. As he stared at her, a feeling of certainty washed over him. He'd sensed it as he held her in the water, but now that he'd admitted his feelings, he had no more doubts. "Madeline, I need ye to ken something, and I pray ye believe me."

"What is it, Fin?" Madeline's voice had grown thready again, and Fingal wavered, fearing he was pushing her too much.

"Nay matter what happens between us, there'll never be anyone else," Fingal promised as he raised her palm to his mouth. He placed kisses at the base of each finger and her thumb before brushing his thumb over her palm, then planting a kiss there. "I only want what ye can give. I dinna need or want anyone else, Maddy."

"Ye say that now because ye feel guilty," Madeline struggled to say. Fingal knew he was running out of time.

"I've kenned that all along. I kenned each night I went to a tavern looking for a distraction, a way to forget how I feel aboot ye. I couldnae do it. Nae once. I was angry that I couldnae get ye out of ma mind, that I couldnae continue on as I always have, as I always thought I would. I once told Cairstine that it didna matter whether I liked ma wife as long as she bore me children. Even when Fenella married her husband Kennon and Cairstine married Eoin, I didna think such soft feelings mattered. Christ on the cross, I was wrong."

"Will ye sleep near me tonight?" Madeline asked as Fingal helped her into his leine. He wrapped the plaid he'd given her around her body before wrapping the plaid he'd worn earlier as a third layer.

"I'm nae letting go," Fingal whispered against her ear as he lifted her into his arms. She was asleep before they entered the camp. His men turned expectant faces toward him, but he didn't know what to say. They must have understood because they each nodded. One of his men, Tommy, slipped down to the shore, and Fingal hoped he was collecting what he'd left behind. Someone had laid out his bedroll, and he noticed Madeline's was next to his. He lowered her to the ground, but she moaned when he released her. He soothed her as he took his place beside her. She laid closer to the fire but a safe distance, so Fingal didn't have to worry about her rolling into it in the middle of the night. Harry offered him some rabbit, then a bannock, but Fingal wasn't interested. He lay on his side watching Madeline sleep until he couldn't keep his eyes open.

CHAPTER NINETEEN

M adeline was certain her skin would melt off her bones. She was broiling, but some type of web wouldn't allow her to free her arms. She fought to open her eyes, but they didn't cooperate. The more she struggled, the more a weight pressed across her middle. The more restricted her movement became, the more she panicked.

"Fingal!" she called out. "Fin! Fin!" Madeline tried to break free, but everything around her shook. She whimpered, "Fin," before it went black and still again.

Fingal watched as the fever ravaged Madeline throughout the night and well into the next afternoon. He hadn't dared move her since she alternated between the sweats and the chills. Her face would grow deep red, then go ghostly white. The sweat poured from her, and Fingal had to fight to get water down her throat. He cooed soothing words to her when she grew agitated and mopped her brow when she rested. He second guessed himself about keeping her bundled in the plaids when she could barely swallow the water. He tried to get Madeline to sip the willow bark tea Harry made, but she coughed and gagged.

She'd called out to him several times. His name was always clear and intelligible, even when he couldn't make out her other ramblings. If he weren't desperate to make her well, it would have flattered him. When she twisted and turned as though she searched for him, he laid beside her, whispering promises that he would go nowhere, that he would never leave her side. She calmed when he kissed her temple and stroked her hair.

Before the sun set after a full day of watching over Madeline, Fingal carried her back down to the river. When Tommy returned the night before, Fingal discovered he'd not only gathered the jar of salve, the jug of whisky, the soap, the washcloth, and Fingal's other clothes, he'd scrubbed Madeline's tunic and Fingal's leine. Fingal thanked him, knowing that he would need the clean clothes for Madeline. He bathed her as he had before, and once she was clean, he inspected her wounds. They didn't appear as angry as they had the previous night. There wasn't as much accumulated pus, despite Madeline's night sweats and tremors. Fingal could even see hints of fresh pink skin beneath. He breathed a sigh of relief, praying that they were moving in the right direction. As he smoothed the balm over her skin, Madeline's eyes fluttered open.

"Fin," Madeline's voice broke as she said the single syllable.

"Wheest, wee one," Fingal cooed as he glanced up from his ministrations. He noticed Madeline looked more lucid than she had the previous night when they'd spoken in the same spot.

"Fin? Am I dying?" Madeline wondered. Fingal froze, then put aside the jar and rubbed his hands together. He'd already slipped the leine Tommy washed onto her, so he lifted her into his arms, cradling her in his lap.

"I willna allow it, Maddy. I just found ye. I amnae anywhere near ready to let ye go," Fingal smiled.

"I dinna think ye control that." Madeline attempted a smile. She rested her head against his chest, recognizing his scent from when she'd been incoherent. She felt much cooler than she had. "Did ye leave me too close to the fire?"

"What? Nay, Maddy," Fingal hissed.

"I just canna figure out why I thought I was lying among the flames. I can recall being miserably hot when I've had other fevers, but nay like that. I dreamed that I was in a spiderweb, and I couldnae get ma arms free. I must have dreamed it was an enormous spider because it felt like it was pressing on ma middle, pinning me to the ground."

"Och, lass. It wasna any of that," Fingal explained. "I had ye wrapped as snug as a bug in a rug, but it was to get ye to sweat out whatever poisons ye have trapped in ye. That's why ye couldnae move. There were two plaids around ye. The weight was ma arm holding ye still when ye thrashed. I feared ye hurting yerself, and I wasna certain how I'd get ye covered again if ye threw off the plaids."

"Ye laid beside me? I can remember calling out to ye. One moment I didna think ye would come, then everything seemed calm. I was certain I could hear ye, even smell yer soap."

"I didna move from yer side, Maddy."

"Thank ye, Fin. I dinna ken what I would do without ye."

"Be a far sight better off than ye are now," Fingal muttered.

"Please dinna say that. I dinna blame ye for any of this." Madeline looked toward the water as the current flowed over rocks and splashed against the shore. Despite the continuous pain between her legs, she felt more herself than she had in days. "I wish we could sleep here tonight, by the water. It sounds like home, ma old home. It's like the waves crashing on the cliff below Stornoway."

"Maddy—"

"Nay, I ken, Fin. It's nae safe to be away from the camp. I was just rambling."

"If this is where ye wish to sleep, then we will stay here. The men willna mind moving such a small distance."

"Och! Yer men." Madeline tried to scramble to her feet, but her head bobbled from side-to-side. "I'm keeping them from returning home to their beds and their families. I'm well now."

"Madeline Grant, that is the most ridiculous thing I've ever heard ye say. Ye were on death's doorstep nae an hour ago, and now ye think to be herding ma men back onto their horses." Fingal shook his head in playful disbelief. He pulled the plaid he'd given her tighter around her shoulders before whistling. His men rushed to find them, but they all halted when they found Fingal sitting with Madeline in his lap.

Fingal bit back his laughter at their stunned faces. He understood why none of his men could have expected to see the couple in such an intimate and comfortable position. For the whole trip they'd been at one another's throats one moment, then ignoring each other the next. Now sitting with Madeline cradled in his arms felt more natural than anything else. "We're moving camp down here."

The men looked at one another, then at Madeline. Harry stepped forward and looked down at her before glancing at Fingal. "Ye look improved, Lady Madeline. Are ye nae feeling better?" Harry shot Fingal a questioning look, worried that Madeline's fever was worse if Fingal wanted her so close to the cool water.

"I am," Madeline nodded. "Fingal's being ridiculous. I mentioned that I wished I could sleep down here because it reminded me of Stornoway. He's being too indulgent."

Madeline listened as the men decided who would bring the firewood down to the riverbank, who would carry the saddles, and where they would tie off the horses. It was as if Madeline had said nothing. She rested back against Fingal as he pressed a kiss to her temple.

"They care aboot ye too, Maddy. If sleeping here is what ye wish, I think ma men would move heaven and earth to make that happen. Ye've given all of us an awful fright." Fingal looked down and noticed Madeline's eyelids were drooping. Her moments of clear-headedness were getting longer, but he had to remind himself that she wasn't yet out of danger. Between her illness and her own need to avoid inconveniencing anyone, Madeline's health was still fragile.

Once the fire was burning again, Fingal was able to get Madeline to drink a mug of willow bark tree, and she asked for some privacy for the first time in a day. He helped her to a secluded spot but turned his back to keep from embarrassing her. When they returned to the camp, Madeline drifted back to sleep leaning against Fingal.

"What do ye think aboot tomorrow?" Harry kept his voice low, so he wouldn't disturb Madeline.

"I dinna ken. Mayhap half a day's ride in the afternoon. I still want to take her to an inn. I think a healer should take a look just to be sure. Let's see how tonight goes and how she fares in the morn," Fingal responded. At the sound of his voice, Madeline sighed and nuzzled her face into his chest.

"She trusts ye," Harry commented.

"For better or for worse, she's always said she does. I took it for granted, but now I want to be worthy of it," Fingal explained. "I wouldnae ever wish for her to be this ill, but it's made me wake up. Ye were right. I thought I wanted a wife, and now I have one. Nay one forced me. I'd say I'm a bluidy lucky mon to be married to the lass. I would do aught to heal her right this vera moment, but I dinna think I would have come around so quickly if this hadnae happened."

"And when she's recovered, and ye dinna feel guilty, what then?" Harry pressed.

"Then we can begin our life together. Ye ken what I tried to do before ma wedding, and ye ken I couldnae go through with it. Nae even a little. It angered me because it felt like she already had control of ma life, because I couldnae go through with what I'd believed ma marriage would be. I thought having a wife wouldnae interfere with the way I wanted to go aboot ma day. That's why Madeline seemed ideal. She said she'd turn a blind eye if I continued with other women because it suited her too.

"But I canna do it. I dinna want anyone else but ma wife. Even now, even though I dinna ken if she'll ever want me the way I want her. But I'm nae a lad anymore. I canna let ma cock lead the way. Nae if I want a life with a woman far more wonderful than I deserve."

Harry stood silently as he listened to Fingal, and he knew his friend had changed. Never had he imagined Fingal changing his life for any woman, not even a wife. He'd said for years that it didn't matter whether his wife had tender feelings for him, because he didn't see the need to have them for her. Now it was Fingal who wasn't sure if Madeline could reciprocate his emotions. It was a turn of events neither man could have predicted.

"Just dinna muck this up, Fingal. Go slowly with her," Harry warned.

"I ken. She's skittish as a day-old foal. I dinna want to hurt her. She deserves to have someone look after her for a while." With nothing more to say, Harry found a spot near the fire, and Fingal lifted a sleeping Madeline back into his lap. As he adjusted her position, her groggy voice made him regret moving her.

"Fin?"

"Aye, Maddy."

"Comfy," Madeline sighed. "But vera thirsty."

Fingal stretched for the waterskin attached to his saddle. He held the water vessel to Madeline's lips but had to urge her to slow down when she gulped several mouthfuls. She settled back to sleep, and Fingal leaned his head back. A boulder may have propped him up, but Madeline in his arms was all the comfort he needed.

CHAPTER TWENTY

F ingal watched Madeline throughout the next morning, and by afternoon she appeared much improved. He helped her to the river in the morning, so she could bathe. They moved further upriver and away from his men to give Madeline privacy. While her balance was still unsteady, she could stand while Fingal passed the lathered linen square over her body. Now that she was fully lucid, her awareness of her body's reaction to Fingal touching her so intimately returned. She turned her head away in embarrassment when he inspected her legs and applied the salve. She appreciated his concern and how he'd tended to her while she was unable, but she was uncomfortable with his nearness.

When they returned to the camp, Madeline rested against the large rock and managed a cup of willow bark tea and a couple of bannocks. As the morning progressed, Madeline was certain her fever had broken, and Fingal assured her that her wounds had improved far faster than he expected. By midday, Fingal thought Madeline might tolerate riding again if she sat in his lap, where he could keep her from being jostled.

"Maddy, do ye think ye're well enough for a few hours of riding?" Fingal asked as he came to sit beside her. He handed her a rabbit leg that had just come off the spit. Fingal had his men hunt for their midday and evening meal, insisting Madeline needed more than bannocks and dried beef. "If ye can manage this afternoon and all day tomorrow, I can have ye at an inn before the sun sets. We are nearly to the mountain passes, and I need ye to be able to walk on yer own. There are parts of the path so narrow that we will have to guide our horses, and they canna have the extra weight of a rider. I dinna want to attempt it until I'm sure ye're well. A couple nights' rest at an inn and having a healer check ye would make me feel more comfortable."

"If I dinna have to ride astride, I can make it," Madeline nodded. Fingal took a long, hard look at Madeline, as though he wasn't certain if he should believe her. "Really, Fin. Ma fever broke, and I amnae so sore after a day and a half off the horse. The salve helps more and more each time ye put it on."

"Vera well," Fingal decided. "We'll break camp when we're done eating and be on our way."

Once Fingal was in the saddle, Harry helped pass Madeline up to him. He settled her as best he could, so her legs draped over his right thigh. If someone attacked, he could draw his sword from the scabbard he wore across his back and not worry about decapitating Madeline. She'd donned one of her tunics again and wrapped her Grant plaid around her waist. She sat up and looked around for the first half hour they were on the road. But the movement of the horse beneath her, and the feel of Fingal's arm wrapped around her waist with his warm body beside her, made her drowsy. He'd encouraged her to sleep, and she relented. She didn't realize she slept the entire afternoon until they stopped to make camp at sundown. Her appetite was improved, and she happily ate the meat given to her, washing it down with yet another cup of willow bark tea. She assured Fingal it was to keep the fever away rather than treat it.

The next day followed much the same pattern. Madeline slept throughout the morning, woke to eat at midday, then fell back to sleep. When they arrived at the inn, Madeline remained outside with Harry while Fingal arranged for a room. She insisted that she could walk on her own two feet rather than be carried like an invalid. Fingal opened his mouth to argue that she was an invalid, but Harry's warning look and shake of his head made him think better.

She devoured two bowls of beef stew and a mug of ale before she sagged against Fingal's shoulder. He wrapped his arm around her and nudged her awake. He offered to carry her to their chamber, but Madeline refused his offer with a smile. Once Madeline entered the chamber, her stomach dropped. She hadn't thought about there being only one bed. When she'd been on her deathbed, Fingal's presence had been comforting and practical. His body heat often warmed her when she shivered with the chills. While her husband was far more intimately aware of her body than she'd expected, she grew uneasy knowing they would share a bed now that she wasn't unconscious most of the time.

Fingal watched Madeline as her eyes darted around the chamber, returning to the bed and lingering before looking at the floor and the fireplace. He sensed her unease, and while he wanted to groan because he thought they'd made great progress, he knew Madeline was apprehensive about sharing a bed with him.

"Maddy, that coverlet doesnae seem vera thick.

Be sure to have both plaids tucked around ye," Fingal suggested. Madeline turned toward him, her brow furrowed.

"Ma fever's gone, and ye give off quite a lot of heat. I dinna think I'll need them both." Madeline couldn't meet his eyes as she replied.

"I'm sleeping on the floor, Maddy."

"What? Nay, Fingal. That isnae right. Ye deserve a bed too. Ye've been sleeping on the ground just as I have," Madeline argued.

"It's fine, Madeline. Ye need yer rest, and I dinna want to disturb ye."

Madeline opened her mouth, then snapped it shut before nodding her head. He'd sensed her discomfort and had tried to ease it, but Madeline suddenly felt bereft. She'd grown accustomed to Fingal's body wrapped around hers. She wondered if she would sleep as well without him. She'd pulled a chemise Laurel gave her from her chest and slipped behind the screen to undress. She reminded herself that it was ridiculous to be so modest after the past few days, but she hadn't thought about what she was doing as she crossed the chamber. She hurried to undress and climbed into the bed. Fingal settled on the floor in front of the fire. He pulled the extra length of his plaid over his head and around his shoulders. His sword rested on the floor before him. Madeline sighed as she closed her eyes. She didn't know what to make of her situation with Fingal.

Two more days of rest and hearty meals greatly improved Madeline's spirit and gave her body time to heal. Fingal sent for the village healer, who tsked several times when she saw Madeline's legs but agreed

186

that they were healing well. She admitted there was nothing more to be done than to continue using the salve and wait until the wounds healed on their own.

By the evening of their fourth day after camping alongside the riverside, the Grants reached the base of the Cairngorms. Madeline stared at the peaks in the distance, awed by their height and rugged terrain. She knew Fingal and his men had made the journey along the pass many times, traveling to Stirling or to see other clans, so she was confident that they knew the best route to traverse. She bit her bottom lip as she considered what she faced the next day.

"Are ye scared?" Fingal asked, and Madeline jumped. She hadn't heard him approach, and she had a sudden memory of the evening the king announced their betrothal. He'd snuck up on her in the royal antechamber and made her jump then, too.

"Nae of the heights. They dinna bother me. I ken we must make our way through the pass tomorrow and come out the other side before nightfall. I'm worried that I willna be able to keep up. Is there snow up there? I dinna see any."

"Nay. There wasna any when we came through earlier in the summer, but it's nae impossible. Ye will be able to ride with me for most of the way, and there are a few stretches where ye could ride while I lead. The parts where we must all walk are vera narrow but nae too long."

"Would ye—uh…" Madeline shook her head as if to dismiss her thought. She smiled at Fingal and made to move past him, but he held his arm out in front of her as a barricade.

"What is it? I told ye, I dinna want ye ever to be afraid to talk to me," Fingal murmured.

"I'm nae afraid. I just changed ma mind," Madeline assured. She'd gotten too embarrassed to ask if Fingal would hold her hand through the parts where she would have to follow him on foot. She'd caused them enough delay. She wouldn't make Fingal worry that she was afraid to walk by herself. Fingal lowered his arm and nodded, but he was unconvinced that all was well with Madeline. He vowed to himself that he would keep better watch over her, and the moment her strength seemed to flag, he would make them stop.

It surprised Fingal when Madeline shook him awake the next morning. The pink and purple rays were barely visible, and the sun was yet to be seen. Fingal sat up and yawned before stretching. Madeline looked wide awake. She looked more like her normal self than she had since they left Stirling.

"Ye seem in fine fittle this morn, wee one," Fingal grinned.

"I feel better than I have in days. I assumed ye wished to have an early start," Madeline explained.

"I do, but the sun could be awake before the rest of us," Fingal teased.

Madeline shrugged. "I told ye, I always rise before the sun is up. I canna help it."

"Mayhap ye will learn to sleep in a wee longer once ye have a proper bed to sleep in," Fingal suggested. At Madeline's blank stare and jerky nod of her head, Fingal realized they had made less progress than he'd hoped. Seeing the bed in the inn's chamber, and then the mention of one in their home, made Madeline shy away. Fingal wasn't interested in exploring Madeline's feelings about what would become of their physical relationship. He was grateful that she was well, and he wanted to cross the mountains without anyone or any horse falling into a ravine.

That morning Madeline mounted in front of Fingal by using the stirrup. She was pleased that much of her old strength had returned. She'd been helpless to mount without either Fingal or Harry lifting her into the saddle as she recovered, but she preferred doing it herself. She still enjoyed the feel of Fingal's body beside her, but as she spent more hours awake, she spent more hours in prayer begging for forgiveness for her sinful thoughts about what she'd like to do with him. The ache between her legs no longer had anything to do with her wounds. Her breasts grew heavy when Fingal wrapped his arm around her middle to keep her from sliding off the horse. When she leaned against him, she knotted her fingers together to keep from exploring his chest and abdomen.

Fingal was acutely aware of Madeline's lush feminine body brushing against his, and how her bottom rubbed against his thigh. Despite it being awkward, he kept his sporran in front of him to create a barrier between Madeline's hip and his rod. He'd made the mistake of pushing it aside the first time Madeline rode with him. He counted his blessings when she slept through most of the first couple of days back on the road, so he didn't fear terrifying her with his arousal.

Now that Madeline was alert and aware of her surroundings, he suffered the annoyance of the pouch resting against his groin to keep Madeline from knowing how her body affected his. He ached to touch her as he had on their wedding night. He longed to discover if her body would react to him as it had the one time they'd coupled. He wanted to know if Madeline might be more receptive to intimacies while they were together. He wasn't so lust driven that he didn't know Madeline would only accept his advances if she believed it was an attempt to conceive. He was in enough agony to consider convincing Madeline that he expected a child soon, so that once she was well enough, he could be with her again.

CHAPTER TWENTY-ONE

Madeline steeled herself for the several miles they would walk while guiding their horses. She knew her wish that Fingal could hold her hand was impractical. Each of them would walk in front of their horse, so there was no way for Fingal to walk close enough to hold her hand. She was anxious about walking for so long since her thighs would rub together. She'd tolerated riding with Fingal because she could keep some distance between her legs. There was no alternative now.

They dismounted and let the horses rest before moving onto the narrow strip of mountain. Fingal wanted the horses fresh to make them less likely to spook. Even though all the horses but Madeline's had traversed the pass before, Fingal knew a tired horse would be unpredictable.

"Maddy, Harry will lead us. I'll be behind him, and ye'll follow me. Watch the hoofprints our horses leave and guide yer horse over them. If ye need to stop, ye need only to tell me. It's dangerous, but I dinna want ye walking if ye dinna think ye can. Will ye promise me that?"

"Aye, Fingal," Madeline nodded.

Fingal gave into his impulse and pulled Madeline

against him. His hands cradled her skull as he pressed his mouth to hers. He didn't move slowly to prepare her. He didn't pause to see if she would pull away. He devoured her mouth, and she opened to him, welcoming his tongue into her mouth. Her hands fisted his leine at his waist as one of his arms moved to hold her tightly against him. The fire between them roared to life as they clung to one another. The sound of the men moving near them slowed their kisses until they were tender nips.

"Ye have nay idea how much I want to touch ye and taste ye, just hold yer body against mine, Maddy. I ache to be inside ye, to feel that pleasure again, to share it with ye." Fingal knew the moment he said the word pleasure that he'd ruined the moment. Madeline's eyes widened as she took a step back. He could see her clenching her jaw as she swallowed. He opened his mouth to say more, but he didn't know what to say. Should he retract his words even though they were the truth?

"Dinna fash," Madeline said. "I will follow yer lead, and I will let ye ken if I need aught." Madeline mouth twitched in a brief smile before she stepped around him. Fingal hung his head and wished he could swallow his tongue. The kiss had felt like a leap forward. He was certain he hadn't imagined how Madeline's desire matched his, how she'd been an equal partner in the exchange. But the instant he said he wanted their joining to be for enjoyment alone, he'd known she would retreat.

Fortunately, their concentration remained focused on navigating the precarious ledge. Madeline kept her eyes on Fingal's horse's hooves. She'd looked down as they entered the pass, and the height hadn't bothered her. Even as they climbed higher, the height had no impact on her. She was more concerned about doing something that might harm the horses and guards behind her. She breathed easier as they began their descent, then sighed with relief when they reached the foot of the mountains. She looked back at whence they came, glad that they would have no more dangerous stretches before reaching Freuchie.

When they made camp that night, Madeline insisted upon helping. Fingal thought to approach her to try to clear the air, but he retreated to his side of the fire. He pulled a jug of whisky from his saddle and took several long drags before forcing himself to put it away. He wanted to groan when Harry came to sit beside him.

"I've noticed a frost has settled across the land," Harry said as he settled against his saddle. "What did ye do?"

"Naught to a reasonable woman," Fingal grumbled. At Harry's raised eyebrows, Fingal huffed. "I kissed her."

"And that's what's made her avoid ye?"

"It was what I said afterward. I may have let it slip that ma intentions were nae for making a bairn. The bluidy woman is convinced that if she enjoys one moment of pleasure, God will send down the Holy Spirit to smote her where she stands."

"Mayhap ye've had enough whisky for this eve," Harry muttered.

"And mayhap ma bollocks have turned blue. Ye try riding with her in yer lap for days," Fingal snapped before he turned a thunderous look at Harry. "Suggest it to her, and I will make sure yer twig and berries never work again."

"Twig?" Harry guffawed. "More like a mighty elm."

"I'm serious, Harry. Dinna touch her," Fingal warned. Harry grew serious as he glared at his friend.

"I told ye. I will never betray ye, and I would never disgrace Lady Madeline. Dinna take yer frustrations out on me."

"I just dinna ken if I can live with a blizzard after every heatwave. I ken she enjoys the bluidy kisses. But the moment she realizes what she's done, she turns frigid. She doesnae trust me. It's insulting," Fingal hissed as he pulled his whisky jug out again.

"Have ye considered that it isnae aboot ye for once? Mayhap the lass doesnae trust herself."

"Aye. She's said she's worried she'll go back to being who she was before Kieran banished her," Fingal muttered. "Five years she's been cloistered away, earning her bluidy halo. She thinks a few moments of indulgence will kill her. If that were the case, I'd have been in the ground years ago."

"How old is she?" Harry asked. Fingal shrugged. He had no idea. He didn't even know what month she'd been born in. He'd never bothered to ask. "She's likely close to four or five-and-twenty. She was her old self for far longer than she's been her new self. Can ye blame her for worrying that she might throw it all away for a moment of pleasure?"

"It'd be a damned sight longer than just a moment, even if ma bollocks feel like they'll explode," Fingal grumbled.

"Then take yerself into the trees and take care of it rather than being foul tempered with the rest of us," Harry suggested.

"I'd like to drag her into the trees and have her take care of it," Fingal grunted as he looked down at his plaid. Behind his sporran, his cock was hard as a rock. He scowled at Harry, then rose. He opted to take his friend's advice before he dragged Madeline along with him. He found a spot close enough that he could see the glow of the fire, but couldn't make out anyone in the camp. He slipped his hand beneath his plaid and gave his cock a long tug.

He pictured Madeline as she'd been when she removed her chemise on their one night together as husband and wife. He groaned as he thought about how her breasts felt when they brushed against his arm while she rode between his legs. He'd thought more than once during those rides how easy it would be to turn Madeline around, so she straddled him. How he could sink into her, letting the horse's rocking gait move them together.

Leaves rustled to his left. Fingal froze as he strained to hear. Nothing moved, but he sensed someone was there. "Who goes?" He called out softly. When no one responded, he reached for his sword. A second later, Madeline appeared.

"It's me, Fin." Madeline held her hands up in surrender, proving she wasn't an intruder.

"Were ye spying on me?" Fingal demanded.

"Nay. I swear. I needed privacy. I was about to return to camp when I heard a groan. I feared one of the men was ill."

"The only illness plaguing me is in ma bollocks," Fingal muttered.

"I didna catch that," Madeline said as she approached. Her sharp intake of air made Fingal realize that his plaid was still folded back, and his left hand was wrapped around his rod.

"Aye, Madeline. It's exactly how it looks. Since ye never want to let me touch ye, I dinna have much choice."

"But ye shouldnae—That's a sin," Madeline hissed.

"Then I'll be burning in hell for all the times I've done it in ma life. And only women will fill Heaven since every sane mon does it to keep from going insane."

Madeline crept a little closer, making the mistake of stepping within arm's reach of Fingal. His hand shot out and snagged her around the waist. He pulled Madeline to him before spinning them, so her back was against the tree. When he felt her trembling, he made a sound of disgust.

"I told ye before. I dinna rape women, and I would never rape ma wife. I amnae going to force ye to couple with me."

Madeline could smell the whisky on Fingal's breath. It was earthy and rich, and she had a sudden urge to taste him. She felt her tremors subside as Fingal didn't press closer.

"Ye dinna trust me, Madeline, but ye're curious. Ye are stubborn to a fault. Ye have the healthy body of a woman of, what, five-and-twenty."

"Seven-and-twenty," Madeline murmured.

"Ye want to ken what it feels like to give in, to enjoy the feel of me buried inside ye. Ye want to touch me as much as I want to touch ye. Ye want to ken what I feel like in yer hands. Ye liked it when I touched ye. Yer body told me so. Ye were so wet for me that night, Madeline. So stop pretending otherwise," Fingal growled.

"There's a difference between what I want and what is right," Madeline stated matter-of-factly.

"It isnae right to leave yer husband with aching bollocks for days on end," Fingal snapped.

"Do ye wish to couple right now?" Madeline asked.

"Of course I do. I've wanted to since the night ye found me drunk in the passageway outside the chapel," Fingal admitted. Fingal's head fell forward in disbelief when Madeline started pulling up her tunic. "What're ye doing?"

"Ye wish for yer husbandly rights. I told ye, I willna say nay."

"Ye really believe me to be a beast, dinna ye? Madeline, ye nearly died a few days ago. I amnae quite that selfish that I would rut on ye like an animal."

"Then what do ye want, Fingal?"

"For ye to touch me. To pretend ye want me for one damn night. To ease ma need to be inside ma wife. I meant it, Madeline. There willna be anyone else. I dinna want to share the pleasure we could have with anyone else."

Madeline considered what she was about to say and reasoned that it wasn't for herself but for Fin. She wasn't the one who would benefit if she gave into his wishes. She could ease his discomfort without committing her own sins of the flesh. In fact, she'd be keeping Fingal from sinning if he pleasured himself. She dropped her tunic and reached for the hem of Fingal's plaid.

"Tell me what to do, Fin," she whispered before she wrapped her hand around his rod. Fingal groaned as his hands bracketed her head against the tree trunk, keeping him from collapsing as a burst of satisfaction shot through him at Madeline's first touch.

"St. Columba's bones," Fingal hissed. "Just—just move yer hand up and down. Aye. Like that. Maddy." Fingal said her name with reverence. Madeline worried that she wouldn't please him, but the sound of Fingal's rapid breathing convinced her that he enjoyed what she was doing. She moved slowly at first, but as she gained confidence, she tightened her grip and moved faster. Fingal's hand grasped a fistful of her hair as he pressed his mouth to hers. His other hand slipped down the neckline of her tunic until he could cup her breast. He'd been so terrified of losing her, and so focused on healing her, that he hadn't allowed himself to think of her as a woman he lusted for while she was ill. Now all he could think about was suckling her breasts before tasting her most intimate parts.

Madeline moaned as the ache low in her belly turned into a fiery burn between her legs. This sensation had nothing to do with her injuries. Her body screamed for her to guide Fingal's sword into her sheath. The temptation to pull up her skirts and beg him for relief was overwhelming. She suspected if her mouth were free, she would have demanded just that. Fingal's kisses were drugging her. He gave a sudden thrust of his hips, and she felt his seed spill onto her hand. He grunted before pinching her nipple then pulling away. He brushed down his plaid before casting her a withering glare.

"Dinna dally tomorrow, or I will leave ye behind."

Madeline watched as Fingal stalked back to camp, leaving her breathless, achy, confused, and miserable. She banged her head on the trunk several times before giving in to her tears. She wanted to believe the whisky Fingal had drunk made him like that, but it was too much like the sober Fingal from before she was sick. She'd rationalized with herself, but she knew she'd done it to satisfy her own curiosity. She'd enjoyed the touching, the kisses, the feel of him palming her breast. What she didn't like was being abandoned by him. Again.

She blamed herself for her naivete when she put her faith in Fingal. He was wrong. She had trusted him. She kept trusting him, and it was always to her regret. Conflicting thoughts raced through her mind as guilt pressed down on her. Part of her wondered if she should give in to Fingal and leave behind her dogmatic beliefs if it would create peace between them. Another part of her wondered if it was pure lust that made her consider changing course. She knew either would bring her some level of happiness. But guilt and fear were still more powerful.

Madeline drew in a breath and composed herself before she returned to the camp. She knew the men pretended not to notice that Fingal returned well before she did. She didn't look in his direction, but in her peripheral vision she saw him drinking once again. She accidentally met Harry's gaze. He frowned and shrugged. She knew there was nothing more to be said, so she bedded down. She was asleep sooner than she expected.

CHAPTER TWENTY-TWO

"Dinna dally, or I will leave ye behind." Fingal's threat replayed over and over in Madeline's mind as she moved around the camp before any of the men stirred. She hurried to pack her bedroll before slipping to the stream nearby to complete her morning ablutions. It surprised her that her moving around the camp didn't wake the men. She suspected a few might have been keeping their eyes closed because it was still very early. She did her best to move silently as she carried her saddle to her horse. She worked by feel, knowing she would need to check the bridle and girth before they set off, but she moved efficiently despite not touching a horse for nearly five years.

When the men finally stretched and moved around, Madeline had already prepared a stack of bannocks. She passed them out before dumping water on the fire. The men watched her in silence, and she appreciated it. She wasn't in the mood for small talk, and she didn't want to force a smile. She noticed that Fingal's eyes were bloodshot, and he scrubbed his hands over his face several times. She suspected he'd finished the jug of whisky the night before and now had a sore head. While she felt no sympathy for him, she didn't intend to incur his wrath either. She kicked dirt over the dying embers before going to her horse to check over her saddle now that there was enough light to see.

Fingal watched Madeline as she worked in silence. He thought not hearing her voice would make it easier to forget she was there, but it didn't. It only made him think about how she must have learned to move so quietly while she was a nun. He'd been awake from the moment she sat up.

Despite his foul mood from the night before, he still worried that she wasn't fully healed. He'd ground his teeth when she hefted her saddle into her arms before tossing it onto her horse's back. It was clear to him that she was more than fine; in fact, she didn't need him anymore, not to care for her nor to make her body hum as it had on their wedding night. But he'd desperately needed her the night before. He fumed at himself for letting her see how much he wanted her, knowing she didn't feel the same way.

His cock ached with the memory of her hand wrapped around it. He was certain no other woman's touch had ever felt so good. The more he thought about it, the more he wanted her to do it again, and that only made him angrier. He knew he was a glutton for punishment when he grasped her waist as she was about to mount. He lifted her into the saddle and wanted to laugh at her stunned expression. She mumbled her thanks. As he was about to turn away, he realized it would be the first time in nearly a week that she rode astride.

"I'm well, Fingal. Dinna fash. I'll keep up," Madeline assured him. Fingal felt as though she were reminding him of something, but he couldn't remember what. He nodded and moved to mount his horse.

"She came out of the woods in the same spot

that ye did, and ye both were gone for a long time," Harry whispered as he glanced at Fingal, then back at Madeline. "But rather than looking like a mon well pleased, ye drank yerself to sleep. And the lass was so eager to get underway that she woke the horses. What did ye do?"

"Naught. Leave it, Harry. It's between me and her," Fingal warned.

"It is until ye make her cry again. Ye werenae looking, but her eyes were red and puffy from crying when she came back."

Fingal kept his thoughts to himself as they rode on throughout the day. He remembered to stop several times to let Madeline rest. He might have been frustrated and disappointed, but he didn't want to cause her to reinjure herself. But as evening drew near, they weren't near a place that he trusted to make camp.

"We canna stop near here," Fingal told Harry. "There have been too many incidents with highwaymen. Do ye think we dare cut through the trees to make camp in the glen on the other side, rather than losing all the light while we ride around?"

"It'll grow darker among the trees sooner than if we stay on the road. But we won't have to ride as long to get to the glen. It's yer call, Fingal. I dinna think one is really better than the other," Harry demurred.

Fingal looked back at Madeline. She'd held up well all day, but he could tell she was growing too tired to remain on her horse for much longer. "I need to get Madeline settled sooner rather than later. She's good for a little longer, but she's exhausted. We cut through the trees."

Fingal called the party to a halt and explained their change of course. It was a densely packed forest, so they would have to spread out rather than following single file. Fingal warned to watch for low-hanging branches and protruding roots. Madeline nodded when he looked directly at her as he issued his commands. Fingal and Harry would ride ahead while Tommy and Simon rode on her right, and Nichol on her left. They trod through the leaves at a slow pace. The dim light filtering through the trees made it difficult to see. Madeline glanced up several times, thinking the light was fading too fast, but it was just the canopy made by the trees. Her horse spooked when a crack of thunder sounded right over head. In a matter of moments, torrents of rain fell through the leaves, and the dim light disappeared, casting them into total darkness.

Madeline's horse grew anxious between being unable to see and the constant noise from the thunder. Madeline strained to hear the other riders, since she could no longer see them. She held one hand out before her, hoping to catch any branches that might unseat her before they crashed into her head. She caught a few, but one thick limb banged against the top of her head hard enough to make her see stars. She had to pull her horse to a stop lest she vomit.

With her own horse's hooves silent, she turned her head left and right. She couldn't hear any of the men. Nervous that she would fall too far behind, she urged her horse on. Her heart beat harder when she still couldn't hear anyone from the Grant party, and she didn't catch up to them. She reasoned that if she continued on as straight a path as she could, she would eventually come out the other side, where Fingal would be furious, but waiting for her.

When it grew pitch black, Madeline laid flat over her horse's withers, praying that no branches injured her mount. But it was a wayward root that forced Madeline to stop. Her horse stumbled, then whinnied and snorted in pain.

"Fin! Harry!" Madeline called out, but she knew her voice wouldn't carry over the sound of the on-going storm. She tried again. "Fingal! Harry! Fin!"

Madeline thought for a moment that Fingal and Harry wouldn't hear her since they led the way, so she called out to the guards. But it dawned on her that if the guards could hear their own names, they would have heard her calling for Fingal and Harry. No one called back to her or approached. She dismounted and felt around in the dark as she checked the leg that her horse refused to put pressure on. She felt a large bump as her hands moved up and down the length of the steed's limb. She lifted its hoof to check the animal's shoe. She groaned when she felt nothing. She didn't know if hitting the root made her horse throw its shoe or if it losing its shoe made it trip. Either way, Madeline couldn't make her horse go on without endangering it. She was certain the animal would go lame, then she would have no way to ride out of the woods in the morning.

With no more options, Madeline tied her horse's reins around a slim tree trunk. She urged the horse to lie down before she pulled her crucifix, two sticks of dried beef, leftover bannocks, and an apple from her sack. She dropped the necklace over her head, then kissed the cross before letting it dangle down her chest. She missed wearing it, and it gave her a sense of reassurance. She unwound the plaid Fingal gave her from around her waist and wished she hadn't left the spare plaid Harry lent Fingal on the bedroll that morning. She swept the yards of wool around her, bundling herself from head to toe. She sat down beside her horse, its belly giving off heat. She ate the beef and bannocks, then offered the apple to the horse. Exhausted from her first full day of riding alone coupled with the dark beneath the trees, Madeline laid down along the horse's side and let her eyes drift closed.

"Where's Madeline?" Fingal demanded as he and his men entered the glen. He looked past the men and waited to see if Madeline emerged behind them. When she did not appear, he glared at each man. "Where is ma wife?"

"I dinna ken," Tommy admitted. "She was beside us when the storm began. When it grew too dark to see, I assumed she was still with us since I didna hear her say aught or call out."

"We wouldnae have heard her anyway," Simon added. "It was far too loud."

"So ye left ma wife in the woods?" Fingal swung his horse back around and kneed it, but Harry grabbed his mount's bridle.

"If ye go charging back in there, we're likely to lose ye both. Lady Madeline has enough sense to ken she needs to stop. She'll find somewhere to tie off her horse until there is enough light for us to find her or for her to find us. Ye're likely to get yerself killed going back in. As is, ma head hurts like the devil from the branch I couldnae see. Do ye want to be thrown from yer horse?"

"Then I'll go back in on foot," Fingal argued.

"And end up completely lost?" Tommy asked. "I dinna like it, but Harry is right."

"Stay if ye want, but I am nae bedding down to ma sweet dreams while ma wife is alone, unarmed, and barely healed. How do we ken she isnae already injured? She'll freeze tonight." Fingal attempted to keep the panic from his voice, but he felt more agitated by the moment. "I shouldnae have let her ride by herself. She should have ridden with me. I should have stopped us when the storm started and taken her up in front of me."

"And had yer horse go lame if it tripped while carrying two riders?" Simon pointed out.

"At least I would ken where she was, and that she isnae likely to be an icicle by morn," Fingal barked. He ran his hands through his hair, making it stick out in all directions. Once more, acting the arse had endangered Madeline. He'd remembered what he'd said the night before that explained why she'd been so anxious about leaving that morning. He recalled threatening to leave her behind. "Ye dinna understand. I was angry with her last night and threatened to leave her behind if she dallied. I didna mean it, but after how I've acted, she doesnae ken I would never do that. She must think that's exactly what I've done. Christ on the cross, I have to find her."

Fingal dismounted and walked to the edge of the woods. He couldn't see the hand in front of his face, let alone guide his horse back into the woods. "Madeline!" He stepped a little further into the woods as he listened for anything that might tell him that she heard him. "Maddy! Maddy! Can ye hear me? Madeline!"

No sounds met his ears, not even the sounds of ground animals scurrying around. The rain continued to fall even if the thunderclaps were further apart. He and his men had ridden through the forest for at least an hour, so he didn't know how far back Madeline might have gotten separated from them.

"Fingal," Harry kept his tone low as he came to stand beside Fingal. "There is naught ye can do. We'll build a large fire and keep it going all night. Mayhap she'll see the light and find her way back to us."

"Mayhap." Fingal didn't believe that in the least. He was certain he would recover his wife's body the next morning, not the gracious and selfless woman he feared he was already in love with. He'd admitted to her that he cared about her, but he'd done very little to show her those weren't hollow words. He'd bitten back the temptation to say "I love ye," since he feared they would meet with silence, or worse, Madeline saying she could never reciprocate his feelings. Fear of Madeline's rejection had driven him nearly every time he'd lashed out at her.

Fingal sat in silence as his men built the fire, stoking it to grow far larger than they would normally do while they traveled with so few men. He sat and stared into the flames as he prayed. He didn't clasp his hands, and he didn't mutter any words. He sent his thoughts directly to the Trinity, praying to each and all throughout the night. He begged forgiveness for discounting Cairstine's warnings about being coldhearted to his future wife. He begged for forgiveness for thinking he could conduct his marriage like a business arrangement, rather than a relationship between two people. He confessed his resentment that Madeline made him want to change, even though it would make him a better man. He acknowledged how selfish and petulant his motives were. He begged that God spare Madeline any more pain and accepted that it was his coldness and detachment that drove Madeline to push herself too hard. As he prayed for divine intervention, he recognized the hypocrisy of asking God's help when he'd disdained Madeline's devotion and piety. He was ready to swear a life of celibacy if it protected Madeline. He drifted off reciting the rosary, something he hadn't done outside a kirk in decades.

CHAPTER TWENTY-THREE

Madeline came awake with a grunt. She doubled over as a sharp pain stabbed through her middle. She blinked several times and tried to look around. Her horse hadn't kicked her, so what had?

"Wake up, ma lady," said a mocking voice. Madeline knew it wasn't a Grant who stood over her. She looked to her left and found a nearly toothless man grinning down at her. "What have we found?"

"Good horseflesh and some bitch," another voice came from behind Madeline. She struggled to sit up and looked around. She was disoriented from the night before. "We'll take her back with us. He'll want to see her."

Madeline wondered who "he" was and where they intended to take her. Before she could ask, a grimy hand reached out and yanked her arm, bringing her to her feet. Her horse lumbered to its feet.

"He's lost a shoe," Madeline whispered. "And he might be lame." She didn't know if she was trying to the spare the horse pain, trying to leave a clue behind for Fingal, or foolishly losing any chance to escape if they left the animal behind.

"Then ye can both walk behind us," the first man said. Before Madeline could fight him off, the man produced a long piece of rope that he tried to wrap around Madeline's wrists. She fought back, tugging on it as she kicked her booted foot in to his shin. She kneed him in the groin, and when the man doubled over, she wrapped the rope around his neck. But she was no match for his strength or his height. When he jerked upright, she couldn't reach well enough to keep the tension. His massive arm whipped out and tossed her aside like a rag doll.

"We dinna have time for this," grunted the second man. "Ye can dole out yer justice once we get back to camp."

The man who'd pulled her to her feet the first time did so again. He shook Madeline before slapping her. He bound her wrists and dragged her to his horse while the other man took hold of her horse's bridle. The two men mounted their horses, and the rope was given just enough slack for Madeline to trudge behind the men and alongside her horse. She glanced down and noticed the horse wasn't limping despite missing a shoe.

"Where are ye taking me?" Madeline asked evenly.

"Dinna ye worry aboot that. Ye will ken when we get there." Madeline couldn't tell which man spoke, but they were the least reassuring words she'd ever heard. She followed behind for miles, a periodic jerk on the rope making her stumble. She fell to her knees more than once and fought to get back onto her feet before she was dragged on her belly. When they left the trees, she got her bearings. The sun was to her right when they emerged from the woods, and it moved around her back as the time passed. The mountains remained behind her, so she estimated that they were heading northeast. She knew the

Chattans, Gordons, and Farquharsons were clans that bordered the Cairngorms along with the Grants. But she didn't know which clan's land they were on, and the two men wore breeks rather than *breacan feile*s, so she didn't know from which clan they hailed.

When the men drew their horses to an abrupt stop, Madeline stumbled and fell to her knees. She looked around and noticed a group of five men sitting around an extinguished fire. They all looked worse for wear, tattered leines and breeks with stains covering them. The men looked like feral beasts, as though they hadn't seen the inside of a dwelling in years.

"Just how I like a woman. On her knees," said a dark-haired man as he sauntered toward Madeline. He grasped her chin in one hand before striking her across the cheek with the other. "With ma mark on her."

Madeline clenched her entire body to keep from crying out. She refused to make a noise or give a sign that would make any of the men feel more empowered. The man who held her in place laughed as he turned Madeline's head from one direction to another. He yanked her hair back and used his thumb to pry her mouth open. When he made to examine her gums like a horse, she snapped her mouth shut, barely missing his fingers. It earned her another slap, but he abandoned his investigation.

A younger man who bore a resemblance to the one who still had a fistful of her hair ambled toward them, using a *sgian dubh* to clean the dirt from under his nails.

Even if he is doing that to intimidate me, at least one of them has some sense of hygiene.

Madeline noticed that the younger one had one eye that was milky and cloudy; she realized that he was blind in that eye. If she were to get on his right side, he wouldn't be able to see her if she attacked or if she ran. She swept her eyes over the motley crew of men and deduced that these were the highwaymen Fingal wanted to avoid. The man she attempted to strangle had the evidence of a rope burn around his throat. The other man who captured her was missing both thumbs, indicating that he'd been caught thieving twice.

"Getting a good look at us are ye?" the dark-haired man said. "Thinking to see if ye will remember us once we're gone? Ye willna see aught when we leave ye with yer throat slit."

"Dee, we canna stay here," the younger of the two looked in the direction that Madeline and her captives came from. "We're too close. They'll find us before we've had any fun." He leered at Madeline and flicked his tongue at her several times. She didn't understand what it meant, but she was certain it was vulgar.

"True," the older of the two said speculatively. "Mount up. The bitch rides with me."

With her hands still bound in front of her, Madeline scrambled onto the man's horse. She didn't want to rely on him to keep her safe, so she swung her leg over to ride astride. She noticed her stockings were showing beneath her tunic; this gave her an idea.

"I need to move ma plaid," Madeline announced.

"I dinna care," snapped the man as he made to mount behind her.

"The Lord does. Ours is an angry and wrathful God when we break His covenants," Madeline intoned in a pious, authoritative voice. Dressed in her plain wool tunic and with her large crucifix hanging down her chest, she looked like a disheveled nun, and she knew this might save her life. "Be He nae just in His vengeance when we sin? He demands women remain chaste and modest at all times. I canna ride around with bare legs. I must drape ma plaid over maself or surely He will cast down his judgement on us. After all, ye will share a horse with me. His punishment may hit ye too."

Madeline pushed aside the flash of guilt she felt for using the Lord's name to manipulate the men. She noticed at least four of the seven looked uncomfortable with her proclamation.

"Let the bampot cover herself," one man muttered.

Madeline didn't hesitate to shift around as she moved her plaid. She made it look as though she was struggling to adjust the yards of fabric, but it disguised her knees as she squeezed the horse's flanks. The steed lurched forward, pushing Madeline backwards into the saddle. The man holding the reins was trying to pull her leg as she fought to get her feet into the stirrups. She kicked out at him, missing him but spurring the horse on. She gripped handfuls of the horse's mane since she didn't have the reins. As the horse picked up speed, her captor couldn't keep up and dropped the reins. Madeline lunged to grab them before they could become tangled around the animal's legs. She felt herself slipping as her hands caught the leather strips. She fought to right herself, but she landed on the ground with the wind knocked out of her when a piercing whistle made the horse halt.

Madeline lay on her back, fighting to draw air into lungs that felt crushed. Her head pounded from where it had hit the ground. Her vision cleared in time to see a booted foot swing back in preparation to kick her. She rolled to her side so that the boot landed near her kidneys rather than her stomach. "Stupid bitch," snarled her captor. "Ye will pay dearly for that. I hope ye like the taste of cock."

"Does yers taste like rotted death?" Madeline muttered. A streak of her old defiance reared its head; she refused to be cowed by any of these men. "I shall ask our Lord God to avenge me, His bride of Christ, and make yer twig shrivel up and snap."

Madeline felt a twinge of guilt for lying to the men about being a nun, but she would do anything to plant the seed of doubt or fear in any of the men. One of the highwaymen might feel guilty enough to help her escape or insist they let her go before the Grant men found them. Madeline desperately wanted to believe that Fingal would come for her, and she hated doubting him. She knew at the very least Harry would search for her. But until they rescued her, she would have to rely on herself to gain her freedom.

"Ye talk a lot for a woman who's supposed to spend her day in silence," snapped the younger dark-haired man as he approached.

"I have nay need to be silent when I pray for our salvation. It shall take me quite a while, since I suspect it shall take quite a lot of convincing for Him to absolve ye lot." Madeline looked around the group of men as though she were in deep contemplation. "What're ye called?"

Madeline didn't expect an answer. The two that had originally snagged her had only referred to their leader as "him." The younger man called him "Dee." Since then, she'd heard nothing that could help her identify one from another. She drew out the moment as she frowned and nodded.

"Then I shall name ye." She looked at the man in charge, whose horse she'd tried to steal. "I shall name ye Herod, for the king who tried to kill our Savior when He was but a wean."

She looked at the younger man and squinted. "I think ye and Herod are brothers, but I dinna ken if

214

that's the case, and I dinna ken if King Herod had any brothers. So I shall name ye Judas. For I suspect ye would do aught for thirty pieces of silver. Ye—aye —ye, the one who kicked me when I awoke, I name ye Doeg the Edomite, for he knocked down the priest."

In turn, Madeline raised her bound hands and pointed to the other four men. "Ye shall be Cain for the scar on yer arm. God has marked ye just as He did Cain to tell the devil who he should claim. Ye are Achan, for the mon partook in the fall of Jericho. Because I suspect ye fell from the grace of yer clan. And finally, ye—ye will be Barabbas. I dinna ken why. I just like the name. Definitely nae the mon they chose over Jesus Christ, just the name."

Madeline lifted her chin with a self-satisfied smile, then nodded her head as if she were pleased with herself. The man she called Judas pushed her toward Herod's horse. Once Herod was in the saddle, Judas tossed Madeline up to him, and none too gently. She hummed one of her favorite hymns as the men urged their horses into a canter. She prayed that her horse could keep up. She remained quiet for a long stretch, letting the men believe she'd grown complacent. She doubted she could force them to leave her, but she could make them regret taking her. As they rounded a bend in the road, Madeline grasped her cross and suddenly held it up toward the sun.

"We believe in God, the Father almighty, creator of heaven and earth." Madeline launched into the Apostle's Creed, being sure to make it sound as though her prayer was as much for the men as for herself. "We believe in Jesus Christ, his only Son, our Lord. He was conceived by the power of the Holy Spirit—"

"Shut up," growled Herod. Madeline ignored him as she continued the prayer.

"And born of the Virgin Mary. He suffered under Pontius Pilate—" Madeline paused and leaned to the side to look back at the other men. "Achan, I've changed ma mind. Ye're now Pontius Pilate. Was crucified, died, and was buried. He descended to the dead. On the third day, He rose again. He ascended into heaven and is seated at the right hand of the Father. He will come again to judge both the quick and the dead. We believe in the Holy Spirit, the holy catholic Church, the communion of saints, the forgiveness of sins, the resurrection of the body, and the life everlasting. Amen. There. Dinna ye feel better now? I do." Madeline chirped her last words. Before any of the men replied, Madeline launched into her next prayer.

"Our Father, who art in Heaven, hallowed be Thy name, Thy kingdom come, Thy will be done on earth as it is in heaven. Give us this day our daily bread and forgive us our trespasses as we forgive those who trespass against us. Lead us nae into temptation, but deliver us from evil, for thine is the kingdom, and the power, and the glory for ever and ever. Amen."

Madeline could hear the grumbles from the men, but she ignored them. She raised her voice as she began the next prayer, drowning out the sounds of her kidnappers' disgust.

"Hail Mary, full of grace, the Lord is with thee. Blessed are thou amongst women, and blessed is the fruit of thy womb, Jesus. Holy Mary, Mother of God, pray for us sinners, now and at the hour of our death. Ah-men." Madeline emphasized the "so be it" at the end of the prayer each time as she recited it thrice. She tried to keep from grinning even though she was once again facing forward, and none of the men could see her.

"Make her stop," barked one of the men. Madeline suspected it was Pontius Pilate, but she couldn't be certain.

"Dinna continue, lass. I'm warning ye," Herod snarled.

"It's yer soul I'm praying for. I'm nae the one who's taken a nun and threatened to violate her." Madeline struggled to keep her voice light, when she wanted to snarl and hiss as she thought of the man's indication of what she would do later.

"Ye would do better to pray for yerself. Pray that sucking ma cock is all that I make ye do," Herod hissed beside her ear. "But yer prayers will be for naught. Ye're too bonnie to be a nun, so keep playing yer game. We shall see if God comes to yer mercy when I stuff yer cunny full of ma cock. I havenae had a virgin in years."

Madeline's gut clenched as the man's foul breath wafted around her and his warning filled her ears. She gritted her teeth, unwilling to cave under his threats of violence. She might not convince him, but she would continue to work on the others.

"O Lord, open ma lips, and ma mouth shall declare Yer praise. O God, come to ma assistance. O Lord, make haste to help me." Madeline stopped to take a breath as she awkwardly made the sign of the cross. "Glory be to the Father, and to the Son, and to the Holy Spirit. As it was in the beginning, is now, and ever shall be, world without end. Amen."

"Are ye done?" demanded Judas.

"Done? Of course nae. Have ye never prayed a rosary? I just started. I must pray the 'Our Father' as I proclaim God's First Mystery. Then I have ten more 'Hail Marys' while I meditate upon that Mystery. After that is another 'Glory Be.' I can move onto the next Mystery with another 'Our Father' and all those 'Hail Marys.' I say the same prayers and meditate on each Mystery. Once I make it through all fifteen Mysteries, I can say the 'Hail Holy Queen' and the 'Final Prayer.' I'm finished when I beg God's Divine Assistance and make the sign of the cross." Madeline tilted her head back and looked up at the sun. "I like to spend a good long while meditating to be really sure I ken each of the Lord's acts. I'd say that I should finish around midday. Do ye ken, I pray the rosary twenty times each day?"

"Nay!" came a chorus of groans.

"Dinna say another word, or I will slit yer throat and let ye fall to yer death," Pontius Pilate vowed as he rode abreast. Madeline cocked an eyebrow and pursed her lips. She began reciting the prayers in silence, but she moved her lips with each word. She stared at Pontius until he growled at her. Madeline sucked in her cheeks as she struggled to keep from laughing. She'd tormented Kieran with the same tactics when they were children, finding ways around his warnings, so that she neither disobeyed nor obeyed him. Granted, Kieran never threatened—and meant —to slit her throat.

"The day of wrath, that day will dissolve the world in ashes, David being witness along with the Sibyl," Madeline launched into the Latin hymn "Day of Wrath, Day of Burning." "How great will be the quaking, when the Judge is aboot to come, strictly investigating all things."

"I warned ye," Pontius reached for his dirk.

"Ye said 'dinna say another word,'" Madeline crooned. "I'm singing. The trumpet scattering a wondrous sound through the sepulchers of the regions, will summon all before the throne."

"Enough," barked Herod.

"But that was only three verses. There's still sixteen more," Madeline sang.

"We have her horse. The Grants willna find her. Leave her, Dougal," Barabbas begged. Madeline pretended not to hear the man slip and use Herod's real name.

"I agree," Cain called out. "She obviously has nay coin. Finneas, make yer brother see reason." Madeline wondered if they would all abandon their secrecy. She listened as the men went back and forth. By the end, she knew all their names. Dougal and Finneas were the brothers in charge. Cain was really named Arthur, Barabbas was another Dougal, Pontius Pilate was David, and Doeg the Edomite was Harris. Judas's real name was Lewis, which made her scowl, since he shared a name with the island upon which she was born and raised. While she learned all their given names, never did she hear a clan mentioned.

With no clan name and no plaids, Madeline could only deduce that they were lawless men who their clan or clans had banished. They knew she was a Grant from her plaid and had said as much. She wondered if it would benefit her to say she was Fingal's wife. She kept that to herself, since their belief that she was a nun had kept her unmolested so far. She would bide her time in deciding her next move.

CHAPTER TWENTY-FOUR

"Where can she be?" Fingal was beyond desperation. He and his men had fanned out and retraced their steps from the night before. They'd traveled from one side of the woods to the other twice, but they found no sign of Madeline. When they made their first sweep through the woods, Fingal had been optimistic that they would find Madeline alive. He'd called out to her several times, but when no response came back by the time they reached the middle of the woods, he grew impatient.

"Madeline, if ye think to hide from me because ye're angry at me, I will turn ye over ma knee," Fingal had called out. "I'm serious, Maddy. We dinna have time for this. Come out." When silence greeted his warning, they pushed on. As they turned back toward their camp, Fingal feared they would find Madeline's body, frozen from the night before or ravaged by starving wolves. It was as they walked toward their camp for the second time that Tommy's boot made contact with metal. He bent down and found a horseshoe. He turned it over and brushed mud from it.

"Look," Tommy pointed to an etching. "A

blazing sun. The MacLeods of Lewis. It's from Lady Madeline's horse."

"Aye, and here's an apple core she must have given her horse," Nichol pointed.

"Madeline!" Fingal bellowed as he spun in a circle.

"She slept here last night. Look," Simon pointed. "Ye can see the imprint from her horse and her. And here are boot prints."

"And another set here," Tommy said as he kicked away leaves that covered two sets, one large and one small. He followed them until he found the beginning of hoofprints. Fingal followed Tommy and squatted to examine the ground.

"They made her walk," Fingal said as he stood. "Ye can see her smaller prints behind the horses'." Fingal followed the trail, stopping periodically to study the ground. "They must have been dragging her because I see where her prints are smeared, and she fell at least once."

"Who do ye think did it? Highwaymen?" Harry wondered.

"Likely," Fingal sighed. The exact people they'd tried to avoid by cutting through the woods were the ones who probably had Madeline. "The Chattans and Farquharsons might take her, but the Gordons wouldnae. She'd tell them that she kens Allyson and Cairstine. The Gordons would ken our plaid, anyway. They'd likely be searching for us."

"If it was highwaymen, that opens up a lot of land to search," Harry mused as he stared at the tracks.

"Aye. We follow these as far as they go, then figure it out from there," Fingal announced as he mounted. Once they were in their saddles, they followed the tracks out of the woods and onto the road. The prints were easy to follow at first, and Fingal reasoned they were made shortly after the rain stopped and the ground was still soft. But as they traveled further from the woods, the road grew drier and dustier, making the tracks harder to follow.

"Look here," Simon pointed as he pulled his horse to a stop. The men maneuvered their mounts near a deeper set of prints. "One of the horses galloped with a light rider or with no rider."

"Then it stopped suddenly," Harry observed as he walked his horse along the road. "And now there are several more tracks. Whoever has Madeline is now with a larger group. There are at least six or seven sets of prints, and there are no footprints. She's either riding her horse or with someone."

"She's with someone. Here are her horse's prints. Ye can see how a shoe is missing. They're lighter than the others. Her mount's smaller to begin with," Fingal noted.

With a course set and clues to follow, Fingal tried to reassure himself that it wouldn't be long before he found Madeline. He would do anything she asked from now until the end of their lives if it meant she was out of harm's way. As they searched the forest, he found himself questioning his faith and wondering what good his prayers had done. Even now, knowing that Madeline was very likely hurt and with men who wouldn't think twice about abusing her, he wondered if God could hear him.

While the men periodically talked to one another, Fingal remained silent and lost in his thoughts. As the morning dragged on, an urge to pray the rosary swept over him. He'd never in his life voluntarily recited the retinue of prayers. But the thought grew stronger until it was all he could think about. He wondered if it was Madeline sending him a silent message. He struggled to remember all the prayers, but as he moved from one invocation to another it got easier. He admitted to himself that he wasn't meditating on God's mysteries so much as he was thinking about how saying these prayers were part of Madeline's daily rituals for nearly half a decade.

As he repeated them over and over, he better understood how Madeline held her beliefs so deeply. The rosary didn't eliminate his fears, but it calmed him enough to think rationally. For the first time, he tried to imagine what Madeline's daily life consisted of while she was at Inchcailleoch. He knew she attended eight prayer services a day, plus full Eucharistic Masses on Sundays. He assumed there were more hours of meditation between the Liturgy of Hours. He remembered she said she enjoyed working in the gardens. He wondered what else she did to fill her days. He'd never thought to ask.

As Fingal considered how little he knew about Madeline's past, he realized she likely knew far more about him. At the very least, she had a better idea of what he did with his time. He was certain she knew he trained in the lists most mornings, and sometimes all day. She would have known that he met with his cousin and the clan council at least once a week. She'd alluded to him adjudicating disputes while they had one of their many arguments. Being the daughter and sister of lairds, she knew all the responsibilities that a clan leader shouldered.

He'd only known she prayed a lot.

He could hear Madeline's angry words ringing in his ears when he accused the nuns of brainwashing her. She said she'd come to her conclusions on faith by herself. She'd accused him of thinking she wasn't smart enough to develop such ideas on her own. He realized she was partly right. When he thought of nuns and convents, he pictured women floating around in their long robes and wimples, all chanting the same words over and over. He assumed they worked in gardens and tended the sick. He never considered what they thought or felt.

If Fingal was going to be really honest with himself, he'd never considered what any woman thought before Madeline. He'd tried to convince Cairstine to marry him simply because it would have been easy. His life wouldn't have changed at all, except he would call her wife rather than friend. Even as he thought about that, he wasn't sure "friend" was the right label for Cairstine. They were distant cousins, but Harry and his men were more his friends than Cairstine was. Cairstine was just a convenient choice for a wife, just as Madeline had seemed in the beginning. He wouldn't have had to do anything different other than bedding Cairstine from time to time.

As he chewed on a strip of beef, Fingal realized he'd spent more time in self-reflection over the past week than he had in all of his life. He was often displeased with what he discovered. Waves of shame, annoyance, and frustration washed over him each time his mind grew introspective Occasionally, it was enough to make him want to never think about himself again. But most of the time, it made him think about the husband and laird he wanted to be. His behavior was so drastically different from the current Laird Grant that he wondered if the clan would accept him if he remained on his current path. Laird Edward Grant was a deeply devout man who'd intended on becoming a monk, but family and clan duty forced him into the lairdship. Even to this day, nearly thirty years after marrying, he still acted very much like a monk, with his insistence upon attending both Lauds and Prime every day and strict fasting on holy days. Fingal chuckled to himself when he realized in many ways, he'd married his cousin—and he didn't mean Cairstine. It was only during Cairstine's courtship with Eoin did anyone discover how loving a marriage Edward and his wife Davina shared.

It must have been bluidy difficult for Edward to give up his plans to become a monk and suddenly find himself both married and laird. That isnae all that different from Madeline. I wonder how Edward came around to Davina. They've shared a chamber for as long as I can remember, and Edward would never think of being unfaithful to Davina. It took everything that happened to Cairstine and with the Gunns to make Edward express how much he cares aboot his wife and daughters. But it's there. I suppose it always has been if any of us bothered to really look.

I canna ask Madeline to discuss our intimacies with Edward, but mayhap Davina might have some wisdom. If Madeline doesnae wish to change, I willna force her. But mayhap she could grow more comfortable with me and nae fear damnation any time we touch.

"Fingal."

"Eh?" Fingal pulled himself out of his woolgathering as he looked at Harry.

"The tracks stop," Harry told him.

"What?" Fingal looked at the ground and realized Harry was right. Fingal looked back and saw the prints they'd followed, but when he leaned forward there was nothing. "Did they move off the road and into the grass?"

"Mayhap," Harry shrugged as all the men dismounted.

"They couldnae just disappear," Fingal muttered. But that was exactly what seemed to have happened.

CHAPTER TWENTY-FIVE

M adeline's teeth chattered as she huddled under her plaid. The day's warm summer weather turned at night, leaving the air brisk and the ground cold. She glanced at the men who surrounded her. Soft snores came from several of them as they wrapped themselves in plaids. She'd strained to see the pattern as they bedded down for the night. The firelight only showed that they were dyed black, or perhaps deep blue. There was no pattern to them, no interwoven colors, or different hued squares. There was nothing to help her identify them. None seemed to notice the change in temperature, which was no surprise if they had always lived outside. With no clan or keep to return to, they must have made their home under one tree or another.

Once the men began talking while they rode that afternoon, Madeline had grown silent, listening to everything they said. They referred to villages and landmarks that she didn't know. Their names meant nothing to her, so none gave her a clue as to whose land they were on. She didn't know if they'd passed through more than one territory, or how they would be received if a patrol found them. If men riding a border found them, she couldn't guarantee that they would rescue her or be any improvement upon the men she was with. She was a woman alone, with no weapons beyond a dull knife for eating. She'd carried a dirk when she lived at Stirling, but there had been no need for it once she was at Inchcailleoch. It had been so long that she didn't think to return to carrying one when she visited Stirling before her marriage. Fingal never suggested she should do anything to protect herself; she was certain he'd never even thought about it.

Madeline had barely drifted off when someone kicked her awake for the second morning in a row. She rubbed her eyes and looked around. The sun was higher than she expected, and the men had already broken down their camp.

"Be quick with what ye need to do. We only let ye sleep, so we wouldnae have to hear ye blathering on aboot God and His lot," Harris said. Madeline nodded, but as she rose, she couldn't help but wince. "What's wrong with ye?"

"Naught. Just slept wrong," Madeline dismissed the question. Two days back in the saddle, one of which with no salve, had reopened some of her still-healing wounds. She hurried to relieve herself before any of the men came in search of her. She looked at the insides of her thighs as best she could. The skin was chafed, and a few scabs had fallen off, but the cuts were nowhere near as bad as they had been. Madeline realized that she was likely to have scars. She wondered if they would make Fingal less interested in bedding her.

She rubbed the tightness that enveloped her chest as she thought about Fingal never wanting to touch her again. She'd keenly felt the absence of his reassuring warmth and strength the night before. She had an unexpected longing to open the chest that carried her clothes and pull out the dove-gray gown that reminded her so much of Fingal. If she couldn't look into his eyes, at least the gown that reminded her of those eyes would make her feel connected to him.

"We should reach *Bràigh Mhàrr* before sundown," Dougal, the leader, said to Finneas. Madeline strained to listen as she moved closer to the horses. She tried as best she could to remember any towns or villages they mentioned. *Bràigh Mhàrr*, or Braemar, meant the upper Marr. She'd never heard of such a river, so she still didn't know where she was or where they were going. She knew little of the geography of the eastern Highlands. She was aware that they were in Aberdeenshire, and the River Dee was important in the region, but she knew no more than that.

"Aye. We can be rid of them both at the market," Finneas said. "Dinna ken which will bring the better price." Both men snorted, and Madeline deduced that they intended to sell both her and her horse once they reached their destination. Madeline swallowed the gorge that rose in her throat. There was only one occupation they would sell her into. If they reached Braemar, there was little chance Fingal would find her before she become someone's property.

Bluidy luck of mine. I fear bedding ma own husband because I'll risk ma eternal soul, but I'm aboot to be made a whore. I suppose I dinna have to fear enjoying it. I'd rather face damnation for coupling with Fingal and liking it than what awaits me. Merciful God, this canna be what Ye planned for me. Was ma path meant to be with Fingal all along? Why did Ye bring him into ma life, if all Ye meant to do was take him away? Why would Ye let me fall in love with him?

Madeline's heart lurched as she realized the truth. She wasn't certain if she was in love with Fingal, but she knew she was moving in that direction. At this point she would gladly welcome passion and

229

pleasure with Fingal if it meant no other man touched her.

I canna let this happen. Dear God, what if Fingal doesnae find me in time? He'd never accept me if I'm with another mon, let alone because I was a whore.

Madeline rode with Finneas that day. She wondered if she could get hold of a dirk and stab him on his blind side. They'd freed her hands the night before, certain that she wouldn't run. She could manage the horse if she could get him off it. While she remained as still as she could, her eyes swung across the landscape, searching for any landmark or sign. She'd tried to think of a way to leave a trail the day before, but she had nothing she could drop. She wished she had a set of prayer beads that she could have used to leave Fingal signs. When the men urged their horses into a gallop, Madeline slid backwards into Finneas. He palmed her breast when Madeline gasped from bumping his arousal.

"If ye dinna want to hear every liturgy and prayer I ken, get yer hand off of me," Madeline hissed.

"I'll do as I please. It willna be long before any mon does as he pleases with ye," Finneas sneered. Madeline grabbed hold of his pinky and wrenched it backwards until she felt it pop. Finneas howled in pain as his arm dropped away from her. Madeline took advantage of his stunned outburst to swing her head back and smash it into his nose and forehead. She spotted a dirk in the boot on his blind side; she yanked it from its sheath and stabbed at anything behind her. She felt the blade enter him twice before she yanked his arm as hard as she could.

When Finneas fell from the saddle, Madeline didn't look back to see what became of him or the other men. She leaned far over the horse's neck, squeezing her thighs as she dug her heels back on the stirrups. She gathered fistfuls of mane along with the reins as she fought to stay on the charging animal's back. He was the largest horse she'd ever ridden alone, and it was a struggle to maintain control of him once he ran at full speed.

Madeline scanned her surroundings, looking for any way to get off the road and away from her pursuers. She could hear the horses behind her. When she saw a thicket to her left, she waited until the last minute before yanking on the rein and turning her horse. She tucked herself tight against the horse, avoiding branches as best she could. Twigs scratched her cheeks and arms as she raced through the trees. She wanted to close her eyes and hang on for dear life, but she knew she had to steer the horse, or they would both end up injured. A lame horse is how she wound up in her present situation. She didn't know how long she rode, but no riders caught up to her. She wondered if it could really have been that easy to lose the highwaymen.

She broke through the trees into a clearing, but her horse reared and pawed the air with its front hooves when they nearly plowed into the very men she'd tried to escape. And just behind them was a village holding a market. Madeline's shoulders sank along with her heart. Rather than evade the men who meant to sell her, she'd ridden right to the town's gates.

"Doesnae do ye much good to run if ye dinna ken where ye're going," Arthur sneered as he yanked her from the saddle. His fist plowed into her middle; and if she'd eaten anything that day, it would have come back up. Instead, Madeline was left wheezing as they dragged her into the village. "Speak, and I will beat ye until ye wish ye were dead."

Madeline searched for anyone who might help her. As the men pushed her through the crowds, she noticed people turned away without making eye contact with any of their group. People scurried to the sides of the road or behind market booths to avoid them. Suspicion crept along Madeline's spine as she watched the townspeople more closely. There was recognition in people's eyes, and wariness, but not outright fear.

When they stopped at the blacksmith's shop, she spotted a young girl just entering adolescence. She smiled warmly at her and received a shy smile in return. Madeline turned to Harris, who now had hold of her. The two Dougals haggled with the blacksmith over re-shoeing her horse. Finneas leaned against the building; his face was pale and clammy, and blood still seeped from the stab wounds Madeline gave him. She tried not to look smug.

"I need to relieve maself," Madeline whispered to Harris.

"Too bad," Harris grunted.

"Do ye really want to be standing so close when I wet maself?" Madeline asked with a pointed look.

"Vera well, but I'm coming with ye," Harris stated.

"Nay. I dinna need a nursemaid. The lass over there can show me where to go," Madeline pointed to the girl she'd spotted. Madeline waved her over. The girl dipped a wobbly curtsy and kept her eyes down. Madeline made the sign of the cross over the girl's head. "Bless ye, ma child. Can ye show me where I might have a moment of privacy?"

"Aye, Sister," the girl nodded. Madeline didn't bother to look at Harris as she pulled free of his grasp. She followed the girl around the back of the smithy to the cottage the family lived in. "Ye can go right there." The girl pointed to a large oak tree.

"Thank ye, ma child. Our blessed Lord looks kindly upon children who are so gracious," Madeline smiled warmly at the girl before hurrying to the tree. She made use of the moment alone, then looked around. There was a bramble bush covering an exposed root. She pushed her skirts among the needles, then called out to the girl, who dashed to help. "I've gotten maself caught, as ye can see. Could ye give me a hand, lass?"

The girl approached cautiously, as though she feared Madeline might bite her. They stared at the fabric for a moment before Madeline reached down to grasp the stem of a branch.

"Sister, ye need to mind yer hands," the lass warned.

"Christ bore the pain of five nails in His body. We should be able to bear the discomfort of brambles. It reminds us of our Savior's sacrifice," Madeline said reverently. "What's yer name?"

"Mary."

"Like our Lord's own mother. That is a name ye must strive to be worthy of, Mary." Madeline pointed to her skirts, and Mary gave them a tug. "Was it yer mama who chose it?"

"Aye. Her name is Mary too," the girl giggled. "And ma da is Joseph."

"Then ye must be a family of great faith," Madeline mused. "Ye are a good lass, Mary. Ye have come to the aid of a bride of Christ. Those who would ignore a person crying out for help, who would ignore a person—a woman of God—when she is in a time of need, they face ruination and damnation." Madeline tried not to cringe as she spoke the half-truths. She prayed that God understood her motives were pure, and that he would forgive her manipulation of the girl.

"I try to be, Sister," Mary said as she pulled Madeline's tunic free. "There ye go. Ye are free now."

"If only that were true," Madeline sighed.

"Are ye nae free? Do ye belong at a convent?"

"I amnae free from those men, who took me. And I would vera much like to return to ma priory," Madeline sighed again.

"They took ye?"

"Aye. A Godly woman. They say they will sell me. I pray the Lord hears ma prayers in time, but He is so vera busy with all those prayers to answer. I dinna ken what to do."

"Isnae everything God's will? Mayhap He meant for ye to be with them," Mary said skeptically.

"God also gave mon free will. It is why we are all sinners. Do those men look like they follow God's teachings or His will?"

"Nay, Sister. They dinna. They scare me when they come here," Mary admitted.

"Who are they?" Madeline pressed, knowing she would have to return soon, lest Harris or one of the other men drag her back.

"I dinna ken, but they come here often," Mary explained.

"They dinna wear their plaids. Were they banished?" Madeline brushed down her skirts and stepped around the tree back into the sunlight.

"Nay. They come and go as they please. I think they see the laird," Mary said as she pointed to a turret at the far side of the village. "That's Braemar Castle, home of Laird Farquharson."

Madeline held her breath, relieved to learn where she was and who had taken her.

If I can make it to the castle, then mayhap I can seek shelter. Mayhap they would send word to Fingal. I need to get to their gates to beg sanctuary. Highland hospitality will demand they let me in.

Madeline looked down at Mary just before they

rounded the smithy. "Is there a kirk in the village or is it at the keep?"

"At the keep, Sister."

"Do ye think I could seek refuge there? I fear what these men will do to me. They spoke of selling me." Madeline infused a tremor in her voice and prayed that she'd built trust with the girl. Mary's eyes widened, and Madeline knew the girl understood what that meant. "Aye. I dinna ken what to do."

That was the last Madeline could say as seven livid faces stared at her. She noticed Finneas leaned against his brother Dougal, the leader of the outlaws. The other Dougal and Arthur stepped forward and forced Madeline to stand between them. She darted a glance at the girl, who nodded her head before disappearing within the smithy.

CHAPTER TWENTY-SIX

T he sun was moving lower over the western horizon, and many of the vendors were packing their wares. People continued to stare, but they didn't look directly at the men. Madeline's hopes that she might find refuge at the keep evaporated as she recalled Mary said the men knew the laird. Madeline now understood that everyone knew. Laird Farquharson protected Dougal and Finneas. She wondered if the laird condoned their highwaymen thievery. It was obvious none of the villagers would come to her aid.

"We take her to Lileas to get cleaned up and made presentable before tonight," Dougal, the leader, declared. Arthur and the mere thief Dougal grasped her arms and dragged her behind the others. Madeline could reach her cross, so she held it as high as the thong it hung from allowed. She drew a deep breath. Her last hope for rescue would either come now, or she would be left to the wolves.

"Ma God, ma God! Why hast Thou forsaken me?" Madeline screamed. "Hail Mary, full of grace. The Lord is with thee. Blessed art thou among women and blessed is the fruit of thy womb, Jesus. Holy Mary, mother of God, pray for me, a sinner, now and at the hour of ma death! Ma God, ma God! Why hast Thou forsaken me?"

"Shut up," snarled Arthur. He shook Madeline, and she cried out in exaggerated pain. She went limp and dropped to her knees.

"Like our Savior Christ, who the Romans placed on the cross but not before dragging Him through the streets, I go to ma death forgiving those who did naught. But, as a bride of Christ, I ask God that He may rain down His holy justice upon those who would ignore Christ's own teachings. Go forth, ma children, and share the word of the Lord," Madeline called out her warning even as the highwaymen's leader reared his hand back to slap her. His hand crashed down upon her face, and Madeline saw stars before she spat blood on his boots.

"Dougal," Finneas warned. "She willna go for as much if she's too battered. We need her bonnie face to bring in the bids."

"Speak again," their leader hissed. "And I will slit yer throat maself. Once I have ma coins."

Madeline glanced around at the people who stopped to stare. Horror was clear upon every face she saw. She hoped her twisted benediction would spur someone to action. But no one called out. No one rushed to stop them. No one moved but the highwaymen and Madeline. They wound through the streets until they approached a tavern. Madeline could smell it before she could read the shingle that advertised The Three Merry Lads.

From the sounds coming from the building, Madeline reasoned there were far more than just three merry lads within. The crowded main room forced people to squeeze together. Madeline was jostled in every direction. She was elbowed and pinched more than once until she was thrust before an aging woman with a massive bust overflowing from an un-laced blouse.

"Lileas, clean this bitch up and make her presentable for the auction. If she speaks, cut out her tongue. She doesnae need it to swallow cock," Finneas snarled. Madeline gauged the woman's reaction and knew she would find no help here. "And get her something to wear besides that tunic."

"That will cost ye," Lileas purred. Dougal flipped a coin at her that Lileas shoved down her cleavage. The older woman pulled Madeline along until they reached the stairs. "Try any funny business, lass, and I dinna care if Jesus himself comes to yer side."

Madeline nodded as she followed Lileas up the stairs and down a long hall. Lileas pushed her into a chamber where three other women looked up at the interruption. They were in various stages of undress, but all three looked terrified. Madeline suspected she wasn't the only woman up for sale that night. The madam steered her toward a basin and ewer before taunting Madeline with a bar of soap. Madeline held out her hand but did nothing else as Lileas leered. When Madeline didn't react, Lileas grabbed Madeline's breast before twisting her nipple. Madeline wanted nothing more than to cringe and whimper, but just as she refused to empower the men by making her discomfort obvious, she lifted her chin and looked down her nose at Lileas.

"Wash and be quick aboot it," Lileas snarled. She dropped the soap into Madeline's hand and spun around to address one of the other women. Madeline didn't waste a moment. She lathered the soap onto a washcloth before pulling her arms out of her sleeves. She scrubbed what she could without removing her tunic. It was awkward, but she would maintain the guise of modesty for as long as she could. She hummed another hymn as she patted herself dry, making the three other woman stare at her.

Lileas handed out chemises to each woman. Madeline held hers up and discovered it was virtually sheer. It would hide extraordinarily little of her body, leaving nothing to anyone's imagination. She held up a sleeve and wondered if she could hide her cross by wrapping it around her wrist beneath the cuff. Then another idea struck her. It would either frighten some of the bidders or their reactions would give her a good laugh at their expense.

She tucked her cross beneath the neckline of her tunic. She noticed the opening at the top of the chemise was wide enough for her to step into and draw it up over her hips. She shimmied the chemise up her legs as she pushed the tunic up too, leaving none of her visible to the eyes that kept swinging in her direction. As she drew each arm out of the sleeve of her tunic, she worked the crucifix's long, loose thong over each shoulder. As the chemise came up to cover her breasts, she used her thumbs to push the leather cord over her bust.

Once she exchanged the tunic for the chemise, she pretended to arrange the sheer garment around her waist and legs. All the while, she pushed the necklace until it sat around her waist like a girdle. She looked down and prayed that the undergarment might not be so sheer as to show the outline of the cross. She knew her nipples and the thatch of hair at the top of her legs were visible. She waited for one of the women to comment, but when nobody said anything, she assumed she'd succeeded. As Lileas opened the door and shooed each woman into the corridor, Madeline steeled herself for what would come next.

CHAPTER TWENTY-SEVEN

The Grants rode into Braemar after an exhausting day on the road. They'd lost the tracks left by the highwaymen, but continued on until darkness forced them to make camp again. The men avoided Fingal, who looked haggard and distraught. He offered to stand first watch, then refused to relinquish his position as each man attempted to relieve him because he couldn't sleep.

His mind buzzed with images of Madeline lying dead in a ravine, or her body picked over first by wolves, then by crows. He imagined her wandering, calling out his name until she gave up all hope that he would find her, that he was even looking for her. He wondered what she must think of him. She'd been too delirious to see the good side of him, always on the receiving end of his disregard for others. He wanted to believe that he was becoming a better man, but he doubted that himself. He knew that every moment that his fear intensified, it was because he worried about Madeline as a person, rather than a responsibility.

Fingal wanted to find his wife, not because he knew he was obligated to protect her and provide for her. He wanted to find her because he couldn't imagine living without her robin's egg–blue eyes twinkling when she smiled or throwing shards of ice at him when she was angry. When she was ill, he'd had to use his fingers to untangle her wet hair, afraid her brittle comb would hurt her scalp. Now he wanted to sit before a fire in their chamber and watch her bathe—or better yet, share a bath with her —then comb her hair until her ebony locks shone. He realized that he wanted them to share a chamber. He didn't want "his" and "hers" anything, if Madeline would agree to it.

Fingal's chest ached as he feared he would never ask her when her saint's day was. He would never learn her favorite color or her favorite season. He would never take her to see her family at Stornoway, and his family would never meet her. He doubted she'd gotten with child from their one night together, but he feared that she would lose the bairn if she had. The idea left a gaping hole in Fingal's chest. Having an heir didn't concern him. He simply wanted a child with Madeline. If that child was lost, he knew it would devastate her, and he would be nowhere to comfort her.

Fingal prayed. He prayed that he would find Madeline and that they would grow old together in a loving marriage. He recognized that he didn't need to couple with her to share intimacy with her or to build love. The more he prayed, the more he knew he just wanted Madeline back.

"Do ye think Laird Farquharson would extend us his Highland hospitality?" Harry asked as the rest of the Grants scowled. The Grants and Farquharsons were on amicable terms, but there was growing tension between the Gordons and Farquharsons. Now that Cairstine and Eoin's marriage allied the Gordons and Grants, it was likely that animosity would increase between the Farquharsons and the Grants.

Each Grant warrior riding into Braemar also knew Laird John Farquharson was the least trustworthy leader east of the Cairngorms. The man traded allies with the wind, which was one reason why they and the Gordons got on so poorly. Fingal didn't trust the laird to offer them shelter or aid in finding Madeline.

They'd picked up tracks again that morning, following them until one set turned left into a thicket. The rest continued on for a couple miles before also turning left into a meadow. Fingal suspected that Madeline had somehow gotten away from the men. He doubled back and took the path he thought Madeline likely had while the others followed the tracks into the glen. The men met up just outside the village gates. Simon pointed out hoofprints that looked like a horse had reared then pawed the ground. Fingal feared it might have been Madeline's mount, and that the animal might have thrown her.

"Look," Harry pointed out. "Today was market day. Mayhap someone saw something. We could ask before making our way to the keep."

Fingal nodded. He'd never been to Braemar before, and it struck him as odd that people stared so much. He suspected they got very few visitors, but he was sure that strangers passed through, since the village lay outside the clan's castle gates. They approached the smithy and the stables. They knocked on the blacksmith's workshop door, but no one answered. Fingal and the men led their mounts into a corral where he recognized one horse.

"That's Madeline's," Fingal said under his breath. "She's here, or she's been here."

"Aye. The animal's been recently reshod," Tommy lifted the animal's front hoof. He laid the MacLeod horseshoe they'd found against the horse's hoof. It was an exact match to the new shoe.

"Do ye think she went to the castle? Mayhap the kirk?" Simon asked.

"I imagine so," Fingal said as he took a last look at the smithy. "We take our mounts. I dinna want to be on foot if Laird John has one of his fits of temper." The men led their horses through the streets to the keep's gates. After heated negotiations, the Farquharson guards admitted the Grants into the bailey, but not before they stripped them of their visible weapons. No one discounted that each Grant man had at least one dirk hidden on him. They entered the Great Hall as the evening meal began.

The men approached the dais, where Fingal made their introductions to Laird Farquharson and explained the reason for their visit. It didn't escape his notice that the laird grew more attentive as Fingal described what befell Madeline in the storm. He could tell he was trying to keep his interest inconspicuous, but the laird's attention raised the hairs on the back of Fingal's neck.

"Ma men could help ye track her in the morn," Laird John Farquharson said. When Fingal swung his full attention to John, and the laird smiled, Fingal thought his face might crack.

And show us to our deaths. He kens where Madeline is.

"We would appreciate the help. Ma wife," Fingal watched the surprise register on John's face. "Is a vera quiet and reserved woman." Fingal observed John's reaction, which he altered from surprised to studiously blank.

"What does yer bride look like?" John asked nonchalantly.

"Aboot yay high," Fingal pointed to his heart, and it pinched as he remembered holding Madeline's hand over it. "Black hair cut short. And she looks like a nun, since she was one."

"Yer wife was a nun?" John guffawed. "Bluidy unlikely."

"She was a sennight from saying her final vows when we wed. A more pious woman I have never met. It wouldnae surprise me if she whispers in God's ear while she dreams. And it wouldnae surprise me if God struck down a mon foolish enough to harm her." Fingal narrowed his eyes as they swept the dais. "If God doesnae, I will."

"Ye and ma men can leave at first light," John announced. "Please come, sit, eat."

Fingal looked back at his men and nodded. He and Harry took seats on the dais; Tommy, Nichol, and Simon glared at the Farquharson warriors at the front table just below the salt until they made room for the Grants. Fingal and Harry kept an eye on John, while the Grant men kept an eye on Fingal.

The meal passed and the men made small talk. Fingal and Harry held up their end of the conversation, but when John asked Fingal his opinion on how matters stood between the Camerons and the Mackintoshes, MacThomases, and the Chattans, Fingal's answers were vague. It was no secret that the Grants and Camerons didn't get along. They kept their distance from one another, and both clans upheld their ends of a truce struck two generations ago. Fingal knew that the Farquharson secretly arranged an alliance with the MacThomases, since Fingal was close in age with and knew the Mackintosh heir. Fingal listened as the laird attempted to inflame his temper by insinuating the Mackintoshes and Chattans were eyeing Grant land. His noncommittal answers drew the Farquharson's ire, rather than the other way around.

When the meal concluded, Lady Maris Farquharson offered Fingal a chamber, but he steadfastly declined the accommodation. He insisted that he not be a further inconvenience after the Farquharson fed him and his men. Fingal made his way to the barracks with his men. While none of the clan's guards were rude to the Grants, they made Fingal and his men aware that their presence was unwanted. They were given a tiny chamber with one cot just inside the doorway. The room suited Fingal's purposes.

"I dinna trust Laird Farquharson. He kens where ma wife is," Fingal whispered as the men sat together on the floor. "I suspect whoever has her will do something with or to Madeline tonight. One of us stands watch at all times. If anyone rides out, we follow."

"An event is happening in the village this eve," Tommy murmured. "We didna hear what, but it's secret. The men wouldnae speak of it in the open, but their faces told us they all knew what was going on."

"Aye. It wouldnae surprise me if the men dinna sneak out to it," Nichol said. "It sounded like an auction to me."

The men grew silent, each knowing there were very few types of auctions that took place in the dead of night. None of them were legal.

"If we must follow them, how do we get our weapons back?" Simon asked. "We canna chase after them with just a couple dirks each."

"There's probably only one guard in the armory at night. It shouldnae be that hard to get in there," Fingal thought out loud. "Two of us are on watch instead of one. Our horses are in stalls in the vera back. One of us slips out as though we need to relieve ourselves, but that mon slips into the stables and saddles the horses. I'm nearly certain we will have to go tonight. We have two on watch, and when it's time to go, two of us go to the armory for our weapons while the last deals with the guard at the gate."

"I'll take watch in the stables," Simon offered.

"I'll take first watch here," Nichol nodded.

"Fingal, ye must try to sleep. Ye've been awake for nearly two days straight." Harry shook his head and held up his hand when Fingal opened his mouth to argue. "Ye must rest or ye willna be any good to us in a fight. Lady Madeline will need ye."

Fingal pursed his lips before agreeing. He doubted he would sleep, but Harry was right. If he didn't rest soon, he wouldn't be able to fight with his full strength. And there was nothing Fingal wouldn't do to find Madeline.

CHAPTER TWENTY-EIGHT

M adeline shivered as she waited in the shadows as more and more men filed into the Three Merry Lads. The tavern had seemed to be bursting at the seams when she arrived, but now all manner of men crowded around a makeshift platform. Madeline strained to see if any of the men who'd taken her were in the crowd. She recognized Arthur, Harris, Lewis, Dougal the Lesser, as she thought of him, and David. But she couldn't see Finneas and Dougal.

"Dinna ye fash. They'll be here to collect their coins and to give ye a goodbye rut," Lileas cackled as she pushed one of the three women who'd been abovestairs out into the main room. She was younger than Madeline and blonde, but Madeline had noticed little more than that in the dim light. She'd heard the other women talking when Lileas stepped away. Their situations were all the same: there were too many mouths to feed in their homes, so their fathers were selling them into servitude. Selling a daughter to a man looking for a slave to bed paid better than sending a daughter out to work in a tavern or a shop.

Madeline watched in horror as the men in the

front groped and fondled the blonde woman before the auctioneer ordered her to remove her chemise. Madeline covered her mouth to stifle her gasp as men stuck their hands between the woman's legs. One pulled her down to a table and forced her onto her back.

Lileas appeared next to the auctioneer and held up her hand. The crowd fell quiet as Lileas walked to the blonde's legs and pushed them apart. Madeline choked when Lileas slapped the blonde's netherlips before tweaking the woman's nipples and pulling them.

"Ye can believe me when I swear to ye she's a virgin. She's ready for a mon to claim her maidenhead and break her in," Lileas called out. "Ye ken the rules. The mon who buys the wench gets the first rut here or abovestairs. It's his choice if he allows any of the rest of ye a turn."

The auctioneer started calling out numbers and pointing as hands went up in the air. Madeline watched as silent tears rolled down the woman's face as men ran their hands over her as though they were considering horseflesh. She noticed several of the men fondling the woman up for sale kept grasping their groins and arranging themselves. She feared she would be sick before they paraded her before the men, and she was certain she would be if this was how they treated her.

She looked around, panicking that she had to escape before it was her turn. Madeline spied a door at the end of the passageway in which she stood. She wondered if it was a storeroom in which she could hide, or maybe Lileas's solar that might have a window. She backed away from the other two women, creeping backwards down the hall until she reached the door. She muttered a brief prayer of thanksgiving when the door opened.

From the smell, Madeline could tell it was where the tavern stored its whisky and ale. She pressed the door closed and held out her hands, shuffling her feet as she felt around for a place to hide. As she moved across the small room, she felt a draft swirling around her bare feet. She moved toward it and ran her hands over the wall when she could walk no further. She suspected there would be a door the brewsters and distillers used to deliver their barrels. Madeline felt the handle and jiggled it, but it was locked. She strained to reach the top of the doorframe, but she was far too short.

Turning to her right, she swept her foot out, hoping to find a crate. When she stubbed her toe hard, she bit back a curse she hadn't used since before her time at Inchcailleoch. She pressed on the top of the crate as hard as she could until she was convinced it would bear her weight. Once she'd pulled it in front of the door, she climbed upon it and ran her hands over the top of the doorframe. She found the key she needed, and she was soon outside.

Madeline looked around, unsure of where she was, since she'd seen so little of the village. Taking her chances, she ran in the opposite direction from the entrance to the tavern. But she'd only been free for a few minutes when hands grabbed her hair and yanked her back.

"That wasna a wise choice, Sister," Lewis hissed beside her ear. "Ye can be sure Dougal and Finneas hear aboot this. Nae only will they claim their turn with ye, they'll let each of us tup ye for all the trouble ye've caused."

"I thought only the mon who bought me could decide that," Madeline bit out as she squirmed.

"Those brothers can be vera convincing," Lewis snarled as he twisted her arm behind her. "Back in ye go."

CHAPTER TWENTY-NINE

L ewis forced Madeline through the door from which she'd escaped as she tried not to sob out loud. He guided her back to where the auction for the blonde had just finished. Madeline ground her heels into the floor, but Lewis gave her a firm push. She looked back to find Lewis running toward the kitchens, then disappearing through a doorway. When she glanced around the crowd, she no longer saw any of the men who'd captured her.

Madeline looked down when someone grasped her wrist. A woman's bony hand was wrapped around her joint. Her eyes followed the papery-skinned arm up to Lileas's face. Madeline drew in a deep breath, trying to avoid inhaling the stench of so many unwashed men, and prepared herself for the groping hands that would travel over her body. Madeline pushed the sights and sounds around her to the side and focused on picturing Fingal as he'd looked their one night together. She told herself that if any man forced himself upon her, she would close her eyes and remember how things had been between them.

Despite the confusion and doubt, and despite the

pain, Madeline had enjoyed Fingal's touch. She knew she had been aroused when Fingal joined their bodies together. It was her mind that was at war with her body. But as she considered the opportunities she'd missed to experience an emotional connection and physical and emotional intimacy with Fingal, Madeline swore she wouldn't make the same mistake again. She'd done it enough times. The elements of Fingal's personality that disheartened her and those that drew her closer left her conflicted. But she'd observed enough to know Fingal was a good man who needed as much time to learn to be a good husband as she did to become a good wife.

"Get yer arse up there," Lileas snapped, making Madeline jump. Madeline stepped onto the platform and looked over the crowd. It was easy to spot the two dark heads that belonged to Dougal and Finneas. Her icy glare made Dougal shift, but Finneas smirked. Madeline found a spot on the wall across from her to stare at and pictured herself riding with Fingal. She imagined the way she'd felt when she leaned against his chiseled chest and abdomen, how it felt when his arms grazed her breasts as he held her securely against him. Just as she had moments earlier, she shut out the world around her and focused all her thoughts on her time with her husband. She noticed the hands on her, but she felt as though she were floating above herself. The touches didn't register with her, so they no longer terrified her.

"Take off yer bluidy chemise, ye halfwit," Lileas hissed. Madeline looked down at the madam and realized she'd lost track of the auction. She knew she would have to strip bare, then turn around as the men ogled her before Lileas examined her.

What a surprise she'll have inside and out. Let's see what they have to say when I dinna have a stitch on me.

Madeline slowly drew the chemise up her legs, watching the crowd. She moved slowly, taunting the men who watched her just as much as they taunted her. As the hem came to just below where her crucifix hung, Madeline shifted her gaze to Dougal and Finneas, who watched her with suspicion and lust. She pulled the gown to her ribs, listening to the gasps and reveling in the buzz she created. When Dougal and Finneas both looked ready to explode, she shot them the smarmy smile she'd perfected when she was a lady-in-waiting.

The men standing before Madeline stared at her, some shaking their heads, others pointing at her cross. She'd watched a few step away from her, bumping into other men and receiving a shove in return. She held her hands out at her sides, raising them inch by inch until they were nearly shoulder height. Her movement drew the crowd's undivided attention back to her.

"He that dwelleth in the secret place of the most High shall abide under the shadow of the Almighty. I will say of the Lord, He is ma refuge and ma fortress: ma God; in Him will I trust." Madeline recited the first two verses of Psalm Ninety-One as she looked up at the ceiling.

Madeline lost her balance as Lileas and the auctioneer pulled her to the table and forced her onto her back. She looked directly at Lileas as she let her thighs fall open without prompting. Lileas jerked backwards as the auctioneer squealed and pushed Lileas in front of him. Men jostled for the same view as Lileas but turned away when they caught sight of the newly forming scars, the old scabs, and the recently chafed skin near the juncture of her hips and thighs.

"She's nay virgin," Lileas squeaked. "She wears the cross, but she is marked by the Devil!"

Madeline released a raucous, shrill laugh. She continued to laugh hysterically as men shook their heads and began moving toward the door. She turned her laughs into howls as she reached out her hand and pretended to claw at whoever stood near her.

"What the hell do ye mean she isnae a virgin?" Dougal demanded as he shook Lileas.

"It's clear to see. The Devil has been betwixt her thighs!" Lileas shrieked as she trembled. "Ye didna say aught aboot bringing the Devil's handmaid to be sold. Out! Out! The lot of ye. Get the raving bampot out."

"Ye will regret this more than aught ye have ever done," Finneas hissed before his fist rammed into her stomach. Madeline had no chance to recover before Finneas's yanked her to her feet by her hair. "Ye stabbed me and cost me a pouch of coin. Ye will die for this."

"Did ye—ye stop—to—" Madeline stammered as Finneas dragged her toward the door. "Who really —bedded me? Nae a—nun. A—a—wife."

"What?" Dougal demanded as he held out his arm to block Finneas.

"Fingal Grant is ma husband," Madeline wheezed. "Ye kenned I was a Grant, but ye never asked why a nun would carry a plaid. Ye never asked why a nun was alone so far from any priory or abbey."

"Ye bluidy, conniving bitch," Dougal spat as he drew his dirk from his waist.

"Nae in here!" Lileas squawked. "I dinna care what ye do with her, but I amnae scrubbing blood from ma floors. I'll be lucky if anyone ever walks through ma door again. I'm nae having that cursed blood on ma floor."

"She's nay more cursed than I am," Finneas spat.

"I'd say between tonight and whatever happened before," Madeline pointed to his milky eye. "I'd say it isnae the Lord who is on yer side."

Finneas and Dougal each grabbed an arm and yanked her outside. Naked, with only her crucifix dangling from her waist, Madeline twisted and writhed as though some demonic power had truly possessed her. She snarled and attempted to bite their arms, going limp over and over, forcing them to stop and pull her up lest she pull them down.

"Where are the others?" Finneas asked as he looked around.

"Dinna ken," Dougal replied as they passed through the village gates. They dragged Madeline to the edge of the thicket that had brought her to Braemar. "Once she's dead, we leave her here for whatever beast wishes to have her."

"Let Fingal Grant find his wife's body naked and battered. Let him think we all had a turn." Finneas pushed her forward, causing Madeline to stumble before she fell into the high grass. When a booted foot landed at the base of her skull, she swallowed down the bile that rushed up her throat. She forced herself to go limp and not breathe.

"What did ye do?" Dougal demanded.

"Ye saw exactly what I did. Bashed her skull in. Shame she died so fast," Finneas mused with disgust. "Leave her. We need to find the men. This willna please him. Only one woman sold."

Madeline didn't dare move but to draw in the shallowest of breaths that didn't move her shoulders or chest. She waited until nothing but the rustles of leaves met her ears. She opened her eyes and looked around. Everything was blurry, and her head viciously pounded. When she could no long control it, she raised herself onto her elbows and retched.

"Sister? Sister, I'm coming."

Madeline was certain she recognized the girlish voice, but she couldn't remember from where before everything went black.

CHAPTER THIRTY

"Fingal," Harry said as he shook his friend awake. "It's time."

Fingal sprang from the cot and looked around. He realized he'd fallen into a deep sleep once he closed his eyes. His mind felt groggy, but his body felt better than it had in days. He drew a dirk from his boot and crept out of the tiny hole in the wall, following Harry and Nichol.

"Simon's still with the horses, and Tommy was on watch but has gone to tell Simon we're coming," Nichol explained.

"Nichol, ye and I go to the armory. Harry, ye see to the guard," Fingal ordered. He and his warriors slipped along the passageway in the barracks to where their weapons were stored. They moved silently as they passed sleeping Farquharsons. Without a sound, Fingal and Nichol overpowered the armorer and collected their swords and knives. They went back the way they came, leaving the building as Simon and Tommy met them with the horses.

"Where's Harry?" Tommy whispered.

Fingal looked around, then pointed. "There." Harry leaped down the last four steps from the guardroom and sprinted to them. The men mounted and charged out of the Braemar Castle bailey. Fingal didn't need a clan war breaking out, at least not yet. He leaned forward to see Harry. "Did ye kill him?"

"Nay. The mon was sleeping at his post. The hilt of ma dagger to his temple will ensure he keeps sleeping."

"Simon, did nay one notice our horses were saddled?" Fingal asked.

"Nae a one. And there were half a dozen guards who rode out," Simon replied.

Fingal squinted in the pitch-black night. The moon and the stars offered barely enough light to see the road in front of them as they trotted toward the village. They'd spotted the riders from the castle as soon as they passed under the portcullis because the battlement's torches illuminated the road just beyond the wall. The Grants hung back so the Farquharsons wouldn't hear them following. As they entered the village, the narrow streets forced the men ahead of them to slow to a walk. Unfortunately for Fingal and his men, the buildings blocked much of the moon's light. Soon there was no one in front of them.

"Where'd they go? Harry muttered.

"I dinna ken," Fingal shook his head. Anger and frustration boiled within him, making the pulsing blood in his head ring between his ears. "I dinna ken if they went inside somewhere or they took a turn we couldnae see."

"Do we spread out or stay together?" Simon asked.

"Stay together. There are too few of us for anyone to go alone. We dinna kill unless it's us or them. When we find Madeline, cover ma back while I get her out." Fingal refused to think about "ifs" and told himself that when they found Madeline, he would pull her into his arms and never let her go.

Fingal and the four Grant warriors combed the

streets of Braemar village, but they couldn't find anything or anyone connected to an auction.

"It must be at a tavern," Tommy said.

"Aye, but we havenae passed even one yet," Harry observed.

"That's odd. Do ye think they only have one?" Simon asked.

"This isnae a large village. I would imagine only one, mayhap two at most. They must be on the other side of the village. We—" Fingal's thought was interrupted when five men stepped in front of them with swords drawn. The men dressed shabbily, and Fingal wondered if they'd just found the highwaymen who likely had Madeline.

"Thought ye were guests of Laird Farquharson," a nearly toothless man spoke up.

"We were, but we got bored," Fingal responded.

"Bored? After all that bemoaning the loss of yer wee bride," the man snickered. "Whoring in the wee hours of the night, then searching for yer wife in the morn. Dinna sound likely."

"But here ye are," said Fingal. "Point us in the right direction, and we will be sure to tip well."

"Tavern's closed," a second man stepped forward, his sword in his right hand and a dirk in his left.

"That's unfortunate," Fingal called back. "I'm mighty thirsty."

"The well's over there," the man with the sword and dirk pointed toward the village water source.

"We wish to enjoy yer tavern's ale. It's nae like we crept into the laird's solar to steal his whisky," Fingal grinned.

"Tavern's closed," the first man droned.

"Then a wee stretch of the legs for me and ma horse before we return to bed," Fingal suggested.

"Yer bed shall be in the ground," spat the second

man as the line of outlaws charged toward them. The Grants drew their swords and stood their ground. Each of them rode battle tested, loyal horses, so they didn't worry that their mounts would run off once the fight began.

"Maim, dinna kill, if ye can help it," Fingal ordered just before the onslaught began. While the highwaymen were better fighters than Fingal expected, moving like trained warriors, they were unprepared for the Grants' tactics. The Grant guards kicked and punched as much as they swung their swords. Fingal backed the first man who spoke against a wall, lunging from side-to-side when the toothless man tried to evade him. Fingal sized the man up before drawing him back into conversation. "Ye dinna look like the kind of mon to break bread with Laird Farquharson, yet ye kenned we were guests at the castle. How could that be?"

"Saw ye ride in," panted the toothless man.

"Do highwaymen often lurk in the village?" Fingal asked.

"Who said we were thieves?"

"Nay one, but yer clothes and stench tell me ye are. I've answered yer question. Now answer mine," Fingal demanded as he swiped the end of his sword across the man's sword arm. It was more of a graze than a cut, but blood soon blossomed through the man's leine. When no information was forthcoming, Fingal jabbed his sword into the man's thigh. "I'm nae kenned for patience."

"Go fu—"

"Dinna finish that," Fingal warned. "Why are highwaymen guarding the village? What's it matter if we discover for ourselves that the tavern is closed?"

"Go fu—" the toothless man attempted to insult Fingal a second time. Fingal lunged forward, using his sword to block the other man's. He drove his fist into the man's face and watched him slump to the ground. He looked around and found his men standing while the outlaws laid about in semi-consciousness or knocked out.

"Learn aught?" Fingal asked.

"Aye," Tommy panted. "The one ye fought is called Arthur, and the one I fought is Dougal."

"Daft bastards thought if they talked to one another and coordinated their fight, they would overpower us," Harry smirked.

"This one," Harry kicked a man who groaned. "Is Lewis. That one is Harris. They look like brothers. Wonder if their mother is from the isles. Lewis and Harris. Bluidy stupid."

"They call the one I fought David," Nichol said.

"Ye learned more than I did," Fingal grunted. "But I learned they watched us when we arrived. They already knew we were coming for Madeline. God only kens what they've done to her if they kenned we're close."

"Whatever this auction is, it's at the tavern. Otherwise, why would they have kept us from there?" Harry asked.

"It must be a stone's throw since I can see where the village ends up ahead," Fingal said as he sheathed his sword and gathered his horse's reins. "Despite how much I want to, we dinna barge in. We scout the building, then decide what's best." Fingal clenched his jaw and curled his free hand into a fist. He'd ordered his men to maim, not kill the ruffians. He wouldn't make the same order for whoever held Madeline.

CHAPTER THIRTY-ONE

Fingal and his men made their way to the far side of the village and stopped just before they reached the village gates. Simon collected the horses' reins and drew the animals into a secluded spot out of sight of most windows. Fingal, Harry, Nichol, and Tommy moved silently along the dirt road as they searched for the tavern. Fingal threw up his fist to signal the Grant warriors to stop before he pointed to his ear.

A commotion further along the street near a row of cottages made the men even more vigilant. Angry voices carried as men cursed and bellowed. The Grants crept forward until Fingal called them to a stop once more. He glanced back at his men and pointed to his eye before pointing up to a swinging shingle above his head. While none of his men could read, the shingle made it obvious that they'd found the village's alehouse.

Fingal pushed open the door to the Three Merry Lads and found it nearly empty. He swept his eyes over the inside of the tavern as his brow furrowed. He was certain that the illicit event was to take place at a tavern, and they hadn't passed any other establishments large enough to hold an auction. He wondered if the arguing they'd heard was the event. He turned to leave when a woman's voice called out.

"Ye're too late," an older, generously endowed woman approached. "But I'm certain I can find ye some entertainment with ma regular lasses. Braw mon that ye are shouldnae go lonely. They call me Lileas." Fingal realized he was looking at the proprietress of the tavern, and wondered if she knew where Madeline was. As the tavern owner purred, she attempted to reach out her hand to run it over Fingal's chest.

"We came for a reason. How could it be over so soon?" Fingal asked as he turned his body away, making it appear as though he were looking around.

"Bluidy daft bitch," Lileas snarled. "I told her to strip, and she hid that blummin' cross."

Fingal's hackles went up as he peered down at someone who abetted the highwaymen responsible for Madeline's disappearance. A wave of bloodlust washed over Fingal unlike any he'd ever experienced. He wanted nothing more than to crush the woman's skull between his bare hands. But he knew that would gain him no information about Madeline.

"A cross? What would that matter?" Fingal attempted to sound confused.

"She wore the bleeding thing around her waist. Made it look like a blummin' shield over her cunny. Then she wasna even a virgin. And it was the Devil who'd been between her legs. He'd marked her!" Lileas shrieked at the end. "I'll be lucky if another God-fearing mon walks in here after that."

God fearing indeed. Fingal struggled not to snort, clearing his throat instead.

"And that ended things? What aboot the other women? Was this Devil woman the last one?"

"Nay. That makes it worse. There were still two more after her," Lileas snarled.

"Is that what all the fuss is aboot down the street?" Fingal wondered.

"What fuss?" Lileas pushed past him and stormed out of the door. "Bluidy bleeding hell! Those sods are still holding the auction but nae in ma tavern. I willna get ma coin." Lileas rushed toward the crowd, with Fingal and his men close behind.

When the Grants approached the gathered men, Fingal looked back over his shoulder, and each of his men understood his expression. They were to remain inconspicuous until they knew what they faced, and they were only to draw their weapons if there was no other choice. The Grant men eased their way into the crowd, pausing every so often to blend in. Fingal strained to hear over choruses of taunts and curses.

"This one has hair so black ye would think ye were looking at a raven." The auctioneer's voice floated to Fingal. He forced himself not to ram into the men who stood in his way and the woman who must surely be Madeline. He fished into his sporran and pulled out a pouch of coins, ready to give them all away if it meant he could get Madeline away from the lechers ogling her.

He opened his mouth to make the next bid but snapped it shut when his gaze landed on a naked young woman who definitely was not Madeline. While they had the same color hair, this woman's tresses reached her waist. She stood shivering in the cool evening air, which made her nipples into pert darts. Fingal turned his head away, unwilling to look at the woman. He realized that only weeks ago, he might have cast a long assessing look over the woman before turning away. Now all he could think about was Madeline. Fingal leaned back and hoped to catch Harry's eye.

Harry raised his eyebrows and shrugged. Fingal

knew the man was as torn as he was whether they helped the woman up for auction or turn their backs in favor of finding Madeline. There weren't nearly enough Grant men to put up a fight to stop the bidding, but when he glanced at his other men, he knew they would all fight if they had to. Fingal considered buying the woman to set her free, but before he decided, the auctioneer bellowed "sold." The Grants stared as a man stepped forward who was clearly a lesser noble. His clothing was clean, and Fingal noticed his nails were groomed when the man stuck out his hand to grasp the woman's breasts. He held up a pouch the tinkled with the sound of coins.

"Ye may all watch as I tup her first," the man announced, and Fingal felt ill. "Then Dougal and Finneas may have a turn, as ma thanks for finding such a ripe plum. If there is aught left of her this eve, I will consider letting some of ye have a go."

Fingal searched the crowd, but it didn't take long for him to discover two men staring back at him wearing matching smirks. The half-blind one went so far as to wink with his good eye. Fingal had had all he could stomach of this scene. Once more, a wave of regret flooded him that he didn't have enough men to fight those around him, so they could free the woman who was already being led off the crate she'd been standing on. Fingal pushed forward and turned in a circle.

"Where is ma wife?" Fingal's voice boomed. "The wee little thing that scared the shite out of ye all. The one with the cross."

Men backed away as Fingal continued to look around, noticing the varying expressions on the faces in the crowd. Some were shocked, others disgusted, but many appeared terrified. Fingal suspected it was not he who terrified them so much as the mention of

Madeline. He laid eyes on a medium-sized man who began to tremble and grabbed him by his shirt.

"Who bought ma wife?" Fingal demanded. He knew the auction had broken up within the Three Merry Lads before anyone bought Madeline, but he assumed she'd been sold amongst this crowd. He shook the man when he didn't answer quickly enough.

"Nay one," the man wheezed as Fingal shook him once more. "From ma mouth to God's ear. I swear it. We seen the Devil's brand between her legs. Nay mon would touch her. She might be carrying the Devil's spawn."

"Then where is she?" Fingal kept the man in his grasp, but he turned to look at the two men he suspected orchestrated the auction.

"Dinna ken," the villager spluttered. "I just came to watch. I dinna have the coin to bid."

Fingal released him with a shove, sending him backwards into several other men. He turned in a full circle as he assessed who might have the coin to purchase a slave. He soon noticed there was only a handful of men left, among them the two men who looked like brothers; Fingal was confident that they were the slavers. He stood before them, his men at his back, with one hand on the hilts of their swords and a dirk in the other.

"Where is she?" Fingal seethed.

"Who?" The man with the blind eye drawled.

"Where is she?" Fingal repeated. He used all the restraint he could muster not to lash out when he was so outnumbered.

"Nae here," the other man taunted.

"Do ye wish for me to return with the Gordons?" Fingal's strident tone carried. "Ye ken we are now family." He watched as a moment of doubt flashed through Dougal's eyes, but Finneas remained resolute.

"By all means, run away and cry to yer neighbors. By the time ye get back, she will be food for the worms," Finneas said with a one-shouldered shrug. "But do ye really think ye are going anywhere? Ye're outnumbered."

"Touch me, and nae only will every Grant mon auld enough and young enough to swing a sword descend upon ye, but so will the Gordons, the Gregors, and the Frasers of Lovat. The MacThomases might join in just for fun. Do ye think the Chattans and Buchans can gather before ma family arrives? Do ye think they would come to rescue slavers?" Fingal narrowed his eyes into a glare. "What will the laird say when four angry clans arrive ready to raze this village and besiege yer keep?"

Voices around him muttered warnings, not to Fingal, but to the outlaw brothers. Men began backing away from him, seemingly evaporating into the air. Soon it was the brothers and a handful of Farquharson guards against the five Grants.

"Seems yer people dinna care for the idea of being raided," Harry muttered.

"Ye ken I speak the truth," Fingal warned.

Dougal and Finneas exchanged a look before Dougal turned a gloating smile on Fingal. "We dinna have her anymore."

"Who bought her?" Fingal demanded.

"Wolves dinna pay coin," Finneas taunted. "I doubt she's alive. Mayhap ye'll find bits and pieces. If ye're lucky."

Fingal lunged forward, making both brothers take a step back. A malicious grin crossed Fingal's face as he realized he intimidated them. They would have stood their ground if they weren't worried Fingal would kill them.

"Tell me where she is. I dinna give a shite what happens to either of ye. I want ma wife, and I want off yer godforsaken dung heap."

Dougal pointed toward the town gates. Fingal drew his sword, and the Grant men followed suit. The sound of metal sliding along metal filled the air. They backed away as the Farquharsons reached for theirs, but Dougal raised a staying hand. The last sound Fingal heard as he turned to mount his horse and ride through the gates was laughter.

CHAPTER THIRTY-TWO

"Sister, ye must wake up. Ye must. I canna move ye."

Madeline's head throbbed as she tried to lift it to find the owner of the voice. She turned it with a groan, but found the young girl, Mary, staring into her eyes. Madeline felt the girl's hands pushing against her shoulders.

"I'm awake, lass," Madeline croaked as she tried to sit up. As soon as her body lifted off the ground, she twisted to her other side and retched. There was nothing left in her stomach to come up, but the bile that spewed forth burned her throat. Mary handed her a waterskin, and Madeline put it to her lips. She caught a waft of the whisky scent just as she tipped the container. It was a different sort of burn that slid down her throat and into her belly. It warmed her in a way that even the thickest sealskin cloak couldn't. When she handed the waterskin back to Mary, she looked down at her bare body. She didn't bother looking around, knowing there would be no clothes for her to find.

"Here," Mary said as she shoved fabric at Madeline. "It's ma mama's."

Madeline held up the kirtle and breathed a sigh

273

of relief. It looked like it might be a bit loose, but it would cover her. She reached for her cross but realized it was no longer around her waist. She had no idea where she'd lost it, but the sense of emptiness she would have expected to feel eluded her. Instead, she scrambled to her feet and pulled on the gown, looking around her to see who might be watching.

"Nay one kens I'm here. I slipped out and came to find ye," Mary explained.

"Came to find me? How could ye ken I was lost? Dinna ye understand how dangerous it is for ye to be out in the dark, regardless of what is happening in yer village?" Madeline asked.

Mary shook her head. "Ma uncle is the priest. Nay one will ever touch me," the girl said confidently. Madeline sighed, but didn't say anything. She knew warning the girl would have no impact.

"How did ye ken to look for me?" Madeline went back to her original question.

"I stayed awake. I prayed and prayed for ye, Sister. When some men passed near our cottage, I could hear them grumbling aboot the auction being broken up at the tavern. Then they were talking aboot how some Grant mon caused a commotion claiming he was looking for his wife. The mon talking made it sound as if the Grant claimed ye were his wife. I dinna understand."

"Fingal," Madeline breathed and looked over the girl's head toward the village gates as five horses charged through. She lifted her arms over her head and waved. "He is ma husband, Mary. I never said ma final vows, but I trained as a nun."

Madeline didn't look down at Mary as she watched Fingal ride closer. Her breath caught as Fingal threw his leg over his saddle before his horse came to a full stop. She didn't feel her feet on the ground as she launched herself into his arms. Fingal's hold was so tight that Madeline had to gasp, but she didn't ask him to loosen his hold. She burrowed her face into his neck and inhaled. She would know his scent anywhere.

Fingal felt Madeline trembling in his arms, but the relief he felt as she returned his embrace was unparalleled. He tunneled his hand into her hair and noticed it had grown since they met. She lifted her head from his shoulder, and their eyes met. Their need was mutual as their mouths sought each other. The kiss was wild and passionate as they finally knew the other was safe. Fingal lifted Madeline's feet off the ground as he drew her closer. He pulled away long enough to bark, "Stay here."

Madeline looked over her shoulders to the dark forest behind her then at Fingal, who carried her into the trees. She wrapped her legs around his waist as he continued to walk. When Fingal was confident that they were far enough into the woods for privacy, but not so far that he couldn't hurry Madeline back to his men, he stopped. He was prepared to ease her to the ground, but she clung to him. She dove in for another searing kiss that Fingal gladly reciprocated.

"Fin, I need ye," Madeline panted.

"I'm here, wee one. I'm nae going anywhere," Fingal reassured.

"That isnae what I mean. I need ye," Madeline repeated as she pulled at his leine. "Please, Fin."

"Maddy, are ye hurt? I dinna think this is a good idea. I need to speak with ye."

"Later, Fin. Please. Before I lose ma nerve," Madeline confessed. "I want ma husband. I want to be yer wife. I thought I'd never see ye again."

It was Fingal's turn to swoop in for a passion-filled kiss. Awkwardly, they shuffled until Fingal's plaid and Madeline's gown were bunched between their chests. They looked into one another's eyes as

Fingal sank into Madeline's channel. Madeline's sigh was music to Fingal's ears. Their gazes didn't shift as they rocked together, and Fingal's fingers bit into Madeline's backside as he gripped her to keep from slipping. Madeline pulled Fingal's leine free from his belt, her hands roaming over the muscles that bunched in Fingal's back.

"Maddy, I never want ye out of ma sight again," Fingal murmured as he kissed her neck.

"Dinna let go," Madeline moaned with each word.

Fingal pulled the sleeve of her loose kirtle over her shoulder until it sagged and revealed her breast. He lowered his mouth to kiss the swell then flicked his tongue over her nipple, which tightened in response to him and the cool night air. She moaned once more as he took her breast into his mouth and suckled. She felt her needs shifting as her body strained for something she didn't understand. She grew restless and eager, her body clamoring for more. Fingal sensed Madeline's changing needs, speeding his thrusts as he drove her closer to the brink. "I need—harder."

Fingal heard the uncertainty in Madeline's voice, knew that her body's cravings confused her. But he also knew that he would give her anything she wanted and more. He bent his knees until he found the soft ground beneath them. Madeline clung to Fingal as he shifted their position. Cradling her head, Fingal encouraged Madeline to lay back. Her moan, as he surged into her, told him that she was as desperate for more as he was.

Days of unspent lust threatened to overwhelm him, but he refused to finish before Madeline. He longed to draw out the moment, even as his body sped toward climax. When Madeline's breath caught, and she clawed at him to bring his head down to hers, he knew she was close. His kiss devoured her, and he swallowed her moan as her body arched off the ground and stiffened.

Fingal still wasn't ready for their lovemaking to end. He would draw out Madeline's pleasure for as long as he could. A quiet but insidious voice in the back of his mind warned that he should make their coupling last because there was no guarantee that Madeline would let it happen again. He gentled his kiss as he tried to make her understand his feelings without having to say them out loud.

Madeline's body floated down from whatever cloud it had sailed away upon, but she still felt the same need to move with Fingal that she had moments before her climax. She experienced a tenderness toward him that she'd never imagined she could feel. Her frantic pawing at him became caresses, and she felt a shift in Fingal's kisses. They were gentler and no longer frenzied. He continued to piston his rod into her, and her hips rose over and over to meet each thrust. But their joining was no longer driven by the panicked need to come together.

"Maddy," Fingal whispered, his soft tone reverent. The simple word, almost just a sound, pushed Madeline over the edge once more. Her legs wrapped over his as her arms encircled his neck. Fingal thrust once more before he felt his release. Neither of them moved except to push the hair away from one another's face. It was too dark to look into each other's eyes, but they both sensed the other's gaze. Fingal's thumb brushed over Madeline's cheek until he found her lips. His kiss was as soft as her whispered name. He pressed more tender kisses over her cheeks as she kissed his neck. Neither was ready to let go.

"Fingal?"

"Aye, wee one."

"I ken we canna stay here tonight, but wherever we go, will ye hold me while I sleep?" Madeline asked. She held her breath, praying that the moment they'd just shared could last throughout the night, if not forever.

"I wasna planning on letting ye go," Fingal replied, and Madeline could feel his smile as he kissed her cheek again. He pressed up onto his hands, but Madeline didn't let go of his neck.

"I ken we should go, but can we have just a few more minutes like this? Alone." Madeline feared that she sounded like she begged, but Fingal didn't hesitate to lower himself onto his forearms, using both thumbs to stroke her temples and forehead.

"I would stay just as we are, the two of us, for eternity, Maddy."

Madeline sighed as her eyes drifted closed. She marveled at how peaceful she felt after such vigorous coupling. She knew she hadn't asked him to couple with her so she might get with child. The thought hadn't crossed her mind. She'd simply needed to be as close as she could to Fingal. She needed the reassurance that they really were reunited, and that he was as happy to find her as she was to find him. Nothing about what they'd done felt sinful to her. It felt reverent and spiritual. She wondered why she didn't feel any guilt or fear about seeking pure pleasure. But she pushed the thoughts from her mind as she concentrated on the feel of Fingal's larger body pressing against hers. Sandwiched between the ground and Fingal, she finally felt safe and shielded from the world.

"Maddy, if we were in a bed, I wouldnae suggest moving us for aught in the world. But the ground must be damp beneath ye, and I'm truly petrified that ye might grow ill again. I canna live through that again," Fingal explained, and Madeline heard anguish in his voice. It gave her pause, considering what Fingal had experienced while tending to her. She remembered his kindness and gentleness through the haze of her fevers. But she'd assumed that he'd simply tolerated the inconvenience. His tone now made her wonder just how her brushes with death affected him.

Once their clothing was back to rights, Fingal led Madeline from the forest. The Grant men milled together, two facing the woods and two facing the town. None looked at the couple as they emerged from the woods. Madeline looked around but didn't spot Mary.

"Where did the lass go?" Madeline asked softly.

"We sent her home," Simon answered. "We didna want to explain—uh—why ye werenae out here. And we told her that ye would want her tucked away safely in her bed where her mama and da wouldnae worry."

"Thank ye," Madeline smiled.

"Where are yer shoes, Maddy?" Fingal whispered in her ear, and his brow furrowed as he finally took in the gown she wore. Madeline shook her head, and Fingal wished he hadn't brought it up. Madeline's expression was a mix of fear and shame. Fingal led her back to the tree line, but they remained where his men could see them. He squeezed the hand he hadn't realized he held. "What happened while we were separated?"

Madeline opened her mouth, but no sound came out. She watched Fingal's expression crumble, and she thought for a moment that he might cry. She understood his look, because she'd experienced guilt and remorse as well.

"Fin," Madeline stepped closer and pressed a kiss to his lips. "This wasna yer fault. Naught of it."

"It was. It is," Fingal disagreed.

"Nay, it wasna. I ken what ye said, but I dinna believe for a moment that ye could have kenned that the weather made Noah's storm look like a sprinkle. Ye couldnae have kenned ma horse would throw its shoe. Ye couldnae have kenned we would become separated. Ye couldnae have kenned someone else would find me. And ye certainly never would have imagined what those men were doing."

"Ye should have been riding with me," Fingal argued.

"So we could have two lame horses?"

"I'd take a dozen lame horses than kenning men planned to sell ye," Fingal's voice cracked.

"Fin, ma horse threw its shoe and tripped over a root. I dinna ken for sure which happened first. The weather was too foul for any of ye to hear me calling out. I survived the night and would have been fine to search for ye if Dougal's men hadnae found me. I'm certain it was blind luck and naught that any of us did that they stumbled upon me." Madeline bit her top lip as she looked at Fingal. "Fin, men saw me naked in the tavern. Some even tried to touch me. But I swear to ye, I havenae lain with a mon other than ye. Please believe me." Madeline fought to keep from choking on the lump in her throat, but she couldn't keep her tears from falling.

"Maddy, I wouldnae care if any had. All I want is ma wife," Fingal reassured her.

"But I need ye to ken that if I get with child, or if I already am, the child can only be yers," Madeline pressed.

"Maddy, if a child were born in nine moons and didna look like either of us, I wouldnae care. I would claim the bairn as mine and be grateful that ye are living under the same roof as me."

"Ye say that now. But ye need an heir. A legitimate one," Madeline said as she brushed away tears.

She didn't understand why Fingal's face darkened and his stance went rigid.

"Is that what that was all aboot?" He jerked his chin toward the woods. "To try to make certain that I'd believe the child is mine if ye told me ye were carrying? Is it only ever aboot a damn heir to ye?"

"What?" The look of shock on Madeline's face made Fingal blink several times as he relaxed. The tears fell faster until Madeline struggled to push out her words. "That was because I needed ye, Fin. I needed to feel ye were truly there. That I was safe again. And because I couldnae bear the thought of being apart from ye for another breath."

"Maddy," Fingal sighed as he pulled her back into his embrace. She shrank against him and suddenly shivered, as though she needed his warmth. "So that had naught to do with trying to have a bairn?"

Madeline shook her head against his chest. Once more, she fought to speak around the heaving sobs that overcame her the moment Fingal wrapped his arms around her again. "I didna think of that until after. And I didna care when I did. I wanted us to be like a couple who—care aboot one another." She'd caught herself before she'd said love. She hadn't a clue about Fingal's true feelings; she was still sorting through her own. And she didn't want to give him any false hope about how she would feel once they'd put danger behind them. But she did want Fingal to know that their coupling meant something special to her. "When I feared I would never see ye again, bearing yer child wasna what I thought aboot. All I wanted was ye."

"Madeline, I am taking ye far away from here. Ye dinna ever need to look back," Fingal promised. He wished she understood that he meant more than just leaving Braemar behind.

"I dinna want to look back, Fin."

Fingal swept Madeline into his arms and carried her back to his horse. He mounted behind her and spurred his steed. His men fell in around them, creating a protective circle around Madeline just as Fingal's arms did.

CHAPTER THIRTY-THREE

"We seek a meal and a place for ma wife to rest," Fingal spoke clearly but softly, afraid to wake a slumbering Madeline. They'd ridden through the night until they came across Abergeldie Castle, home to a Gordon chieftain. Fingal had last seen Seamus Gordon at Cairstine's wedding. Seamus looked at Madeline, who was curled into Fingal's lap with the extra length of his plaid draped around her. "She's been ill, and I fear she may have a relapse," Fingal explained

"I willna have a sickness coming through ma gates," Seamus said as he passed under the portcullis.

"It's naught anyone can catch. She fell ill when a cut grew infected," Fingal hedged. "But she wasna back to her full health before the storm a few nights back. We just had to ride through the night, and she is exhausted and chilled."

"Ride through the night? Where did ye come from?" Seamus asked. Fingal knew the question was from more than idle curiosity.

"Southwest of here," Fingal hedged. Seamus narrowed his eyes as he stared at Madeline, who still hadn't woken despite Fingal speaking above her head.

"There's naught much in that direction but Braemar," Seamus mused. The two men exchanged a look, and Seamus nodded. Fingal wondered how aware the chieftain was of what went on with his neighbors. After Harry dismounted and handed off the reins to a stable boy, Fingal handed Madeline down to him. But she woke and flailed her arms and legs, trying to grasp hold of Fingal. He jumped down from his horse and pulled Madeline back into his arms. She wrapped her arms around his neck and cried against his shoulder.

"Wheest, wee one. I'm here," Fingal cooed.

"I thought I was falling. Then I thought someone was taking me," Madeline whispered.

"We will get ye settled soon enough," Fingal promised.

"And ye willna leave me?" Madeline swiped at her tears, but kept her head against Fingal's shoulder.

"And I willna leave ye."

The chieftain's wife took one look at the bedraggled couple and issued orders for a chamber to be prepared and water boiled for a bath. Fingal watched as servants hurried to follow the woman's orders as though she were commanding an army. He supposed she was.

"Is yer lass poorly?" The woman asked softly as she approached.

"She was. Now I think she is exhausted," Fingal explained. Madeline turned her head and looked into the kind woman's face. There was something about her that reminded her of the Mother Abbess. She would have asked Fingal to put her down if she'd had her plaid to wrap around her shoulders. The gown sagged too much in the neck to cover Madeline modestly while standing. In any case, Fingal didn't seem to be in a hurry to put her down.

"Come to our table. Lass, ye look like a wee thing. Ye could do with a little meat on yer bones," the woman said. "I'm Ceana."

Madeline blinked several times as she thanked the chieftain's wife, remembering the prioress had once had the same name. The similarity in appearance, and then the same name, was uncanny. It put Madeline at ease as Fingal carried her to the dais.

"I dinna have yer plaid anymore," Madeline whispered. "Is there one I can borrow? This gown is far too loose in the bust." Fingal nodded and turned his head to look back at his men, mouthing the word "plaid." Simon was closest, and pulled a spare from his saddlebag. Madeline peered over his shoulder as she reached for it, offering him a smile of thanks. Madeline quickly wrapped the plaid around her shoulders before turning toward the table. Fingal pulled out a chair for her, but thought better of it. He slid into the seat and pulled Madeline into his lap.

"Fin," Madeline hissed, looking around in shock before glancing at Fingal.

"I told ye I wasna letting ye out of ma reach," Fingal shrugged.

"Ye said out of sight," Madeline corrected. Fingal grew serious as he looked at the chair that should have been his.

"Do ye need yer space, Maddy? Ye need only tell me." Fingal dropped his arms, prepared for Madeline to slide off his lap, but she surprised him when she leaned back against him. It shocked him that she would allow such an intimate display of affection. He glanced down to see her eyes were closed once more.

"Mayhap it was me who said I didna want ye out of ma reach," Madeline said around a yawn. Fingal wrapped his arm around her middle as his other hand stroked her hair. He kissed her forehead, and Madeline sighed.

"Will ye stay awake long enough for a meal and a bath?" Fingal wondered.

"Aye. And if nay, wake me please. I'm starving." Madeline didn't have time to fall asleep before Ceana returned with servants carrying platters of cheese, cold meats, and bread. "I shall make a pig of maself, but I feel like I havenae eaten in a sennight."

"Ye havenae eaten properly in aboot that time. Enjoy, wee one. Then I'll assist ye abovestairs," Fingal offered. Madeline still leaned against Fingal as she ate, accepting the pieces of food he passed to her. It wasn't long before Ceana informed them that Madeline's bath was ready. Fingal carried her abovestairs and set her down as the last servant slipped past them into the passageway. When he turned to leave, Madeline grasped his hand.

"I'm vera stiff, and I dinna think I can lift the gown over ma head," Madeline admitted as her cheeks burned with embarrassment, but it wasn't an exaggeration. Madeline's lips thinned, and she squeezed her eyes shut as Fingal lifted the dress up for her to pull her arms from the sleeves before pulling it off over her head. At Fingal's sharp inhale, Madeline's eyes flew open. She looked down to where Fingal was staring. There was a livid bruise across her kidney. "I'm all right."

"Nay. Ye are nae." Fingal reached out a tentative hand, his fingers feathering over the injury. He looked at Madeline's face as he turned it to see the bruise that he'd tried to ignore. "Where else, Maddy?"

"Just the back of ma head. I think I have a bump." Madeline lifted her hair and felt around, wincing when she came to the place where Finneas kicked her. Fingal eased his fingers under her hair and cringed when he felt the goose egg at the base of her skull.

"Och, Madeline. I shouldnae have put ye on the ground like that," Fingal lamented, but Madeline kissed his cheek softly.

"Please dinna ruin ma memory with yer regret," Madeline whispered. Fingal pressed his mouth to hers, and she opened her lips without hesitation. When they drew apart, Fingal looked into Madeline's eyes and saw no hesitation or fear.

"I dinna regret any of it either, wee one," Fingal murmured before he stepped back. "I—ah—shall wait outside."

"Fin, dinna go," Madeline said before biting the side of her bottom lip. "I canna keep ma arms up to wash ma hair." Once more, her cheeks radiated fire as she admitted that not only did she need help, but she needed help with something so intimate. She glanced at the tub and then back at Fingal. "Do ye plan to use the water after me?"

Fingal looked at Madeline for a long time before his eyes darted to the tub then back to her. He nodded before looking around for a screen. "I dinna want ye to have to wait for me in the passageway. I can put up the screen, so ye dinna have to see."

Madeline wiggled her toes as she looked at Fingal nervously. She was torn between the daring request she wanted to make and fear that God would smite her right where she stood. But she didn't want Fingal to go. Trepidation filled her as she cast caution to the wind.

"The water will be cold by then, Fin." Madeline hoped Fingal would intuit her meaning without her having to say it aloud. He took a step closer until his booted toes touched her bare ones, and they rested their foreheads together.

"I need to hear ye say it, Madeline," Fingal

rasped.

"I dinna ken if I can," Madeline confessed as she closed her eyes.

"Do ye fear God will punish ye where ye stand?"

"A little," Madeline admitted. "I dinna want ye to think me wanton. I dinna want ye to think that I lied aboot what didna happen, and that is why I'm acting loose now."

Fingal shook his head. "I believed ye, and I ken naught happened. As for being loose, Madeline, that word canna describe ye. It'd be ridiculous. Ye're barely able to let me, yer husband, ken ye wish to be with me. I hardly think ye're going to be soliciting anyone else."

Swallowing, Madeline took a deep breath. "Will ye tell me what happened to ye and yer men while ye bathe with me?" She nearly tripped over her tongue as she hurried to blurt out the last five words. Fingal cupped her jaw and smiled down to her.

"I want naught more, wife." Fingal moved to sit on the end of the bed, and Madeline followed him. She supposed she wasn't embarrassed to be naked in front of him after the times he bathed her while she was ill. She kneeled and unlaced his boots before tugging them off. She rolled down his stockings, marveling at the sinews and corded muscles in his thighs and calves.

Fingal watched every movement Madeline made as he unbuckled his belt and pulled off his leine. He steeled himself against temptation, knowing he couldn't suggest to Madeline what he wanted lest she run into the hills, this time never to be seen again. But as he looked at her kneeling before him, his rod pulsated, and he wished that she would wrap her mouth around him. When their eyes met and Madeline swallowed before her lips parted, he wondered if she shared his thoughts. "Maddy?"

"Hmm?" Madeline looked at him blankly before glancing back at where his plaid tented over his cock-stand. Fingal was slow as he moved to unwrap his *breacan feile.* He expected her to shy away, or even fall backward. But she remained where she was, kneeling on one leg.

"Maddy, if ye dinna back up, when I remove ma plaid, I'll—you'll—" Fingal watched Madeline, but she didn't move. "Madeline, ma rod will be in yer face," he blurted. Madeline still didn't move, so he rose, leaving his plaid behind him on the bed. Madeline reached out but glanced up at Fingal before she touched him. He nodded once, then his head fell back as her hand wrapped around him. She stroked him as he'd taught her during their brief interlude in the woods several nights earlier. The night he threatened to leave her behind.

"Fin?"

"Mmm," Fingal couldn't manage more than a hum as the feel of Madeline's hand wrapped around him filled every inch of his concentration.

"I've never done, or even seen it done, but I ken what a woman can do for—" Madeline waited for Fingal to reject her, to be horrified by what she suggested. She couldn't even explain why the idea presented itself to her, let alone why she was entertaining it. But she didn't want to have a conscience while she was alone with her husband. She didn't want to think about what the pious choice would be. She didn't even want to think about whether she would be disgusted with herself by morning.

"Do ye mean, ye wish to take me into yer mouth? How the devil do ye ken aboot that?" Fingal's dumbfounded expression made Madeline smile.

"Fin, I was at court as long as I was at the convent. I learned a great deal aboot what can go on between a mon and a woman because people are hardly discreet. They arenae discreet aboot their conversation or some of the places they choose to tryst. It's why I ken it's such a—" Madeline caught herself before she said "sin." She pushed her conscience back into the box in which she wanted to keep it that night. "If ye dinna want me to…"

"Praise the saints, Madeline. I'd like ye to. Of course. But that isnae something a mon should ask his lady-wife to do. I dinna expect aught from ye."

"I ken, and that's why I want to offer. Will ye let me?" Madeline waited, but when she saw the slightest dip of Fingal's chin, she leaned forward. She knew that if she waited another moment, she would lose her courage and regret for the suggestion would take hold. Her tongue passed over the head of Fingal's cock, and he hissed as his hands balled into a fist. "I dinna ken what I'm doing."

"As long as ye dinna bite me, there is naught that wouldnae feel good kenning it's ye doing it." Fingal was torn between closing his eyes and basking in the feeling alone and the curiosity of watching his modest wife engage in something so carnal. He kept his thoughts to himself as his eyes narrowed to slits while Madeline swirled her tongue over the tip of his staff before sweeping it along the length.

When she wrapped her lips around him, Fingal was certain he would expire. She moved slowly, growing accustomed to the sensations, but it felt as though she teased him as Fingal observed her deep concentration. When she paused, he assumed she'd taken in as much as she could. Then she slid her mouth to the root, the tip brushing the back of her throat before sliding further. Madeline froze, and Fingal could feel her breathing before she began to suck, moving her head in the most tantalizing rhythm.

His climax was nipping at his heels too fast for him to calm himself. The sensations Madeline evoked were unlike anything he'd experienced before, no matter how experienced the women before her were. It was the eroticism of it being Madeline, coupled with the feel of her touching him. He tried to think of something else, anything else, just long enough to slow his racing heart and the need for release. When she hummed as though she enjoyed her task, Fingal reached his limits. He pulled Madeline onto her feet before practically flinging her onto the bed before he pounced. He'd barely slid inside her before he spilled. He rested on his forearm above her as his fingertip trailed over her skin and the back of his fingers brushed over her tightened nipples.

"Maddy, ye mean more to me than anyone else."

"Because I—I pleasured ye?" Madeline asked in confusion as her heart sank.

"Nay. I mean, the fact that it was ye who gave me pleasure. That ye would do such for me makes ma heart feel too large for ma chest. I'm sorry that I didna tend to ye before I spilled. I couldnae let it happen in yer—"

"Ye couldnae spill in ma mouth. Is that only for whores?" There was no rancor in Madeline's voice. Fingal only heard curiosity.

"Mayhap for some. I didna want to disgust ye," Fingal smiled ruefully. "But I didna seek to bring ye —ye—" Fingal didn't know what word to say. He was fearful that if he said pleasure or satisfaction, she would push him away. But she'd called what she'd done for him "pleasuring." He was out of his depths as Madeline tucked hair behind his ear.

"The bath will be cold by now." Fingal stared at Madeline as she changed the topic of conversation so unexpectedly. "Will ye still help me?"

Fingal climbed off the bed and helped Madeline

to stand before they crossed the chamber to the tub. Fingal dipped his finger in the water and found it was still warm, but it wouldn't be for much longer. He helped Madeline step into the tub, but she waited until he was settled before she tried to determine how to sit. Fingal guided her to sit between his legs, her back resting against his chest. He lapped water over her shoulders as she sighed. They sat in silence, but Fingal knew Madeline was still awake because her hands kept rubbing over his lower thighs and knees. When he knew they shouldn't linger much longer, he reached for the soap and a linen. He ran the cloth over her body before she dipped her head under the water. He scrubbed her hair and poured clean water over it. When Madeline looked back at him, he smiled at her ponderous expression. She gestured for him to slide forward as she rose. She maneuvered herself to sit behind him and pulled him to lean against her just as she had done with him. Fingal wrapped her calves over his thighs as he massaged her lower legs.

Madeline pressed gentle kisses against his neck before washing everywhere she could reach. As intimate as it was to run the soapy linen over his body, enjoying her exploration, she found something uniquely intimate, wifely, about washing Fingal's hair. Rather than being sexual, it was something she could do simply to tend to him. She wondered if he'd felt anything like that as he scrubbed her scalp. He'd been cautious to avoid the bump and apologized profusely when the side of his hand grazed it. Madeline smiled to herself and wondered if the bliss would disappear once morning came, and they were back on the road. They were both too exhausted to do more than sleep once they climbed into bed. Just as he promised, Fingal slept beside her, not once letting her go even in the midst of deep slumber.

CHAPTER THIRTY-FOUR

Madeline came awake to the feel of a rock moving up and down beneath her head and chest while something stroked along her back and arm. She lay still and smiled as Fingal's warmth and comfort made her want to laze away the day. She tilted her head back and gazed up at Fingal with her smile still in place, before closing her eyes and nestling closer.

Fingal was surely in a heaven built just for him. He'd woken with Madeline nestled against his side. He'd known she was still in a deep sleep as she barely stirred when he lifted his head to look down at her. He knew it was well after sunrise, and the morning meal would soon be served, but he couldn't bring himself to disturb her—or to end the way he felt when he held her. He'd spent at least a half hour looking at the ceiling while his hand trailed over her, at peace for the first time in years.

Assuming Madeline would expect to rise soon, Fingal shifted to release her. The arm that had been tucked beneath her shot out and wrapped around his ribs. "Nae yet. The rest of the world can wait. I dinna want to face that yet."

"Whatever ye wish, Maddy," Fingal returned her

smile. But before he could grant her request, someone knocked at their door. Madeline scrambled to pull the covers up to her chin before turning horrified eyes toward Fingal. He wanted to groan as the reality they both wanted to escape came banging on their door. Madeline's nervous eyes darted around the chamber, but Fingal was already calling for whoever interrupted their seclusion to enter. When Madeline noticed it was a man coming into the room, she ducked beneath the covers. With a glance at his hidden wife, Fingal sighed and thanked the man for bringing Madeline's chest up. "He's gone now."

Madeline slowly lifted the covers from her head, her face beet red. Fingal knew someone seeing them together in bed decimated any progress they'd made last night. Madeline would likely say the rosary for the rest of the day. He opted not to say anything as he rose and pulled a fresh leine from his saddlebag. Madeline surprised him when she crawled to the end of the bed and kneeled, the sheet still wrapped around her.

"Do ye have another plaid in there?" Madeline whispered, still mortified.

"Nay," Fingal shook his head as his forehead creased. From the disappointment on Madeline's face, he feared she might cry.

"I dinna want to wear another mon's plaid," she closed her eyes, but her disappointment was still clear. Fingal sat beside her and pulled her into his lap. Perhaps not all hope was lost. "Fin, I feel as though I should feel guilty, but I dinna. I'm more upset that I lost yer plaid than I am that I lost ma cross."

"We can replace both," Fingal assured her. Madeline nodded, but he could tell his words didn't console her. "Maddy?"

"Both were vera special to me. Things didna start out well between us, but that was the first thing ye ever gave me. It was yers, and ye made it mine."

Fingal kissed her temple, and Madeline turned her face into his chest. He was touched that his gesture, which he'd thought little of at the time, made such an impression on Madeline. She'd said it was special to her that night, but he knew he'd offered it out of jealousy. While Madeline grieved its loss, Fingal felt relieved that he could offer her another and truly mean the sentiment she clung to. "Maddie, we still have another night on the road, so ye need someone's plaid. But once we're home, ye may pick as many of ma plaids as ye wish."

"It's silly that it matters so much to me. It's far too long for me to wear as an arisaid while I work, but I'd planned to spread it over ma bed." Madeline inched off Fingal's lap with a sad twitch of her lips. She slipped out of bed and kneeled before her chest before looking up at Fingal. He hadn't moved. When she cocked an eyebrow, he stood and finished dressing.

"Dinna rush, Madeline. I will be with Seamus, either in the Great Hall or his solar," Fingal stated as he walked to the door. He looked back at Madeline and found confusion on her face rather than sadness. He knew he'd only called her Madeline once since they were separated. And that time, it was to tell her how much he wanted her to pleasure him with her mouth. But she'd knocked the wind out of his sails when she said she wanted to spread it over her bed, not theirs. Hers. And she'd mentioned working. He feared she would return to toiling as hard as she had at Inchcailleoch. He wanted her to have an easier life than that. She nodded before easing the door open.

Madeline watched as Fingal left the chamber they'd shared. She looked at the bed for a long time as she tried to sort out her emotions. She'd never felt so content as she had when she woke to find herself tucked next to Fingal. She'd felt cherished the night before. But when the servant arrived to deliver her chest, shame and guilt flooded her. There would be no doubt in anyone's mind about what they'd been doing the night before. She was certain people would know they'd shared a chamber. As she continued to gaze at the bed, she tried to push embarrassment and shame aside, refusing to allow regret to worm its way into her heart.

As Madeline looked at the gowns packed in the chest in front of her, it reminded her of her life at court before being sent away. Memories assailed her of the hideous things she'd said and done to the other ladies, particularly Maude. That Madeline was incapable of feeling remorse and delighted in Maude's misery. She'd been frivolous, caring only for her sense of style and the attention she could garner. She wouldn't regret what she'd shared with Fingal because her feelings for him were real. But she couldn't allow herself to return to the version of her that she despised. She lifted out a gown, deciding to wear a kirtle while they were at Abergeldie, but she would change into the serviceable tunic she still had for the rest of their journey.

"They sell women," Fingal told Seamus as they sat together in the chieftain's solar. He'd already recounted how Madeline got separated from their party and how the Grants tracked her to Braemar.

"I kenned something was amiss. We've had two lasses go missing in the past three moons. They'd gone foraging for mushrooms, and when we found their baskets, we feared that they'd drowned trying to cross a swollen stream. We thought the current carried them away. Now I wonder if they were taken."

"If ye never found their bodies, I would say it's likely. I dinna ken how often they hold these auctions, so I dinna ken how long they keep the women. What do ye ken of the laird's men?"

"I ken they arenae to be trusted. He allows outlaws to roam his land," Seamus growled. "Nay love lost with that lot. Nae an honest one in the bunch."

Fingal considered his next questions because he needed to have more facts before he said anything that might sound like an accusation. "I wonder how it started. I ken it's done, but who do ye think came up with it?"

"I dinna have any idea, but it must be men the laird kens."

"Oh?" Fingal pressed.

"To be carrying on as they are just outside the gates? John must ken," Seamus mused. Fingal was about to ask another question when a soft knock came at the door.

"Come," Seamus bellowed. The man seemed to have no sense of volume in the small chamber. The door opened a crack, and Fingal recognized Madeline's blue eyes before she pushed the door open wider. Fingal drank in the sight of her. She'd chosen the subdued dove-gray gown he'd seen her wear more than once at court. He stood from his chair and crossed the room.

"Is aught amiss?" Fingal worried.

"Nay," Madeline replied, squeezing the hand Fingal hadn't realized he'd claimed. "I thought to offer ma thanks to the chieftain for allowing us a night under his roof, and to ask if ye wish for me to set something aside to break yer fast. Lady Ceana said ye hadna eaten yet." Fingal was put off when Madeline's eyes darted to Seamus, then remained downcast. He understood it was deference, but it wasn't the spirited Madeline he'd grown to know. Fingal looked over his shoulder at Seamus before stepping aside, so Madeline could see Seamus. "Good morn, chieftain. I wished to thank ye for yer hospitality. I'm certain ye dinna have unexpected guests turn up at yer gate vera often. Especially nae at night. I am grateful for yer kindness."

Fingal watched as Madeline looked at Seamus as she spoke, but then dropped her gaze when she finished. He knew she'd already retreated into her shell. He didn't want her to regret their time together. He didn't want the rejection that would come along with that, but he didn't want Madeline to bury herself in self-recrimination either.

"Dinna fash, Lady Madeline. Ma wife would have had ma bollocks if I turned ye away," Seamus grinned. Madeline dipped a shallow curtsy before turning back to Fingal.

"I'll accompany ye to the Great Hall," Fingal offered. "Did ye eat?"

Madeline shook her head. "I wanted to wait until I kenned if ye needed aught."

"Ye're a good wife, Madeline," Fingal whispered. Madeline's eyes darted to his and filled with tears. She dipped her head in a nod before turning around. Fingal didn't understand Madeline's reaction to what he'd intended as a compliment. He supposed her sudden change in behavior shouldn't have surprised him, but it frustrated him.

Once they'd broken their fast, Madeline slipped back up to the chamber she'd shared with Fingal and changed into the tunic she had left. She noticed Fingal flinched when he spotted her in her tunic. She stopped him before he lifted her onto his horse.

"Fin, that gown. I dinna want to ruin it. It reminds me——" Madeline caught herself, having said more than she intended.

"Reminds ye of what, Madeline?" Fingal snapped, expecting her to name something from the priory. Madeline's head jerked back as she fought back more tears. She was annoyed at herself for being so emotional that morning.

"Yer eyes," she muttered. It was Fingal's turn to be taken aback. He tilted Madeline's chin up until her eyes met his, and he saw her shoulders droop as he sighed. He pressed a gentle kiss to her lips before cupping her cheek and leaning his forehead against hers.

"Ye are the sweetest lass," Fingal kissed her forehead before lifting her into the saddle and following her. He nodded his thanks to Seamus and Ceana once more before the Grants rode out.

CHAPTER THIRTY-FIVE

Fingal felt the weight of the world lifted from his shoulders, even if for only a moment, as they rode through the gates of Freuchie Castle. They'd ridden hard both days they'd been on the road. Madeline had spoken little except to relay what happened while she was a captive and what she knew of the men. Fingal shared his experiences in the village, and they concluded that they'd seen the same men. But neither could deduce more than they already had.

Madeline moved around the camp as she had before she'd fallen ill. Helping build the fire and cooking. With no bedroll of her own, she'd readily curled next to Fingal to share his. She'd even pulled his arm around her before falling asleep nearly as soon as they laid down.

It was agony for Fingal to ride with Madeline's body pressed against him. He was in a permanent state of arousal with no way to ease the discomfort. He sensed Madeline's restlessness being near him. When he'd brushed the underside of her breast with his hand as he wrapped his arm around her, he'd felt her sharp inhale, but she hadn't squirmed away or moved his hand. Instead, she'd rested further back against Fingal's chest. He'd kissed her crown, her temples, and her cheeks several times over the last two days of their arduous journey, and she offered him a shy smile each time. But Fingal felt like he was in limbo. Madeline didn't outright reject him, but neither was she the passionate woman from the night they fled Braemar. He forced himself to accept that it must have been her extreme emotions after her ordeal.

Fingal's brow furrowed when he spotted Ewan and Eoin Gordon leaving the lists as they entered the bailey. He'd just set Madeline on her feet when two women's voices called out in unison. "Madeline?" Her nails bit into Fingal's arms where she'd placed them to brace herself as her legs steadied. He felt her tremble as her grip tightened.

"Maddy?" Fingal murmured. She cast her gaze at him, and he didn't know how to interpret the look in her eyes. When she released him, he turned to greet his cousin and her sister-by-marriage, but neither woman looked at him.

"Madeline?" Cairstine asked in shock. Madeline had recognized both women's voices without seeing them. Her stomach had dropped, then knotted so quickly that she feared she would be ill. She'd known all along that Cairstine would eventually return to visit her family. But she'd been unprepared for Cairstine and Allyson to greet her.

She looked at the two women as they approached, their husbands wrapping their arms around each of them. Madeline realized the one useful thing about the women being with their husbands was she could tell the men apart. The older twin, Ewan, was married to Allyson Elliot. Eoin was married to Cairstine.

"Aye, Lady Cairstine," Madeline replied softly. She was terrified of how the women would respond to her arriving with Fingal. She was certain they'd deduced why she was there.

"Lady?" Cairstine snorted. "When have we ever used our titles?"

Madeline ignored Cairstine as she looked at Allyson. While she and Cairstine had been friends of a sort, Madeline had manipulated both women too many times to count. Allyson was on the receiving end of Madeline's scathing putdowns more than once.

"Lady Allyson," Madeline dipped her head. They were all of equal status, and both Allyson and Madeline would one day be the ladies of their clans. But Madeline hadn't felt like a noblewoman in nearly five years. It felt awkward to be addressed by her honorific, and she'd addressed all the ladies-in-waiting with their titles, even the ones whose sisters she'd known.

"Madeline, what're you doing here?" Allyson's Lowland accent floated on the breeze, and it almost felt like a comfort. As much as hearing Highland accents at court and while she traveled put her at ease, Allyson's accent reminded her of the contentment she'd found at Inchcailleoch.

"Cairstine," Fingal spoke up as he looked at the two couples. "Madeline is ma wife." His arm around her waist was the only thing keeping her from running.

"Yer wife?" Ewan chuckled. Fingal bristled and practically bared his teeth. "How'd she get stuck with ye?"

Fingal, realizing the jest was at his expense, not Madeline's, relaxed and grinned. "I dinna ken how I was so fortunate, but between God and the king, I was blessed."

Four blank faces looked between Fingal and Madeline. She wanted to sink into the ground, knowing no one believed Fingal's boast. She wished he had said nothing. She offered the practiced smile that she'd worn so many times over her years at court, and she feared her face would crack.

"But I dinna understand," Cairstine pressed. "Everyone thought ye were a nun." Madeline decided she appreciated Cairstine's bluntness. She'd rather get the conversation over with while there were only four sets of ears listening, rather than with the entire clan gathered in the Great Hall. Briefly, she related the story.

"Fingal asked you to marry him?" Cairstine laughed. Madeline waited for Cairstine to have her revenge. She felt Fingal's body go rigid. "I ken he went to court to find a wife, but I assumed he'd be dragged before the kirk rather than ask someone to marry him."

"Madeline suits me," Fingal said through gritted teeth. He stepped forward, practically pulling Madeline with him. His path forced the two couples to move aside. "It has been an arduous journey, and I think we should go inside."

"Made his life miserable," Cairstine muttered.

"Figures," Allyson hissed.

Fingal spun around and moved with such purpose that Ewan and Eoin stepped in front of their wives. He glared at the men before he looked down at the women.

"Speak against her like that again," Fingal dared the women, who only stared at him with wide eyes. "She isnae who ye knew. I wanted to marry ma wife, and our reasons are our own. But just so we are clear, she means as much to me as ye do to yer husbands. I will always choose her first." Fingal finished his declaration too quietly for Madeline to hear from where she stood trembling. As if her humiliation weren't complete, Fingal's reaction scared her.

Fingal returned to her side and slid his hand into hers as though he hadn't just spat fire. He guided her into the Great Hall, where a middle-aged man and woman hurried toward them. Madeline recognized them from when the couple had visited Stirling. Madeline braced herself for a repeat of the reactions from outside.

Madeline squeaked when Lady Davina Grant pulled her in for an embrace. She heard more than saw Laird Edward Grant clap Fingal on the back as they exchanged a manly embrace. When Davina released Madeline, she stepped back and ran her eyes over Madeline. The younger woman had never felt more lacking in appearance, but Davina's expression was warm.

"We feared the worst when ye didna arrive sooner," Edward said.

"I'll explain everything later. In private," Fingal gave Edward and Davina a speaking look. "I'd like to get something hot to eat and a warm bath for Madeline. It hasnae been an easy journey for her." Fingal looked down at Madeline, who once again had her gaze averted. When the older couple turned to lead the way to the dais, Fingal leaned over to kiss Madeline's temple then whispered in her ear. "I'm sorry ye heard what they said. But I can promise ye Edward and Davina's welcome is genuine. They ken I wanted to marry ye. Mayhap nae ma original reason, but they ken neither of us was forced."

"Original?" Madeline asked, but Fingal didn't have a chance to answer before they were shown to their seats. While Fingal sat to Edward's right, and Madeline sat to Fingal's right, Davina opted to sit on Madeline's other side rather than her usual seat beside Edward's.

"Madeline, if there is aught ye need, ye have only to ask. I imagine ye dinna have many possessions, so

I ken ye may be in need of some clothes. Cairstine and Allyson will surely share what they brought, and Fenella still has some gowns she left behind when she married. But they're older and likely outdated." Davina stopped speaking when she noticed Madeline's hands knotted in her lap. Her knuckles were white, and the skin was pulled taut. "Ye've seen them already."

Madeline gave a jerking nod. She swallowed before she looked at Davina, forcing her most serene expression. "They were a little more surprised to see me than ye and Laird Grant, ma lady."

"First, I'm Davina and ma husband is Edward. Ye're our family now," Davina offered a warm smile. "And we didna give them any of the details beyond that Fingal went to court to look for a bride. They only arrived yesterday, and we were worried aboot why yer journey took so long."

Madeline nodded and was about to explain what happened, when Fingal's hand brushed her arm as he searched for her hands. Finding them knotted together, he covered both with his larger one and turned his head toward Madeline. She'd whipped her gaze toward Fingal as soon as his hand touched her. It shocked her to find he was still in the midst of his conversation with Edward and wasn't even looking in her direction. She opened her fingers, and Fingal's hand slipped into hers, lacing their fingers together. He glanced at her, but before she could ask what he was doing, he turned back to Edward. Madeline glanced at Davina, but she was uneasy with Davina's speculative expression.

Saved by servants bringing out steaming bowls of pottage along with a wheel of cheese and a loaf of bread, Madeline had an excuse to remain quiet. Fingal glanced at her several times while he continued talking to Edward. When they finished eating,

Madeline wasn't sure what to do next. She longed for a bath and the chance to sleep. Fingal watched Madeline and helped her from her seat, leaning forward to once more whisper in her ear.

"Davina will arrange for a bath, then why dinna ye sleep?" Fingal suggested.

"I would like that," Madeline said with a weak smile. "But we must cease whispering. People will think us rude."

"People will think us married," Fingal grinned and winked. Madeline stood staring at him owlishly before a brief smile made her lips twitch.

CHAPTER THIRTY-SIX

Davina led Madeline along the passageway, with family chambers on either side. She stopped at the last door on the right and pressed down on the handle. When the door opened, she stepped aside for Madeline. Looking around the chamber, Madeline blinked several times before turning to Davina.

"Thank ye for showing me Fingal's chamber. It's good to ken where it is. If I might go to ma chamber, I'd like to rest."

"It will take a few minutes to be made up. I assumed..." Davina trailed off as she noticed Madeline's uneasiness. "I'm afraid that with Cairstine and her extended family visiting, there are nay more chambers on the family floor."

"I'm certain whichever chamber ye show me will be a luxury," Madeline smiled graciously. Davina led their way to the next floor, where Madeline found a spacious chamber with plenty of sun filtering through the window. She gazed at the view while Davina ordered servants to prepare the chamber and a bath.

When her chest arrived, one woman moved to unpack it. Madeline forced herself to remain at the window rather than interrupt the woman's work. She knew she needed to make some concessions or people would talk. She thanked Davina and the maids with a gracious smile, but she felt drained once she was alone. She didn't dawdle, stripping down and settling in the nearly scalding bath. The heat eased her aching muscles, but each time she closed her eyes, she pictured bathing with Fingal. She refused to cry, even within the privacy of her chamber. She rationalized that she'd already cried enough times to release the anguish of her ordeal. But tears dripped down her cheek as she accepted that her relationship with Fingal couldn't continue to progress as it had.

Cairstine and Allyson's greetings were enough to confirm that Madeline's reputation would be all anyone saw. The women wouldn't change their minds, and she didn't blame them. But their lukewarm reception would set the tone for the other members of the clan, no matter how welcoming Davina was. Madeline knew the only means she had to earn her new clan members' respect was through a hard work ethic and moral behavior. With a new resolve, she hurried through her bath and dried her hair before the fire, thankful that it was still short and didn't take long to dry. She pulled on a chemise and slid beneath the covers, falling asleep immediately.

"Edward, I canna let it stand," Fingal growled. "They took ma wife, damn it. She came out with only two bruises and a bump on her head, but they were prepared to sell her as a whore. If I'd had more men, I would have killed the ruddy bastards while I was there. But getting Madeline away and safe was more important. Now I can mete out justice."

"This isnae worth a blood feud, Fingal," Edward countered.

Fingal paced before Edward's desk, but came to a halt and twisted to look at Edward, who sat behind the massive wood table. "Would ye have said the same if it was Davina? Ye were ready to kill Farlane and Arlan Gunn for what they tried to do to Cairstine."

"That was different. I lo—" Edward stopped short when Fingal's glare turned murderous.

"Dinna ye dare say she doesnae deserve defending because I dinna love her. And how the bluidy hell would ye ken how I feel aboot ma wife?" Fingal snarled. He placed both hands on the table and leaned forward. "I have never defied ye a day in ma life, but I will on this. As long as they are alive, they are a danger to Maddy and to any other woman. I canna risk them coming for their own retribution."

"Are ye threatening to leave here even if I ordered ye to stay?" Edward demanded.

"Aye." Fingal's left eye twitched as he continued to glower at the man he'd respected above all others. He hadn't always understood or agreed with his cousin, but he respected the older man. He'd been Fingal's moral compass on more than one occasion when Fingal was tempted to push the limits. As he stood before Edward, he realized what a disappointment he would have been to Edward if he'd continued believing he could break his wedding vows with no consequence. Now, not only couldn't he imagine betraying Madeline, he was ready to lay down his life to ensure Dougal and Finneas Farquharson could never pose a threat to her again.

"Ye seem a vera changed mon from the one who left here. Ye dragged yer feet to find a wife, and I ken ye swore ye would never bother loving the woman ye married. I ken ye didna plan to honor yer vows, but ye're ready to tear apart anyone who speaks against yer wife."

"I would defend ma wife's honor—whoever she might be—regardless of ma personal feelings for the woman. But Maddy has changed everything." Fingal sank into the chair behind him. "Edward, this was supposed to be a marriage of convenience. Even after I met Maddy. I thought we would marry, I would do as I please just as I always have, and she would bear ma children and be content. She drives me mad at times, and I even told her that's why I call her Maddy." Fingal grinned as he recalled telling Madeline that. "She reminds me of ye in many ways."

"Oh?" Edward raised a skeptical eyebrow.

"Aye. Ye both thought ye would dedicate yer life to the church, and ye both ended up married. She's as devout as ye, and mayhap even more pious—most of the time. Edward, she's terrified that if she doesnae work hard and keep her head down, if she dares find enjoyment in—" Fingal stopped and gave Edward a pointed look. "She fears she'll return to the woman she was before she went to Inchcailleoch. She feared being a burden to me so much that she didna say aught aboot her discomfort from so many hours in the saddle. She went days without saying a word. Harry figured it out before me, much to ma shame. She was deathly ill when her legs became infected. That was the first thing to slow us. I have never been so frightened for someone's life as I was when she was sick. Even when Dougal and Finneas had her, it wasna as bad."

Edward saw anguish unlike any he'd seen in Fingal since his parents died when he was a young child. He'd often worried that Fingal had grown cold-hearted after the pain of losing his parents, and he'd wondered if Fingal was selfless enough to lead the clan should Edward die before he was an old man. But as he watched Fingal, who rose and paced again, he saw a man who was more mature than the one who'd left for Stirling.

"Do ye ken that one morn before she became ill, she woke before everyone else and found quail eggs. She cooked ten of them and bannocks too, just as we were waking. I'd been horrid and selfish to her, but she kenned she couldnae eat the eggs without being ill. She still cooked ten and gave me hers. She'd done it to be thoughtful and out of deference to ma position because Lord kens it wasna as thanks for how I'd treated her."

Fingal rubbed his hand across the back of his neck. "She's resourceful too. She told me as we rode from Abergeldie that she sang hymns and recited prayers to convince the men who took her that she was a nun. Even though they still intended to auction her off, I'm certain it kept them from molesting her along the way. She made several of Dougal and Finneas's thugs nervous when she prayed for them."

"Fingal, do ye love her?"

"Aye." Fingal felt no reservations saying the affirmative. He just wished he knew how to tell Madeline without scaring her or pushing her away. Edward sat back in his chair and watched Fingal, who returned to his seat but fidgeted. He sighed before shifting in his seat, uncomfortable about what he would share with his protege.

"I fear the past is come to be the present. When I married Davina, I didna want to be wed to anyone. I resented having ma life changed because ma older brothers died and suddenly, I was the laird. I shut her out. At first, I was cold and distant, and I took ma anger out on her by ignoring her. I resented being expected to sire an heir, and I feared for ma soul if I should see being with ma wife as aught other than duty. I'm a vera fortunate mon that Davina is so patient and giving. I suspect some of what I experienced is the same for Lady Madeline." Edward watched as Fingal nodded, and Edward was certain he didn't imagine the pain in Fingal's eyes because it matched how his wife had looked so many times during the early years of their marriage.

"I was a fool. It took three years before I visited her often enough for me to sire Cairstine. I pray it doesnae take so long with yer wife, but I also pray ye can have the patience Davina did. Ma fear for ma salvation was so real that it felt as though it kneeled beside me every time I went in the kirk. It felt as though it dined beside me and joined me in our marriage bed. Fingal, it took me six moons before I realized I love Davina. But it took me three years to overcome ma guilt and shame for wanting her."

"Edward, I'm nae going anywhere. Ma wife is the only woman I have ever had any tender feelings for, let alone loved. I owe Cairstine a debt of gratitude for refusing to marry me. And I should humble maself before her because she was right aboot how a mon and wife should feel toward one another. I've already accepted that Maddy may never be comfortable with the intimacy I wish for, but I will never seek it elsewhere."

"Good," Edward nodded. "I doubt yer wife would like to discuss this with me or take advice from me, but mayhap she would be willing to speak with Davina."

"That's what I'm hoping." Fingal glanced toward the door, overwhelming need to see Madeline swept over him. The last time they'd been apart this long, Madeline got separated from him in the storm. He knew she was tucked away safely in their chamber, but he needed the reassurance. He returned his gaze to Edward. "I thank ye for this, Edward. I needed this talk. But it changes naught aboot ma decision to ride out."

"And when do ye plan to do that? To leave yer wife among people she doesnae ken except for two women I suspect were less than welcoming."

Fingal wrestled with the same question, because despite his desire for vengeance, his need to ensure Madeline felt welcome in her new home was stronger. "Nae before a fortnight, but likely nae before a moon. How long I wait doesnae lessen ma right to seek retribution. It will only make them believe they've gotten away with it and lower their guard."

"That is likely true. Mayhap ye make settling Lady Madeline in yer priority, then see how things stand after that," Edward suggested.

"Aye. Thank ye, Edward." Fingal reached out his arm, but Edward came around the desk and embraced him for the second time that day, disconcerting Fingal. But he admitted to himself that Edward's support meant a great deal to him. "And I would ask ye and the others nae to call Maddy Lady Madeline. The title makes her vera uncomfortable right now."

"Did she say as much?"

"Of course nae. But I can tell," Fingal answered.

"Vera well. I will tell the others. Now go and check on yer bride before ye expire." Edward grinned, and Fingal nodded.

CHAPTER THIRTY-SEVEN

F ingal eased the door open to his chamber, not wanting to disturb Madeline. But when he noticed the bed was empty and a quick scan of the room showed him it was vacant, he threw the door open.

So we're back to the ice queen. Bluidy hell. Was it aught I did? Was it Cairstine and the others? Was it that the bluidy wind blew the wrong way? I thought we'd made progress, but she's walked away, just as she always does.

Fingal closed his eyes and forced himself to calm down. He knew he was being unreasonable, but he was sad, frustrated, and more than anything, hurt. He made his way to the chest at the foot of his empty bed and pulled out one of his plaids. He would find Madeline and remind her that she was the one who wanted him, or at least his plaid. He was relieved to find Davina in the passageway so he wouldn't have to search the other chambers for Madeline.

"Fingal, she's in the chamber above yers," Davina said without prevarication. "I heard what ma daughter and Lady Allyson said. I dinna blame Madeline for needing her space and for feeling like she shouldnae share a chamber with ye."

"What? Cairstine and Allyson share chambers with their husbands," Fingal argued.

"Aye. But nay one believes ye care for Madeline, and she kens that. I suspect she is much like Edward and I were when we first married. She doesnae ken what to make of her feelings toward ye and what she wants. That was Edward. But I also suspect she doesnae want to disappoint ye by reminding anyone of who she used to be. She wants to earn the clan's respect and yers. That was me."

"How do ye ken all of that from the few minutes ye must have spent with her?" Fingal wondered.

"Fingal, I watched her the entire time ye sat together at the table and her reaction when I showed her yer chamber," Davina pointed out. "The lass was a bundle of nerves sitting there. When ye took her hand, she didna ken what to make of it. My guess is she wanted to hold yers. Her body relaxed, but she was vera uncomfortable. Her eyes darted around to see who might be watching."

"I dinna ken what to do, Davina. One moment she's at ease with me and we seem to want the same thing. The next, she's retreated from me and locked me out."

"And that is why our conscience is a powerful force. In Madeline's case, it might be a wee misguided. But the fact that she has one and listens to it tells me she's a good woman, one who will be ready to take ma place eventually. I ken patience may nae be in abundance right now, but that's what she needs. Imagine if it were the other way around. Imagine if she was the one with experience, and ye werenae. How would ye feel if ye were her? She doesnae want to disappoint ye. But she doesnae want to err and lose sight of the woman she is now. At the same time, I doubt she understands why she feels for ye what she does."

Davina watched Fingal as he listened to her. He hadn't paid such rapt attention to one of her lessons since he was a child. She prayed he would take to heart what she said.

"Remember," Davina continued. "I was a widow before I married Edward. Ma first husband was a lout who beat me, but I'd still already been married. When I married Edward, I was ye, and Madeline was Edward. Think aboot how modest Edward is, even after nearly a score and half years being married. I ken ma husband loves me as much as I love him, but he'll never be like Eoin or Ewan. He doesnae fear for his soul anymore, but he'll never be as demonstrative as the twins are with their wives. At least nae in public. Madeline may be the same."

Davina shrugged and sighed at she looked at the young man she'd thought of as her son for most of his life. She knew she would never replace his mother, but she cared for him just as she did both her daughters. She wished she could lighten the weight that rested upon him, but he was a married man now. She couldn't solve his problems for him.

"I ken ye're right, Davina. It hurts, but I've always been aware of Madeline's reasons and fears. I may never feel those doubts, but I do understand them. Mayhap I should take yer advice and do more than that. Mayhap I should put maself in her place and really imagine how conflicted she must be." Fingal nodded and was about to step away when he looked back at Davina. "I need ye, and everyone else too, to understand that nay matter what, I amnae the Fingal who left here. I choose to put ma wife first, and there will be nay others. Ever." Fingal didn't wait for Davina's response, turning toward the stairs.

Fingal listened at Madeline's door, but he heard no movement, so he let himself into her chamber. He found her snoring softly, and he felt a moment of worry that she wasn't as hale as she claimed. He wanted to climb into bed beside her, but he knew it would drive her further away. She'd asked for the separate chamber because she needed space, and he wouldn't ignore that wish. He walked to the bed and watched her slumber before unfolding his plaid halfway and laying it over the bed beside her. He slipped from the chamber and went in search of Harry to tell him they would return to Braemar. He just wasn't certain of the timeline.

Madeline woke to something soft and fuzzy beneath her hand. As her eyes eased open, she focused upon the deep green and blue hunting plaid. She ran her hand over the fabric and smiled.

Fin. He checked on me. He remembered. Should I have told him ma plans for ma own chamber? I dinna want to hurt him, but I just canna disgrace maself by sharing with him. Cairstine and Allyson will think I'm just as I was. That all I think aboot is indulging ma wants. Then they'll surely tell everyone else.

Madeline breathed a resigned sigh as she forced herself from the bed. She glanced at the window and knew the evening meal was approaching. As much as she would have preferred taking a tray in her chamber and going straight back to sleep, she knew she needed to make an appearance, lest the others think her lazy and entitled.

She opted for the lavender gown with the purple trim, remembering Laurel's excitement when she first lent, then gave, it to Madeline. She wondered if Cairstine and Laurel communicated. She supposed not if Cairstine hadn't heard of her marriage to Fingal. She donned the gown and moved before the looking glass, trying to decide what to do with her hair. It now hung below her shoulders, so it was long enough for her to pin up. She did what she could to arrange her hair, but she kept it simple. It was a stark contrast to how she'd once worn her hair when her appearance was her highest priority. Before leaving, she folded Fingal's plaid into an arisaid. It drowned her, just as the first one had but knowing it was Fingal's somehow gave her courage she'd lacked only a moment ago.

Madeline spotted Fingal as she came down the stairs. She noticed he glanced toward the stairs, looking anxious, then beamed when he noticed her. It appeared to Madeline that he walked away from Ewan and Eoin without saying a word to excuse himself. He met her at the bottom of the stairs and held out his hand. Madeline held her breath as she placed her hand in his, her eyes darting around, taking in all the people staring at them. She wondered if Fingal was doing it for show to impress upon his people that he was attentive to his wife. When Fingal didn't release her hand, rather entwining their fingers, Madeline turned a startled gaze to him.

"Did ye sleep well, Maddy?" Fingal asked in a hushed tone.

"Ye checked on me," Madeline blurted before she felt the heat rise in her neck and cheeks.

"I did. I wanted to make sure ye had everything ye needed and that ye could rest. I worry aboot ye, Maddy. I dinna want ye to fall ill again. Ye canna be fully recovered yet. But ye've been through much since yer fevers."

"I'm well, Fin. I promise I will tell ye if aught is amiss. Ye dinna need to fash," Madeline assured him.

"I will anyway. Are ye hungry, wee one?" Fingal's expression was so filled with concern, that it touched deep within Madeline's heart. It tempted her to drag him abovestairs and prove to him how much she

321

cared for him. But she forced all the restraint she could muster. She nodded and moved to the table where she once more sat beside Fingal.

While he talked merrily with his family, Madeline kept to answering questions posed to her. She was receptive to the others' attempts to draw her into conversation, not wanting to be rude. But when talk moved away from her responding to inquiries, she remained quiet, her eyes down. She was relieved when the meal was over, but her heart sank as musicians tuned their instruments and couples moved to dance while servants cleared away the tables. She watched as Cairstine and Allyson joined their husbands, both couples beaming smiles at one another. Yet another round of tears threatened as Madeline considered how she could never have that with Fingal.

Fingal sensed Madeline's conflicted emotions as she watched his family and friends twirling amid the other dancing couples. He knew Madeline would never suggest dancing, and he knew she would only accept out of guilt if he asked. Rather than forcing the issue, he slipped his hand into hers beneath the tablecloth and gave it a supportive squeeze.

"What do ye wish to do tomorrow, Maddy? Would ye like a tour of the keep and bailey? Would ye like to visit the village? Do ye need more rest?"

"I think I should tour the keep and bailey," Madeline replied. Fingal caught the word "should" and suspected Madeline intended to determine where she should work first. He wanted her to regain her strength before she worried about helping around the keep. But he knew she would balk if he suggested such.

"Then I shall show ye around after we break our fast," Fingal offered.

"Ye? Dinna ye have business to catch up on or

322

need to be in the lists? I'm sure one of the ladies or mayhap a servant can show me around."

"Maddy, ma duties will call me back all too soon. I'd spend more time with ye while I can," Fingal explained. He'd realized that afternoon that not only would he need patience with Madeline. He would need to start virtually from scratch to win her trust back. He knew he had done nothing wrong, but a few words from Cairstine and Allyson had affirmed Madeline's worst fears.

"I would like that, Fin," Madeline admitted in a whisper.

"Maddy, the meal is over. Why dinna ye retire? I'll walk ye to yer chamber," Fingal suggested. But at her horrified expression, he wanted to bite his tongue.

"They'll all think we're—that ye want—" Madeline tried not to panic as she swept her eyes over the crowd. Very few people looked in their direction, and she chided herself for overreacting. But her inner voice told her that as soon as she and Fingal rose, people would watch them.

"We are married, Maddy. And newlyweds at that," Fingal pointed out, and Madeline nodded.

"I told ye the truth, Fin. I will never deny ye yer rights, and I promised to bear yer children. I just would wish for some discretion, please."

Fingal's heart broke. He was certain he could feel each tiny shard fall beneath his ribs. He'd hoped, prayed even, that despite the separate chambers and her nervousness, that she wouldn't abandon their progress altogether. But now she spoke as though nothing passed between them beside dutiful coupling, when Fingal had never been so moved by making love to someone as he was with Madeline. He'd even realized that he'd never before made love in the truest sense of the words because he'd loved no woman but Madeline. Second thoughts about wooing her flooded his mind. He feared she would feel forced rather than cherished. He resolved to give her space.

"Maddy, we have many years ahead of us. One night of ye recuperating willna harm us," Fingal said as he squeezed her hand. Fingal told himself the feeling that flashed in Madeline's eyes couldn't be disappointment. She offered him a gracious smile and nodded. "Perhaps ye would like to retire now?"

"I would. Thank ye, Fin. Nae just for ma plaid, but for everything. Ye told me I was a good wife. I should have told ye then what I'm telling ye now. Ye're a good husband, Fin. Mayhap ye exaggerated earlier, but I ken I was blessed that ye offered for me." Madeline brushed a brief kiss on Fingal's cheek before rising and leaving the dais.

CHAPTER THIRTY-EIGHT

M adeline's eyes snapped open in the dark, and she wanted to groan when she realized that she'd recovered enough that her body reverted to its old routine of waking for Matins. As she dressed, she reminded herself that it had been weeks since she'd been to any prayer service, let alone Mass. Besides Fingal's plaid, Madeline discovered that Davina left her a pair of boots. Many women moved about the Great Hall in bare feet, so she'd thought nothing of it when she joined the evening meal with no footwear. But finding the shoes relieved Madeline; she feared having to ask for a pair but knew she couldn't easily move about the bailey and village with bare feet. She slipped the boots on, then wrapped Fingal's plaid around her shoulders before making her way to the kirk.

The building was empty, but the sanctuary candle burned in its red sconce. It provided too little light to make anything visible away from the altar, but peacefulness swept over Madeline. She felt like she was home. The familiarity and predictability of the church services were a raft as she navigated turbulent seas. She slipped into the third pew and began reciting the Matins' prayers from memory.

By the time she'd finished, Madeline felt confident that she could face the day. She slipped back into her chamber and returned to bed, only to have her eyes spring open once more a few hours later. She slipped into the chapel for Lauds and Prime, relieved to find Edward there for both morning services. He nodded at her and returned to his prayers. It was all Madeline needed to feel welcome. She appreciated that he kept to himself even when they both finished praying.

Opting for the gray gown once more, Madeline joined the others when they broke their fast. While her appetite had returned tenfold while she was recovering from her injuries, Madeline discovered that she once more could eat very little at each meal. The meager meals she'd eaten at the priory had shrunk her appetite and her stomach. She declined Fingal's offer for more food, whispering her reasoning lest he think she was being awkward or ungrateful.

She shied away from holding his hand as he offered her the tour, but she was happy to wrap her arm around his and rest her hand on his forearm. She noted the areas of the gardens that needed more attention, and she realized the laundresses were short-handed. She'd made her bed that morning and ran her used wash linen over all the surfaces. She'd folded Fingal's plaid and left it at the foot of her bed, since the weather was too warm for the additional layers. She made certain she explained why she hadn't worn it because she feared he would think she didn't appreciate the gift. Throughout the day, she worked at remaining observant, quiet, and mindful of being humble.

Fingal wanted to scream. Over and over and over. When Madeline arrived at the morning meal in the gown she'd told him reminded her of his eyes, he'd wanted to drag her into a dark passageway and ravage her. She looked beautiful in the soft colors, and the cut of her gown complimented her figure. The private sentiment she'd shared about why she favored it also made him want to drag her into private, but to cover her in gentle kisses and caresses.

She didn't completely reject his intention to hold her hand by entwining their arms rather than their fingers. She asked astute questions and was warm to all those she met, but she had returned to being reserved and closed off from him. He noticed she looked toward the kirk twice, and he suspected she wanted to attend Sext at midday and None during midafternoon. He'd released her arm both times, but she shook her head and offered him a weak smile. Sympathy prompted him to suggest she retire to her chamber for some privacy before the evening meal. She'd asked him if he meant for her to pray, and he hadn't lied. It was the brightest smile he'd seen since they arrived at Freuchie. It stung that she was more eager to be alone with her thoughts than to be with him.

Madeline rose from kneeling beside her bed when someone rapped softly on her door. She didn't expect to see Fingal when she opened it. She stared at him blankly for a moment before inviting him in. She noticed he carried a sack, but she couldn't guess what was inside.

"Maddy, I brought ye a couple things. It was all I could arrange so far," Fingal explained. He wondered if he should open the sack and make it appear practical, or if he should hand her the sack and make it appear as the gift he intended. He opted for the latter and held his breath. When Madeline reached into the sack, her brow furrowed before her eyes widened. She withdrew a pair of brand-new leather boots. She ran her hands over them and looked at them from every angle. She was certain they were exactly her size.

"How did ye get them so quickly?" Madeline asked in awe.

"I went into the village after ye came inside," Fingal shrugged. "I visited the cobbler, and he was already in the middle of cutting a pair of shoes."

"Those must be intended for someone else, Fin. I canna take someone else's shoes!" Madeline looked horrified at first, then guilty, but Fingal saw the longing in her eyes as she attempted to hand them back.

"Nay. He was cutting the leather large and trimmed it to fit."

"How did ye ken ma size? They look like they'll fit perfectly," Madeline wondered aloud.

Fingal shrugged again. "I helped ye enough days to ken yer feet are aboot the length of ma hand." Madeline's cheeks heated as she knew Fingal referred to all the days he'd bathed her. "There's one more item in the sack."

Madeline shook the bag before reaching into it. Once more her eyes widened before she retrieved the item. She withdrew and let dangle a wooden cross that hung from a purple ribbon. She wrapped her hands around it and pressed it against her heart.

"I ken the ribbon isnae vera practical. Ye can re-place it—" Fingal's breath left him in an oomph when Madeline dropped her boots and launched herself into his arms. He reveled in the feeling of Madeline being in his arms once more, and she made no move to pull away. It wasn't a perfunctory hug merely to show her thanks. She clung to him just as he clung to her. Her head rested on his chest, and Fingal was certain he didn't imagine her sigh of contentment. But soon it wasn't enough for either of them.

Madeline cupped Fingal's cheek and turned his head toward hers as she lifted it from his shoulder. Their mouths came together in a searing kiss. Their hands roamed over one another as they reacquainted themselves, as though they'd been apart for years rather than days.

Madeline dropped the cross, unaware of anything but the feel of Fingal pressed against her. When Fingal's hands slid down to grasp her backside, she moaned with relief, then frustration. Fingal used it as a signal that she wanted more, and she didn't resist as he drew her skirt up her legs until his hands could squeeze bare skin. Madeline mimicked him, drawing Fingal's plaid high enough to run her hands over buttocks she was certain was carved from stone.

"Maddy, please," Fingal begged. It was Madeline who reached between them and pulled at the laces to her kirtle. Neither said another word as they shed their clothes. Fingal lifted Madeline until she could wrap her legs around his waist. He walked them to the chair that sat before the fireplace. The only blaze in the room was the passion between them as Fingal sat and guided Madeline to move over him. He kissed her until she moaned for more. They whispered one another's names as their need intensified, even though they'd joined their bodies. Neither wanted the moment to end, but each strove to experience the release that they only found together. Fingal dipped his head and brought Madeline's breast to his mouth, suckling her. He watched as her head fell back and her fingers bit into his shoulders. They clung to one another as their release swept over them, perfectly timed so they were one in body and soul.

Fingal struggled to catch his breath as he kissed Madeline's shoulder and neck as she rested her forehead in the crook of his neck, gasping from their exertion. When their breathing slowed, their kisses were tender and languid after the frenzy of their lovemaking. Fingal wanted nothing more than to climb into bed beside Madeline and hold her as he'd ached to do the night before. He wanted to send for a tray so they would hide away for the evening. He lifted Madeline and walked toward the bed, but he knew the moment she spied her discarded cross on the ground because her legs went lax and slid from his waist. He released her when she pulled away. She picked up the cross and stared at it for a long moment before looking at Fingal.

"Thank ye for ma gifts. They were thoughtful," Madeline whispered as she pulled the ribbon over her head, settling the cross between her breasts. The contradiction wasn't lost on Fingal. "I will cherish this, Fingal. Please tell me who carved it so I might thank them, too."

"A mon did it in the village," Fingal responded vaguely. He knew the moment was over as Madeline reached for her chemise. She surprised him when she pressed a soft kiss to his cheek.

"I meant what I said earlier, Fin. Ye're a good husband. I ken I'm nae an easy wife to have, but I'm certain the Mother Abbess was right. Ma calling wasna to be a nun. I just need to adjust to being part of a clan again. But I ken I'm happier with ye than I would have been in a lifetime at Inchcailleoch."

Fingal was unprepared for Madeline's confession. He wrapped his arm around her middle and eased her closer without pressing their bodies together. He saw none of the shame and guilt he'd expected, but he knew they would be there once she was alone. She'd already retreated from him.

"I'll give everything ye need and always strive to give aught that ye want, Maddy." Fingal stopped himself before he admitted that he loved her. With a kiss to her forehead, Fingal left Madeline alone. She sat on the end of her bed, more conflicted than ever.

CHAPTER THIRTY-NINE

Fingal came awake to the sound of someone pounding on his door. He reached for his sword and pulled his plaid around his waist as he called for the person to enter. When a guardsman walked in with no sword drawn, Fingal looked at the man with confusion. He'd expected to be told there was a raid.

"Fingal, ye're wife is out again," the guard announced. Fingal bristled when the comment sounded like the man referred to Madeline as an animal that escaped its pen.

"What do ye mean?" Fingal scowled.

"She's traipsing aboot the bailey just as she did last night," the man explained.

"Where's she going?" Fingal knew the answer, but he wanted the guard to admit it out loud.

"The kirk."

"Ye woke me because ma wife went to church?" Fingal snorted and turned back to his bed. "Dinna pound on ma door again unless someone is dying."

"But Fingal—"

"Nay. Ma wife is there to pray the Matins service. She's prayed the Liturgy of Hours for years. Nay different from the laird, except she doesnae mind waking in the middle of the night. Go back to yer post." Fingal dismissed the guard with barely a glance over his shoulder. When his door closed, Fingal moved to the window embrasure where he stood until Madeline left the chapel and crossed the bailey. He couldn't see her enter the keep, but he went to his door and opened it a crack. He saw the flickering candlelight as Madeline made her way back to her chamber.

And so began their life at Freuchie for the next fortnight. Madeline took each meal alongside Fingal, quiet but polite. While he went to the lists or met with Edward, Madeline found things to do around the keep. He knew she spent most of her time in the gardens and the orchard. After he gave her a tour of the village, she accompanied Davina to visit the elderly and those in need.

Fingal had prayed that once Cairstine and Allyson left that Madeline would be more at ease. After their initial snide comments when Madeline arrived, the two women kept away from Madeline. They were never rude again, but neither were they inviting. Fingal deduced that neither Cairstine and Allyson nor Madeline felt comfortable initiating time together, so the women remained distant. Fingal wished he could intervene, but both Edward and Davina warned him not to. He wanted Madeline to make friends, but she was too quiet for anyone to approach her.

He knew she attended Matins, Lauds, and Prime every day, but he grew worried that she'd given up on them as a couple and returned to wanting to be a nun when she returned to the kirk for Terce, Sext, and None. Davina tried to reassure him that she was just filling her day when she didn't have enough duties to keep her occupied.

When Edward asked how things were in private, Fingal admitted that things had cooled between them. He didn't attempt to visit Madeline every night, but when he did, she was more inhibited than she had been the few times they'd been together since their wedding night. She never turned him away; her desire for him always won out. She was hesitant whenever he arrived at her door, but by the time their bodies were one, she was as needy as he was. Edward offered him a sympathetic smile and reminded him that it had only been a moon since they married. She'd spent five years at the convent. They were hardly equivalent.

He drew the line though when he stumbled upon her working alongside the laundresses, stirring the boiling cauldron with the large paddle. He caught her handling the lye soap and nearly threw her over his shoulder. He struggled to remain polite, but he pulled her away from the other women and practically dragged her to his chamber. It was the first argument they'd had in weeks, and Fingal said more than he should have, just to seek the sparks fly from Madeline's eyes. She promised that she wouldn't wash the clothes and linens anymore, but the next day he found her folding them. When he stood before her with his arms crossed, she offered him the serene smile he recognized hid her emotions. She pointed to the cauldron, then to the drying lines behind her, and reminded him that she'd promised not to work with the soap.

It surprised him to learn that she loved to ride. She reminded him that she'd been unaccustomed to being in the saddle for so many hours, and that's what caused her injuries, not being an inexperienced rider. The only time he saw her spirit return to her eyes was when they were galloping through the meadows and along the stream. Her hair would come loose, and her visage was a picture of beauty and happiness. If they hadn't other responsibilities, and if he didn't worry about overtaxing her, he would have kept her away from the keep completely.

But never far from his mind was the need to deal with Dougal and Finneas. He never discussed the matter with Madeline, but he made plans with Edward and Harry. By the time the first fortnight ended, Fingal was confident that Madeline was settled well enough for him to leave. He also knew that his efforts to woo her were in vain. She was no more comfortable with him in public than she had been when they arrived, and she was hesitant with him when they were alone. He decided that a break from one another would do them both some good.

Madeline never imagined her emotions could vacillate so much in a day. She woke each morning wishing Fingal was lying next to her, regretful when he left her chamber and when he did not come. She grew eager to see him as she dressed, then hesitant when they sat together at the dais. She knew no one paid overt attention to them, but she'd overheard servants talking about what they'd heard while Cairstine and Allyson were still in residence. Everyone knew she'd been banished from court, then turned out of the convent.

The women accepted her help around the keep and in the bailey, but none warmed to her. She was too embarrassed to make any attempts to be friendly. Instead, she struggled to bite back the tears every day as she felt lonelier than she ever had before, despite the masses of people who surrounded her.

She sought solace in prayer, but her mind always drifted to one topic: Fingal. On the days after he came to her chamber, guilt consumed her for being so lusty and selfish for wanting his attention. When he didn't visit, she blamed herself for pushing him away. She was certain he was occupying his time elsewhere, since he didn't try to convince her to let him join her nightly. She feared she wasn't doing enough around the keep to earn respect. But when Fingal smiled at her or took her hand, it was as though the heavens opened and the sun shone for the first time.

The only genuinely enjoyable times were when they escaped the keep together and went riding. When the horses needed rest, they'd walk along the stream and talk about their childhoods. They discovered they had many similar interests, and they even learned their birthdays were only a week apart, though Madeline was a few years younger.

If men didn't accompany them each time they left the keep, Madeline might have let her guard down long enough to share more intimate moments with Fingal, but she was too nervous with warriors tasked to watch them nearby. Only when Nichol, Simon, Tommy, and Harry were the men who accompanied them did she feel comfortable holding his hand. Then she would lean against Fin when he wrapped his arm around her shoulders. She'd sigh when he kissed her crown, and she even welcomed brief, but passionate, kisses. Madeline's emotions shifted from the highest of highs to the lowest of lows during the day. It exhausted her, but despite falling into bed each night wishing for slumber, her mind rarely rested. She prayed for a sense of peace that never came.

CHAPTER FORTY

"**A**re ye at least going to tell her before ye ride out? She is yer wife."

Madeline heard Harry's voice as she entered the stables. She'd seen the men enter, and she'd hoped to ask Fingal if they could go for a ride before it grew too late. She knew that she should make her presence known, but she feared Fingal would keep from her whatever they were discussing. It didn't sound as though he intended to share anything with her.

"Of course, I will. But I'll wait until the eve before," Fingal responded.

"Why? So ye dinna have to feel guilty for abandoning her?" Harry demanded.

"Aye," Fingal snapped. "Ye think I dinna see how miserable she is? Ye think I dinna see how much she wishes she hadnae married me? Ye think I dinna ken she wishes she'd stayed at Inchcailleoch? I'm nae as blind as ye believe."

"Then tell her how ye feel. Stop avoiding it," Harry pressed. "If ye lay dying on the battlefield, do ye really want yer last thoughts to be regrets for nae telling the lass how ye feel? Or would ye rather die kenning she'll know even if ye dinna return to show her?"

"Is that what ye would do?" Fingal sneered. "Ye're still in love with ma wife. Touch her once, and I will kill ye, Harry."

"I'll tell what I did the last time ye accused me of that. At least someone does." Harry spun away but stumbled when he came face to face with a stunned Madeline. "Lady Madeline."

Fingal spun around when he heard his wife's name. By her pallor, he feared she would collapse. He pushed past Harry and went to Madeline, pulling her into his arms. She clung to him, just as she had when he found her outside the gates at Braemar. He tried to pull back to look at her, but she wouldn't loosen her hold.

"Where're ye going?" She mumbled against his chest.

"Things are still unresolved with the Farquharsons and the highwaymen. As long as Dougal and Finneas are alive, ye arenae safe," Fingal explained.

As though the hands of death reached into Madeline and tried to pull her from Fingal, a sense of doom engulfed her. She'd never had such an overpowering sense of fear. She'd believed that she could never be more frightened than she was while she was in Dougal and Finneas's clutches. But a voice bellowed in her head that if Fingal rode out, he would never ride back. She wasn't sure if it was God or the Devil, but she reasoned that some invisible but powerful force wanted to warn her. She decided she would pray later to discern whether God warned her with compassion or if it was the Devil with malice. She promised to say the rosary a dozen times for God to forgive her for her sins if it would keep Fingal safe.

"Dinna do this, Fin. I beg ye. I canna give ye a sound reason, but I can feel it in every bit of ma body that ye arenae coming back. Please. Dinna do this. Please." Madeline begged. Fingal eased Madeline away from him, expecting to find hysteria in her expression. But she was somber as she shook her head.

"Madeline, ye've always kenned I would ride out, either on patrol or to fight. Ye couldnae nae know when yer own brother is a warrior and a laird."

"There a bluidy big difference between kenning yer husband is riding out to defend yer people and kenning yer husband is riding to his death because it's yer fault." Madeline pulled away and sprinted across the bailey, Fingal hot on her heels. Her words stunned him, but not so much that he didn't know to chase after her.

"Madeline!" Fingal called as his wife raced up the servant's stairs, focused on getting to her chamber. Fingal reached her as she turned the corner on the second-floor landing and took the first two steps toward the floor with her chamber. He wrapped his arm around her waist and hauled her backward. "Madeline, stop. That isnae the way I wanted ye to learn of this."

"Nay. Ye didna want to tell me at all. Ye would have left me in ma bed and bid me a fare-thee-well, then ridden out before I was awake," Madeline hissed.

"I didna want to worry ye," Fingal explained lamely.

"Of course I'm going to worry. Ye're ma husband. I—I—Damn ye, Fingal. Ye didna tell me because ye were going to do what ye wanted regardless of how I feel. Ye didna tell me because this is more aboot yer pride than it is ma safety. Dinna fash, Fingal. I willna be any more inconvenient to ye than I already am."

"Madeline, I never said ye're inconvenient to me. Just the opposite. I'm inconvenient to ye. I ken ye're miserable here, and ye wish ye'd never married me. Dinna ye fash, Madeline. I willna impose upon ye further," Fingal barked.

"What the hell does that mean?" Madeline snapped.

"It means ye wish ye'd become a nun, and I'm standing in yer way. If ye wish to retire to an abbey rather than be married to me, then I will take ye where ye want. But I will be clear aboot this. I will do everything I must to keep ye safe and to make sure Dougal, Finneas, and their band of highwaymen are nae long for this world."

"Ye're setting me aside?" Madeline's legs gave out from shock, and she crumpled to the stairs.

"What? I never said that," Fingal argued. Madeline nodded and rose but held a hand up when Fingal made to follow her up the stairs. She left him standing alone, wondering once more how their conversation fell apart so abruptly. He hadn't told her he was going because he didn't want to face leaving her. Telling her would be the last step in solidifying his plan, and until he'd told her, it had felt more like just an idea.

He knew part of his motivation was pride. She hadn't been wrong about that because he couldn't let any clan believe that the Grants were weak. But it was as much about protecting her as his wife as it was about securing his clan. One way or another, he had to take a stand as the future laird of Clan Grant. Fingal resigned himself to leaving Madeline alone that night, but he was leaving in two days. He would not, could not ride out without resolving things one way or another.

Madeline didn't bother with a pew as she moved through the kirk for Matins. She kneeled on the steps before the altar, hoping that by being closer to the embodiments of Christ, that her voice would be louder to God. She recited the prayers, but didn't leave when she was finished. She remained on her knees despite how the stone bit into them. She reminded herself that it wasn't that long ago that she spent most of her day in prayer on bended knee.

Heavenly Father, please make Fingal see sense. I ken he believes he must avenge me, and I ken he doesnae want anyone to think the Grants are weak. But nay one in their right mind could think the Grants are weak. It was a band of lawless men who were daft enough to take on the Grants. Please Father, dinna let him go. I canna figure out if it was Ye or the Devil, but I ken he willna come back. I canna lose him. I love him, Lord. I'm too much of a coward to tell him. And I'm ashamed of that as much as I'm ashamed of ma sins of lust and gluttony. I dinna want to go through life without him, even if I canna be as much as he hoped. I certainly dinna want him to set me aside. But Lord, if going back to a convent is Yer wish after all, I will do that if it means Fingal willna come to any harm. If I'm nae his wife anymore, then he has nay reason to fight. Guide me, ma shepherd, for I am but a lost sheep.

Madeline clasped her hands throughout her prayers until her fingers ached, but she welcomed the pain as penance for what she believed was her selfishness and other venial sins. She remained with her head bowed through the night. She decided she would remain in meditation until Prime ended, and she would have to appear in the Great Hall to break her fast.

CHAPTER FORTY-ONE

F ingal sat in the window embrasure, just as he had every night since the guard informed him that Madeline snuck out to the chapel. He watched her each night, worried that some unseen danger would befall her and he wouldn't be by her side. As the minutes drew into an hour, Fingal paced before the window, worrying that something was amiss. He reasoned that she just wished for more time to pray, but when she didn't appear after two hours, he couldn't wait any longer. He donned a leine and wrapped his plaid around his waist, not bothering to pleat it or to put on shoes.

He waved away the guard who approached him as he crossed the bailey before he pushed open the door. It was pitch black inside the kirk except for two burning candles. One was the sanctuary lamp over the alter, and the other was the dwindling candle beside Madeline. He moved silently down the aisle until he was within arms' reach, but Madeline didn't turn. She was folded over as she kneeled, and he feared she was ill. He tried to convince himself that maybe she'd fallen asleep. He kneeled beside her on the step. When she turned her head toward him, he brushed his hand over her shoulder and back.

"Ye scared me, being in here so long," Fingal confessed in whisper.

"How did ye even ken?"

Fingal sighed as he looked at the crucifix. "A guard told me the second night ye came for Matins. Ever since then, I've watched ye come and go to be sure ye are safe. I trust ma clan, but I'm nae fool enough to think a mon wouldnae try to take advantage of ye. I wait until I see ye go up the stairs and then listen for yer tread above me. When I hear the bed creak, I ken ye're safe."

"Every night?" Madeline asked in disbelief.

"Aye. Even after I leave yer chamber." Fingal understood the implication to her question. "Are ye all right, Maddy? Is aught wrong? Can ye nae make it back to yer chamber?"

"There is naught wrong with me, Fin. I just decided to pray through Prime," Madeline explained.

"Ye miss yer life at the priory," Fingal realized with resignation.

"Some of it, aye. But most of it, nay." Madeline pressed her lips together to keep from crying until she could speak again. "Please dinna send me away. I ken I'm nae the wife ye wanted, but I dinna want to stop being yer wife." Madeline turned her head to look up at the crucifix. No light filtered through the windows. Nothing illuminated the cross as it had been that day in the priory. Nothing gave Madeline a clear path to follow.

"I dinna want to set ye aside. But I dinna want to keep ye from the life ye want."

"I dinna want to be a nun, Fingal. I just told ye that," Madeline shook her head. "I'm nae what ye wanted."

"Maddy, bluidy hell," Fingal glanced back at the crucifix and begrudgingly made the sign of the cross.

"What I wanted, or thought I wanted, is nay longer the same. I thought I wanted the wife ye are now, but it's torture. I want the wife I see when we're alone, the one ye only let me catch glances of."

"Ye want me to be a sinner." Madeline shook her head. "Ye'll regret that once ye're laird. Yer people ken aboot me, Fingal. They ken ma past. I will be an even greater embarrassment to ye than I already am."

Fingal stared at her in disbelief. He was at a loss for words, so he could only stare at her and blink. Finally, he inhaled deeply and shook his head. "I have never, nae even for a moment since ye agreed to marry me, been embarrassed that ye're ma wife. I'm proud to be yer husband. I dinna ken a more courageous woman. Both to keep to yer convictions when ye're tested and to adapt to whatever situation ye're in. Ye learned to live at court, and despite it being for the worse, ye survived there for five years. Ye didna ask to go to Inchcailleoch, but ye accepted the path yer life took and ye became a giving member of yer community. Ye braved court again, never showing weakness despite the stares and whispers. Ye've bluidy well been the most forgiving person I ken to have married me and nae throttled me yet. Yer courage and fortitude got ye through the dangers ye faced when I failed to protect ye."

Fingal took Madeline's hands and eased her off her knees before leading her to sit in a pew beside him. In the dark, he brought each of her hands to his lips, kissing the backs, then the palms. He ran his hand up her arms until he could cup her jaw. He wished he could see her eyes as he finally confessed his secrets.

"Madeline, I love ye. I dinna want ye to be aught that ye canna. But I need ye to ken ye arenae the failure ye fear. We're all sinners. But yer virtues far outweigh yer sins. I dinna care if ye never grow comfortable being intimate with me. I will always love ye, Maddy."

"Fin," Madeline whimpered as she felt for his face in the dark. "I love ye. I dinna want to be anywhere but where ye are. I dinna ken how ye can love me when I've made yer life worse. I dinna blame ye for only seeking ma company to do yer duty. I canna blame ye for turning elsewhere. But please dinna turn me out."

Fingal reminded himself that he shouldn't be shocked when Madeline said the least predictable things. "What do ye mean, turning elsewhere?" He knew exactly what she meant.

"Ye are a mon who wants a woman who enjoys the same intimacy that ye do."

Fingal waited for her to say more, but nothing else was forthcoming. "Maddy, I told ye I would never stray. I wasna making false promises. I never have. I lay in ma bed, lonely and pining for ye. I confess to ye and to God ma sin, but I think of ye each night to ease the ache of nae being with ye. I am nae the mon ye met. I dinna want a wife of convenience, nae when I love her."

"I just assumed…" Madeline trailed off.

"Clearly. Maddy, I dinna ken how things will be between us in the future. But I would ask ye to share ma chamber just so I might be able to sleep next to ye. I crave the feel of ye in ma arms more than I do the feel of being inside ye."

"Fin!" Madeline gasped. But she inched forward until she leaned her head against his chest. She closed her eyes as exhaustion washed over her. She tried, unsuccessfully, to stifle her yawn. "I havenae slept well since Abergeldie. Can we go to bed now?"

"Aye, Maddy. Let us get some sleep." Fingal helped Madeline to her feet before collecting the candle that was smoldering. Madeline slipped her hand into Fingal's before they left the chapel.

CHAPTER FORTY-TWO

M adeline knew she was dreaming, but never had her sleeping thoughts been so vivid. She could hear children's voices somewhere ahead of her in the tall meadow grass. She looked around at the field of heather to her right, then at the massive castle to her left. Her semiconscious mind didn't recognize the castle, but somehow, she knew it was her home. She continued to walk toward the voices, and as she drew closer, she could hear two girls and a boy. At first, she assumed they were her nieces and nephew. But a tawny-haired little boy popped up from among the stalks of yellow autumn grass and waved to her.

"Mama! Come see what we've made," the little boy chirped. Madeline joined the children who sat together in a circle, each making a flower crown.

"Are those for yer bonnie mama?" Fingal's deep voice came from behind her. She didn't startle when his arms slipped around her waist. Instead, she leaned into his embrace. Even though it was a dream, she could feel his soft lips and the rasp of his beard against her neck. She didn't recoil or rebel against his affection. Rather, she turned her head to receive his kiss.

"Disgusting," a little girl's voice crowed. "Mama, Da, are ye going to be kissing again? Werenae ye doing that this morn, and that's why ye said we had to wait to go for our walk?"

Madeline stared down at the little girl, her cheeks warming. She squealed when Fingal pinched her backside. "Yer mama gives the best kisses in all the land," Fingal explained. "I canna keep from stealing them whenever I can."

"Mama, can ye help me?" the youngest child said. Madeline moved to sit down, and she realized that her belly was swollen. She rubbed her hand over her pregnant middle as Fingal eased her to the ground. He lay on his side behind her, his hand resting on her hip as Madeline tied off the flower crown and handed it back to the little girl.

"Da! Ye promised to teach me how to slay the dragon," the little boy insisted before diving at Fingal, who rolled onto his back before tossing the boy into the air. Madeline giggled as the boy squealed. The two little girls abandoned their handiwork to climb on and over Fingal. She watched her imaginary family with Fingal; she knew she was dreaming, but it felt so real. When the children tired of playing and began yawning, Fingal helped Madeline to her feet, but didn't release her.

"Tommy and Harry will take ye back," Fingal told the children. "Yer mama is moving a little slower today."

Madeline made to argue as she glanced at the children walking between the two enormous Grant warriors. Fingal's arm wrapped around her waist and cupped her backside as his other hand rubbed her belly. When Fingal dipped his head for a kiss, Madeline raised her mouth to his. She ran her hand over his chest and shoulder until she reached his hair. She gave it a playful tug as she deepened their kiss.

"I would see ye, wife," Fingal whispered.

"Are ye sure nay one will catch us this time?" Madeline chuckled as Fingal began pulling at the laces to her kirtle. He helped her back down to the spot where the grass was flattened. When Fingal eased her skirts up to her waist and then lifted her kirtle over her head, Madeline didn't shy away from his perusal. "Ye are overdressed for the occasion, husband."

Fingal wasted no time undressing and spreading out his plaid. They laid side by side as their hands explored one another with the expertise that came from knowing one another for years. When Fingal pressed Madeline onto her back, she pulled him to follow her, refusing to break the kiss they shared. Madeline heard herself moan in her dream as Fingal's fingers slipped along her seam before dipping into her entrance. When Madeline's hand wrapped around Fingal's cock, he groaned and lowered his head to her breasts. He nipped and suckled as one hand massaged her breast and the other worked her sheath. Madeline stroked him, brushing her thumb over the head of his cock.

Madeline felt no shock when Fingal slid down her body and rested his shoulders between her thighs. She leaned on her elbows to see over her belly as she marveled at the sensations Fingal created as his tongue lapped her seam. His thumb found her nub and rubbed slow circles as his tongue dipped within her. One of her hands came to rest on his shoulder, but as his ministrations became more insistent, her hand cupped the back of his head and pressed his mouth to her channel. She felt no guilt or shame. Instead her body hummed with desire, then satisfaction, as she came apart before him.

"Fin, dinna make me wait. I need ye," Madeline moaned. She rolled to straddle Fingal as he guided his cock into her. As she moved above her husband, she threw her head back, moaning again in pure pleasure. Never did doubt, regret, or guilt enter her mind as she enjoyed the pleasure of joining her body with Fingal's.

Despite it being a dream, Madeline knew what she shared with Fingal was natural. She realized that, in her dreamworld, she and Fingal coupled often and for pleasure rather than duty. In her dream Madeline felt a tightening in her core before a wave of tingling sensations washed over her, and she cried out her release a second time. She sagged forward once Fingal spent, his arms creating the protective cocoon she instinctively knew she wanted. His fingers grazed over her back as they laid together under the warm summer sun.

"I love ye, Madeline Grant," Fingal's whispered in her ear.

"And I love ye, Fingal Grant," Madeline replied as she closed her eyes and sighed with bliss.

Madeline stirred as she woke from her dream. She felt warm and cozy as she recognized where she was. Fingal lay at her back, with his arm draped over her waist. The dream had felt so real that, as she came awake, she wondered for a moment if it had been a memory rather than her imagination. The memory of her conversation with the Mother Abbess floated back to her. She could hear the older woman's voice as she told Madeline the story of how she became a nun. "We'd fallen deeply in love, and neither of us regretted the passion we shared."

Madeline considered what the prioress told her about her life before arriving at the convent. She realized nowhere in the story had the nun spoken of sin or guilt for falling in love with Dugan Sinclair. She cast no judgment on her actions when she made it clear that she'd coupled with the man, even carried his child out of wedlock. Madeline realized that the young couple had come together for pleasure, not duty. The Mother Abbess was a much older woman, and the Lord had never struck her down for what she'd done in her youth.

The prioress had told Madeline twice in that conversation that it was the Lord's will that she be a wife and a mother, not a nun. As Madeline considered what remained unsaid while the nun spoke of her past, Madeline realized that the abbess never thought of her relationship with Dugan as sinful fornication. And as she recalled the prioress telling her that she hadn't been called to be a nun, Madeline realized that she was the only one clinging to the belief that she should live like one. Madeline's memory shifted to when she prepared to leave the priory. Mother Abbess had embraced her and whispered, "this is what the Lord intended for you, my child. He wishes you to find happiness in the secular world with a husband and bairns. Follow His will and open your heart."

As those words echoed in her ears, something shifted in Madeline's mind and her chest. Much like she'd unexpectedly accepted her life at the convent after seeing the glowing cross, a sense of acceptance swept over her as she woke in Fingal's arms. She'd fought against her feelings for weeks, making herself and Fingal miserable. Madeline realized as she laid beside her husband, she accepted her new life as his wife just as much as she accepted the feel of his touch. Feeling him hold her no longer scared her.

They'd returned to Fingal's chamber when they left the kirk. Once in bed, Fingal wrapped his arms around Madeline as she lay against his side. Neither spoke, and neither sought to make love. It was only a matter of moments before they were both asleep. Awake now, it didn't feel like a sin to Madeline to wish to remain exactly where she was. The dream she'd had filled her with peace, not remorse. Just as she'd made a choice that day in the Inchcailleoch Priory chapel when she accepted her unexpected path to become a nun, she chose to accept the path that led her to Fingal.

Madeline sighed as she opened her eyes and found Fingal looking down at her. In the soft early morning light, Madeline smiled at him as she reached up to place her hand against his cheek.

"Ye were dreaming," Fingal whispered.

"I ken, and it was the most wonderful dream I've ever had." Madeline stroked his cheek as she gazed up at him. "Ye told me I dinna need to ask ye to kiss me, but I am now. Fin, will ye please kiss me?"

Fingal didn't hesitate, fearing she would retract her request. Neither hurried once Fingal knew Madeline wouldn't pull away. Fingal drew the hand that caressed his cheek down to cover his heart, wrapping his arms around hers. Madeline's body went lax, the last tether to her life at the priory frayed and snapped. She held no reservations about her salvation or fears of returning to the way she'd once been. She felt free.

"Maddy," Fingal murmured as their foreheads rested together. "I dinna expect ye to couple with me just because ye're in ma bed."

"I didna ask for the kiss because I thought ye wanted to couple. I told ye I had a dream, Fin." Madeline's response confused Fingal. "I saw us with three children, and I was carrying our fourth. We had two lasses and a lad. At first, I thought they were Maude and Kieran's, but they called us Mama and Da. Fin, it was our family, and we were happy together. We—ye and I—when we—it wasna like our wedding night, or the other nights when I was so hesitant. It had naught to do with duty, and since ma belly was vera swollen in ma dream, we werenae trying to conceive." Madeline grinned sheepishly.

Fingal listened with rapt attention as Madeline described her dream. His mouth softened as she implied that they'd coupled in her dream, and they'd done it for pleasure. Madeline's hand fisted his leine over his heart before she dropped a kiss on his chest.

"I remembered something Mother Abbess told me aboot her past, aboot why she'd come to the priory. She'd thought she was going to be a wife and mother to a mon she loved, but it wasna to be. But she told me that ma calling was to be just that, a wife and a mother. Nay one is making me hang on to ma past, ma belief that I would be a nun, but me.

"Her words made me think of Maude and Kieran. I havenae seen them in years, but I can imagine how they are together. I can imagine how many of the ladies I used to ken are now that they're married. I've seen Cairstine and Allyson, and I've seen yer cousin. God hasnae struck any of them dead for enjoying themselves when they're with their husbands. And I dinna think they're fearing for their souls each time they couple. Fin, I kissed ye because I wanted naught more than to do so. I kissed ye nae because I expected more afterward. I kissed ye just because..."

Madeline stretched to kiss Fingal again. This time passion replaced tenderness. Madeline had felt Fingal's rod harden during their last kiss, and now she could feel it pulsing against her hip. His hand slipped beneath her tunic to find the silky skin hidden by the yards of material. He kneaded the soft flesh of her backside, but he tensed, ready for her to reject him. Rather than push him away, her hand slid down to press his more firmly against her.

"Never again will I reject ye, Fin. I'm done fighting for something that was never there. During ma dream, I realized that God would rather a husband and wife love one another than hate each other. Between a husband and wife, passion isnae a vice. It's a way to show one another that they're loved. Fingal, I love ye. I have since nearly the beginning, even when ye were rather difficult," Madeline grinned. "I dinna want a life lived in fear. Irrational fear."

"I feared I'd never hear ye say ye shared the depth of ma feelings. When I grew impatient or felt rejected, I reminded maself that we havenae kenned one another that long. Nae compared to the lives we led before we met one another. Ye've taught me to have patience where I had none. Ye've taught me a great many things that I hope make me a better mon and will one day make me a good laird. I dinna think I would be if it wasna for ye."

"Fin, can we agree to a few things?" Madeline asked as she pushed up on her elbow to see Fingal's face. "Neither of us wants to cling to the way we were before we met each other. We shouldnae hide how we feel. And this is our chamber nae yers."

Fingal rolled Madeline over as he gathered the skirts of her tunic and slid his hand beneath. "I agree to yer terms and ask for one more." Fingal took a deep breath, praying he hadn't overestimated how much Madeline had come around. "Can we agree to nae come to bed wearing a stitch of clothing?"

Madeline looked at Fingal for a long moment before grinning. She pushed him aside and pulled her tunic over her head, tossing it to the floor. Fingal followed suit as Madeline opened her arms to him. He promised her that the next time would be slower. Madeline guided his length into her channel, agreeing that they wouldn't rush next time, or the one after that. But she was just as impatient as he was to make love.

They remained in their chamber throughout the

next two days and nights, opening the door only for food trays and for Madeline's belongings to be moved. Madeline felt no hesitation when servants arrived at their door, aware that everyone in the keep knew what they were doing. She was too happy being with Fingal to care.

CHAPTER FORTY-THREE

Reality crept back in their third morning together in their shared chamber. They'd studiously avoided the topic of Fingal riding out, but Madeline pleaded once more for him to listen to her. Her sense of dread hadn't abated; it had only grown stronger as she accompanied him to the bailey. She knew people watched them, and she understood how she bid farewell to her husband would one day set the mood for the clan when warriors left the keep. They'd shared an unhurried goodbye in their chamber, but Fingal still pulled her into his arms and lowered his mouth for a passionate kiss that left no one in doubt that the unlikely couple loved one another.

Fingal looked back twice as he rode through the gates and led the Grant warriors southwest. He'd told Madeline to expect him to be gone anywhere between a fortnight and a moon. She nodded silently as she fought to remain resilient. She stood between Edward and Davina as only a dust cloud remained as her husband left her fearing for his life. She'd told no one but Fingal, and by default Harry since he'd overheard her in the stables, about her fears. She resolved to keep herself busy throughout the day, but she dreaded the nights when she would climb into their bed alone. They'd just committed themselves, and Fingal already left Madeline alone.

As the days passed, Madeline took comfort in Davina's company. They spent hours together working in the kitchens since they both enjoyed baking. They sat together in the lady's solar while they sewed, and they went for walks in the orchard. As they grew more comfortable with one another, Madeline confessed the struggle she'd experienced becoming accustomed to being a wife and falling in love. Davina shared some of her past with Edward, and Madeline realized that their circumstances weren't that different. She said a prayer of thanksgiving that it only took her and Fingal less than a season to admit their feelings, rather than three years like Davina and Edward.

But Madeline's nights were lonely. She didn't venture to the kirk for Matins, but she prayed in her chamber. She attended Lauds and Prime, knowing Edward would offer companionable silence. She folded Fingal's plaid just as he'd done for her on her first day at Freuchie and laid it beside her, running her hand over it until she fell asleep. When one of the laundresses delivered another one of Fingal's plaids, she wrapped herself in it to sleep while keeping the other beside her. Foreboding was her constant companion that dogged her every step. She suffered nightmares nearly every time she fell asleep, but she never discerned whether it was a holy or unholy message. Eventually, she convinced herself that she just had an overactive imagination.

Fingal gritted his teeth as he listened to Seamus tell him about three more young women who were missing from his branch since Fingal and the Grants passed through. Seamus had already sent a missive to Laird Andrew Gordon, and he expected Ewan and Eoin to arrive any day. Fingal didn't want to wait, but he knew that it would be prudent to double his forces. Seamus said Andrew would likely send at least three score of warriors, if not five. Fingal had five score with him, but even with such a large contingent, more men would improve their odds.

Fingal knew that there was the possibility that Laird John Farquharson expected Fingal to return and had already sent missives to the Chattans and Buchans requesting their aid. He'd agreed Seamus should also send a missive to the MacThomases, inviting them to join the fray. Clan MacThomas wasn't an ally to the Grants or the Gordons, but they were in a decades-long feud with the Farquharsons, and it would take little goading for them to join the fray.

"Do ye think the Farquharson kens why we left in the middle of the night?" Harry asked as they sipped their whisky at a campfire outside the Abergeldie Castle's walls. He and Fingal shared a chamber in the keep, but they'd slipped out to where the rest of the Grants had pitched camp. Only the four men who'd traveled with him and Madeline knew the details about what happened in Braemar, so the five men kept their voices low.

"Likely. He probably assumed we heard aboot the auction and went in search of Madeline. I want to ken why he'd allow such a thing within his village. Madeline said the highwaymen intimidated the villagers, but the men seemed familiar to the locals," Fingal explained.

"I suppose they sell their stolen wares—besides women—there. The vendors dinna make a fuss, since it's goods they can resell," Simon mused.

"I thought the same," Tommy said with a nod. "If the laird kens, then why doesnae he do aught?"

"Because he has the morals of the snake who tempted Eve," Fingal scowled. "The mon is notoriously untrustworthy and only out for himself. If it doesnae benefit him—or his clan by extension—then he isnae interested. He canna be trusted."

"How do ye ken?" Tommy asked.

"When Ewan and Eoin were at Freuchie, we spoke aboot what happened. I already knew the mon by reputation, but the Gordons confirmed ma suspicions," Fingal told his men. He looked around the circle they made around the little campfire, and he realized the men were more than just his guards. He'd known all of them his entire life, and they'd all entered the lists around the same time since they were similar in age. He'd kept himself distant from most of the men, except Harry. But as he looked at Simon, Nichol, and Tommy, he knew he could count them as confidants and friends. "I didna thank any of ye enough for what ye did for Lady Madeline and me. I ken what yer duty was, but ye did more than I expected. Yer help likely saved ma wife's life. And how ye had the patience nae to hang me up by ma bollocks is God's own secret."

"Lady Madeline is a kind lass, and she's a good cook. How could we nae watch out for her?" Simon grinned, downplaying the men's roles in getting Madeline to Freuchie.

"Aye, well, I still appreciate it. I consider maself lucky to have ye nae only as guards but to call ye friends," Fingal raised his mug of whisky.

Thinking back on their conversation, Nichol wondered aloud. "Do ye think the Farquharson is preparing for us? Or do ye think he believes we ran away scared? I assume he kens we connected him to the highwaymen."

"I want to say it's the latter and that his arrogance will be his downfall. But he isnae an eejit. I suspect they'll be ready. When the Gordons arrive, we'll have to decide what we'll do if it comes to an attack or besiegement. I'd rather John turned over the last two men than forcing us to fight, but I dinna ken."

CHAPTER FORTY-FOUR

The sound of riders entering the bailey woke Fingal just before sunrise. He peered out the window as Gordon warriors filled the space between the keep and the surrounding wall. He hurried to dress before dashing down to greet his friends. Ewan and Eoin grasped his forearm in a warrior's handshake before greeting Seamus. The four men moved swiftly into Seamus's solar, where the chieftain pulled out maps of the land between Abergeldie and Braemar, and the surrounding area.

"If the MacThomases join us, we will probably meet them here," Seamus pointed to a spot on the map slightly east of the midpoint between Abergeldie and Braemar. "With the numbers we have, it would be best if we stay off the roads. It will be slower going, especially for the men on foot, but it willna announce our presence. If these slavers are the highwaymen, then they'll be scouting our route, anyway."

"Do ye think Laird MacThomas will send men?" Ewan glanced up at the chieftain, then Fingal, before looking at his twin. "I ken they canna stand one another, but ever since the failed attack on the

Camerons, the MacThomas is much more cautious aboot who he gets into bed with."

"I imagine he will. With the numbers we bring, the MacThomas kens victory favors us. He'll celebrate the glory without shouldering the most risk," Seamus answered.

"How many do ye think he'll send?" Eoin asked.

"I'd say two or three score. There will only be enough to say the MacThomases took part. Like I said, he doesnae want the risk after losing so many against the Camerons. He was an eejit to follow the Mackintosh and the MacBain. He willna make the same mistake twice, so he'll nae commit too many."

"Better than saying nay and giving us a kick up the backside," Eoin smirked.

"The Gordons number five score, the Grants are five score too. Say the MacThomases only bring two score, that's still two hundred and forty men."

"Ma branch can send a score and a half," Seamus added. A much smaller branch than the main cadet branch that Ewan and Eoin belonged to, Seamus answered to the twins' father, and by extension Ewan, as Andrew's heir. Sending thirty men would tax Abergeldie's defenses, but Seamus insisted upon doing more than offering the others a roof over their heads.

"Then we are at two hundred and seventy," Fingal said as he straightened, looking at the men across the table from him. "How many men does the Farquharson have garrisoned at Braemar?"

"Likely ten score," Seamus estimated.

"We may outnumber them," Ewan mused. "But nae by much, and they will have the advantage of kenning the land and being within their walls."

"Then we create two plans. One for a direct attack, and one to lay siege," Eoin suggested.

Fingal looked at Seamus and tapped his fingers

against his arm. "How long do ye think they could last? And could ye bring supplies if we need them?"

"Aye, I can do that," Seamus agreed. "And I'd say two or three moons. Depends on if ye can block their water supply. They have an underground spring that they rely on more than their well. A narrow river supplies the spring. If ye can block that off, then they will fall faster."

"And if John hands over the highwaymen without a fuss?" Ewan asked.

Fingal had thought about that throughout the two days' ride to Abergeldie. "That may have to be enough. But I dinna think it can be. If the laird kens slavers were holding auctions on his land and he did naught, then he is as guilty as the men he turned a blind eye to."

"And what of King Robert? What will he say when he hears we've attacked Clan Farquharson?" Ewan asked as he tried to read Fingal's expression, which had grown guarded.

"I dinna care," Fingal's voice was hushed, but there was steel in it. "He's in Stirling, and I am here. I'll sort that out after I'm certain those men canna come for Madeline."

"Ye really care aboot her, dinna ye?" Eoin asked in surprise.

"I told ye she means as much to me as yer wives mean to ye," Fingal snapped. He missed Madeline, and he worried about her incessantly. He knew Edward and Davina would always keep her safe, but he feared how she was doing with only Davina for a friend.

"We thought ye felt obligated to defend her," Ewan said, throwing his hands up in surrender when Fingal glared at him. "She wasna how any of us remembered. Mayhap there is more between ye than any of us assumed."

Fingal wanted to point out that it was Allyson and Cairstine's careless comments that made the Grants so wary of Madeline. They'd have been none the wiser if he and Madeline arrived without guests in attendance. But sniping at the twins about their wives wouldn't endear him to his allies. "She isnae the woman ye kenned, but she's the woman I love." He offered no more than that, and the twins didn't press. Seamus remained silent as he watched the exchange, knowing better than to interfere.

"So we ride out in the morn?" Eoin asked.

"Aye," three voices agreed.

CHAPTER FORTY-FIVE

Fingal checked his horse's saddle once more before mounting. Since they were on Gordon land, Ewan and Eoin would lead the way. But it was Fingal who would issue the orders once they were in place. He'd explained the plan to Harry and his men, all of whom were the Grants' most experienced warriors. Fingal refused to bring any men who hadn't fought for the clan for at least five years. He didn't want to endanger lives needlessly, and he would do everything he could to ensure victory. As he looked back at his men as the massive force left Abergeldie behind, he felt confident that they could avoid a siege that could keep them from their families for months. He wanted to ride back to Madeline within the fortnight.

Seamus hadn't exaggerated that it would be slow going for such a large force with many men on foot. Staying well away from the road provided some secrecy, but it meant trodding through overgrown meadows and winding through woods. But Fingal decided the detour was well worth it when they stumbled upon the MacThomases just where Seamus expected.

Fingal was surprised to find that the Mac-

Thomases sent four score of warriors, bringing their numbers to nearly three hundred. They made their camp over a ridge from Braemar. It was out of sight from the road and the castle's guards, but they could watch the castle and see some people moving around the village. With the size army they'd gathered, the leaders decided a predawn attack on the castle would decrease the likelihood that any villagers would sound the alarm. The darkness would allow them to circumvent the village and not lead their attack through innocents.

"Rider approaches," a Gordon guard announced as he approached where Fingal sat with Ewan, Eoin, Seamus, and the MacThomases' leader, Donald. "A woman on horseback alone."

The men rose, their suspicions heightened since there were no cookfires lit and they were beyond the castle's visibility. They waited for the rider to crest the hill before three mouths dropped open.

"That canna be," Ewan said, shaking his head. "What is that bitch doing riding out to us?"

The men watched as a familiar face approached before dismounting. The woman was hesitant to approach until she recognized the Gordon twins and Fingal. She hurried over to them and smiled. No one returned her smile.

"Lady Bevan, what are ye doing here?" Ewan demanded with no pretense.

"It's Lady Farquharson," Lady Gwendolyn Bevan-Farquharson corrected.

"Och, that's right," Eoin chimed in. "After propositioning ma brother in front of his wife, ye made the same daft offer to the king, but the queen heard ye. Married ye off to the auld sod. Heard his heart gave out trying to have ye up against a wall."

The five leaders watched, but not an ounce of embarrassment crossed the former courtier's face.

Instead, she appeared to gloat. "Well, I left ye two breathless more than once." She grinned at Ewan and Eoin, but the twins curled their lips in identical looks of disgust. There had been a poorly timed encounter with Allyson outside the courtier's chamber just before the king's announcement that Ewan and Allyson would marry. Seeing the twins leaving Lady Bevan's chambers under dubious circumstances, along with Ewan's poor attempts at jesting, led Allyson to run away. Even though it was obvious the couple returned to Stirling very much in love, the former Lady Bevan had no compunction about asking Ewan for a tryst while he held Allyson's hand.

"Why are ye here?" Fingal cut in. He'd never dallied with the woman like the twins had, but he'd flirted with her while at court. "And ye arenae Lady Farquharson anymore. I didna see ye when I was there a few sennights ago. I would have thought they'd send ye back to yer kin after the auld bastard popped his cogs."

"It was one of the rare eves I didn't dine in the Great Hall. I was waiting for someone," she said with a cocked eyebrow. Her Lowlander accent was jarring to Fingal's ears. "As for now, I saw you make camp earlier. I ride alone when I please. Usually no one is daft enough to approach so close."

"That still doesnae explain why ye are here," Seamus spoke up, tired of the woman's games with her former lovers. "Tell us, or ye shall find yerself bound and gagged to a tree."

Gwendolyn glared at the chieftain before tossing her hair over her shoulder. "I came because I recognized you. I thought to warn you that whatever your plan is, it won't work." She cast her gaze across the men standing before her. "That is, it won't work without me."

"I told ye, ye would be bound and gagged," Seamus warned.

"And if I don't return to the keep soon, to the mon expecting me, then they will search for me. I don't think you're prepared to be found," Gwendolyn taunted. "I may have a lover, but I hate it here. I will help you if you get me out of this hellhole."

The men were unmoved by her words, followed up with a beseeching stare. Ewan and Eoin exchanged a glance that only the twins understood before they shifted their eyes to Fingal, whose grim expression told the twins he shared their disgust. Donald MacThomas had remained silent, but chose then to speak up.

"I dinna trust her. Seamus is right. Tie her up, gag her, kill her even. But ma money says she'd betray ye thrice before the cockerel crows." Donald crossed his arms and glowered.

"Or I can lead you in through the tunnels," Gwendolyn countered.

"Nae on yer cursed life," Donald MacThomas snarled. There was no MacThomas who would enter a tunnel ever again. They'd been part of a failed attempt to use a tunnel dug between Inverlochy Castle and Tor Castle when the MacThomases, MacBains, and Mackintoshes attacked the Camerons. Laird Hardwin and Lady Blair Cameron blocked the entrance within the keep and ordered dirt dumped into the other opening. The men had been sealed in the tunnel for more than a day. "We'll join ye once the gates are open."

"Coward," Gwendolyn jeered.

"We arenae going through any tunnels either," Fingal countered. "And Seamus's idea holds more appeal as ye try to snooker us."

"I told you, I wish to leave. I can't do that on my

own. The current laird wouldn't allow it, and I have no men to accompany me."

"And why wouldn't John allow it?" Eoin said with a pointed smirk.

"Aye, I'm his leman. But he didn't give me a choice. It's that, or he'll turn me out. Destitute." Tears filled the former courtier's eyes, but none of the men believed her. When she saw that her attempt for sympathy garnered none, she took another approach. "I can get you in through the postern gate. I often ride early in the morning. It's how I leave before they raise the portcullis. Have men posted outside the gate before sunrise. When the guard opens the hatch for me to leave, you can sweep in before it's shut. Once he's overpowered, others can come in that way before raising the main gate."

"And when ye warn the Farquharsons that we're waiting in the shadows?" Fingal narrowed his eyes and cast a disgusted look at the untrustworthy woman.

"I told you already. I want to leave. Why would I sabotage the one chance I've had since I arrived at this godforsaken place?"

"And once ye're out?" Donald asked. "Ye said yerself ye havenae any guards. Do ye think we'll ferry ye wherever yer whim takes ye?"

Gwendolyn ignored Donald and turned to look directly at Fingal. "I know why you're here. I heard what happened to Madeline. Once this is done, you'll have to go to Stirling to explain everything to King Robert. Take me that far, and I will figure out the rest."

"Ye were banished," Fingal pointed out.

"So was your wife, but they took her back. They even married her off to you," she countered.

"Aye, because the queen forgave her. Madeline's

sins weren't personal for Queen Elizabeth," Fingal reminded her.

"Bah. That was years ago. The queen got the bairn she wanted and the heir Robert needs. She doesnae care where he sows his seeds now that one took root in her," Gwendolyn's mien was filled with disdain as she waved a dismissive hand.

"Are ye prepared for an agonizing death if ye betray us?" Donald asked. "I dinna hold any mercy just because ye're a woman."

"Then I suppose I had better not do that," she said without flinching as she stared Donald in the eye.

The five leaders exchanged glances with one another, and Gwendolyn fought not to let her face show the smug satisfaction she felt. She could barely remember the last time a man had turned her down for anything. She clenched her teeth as she darted a glance at Ewan, recalling he was that very man. But she would remedy that before they reached Stirling. None of the men had their wives with them. She would use that to her advantage.

"Return to the keep," Fingal ordered. "We'll meet ye at the postern gate. One of the men will bring ye back here and keep watch."

Gwendolyn looked at the men once before nodding and wheeling her horse around and cantering back to the castle. The five men watched her until she was out of sight.

"How do ye think she'll betray us?" Eoin asked. "Have a score of guards waiting inside the postern gate? Tell every mon on the battlements to watch for us? Tell John to send men here?"

"All of that," Fingal mused. "We triple the perimeter guards tonight. And we follow our original plan. A score of us enter the bailey as though we're

376

servants on the way to work. Once we're all in place, we attack."

"And if nay one is there to meet her?" Donald asked. "We dinna need her to get in through the postern. We have the men's plaids that we took off the patrol we captured. I say we still make it look like the Farquharsons captured some of ma men scouting and make it look like we're being turned over to the laird."

"I agree," Eoin nodded. "That's far more sound than relying on her for aught. She will think we stayed away once it looks like we've been found out."

"And once we've won, what aboot her then?" Seamus asked.

"Nae our bluidy problem," Ewan growled. "If she wants to leave so badly, let her walk."

"Ye really dinna like her," Fingal mused.

"She was good for tupping," Ewan smirked. "But the moment she looked sideways at Allyson, she was as good as dead to me. If I have to be the one to make that true, I willna lose a wink of sleep."

"Speaking of sleep, we should catch what we can," Eoin pointed out.

The men sought their bedrolls after ensuring there was no more than two arms' lengths between the guards who stood watch around the camp. Fingal closed his eyes and thought of Madeline, just as he always did. And like every other night, he wondered if she thought about him. During the day they were tucked away in their love nest, Fingal asked her why she'd changed her stance on their marriage so drastically.

Madeline had recounted her experience her first week at the priory, how the glowing cross led her to pray and the peace she'd found from it. She explained she had never in her life had such a powerful feeling influence her. He remembered how she'd slid closer to him in bed as they lay on their sides looking at each other. She'd ran her hand over his chest before resting it over his heart.

Madeline said that the Holy Spirit had visited her that day at the priory, and It had returned to her in her dream. She'd shrugged and said she had no other explanation for it. Neither wanted to speculate if it was divine intervention. They were both too happy to question it. Fingal fell asleep to the image of wrapping Madeline in his arms as they shared their bed at Freuchie.

CHAPTER FORTY-SIX

Fingal, Ewan, Eoin, and Seamus cast disgusted looks at the Farquharson plaids they wore. They would pretend to be the patrol returning, with Donald and some of his men as their captives. They'd agreed that the four men would have been too recognizable trying to enter through the main gate, especially since Fingal had been there less than a month ago. While it was still pitch black, Nichol, Simon, Harry, and Tommy slipped toward the postern gate and positioned themselves among bushes less than a hundred yards from the gate.

When no alarm sounded, Fingal felt confident his men were in position. They would serve as additional force if Farquharson guards recognized Fingal and the others. Otherwise, they would capture the former Lady Bevan-Farquharson. A group of Seamus's men would enter the bailey dressed as servants and craftsmen arriving for work in and around the keep. The rest of their armies spread out to approach the castle from every direction but the village. A few men would sweep through to ensure the villagers did nothing to interfere, but none of the clans wanted to make war on the innocent.

Everyone was in place before the sun cast pink

and purple rays over the horizon. Using the dim light in their favor as villagers formed a line at the front gate when the portcullis rose, Fingal, Ewan, Eoin, and Seamus approached the postern gate. Fingal noticed Harry and the others, but he made no sign that he saw them. They were within sight of the guards on the battlements. They'd all said a prayer of thanksgiving for the light rain that fell since it gave them an excuse to pull the extra length of plaid over their heads.

"What goes?" a Farquharson guard called down from the wall walk.

"Found these maggots across our border," Fingal called out. "Let us in. It's bluidy cold, and I dinna need to be sopping wet for their sake."

The disguised men along with their supposed captives watched as the guard turned away and called down to a man below. The hatch swung open, allowing them entry into the bailey. Without a word, they moved in the dungeon's direction but ducked behind outbuildings, where Fingal and the others discarded their stolen plaids. They breathed a sigh of relief to be wearing their own clans' plaid. They watched as a lone female rider left through the front gate, and the men exchanged knowing smirks.

Seamus signaled that he would go back to the postern gate to let the hidden warriors in. They watched as their men, disguised as servants and workers, slipped into their positions. When all was settled, Fingal counted to two hundred before releasing an ear-piercing whistle that signaled the beginning of their attack. The three clans swept through the bailey like a hoard of locusts. Men took the steps up to the battlements while others charged into the barracks, cornering warriors in the narrow building.

Once warned that there might be secret tunnels,

Fingal assumed the laird would try to make his escape through them. He'd never believed John would come out to fight alongside his men. With Harry and the others at his back, they fought their way into the keep. Fingal spotted the current Lady Farquharson and ran toward her as the woman screamed.

"Go to yer chamber or yer solar and dinna come out. Get as many women hidden as ye can. We arenae here for ye or them," Fingal ordered. The terrified woman didn't wait to be told twice. She darted across the Great Hall that was swelling with people and issued orders to the women and children. It was still too early for people to gather for the morning meal, so the Great Hall wasn't filled with warriors.

Harry, Nichol, and Simon struggled to barricade the enormous wooden doors, but it gave Fingal and Tommy time to search for John Farquharson. They barreled into his solar, but it appeared empty. They turned over the laird's desk and pulled books from the walls as they searched for any hidden lever or crack that would give them entrance to a secret hiding place or tunnel.

Not wanting to waste too much time, they abandoned the solar and bound up the stairs to the family chambers. Kicking open one door after another, they made their way along the passageway. Each chamber was empty except for one. Fingal put his finger to his mouth as the two Grants crept to the door. They'd heard the women screaming, but Fingal had a sneaking suspicion where John was hiding. He put his ear to the door and waited in silence.

When the screams subsided, he heard a distinctly male voice warning them to keep quiet lest their attackers return. Fingal looked at Tommy before both men stepped back then ran toward the door, their shoulders slamming into it. When the wood creaked and splintered, the men thrust their booted feet against it. The door swung open to reveal Laird John Farquharson standing behind his wife, no weapon drawn.

"Why nae just put the skirts on if ye're going to hide behind them?" Fingal chuckled. But there was no mirth, only scorn. "Nae even prepared to defend them."

"He might have if he hadnae been so daft as to think we wouldnae at least check the chamber we told the women to hide in," Tommy pointed out. With a shrug, he tossed out, "But he didna."

Fingal glared at the women who'd been too frightened to move. They jumped aside as John raised a dirk to defend himself. Fingal and Tommy both laughed as their much longer swords backed John against the wall. Within a blink, the laird was disarmed and being dragged down the stairs and out to the bailey. Fingal whistled once more, drawing people's attention to where he kept John kneeling on the ground.

"We have yer laird, so lay down yer weapons," Fingal ordered. The Farquharson warriors looked around, seeing themselves outnumbered. Many turned to look at their laird for guidance that didn't come. Eventually the men decided for themselves, dropping their weapons, the metal twanging as it hit the ground. "We have Laird Farquharson, but we want the highwaymen ye allow into yer village to auction women to the highest bidder. The vera highwaymen who took ma wife."

Fingal looked around as the Gordon twins came to stand beside him. He'd spotted Seamus and Donald fighting when he left the keep, but they now held their opponents at bay. Fingal waited for someone, anyone, to speak. But the silence only intensified the tension still humming in the air.

"Their names are Dougal and Finneas," called

out a woman's voice from behind Fingal's shoulder. He glanced back to see the Maris Farquharson—the current Lady Farquharson—descending the steps. She stepped around Ewan and Eoin, so she could stand before her husband. She spat in his face, and Fingal struggled not to show his surprise. "They're the laird's nephews. Henchmen more like it."

Fingal looked around the Farquharsons gathered in the bailey, and many shifted with unease. While he knew the ringleaders' names from what Madeline told him, he never expected to learn they were close relatives to the laird. He looked back at the lady of the clan, and the amount of loathing she directed at her husband was nearly palpable. He supposed she despised him for his cowardice only moments ago when he didn't defend her. He was unprepared for the woman to pull a *sgian dubh* from her girdle near where her chatelaine's key hung. Without a moment's hesitation, she pierced her husband's eye with the knife.

"Now ye and Finneas can match since ye hold each other in such high esteem. Ye think I dinna ken ye've been swiving yer own stepmother? Ye think I dinna ken she's humping both Dougal and Finneas? Usually at the same time. Ye think I am so daft that I dinna ken what goes on around here. I may nae have had the power to stop them, but I can bluidy well stop ye."

Ewan lurched forward when Maris drew back her arm and prepared to stab the laird in his neck. He pulled the hissing woman away, restraining her as Eoin fought to take her blade.

"Ye canna kill him. Yet," Ewan muttered into the writhing woman's ear. "We still need to ken more."

"There's naught he can tell ye that I dinna ken too," Maris hissed. "Find the slut, and ye will find Dougal and Finneas. Bring her to me, and I'll stitch her quim shut. Nae being able to rut again would be worse punishment for that whore than death. She doesnae just enjoy it, she uses it as her currency. Gwendolyn trades a good fuck for whatever she wants."

Her foot lashed out and caught John beneath his chin, making his head snap backwards. Fingal's hold on his hair pushed his head forward, only for it snap back again when Maris drove her boot into his face. She looked around at the shocked faces who watched their usually demure lady release her wrath. She turned away from John and looked at those staring at her.

"Ye all ken what goes on here. Nae a one of ye has ever tried to stop it. Dougal and Finneas are but mere men. Men who bleed and die. When lasses from our own clan went missing, ye did naught. Nae a husband, a brother, a father. Nay one." Maris spun back to glare at her husband. "When ye let those bastards sell their own sister, I grew a set of ma own bollocks. The king kens and has men on the way. I despise ye with every breath I take. I have prayed for a painful death every day since yer father bought me. *Bought me.*"

"How long has this been going on?" Fingal asked.

"Since before the auld laird died last year. We wed two years ago," Maris explained. She looked at Fingal, Ewan, and Eoin in turn. "Can I kill him now?"

Eoin shook his head with regret. "Nae if the king has men on their way. They will take him to Stirling for the king to mete out justice."

Maris gave a jerking nod before spitting on her husband once more. "I hope ye rot in misery every day of what's left of yer short life. I hope the pox that bitch gave ye makes yer cock burn like the devil before it shrivels up. I never want to lay eyes on ye again." Ewan released her when she pulled away. The Farquharsons and their attackers alike watched as the woman glided back to the steps and entered the keep with dignity and grace. No one would have guessed she'd maimed a man only minutes earlier.

Donald and Seamus approached, and Donald spoke. "We will remain behind to deal with him until the king's men arrive. If ye wish to find his nephews, ye should ride out now. Ye ken that woman went to warn them. They will have scarpered by now. If ye dinna hurry, they'll be in the wind."

The Gordons from the primary sect and all the Grants gathered their dead and wounded before moving back to their camp. The few men they'd left behind to guard the horses had already cleared any traces of their time there. Men mounted and others formed lines, marching behind the horses. They swept through the village to ensure the brothers weren't hiding in plain sight, and they'd almost reached the town's gates, when a young girl darted out before Fingal, Ewan, and Eoin.

CHAPTER FORTY-SEVEN

Fingal dismounted once he recognized the girl who'd helped Madeline when Finneas and Dougal dumped her near the woods. He struggled to remember her name but came up blank. Before he could speak, the girl stepped forward and pointed northeast.

"That way," she blurted. "They have more men. They came to Da the other day when they needed Da to shoe a horse. While Da was working, I slipped to the back of the corral where they were waiting. They were talking aboot the nun. I mean, yer wife. The mon with the blind eye said ye wouldnae expect them to make the long ride to get her. They havenae forgiven her for what happened in the village. The other was saying how much they would have to sell her for to make up for what she cost them and to pay for their new men. They didna ken anyone was listening. Ma da kens I helped her, so I told him everything I heard. He planned to ride for Abergeldie this morn, but the fighting at the keep made him stay home with Mama and me."

Fingal kneeled before the young girl as she spoke. He offered her a genuine smile when she finished recounting her tale. "Ye are a vera brave lass. Ye remind me of ma Maddy. I thank ye for what ye've told me. But I also ken Lady Madeline wouldnae want ye risking yer life as ye have twice for her. She would tell ye to stay safe with yer mama and da. If these men, or any like them, ever come back here, promise me ye willna sneak around. Ye ken what will happen if they find ye. Then what would yer Mama do?"

Mary's eyes opened wide as she nodded. Fingal realized that his warning carried more weight than Madeline's had. He assumed it was because he was a warrior, but either way, he prayed the girl listened to him. She dashed back to her cottage, and Fingal led the men in the direction she pointed.

The hair on the back of Fingal's neck stood up as he scanned the surrounding landscape. Something felt off, but he couldn't tell what. Birds still flew overhead, and he'd seen deer among the trees only a few minutes ago. But his intuition sensed danger. He glanced at Ewan and Eoin and could tell they felt the same.

"Harry, Tommy," Fingal called out and waited for the men to ride alongside him. "I dinna ken what it is, but something is amiss."

"Ye feel it too?" Tommy asked. "I just said the same to Harry. Do ye want us to scout?"

"Aye, but dinna get too far ahead of us. I dinna want ye cut off from us if someone's out there," Fingal warned. The men nodded and set off ahead of the slower-moving army. Fingal turned to Ewan and Eoin. "Do ye think they sent word to the Chattans and Buchans?"

"That's who I think is waiting for us," Eoin speculated. "They ken we're here. If the Farquharson's nephews didna see how many of us there are, then

Lady whatever-she's-called-these-days told them. They couldnae get that far ahead of us."

"Unless they stuck to the roads while we cut across the land," Fingal pointed out.

"With only a handful of lawless men, do ye think they would try to steal Madeline from Freuchie?" Ewan asked, his brow furrowed.

"I willna put aught past them." Fingal strained to see and caught sight of Harry and Tommy galloping toward them. "Bluidy hell. That was fast."

"They're just around the bend. They spotted us. We're an even match," Harry panted. Fingal nodded and gave the signal for all the men to draw their weapons. With the Grant battle cry of "Stand fast Craig Elachie" and the Gordon cry of "An Gòr-donach," their clan name, the army surged forward. The battle between the Grant and Gordon army against the Buchans and Chattans was far worse than Fingal could imagine.

Fingal's side screamed with pain as he swiped his sleeve across his forehead. He swung his sword indiscriminately as he staggered. He'd remained on his mount for as long as he could, using the height as an advantage. It gave him a longer reach, and his horse was trained for battle, with hooves as lethal as his sword. But he'd been unprepared for the man with one good eye to charge toward him. Fingal had been unseated and fallen to the ground. He'd been lucky to land on his left arm rather than his sword arm. But the impact dislocated his shoulder.

"Dinna cry," the half-blind man taunted.

"Which one are ye?" Fingal panted.

"Finneas," the man snarled.

Fingal positioned himself where his opponent

couldn't see, running him through. But not before a Buchan warrior's blade sliced his ribs from behind. As Fingal fought to remain on his feet, he realized that he'd hit his head harder than he realized when he fell from his horse. After Finneas and the Buchan warrior fell dead, Fingal reached back and winced when he found a bump at the base of his head much like Madeline had from Finneas kicking her. He'd taken great satisfaction in killing his foe, but now he cursed when he pulled back his hand and found it bloody. He squinted, trying to make out the various plaids to find where his men fought. But the men were spread out too far, and Fingal's throbbing head kept him from focusing. Between the pain in his shoulder, the pain in his ribs, his throbbing head, the ringing in his ears, and his blurred vision, Fingal wasn't sure if he was even standing upright. No longer able to hold his sword upright, it trailed behind him as he dragged it.

"What a boon for me," crowed a voice behind Fingal. He turned to look, and his head bobbled back and forth. He squeezed his eyes shut before looking at the sneering man. "A shame ye're already closer to dead than alive. I'd hoped to be the one to cause ye pain. Yer wife—lying bitch that she is—cost me a fortune that night. Dinna ye worry, I still intend to have ma pound of flesh from her. Actually, her flesh should go for several pounds." Dougal cackled as he approached Fingal. "But before that, I shall make sure ye can never ride to her defense again."

"If I'm going to die, why nae tell me the truth," Fingal gasped. "I ken ye and the dead one over there are brothers. Ye are the laird's nephews. Why turn highwaymen, Dougal?"

"We're nae more highwaymen than ye are. We belong to our clan, but we rob those we want," Dougal chortled.

"Why the auctions? Selling women?" Fingal fought to say each word.

"Why nae? It's profitable," Dougal shrugged.

Fingal knew the man was trying to wear him out by only giving vague answers. Fingal needed to know before he collapsed. Even if he was taking the knowledge to the grave. "Whose idea was it? Yer uncle's?"

Dougal laughed as he shook his head at Fingal. "Ma eejit uncle is so hot for getting under that tart's skirts that he does aught that she says." Fingal tried to remember what happened in the bailey and what he'd heard, but his memory was hazy. At his confused look, Dougal sighed. "Gwendolyn Bevan, or rather the former Lady Farquharson. Ma step-grandmother. A woman who doesnae care who is riding her as long as she gets what she wants. It was her idea."

Dougal snorted at Fingal's shock. He cast Fingal a mocking look of disbelief.

"Ma grandfather didna care what she did as long as she lifted her skirts when he told her to. Ma uncle turns a blind eye because she lets him pant all over her. And Finneas and I have her simply because we can. She kens we'll kill her or send her back to court. Either way, she'll lose the life she likes. As ma uncle's leman, she has all the luxuries of being the laird's wife with none of the duties."

"But why would she suggest such a thing? If she has all that she wants, why would she devise such an arrangement?"

"She says that she was basically bought and sold by her husbands and the king. She doesnae see why she shouldnae profit from other women being traded just as she was," Dougal shrugged. "Now ye ken. Now ye die."

Fingal attempted to lift his sword, but his arm refused to cooperate. He dropped the weapon and reached for his dirk instead. His mind cleared enough for him to understand that if he killed Dougal, he would eliminate the danger to Madeline. But if he failed, he'd likely signed his wife's death sentence. He was certain Dougal was as adamant about getting to Madeline as Fingal was to protect her. He waited until Dougal drew closer. He held his breath as he fought to steady himself. When Dougal raised his arm and swung, Fingal bent forward and lunged.

Head down but eyes up, Fingal aimed his blade at Dougal's breastbone. The dirk slid into the man's chest to the hilt, but it was the hilt of Dougal's sword that crashed into Fingal's temple and sent him reeling backwards. The last thing he remembered was Dougal pushing him over an embankment into a ravine. As he slid down the hill and crashed into trees and bushes, he watched Dougal collapse. It was only another breath later that everything went black for Fingal.

CHAPTER FORTY-EIGHT

Madeline doubled over in pain as she stepped from the kirk. Edward and Davina reached for her, but she stumbled away before retching. Her stomach cramped over and over until the meager remnants of the previous night's meal spewed forth. Sweat broke out on her forehead as she clutched her middle. Edward and Davina caught her arms as her legs gave out.

"Fingal," Madeline whispered. She looked up at Davina then Edward. "Something's happened. He's nae coming back."

Uncontrollable shivers swept over Madeline's body as she closed her eyes, her chest growing so tight that she gasped for air. Edward swept her into his arms and carried her into the keep, Davina hurrying to keep up with her husband's longer stride. When he laid Madeline on her bed, her hand flailed around until her fingers found Fingal's plaid. She pulled it around her as she curled into a ball, sobbing.

"Madeline?" Davina whispered.

"He's nae coming back," Madeline rasped. "I told him nae to go. I had such a strong feeling before.

But now I can barely breathe." Madeline opened terrified eyes to Edward and Davina. "I'm nae a witch!"

Edward kneeled beside the bed and took Madeline's hand. "Nay one thinks ye are. Ye said ye had a feeling before Fingal even left. The Lord works in mysterious ways, lass. Mayhap the Lord was warning ye."

"He or the Devil," Madeline whispered as more tears fell. "It's nae as though I hear voices. I just feel it within me, all of me. Ma head and body aches with it."

"Madeline, the ancient Greeks had the notion that two people can have souls that are such a match that they become one and the same." Edward squeezed her hand and shrugged. "Mayhap that is ye and Fingal. Ye seem to understand one another in a way the rest of us dinna see. Mayhap the pagan Greeks didna ken it was actually the hand of the Lord that guided soulmates. But ye are a devout woman, mayhap the Lord hears yer prayers loudest when ye are most in need."

Madeline could only nod as she clung to Fingal's plaid. Edward and Davina offered to stay with her, but she declined. Her misery was too intense to share with anyone else. In the solitude of their chamber, Madeline prayed over and over for Fingal. She prayed the rosary throughout the day and well into the night, until her eyes couldn't remain open.

Bells ringing to announce the return of the Grant warriors woke Madeline. She rubbed her eyes as she tried to clear her groggy mind. As the bells continued to ring, Madeline realized what they meant. She rolled from the bed still wearing the kirtle from the day before. She wrapped Fingal's plaid around her shoulders before racing out to the bailey. Standing on the steps between Edward and Davina, she watched as the men flowed into the bailey. Her hands clenched the plaid when she saw Fingal didn't lead the men. She looked over every man as he passed under the portcullis. She wondered if he'd lost his horse and was on foot. But she didn't see him among the men walking. She searched the men carried and pulled in litters.

Unable to wait any longer, Madeline ran down the steps and went from one limp body to another, pulling back the tarps only to find the dead men weren't Fingal. She spun around when a hand rested on her shoulder. She found an exhausted Harry looking down at her. She shook her head as she tried to back away.

"Where is ma husband?" Madeline croaked. Her voice growing stronger, she demanded, "Where is ma husband?"

"Lady Madeline—" Harry's anguished voice broke.

"Dinna ye tell me he's dead. He isnae with any of the others. Where is he?" Madeline stepped forward until she was toe-to-toe with Harry. She scanned his face before she moaned and drew her fists toward Harry, stopping herself at the last minute before she pounded on his chest. "How could ye leave him?"

"Lady Madeline, we searched and searched. We couldnae find him," Harry said as he grasped her upper arms, keeping her from collapsing.

"Ye didna search hard enough if he isnae with ye. Ye gave up. Ye left him behind, and ye gave up," Madeline snarled. "Dinna touch me or yer soul will join the departed." Madeline pulled away from Harry with a glare that would haunt him until the end. She looked around at the people who watched her, stunned at her reaction. People jumped from her path as she stormed past them, shooting murderous glares at Tommy, Nichol, and Simon.

She could see many of the men were injured, and a fragment of her conscience tried to gain strength, telling her that she should help tend to them. But she couldn't think of doing anything but getting to the kirk. She would demand answers from God, and if He didn't give them, then she expected the Devil to supply them.

Madeline looked at the third pew where she usually knelt, but much like the night Fingal found her in the kirk, she went to kneel on the steps before the altar. She closed her eyes and took a calming breath. She breathed deeply until her anger and her fear subsided enough for her to think about her prayers. She remained there for hours as she recited every prayer she knew and made up her own as she went along. She refused to leave even when Davina, then Edward, coaxed her. She ignored the sound of the door opening and closing or the sound of men sliding in and out of the pews. She knew guards took turns watching over her, but she didn't care. When she could no longer kneel or keep her eyes open, she laid down at the base of the steps. The last thing she saw was moonlight shining on the hanging crucifix.

Madeline awoke with a start. Her body ached from laying on the stone floor. The cold and hardness had seeped into her bones, but she'd accepted the pain without complaint. She was certain it was negligible compared to whatever Fingal had suffered. She sat up but scrunched her eyes closed as an image floated back to her from the dream that woke her. She'd seen Fingal lying on the ground covered in leaves, twigs, and dirt. As Madeline forced herself to recall the dream, she remembered that it was dark throughout it. She strained to tell if she'd envisioned it being night or if it was a more ominous darkness, like death. She remembered trees and wind that blew more debris over Fingal's body. She kept her eyes closed and saw herself in the dream looking over the edge of something. There were no stars or moon, but the longer she thought about it, the more convinced she was that it was the nighttime, not the darkness of the under-world. With a jolt, Madeline realized she knew where to look.

She looked at the man slumped in the first pew. She stood up then rushed to Nichol, shaking his shoulder. "Wake up."

Madeline didn't wait to see if Nichol followed her. She barreled through the kirk's doors and dashed across the bailey to the barracks. She pounded on the door until one of the guards opened it, stunned to see Madeline on the other side.

"Where's Harry?" Madeline demanded. She leaned past the man, sticking her head through the doorway and bellowed, "Harry!"

When the guard she looked for staggered into the passageway and limped toward her, she realized for the first time that Harry had sustained several in-juries. She covered her mouth as her eyes widened. She took in his blackened eye, the gash along his left cheek, and how he held his ribs as he limped toward her.

"Merciful God," Madeline murmured as Harry came to stand before her. Her eyes watered as she looked at the man who had cared for her throughout her journey to Freuchie. She knew he'd made Fingal see reason more than once. Her heart pinched as she realized he was gravely wounded. "I'm so sorry for yesterday. I—I didna even notice. I'm sorry."

"Lady Madeline, we did search. We spent hours—"

"Harry, did ye fight near a ravine?" Madeline blurted.

"Aye. How'd ye—" Harry looked at her in confusion, then shook his head. "Ye must have heard someone say that."

"I didna. I yelled at ye like a banshee then stormed into the kirk. I havenae left and havenae spoken to anyone except to tell the laird and lady most ungraciously to leave me alone." Madeline swallowed as she rallied her courage to tell him what she'd seen. She lowered her voice so only Harry could hear her. "Ye remember the day in the stables when I found out ye were all leaving. Ye saw how I reacted, how I told Fingal that I had a horrible feeling aboot this. Harry, I ken where he is. I dinna ken how other than I dreamed it. I couldnae have kenned aboot the ravine. He fell down the ravine. He's at the bottom covered in twigs and leaves."

"Lady Madeline, even if ye're right, and I'll give ye that there's a chance, he couldnae have survived. He'd have been down there for two days already, and it would be another two before we could reach him."

"Could?" Madeline snapped as she rose to her full height. "Dinna ye mean can? Ye are sending men to bring ma husband back."

Harry shook his head. "I dinna have a say in it. Only the laird decides that. But I can tell ye, he willna send anyone. The Buchans and Chattans may nae have cleared out from there. We'd be riding back into a battle that nae enough men are well enough to fight. If they have him, then they'll either ransom him or send his body back."

Madeline backed away before she lashed out at Harry. It surprised the guard to see the hate that filled her gaze. He'd never imagined such a pious

398

woman was capable of such scorn, such loathing. It made any angry look she'd ever cast Fingal appear insignificant.

"The laird—and ye—and every other mon in this clan has a choice. Ye ride with me or ye dinna. But I am going for ma husband," Madeline threatened.

"The laird will lock ye in yer chamber if ye tell him that," Harry warned.

"Then ye can fucking tell him," Madeline seethed before spinning on her heels. Rather than going up the steps to the main doors of the keep, she ducked into the kitchens. Women turned to look at her, but none stepped in her way. She stormed through until she reached the servants' stairs, taking them two at a time as she bunched her skirts above her knees. She swung the door open to her chamber before thinking twice and easing it shut. She went to her chest and began pulling clothes from it. She'd had time to make two pairs of wool leggings that she would ordinarily wear in winter. She laid one pair on the bed as she yanked out a plain kirtle. She changed her clothes and ran back down to the kitchens.

Once more the women stayed out of her way as she grabbed three sacks and filled them to over-flowing with fruit, cheese wheels, bread, and cold meat. She didn't say a word, and no one asked her any questions. She saw one woman dash from the kitchens, and she knew the servant went to warn Davina. It only made Madeline move faster.

She ran to the stables; the bags bumping her legs. She thanked Kieran for all the times she'd accused him of being an ogre. She'd always run to the stables and raced to saddle her horse before he could stop her. Her nimble fingers fastened the girth before she tied the sacks to the saddle. She mounted in the stables and laid over her horse's withers to duck beneath the doorway. She spurred the horse and galloped through the main gates. She heard people calling to her, but she didn't slow. She figured they would either catch up or let her go, but she wasn't returning to Freuchie Castle without Fingal.

CHAPTER FORTY-NINE

"Madeline, we must stop for the night," Edward stated. She hadn't said more than a few words since Edward caught up to her. He'd ordered the men well enough to travel and fight to follow him as he chased after Madeline. She'd spared only enough words to tell Edward what she'd dreamed, what she was certain of. She was surprised when he didn't argue, only telling her they would have to rest the horses now and again and stop when it was too dark to see the road. Madeline nodded, and pulled one of the food sacks from her saddle before handing off her horse to Simon with more of a grimace than a smile.

Looking around, it was easy to see the men all believed her crazy, and they resented being pulled away from home for what seemed to be her whim. But Madeline didn't care. She hadn't lied when she said she would go alone. She sat in silence and ate before wrapping herself in Fingal's plaid and closing her eyes. She wanted to groan when Edward sat down beside her.

"Lass, I ken ye dinna want to talk, so please listen." Edward waited until she opened her eyes and nodded. In a hushed voice he explained, "I dinna doubt what ye dreamed. I told ye as much. I will lead the men wherever ye point, but if we arenae alone along the way or when we arrive, ye will listen to ma orders to find safety. Nichol and Simon already ken ye're to go with them. I ken Fingal wouldnae trust anyone else since Tommy and Harry couldnae come."

"Yes, Edward," Madeline whispered.

"Lass, I also need ye to ken it isnae likely that we are rescuing Fingal. It's likely we're recovering his body," Edward warned.

"I didna see if Fingal was alive or nae in ma dream. After this long, with the injuries I'm certain he has, I ken I'm most probably a widow. But I canna leave his body to wither away in unconsecrated ground, Edward. If I find him only to bury him, at least I ken where his spirit will go."

"Vera well. Get what rest ye can. We leave before sunrise," Edward said with a nod.

Madeline smiled for the first time in days. "Dinna make me wake ye if ye oversleep." Her smile faded when she'd finished speaking, but she wanted Edward to know she appreciated what he was doing. She understood he could have dragged her back to the keep and locked her away, just as Harry warned. Instead, he'd ridden up beside her, pointed back over his shoulder, and showed her how to get to the road. It had shocked her to see Edward leading so many of his men. She offered him a tight smile, then resumed her silence.

The same dream returned to Madeline, except she saw a woman standing at the edge of the ravine looking down. She couldn't tell if she was the woman from her own dream or if it was someone else. But her sense of urgency increased when she realized she wasn't the only woman looking for Fingal.

She woke before anyone else, so she moved

silently and began making bannocks before any of the men stirred. She'd made enough for each man to have one—and some to have two—by the time the camp stirred. She realized her face wouldn't crack when she grinned at the men's surprise. Nichol and Simon vouched for their taste. Everyone was a little more at ease by the time they mounted.

Madeline leaned to look around the men who rode in front and beside her. She caught sight of a steep slope ahead on her right. It was the drop-off that a rider would expect before reaching a ravine. She looked back at Nichol, who rode behind her and pointed.

"Are we close to where ye fought? Could that lead into the ravine?" Madeline asked. When Nichol nodded, Madeline pulled on her horse's reins, drawing it to a stop until the man to her right rode past her. She squeezed her knees against her horse's flanks. She'd chosen a horse much larger than she was used to riding, certain it was a warhorse. But she'd been determined to take a mount who could travel long distances, didn't spook easily, and would be her only weapon besides the dirks she carried. She heard Edward and Nichol calling her name, and she looked back to find Simon pursuing her. She steered her horse down the slope and into the ravine.

"How much further to where ye fought?" She called back to Simon.

"Lady Madeline—"

"How far?" She demanded.

"A furlong or two," Simon answered.

Madeline's eyes swept over the ground, into the trees, and up the hill, trying to find any sign of Fingal. Winding through the ravine reminded her of the night she got separated from the men. The night that began this entire nightmare. She tried to conjure the images from her dream, but none were specific enough to tell her exactly where Fingal might lie. Madeline glanced up to see the Grants riding high above her but still keeping pace.

"Fingal!" Madeline called out and waited. When she heard nothing and Simon didn't warn her to be quiet, she yelled louder. "Fingal! Fin!" She made a pattern of saying his name, then waiting for any response. When the hairs on her arms made her skin prickle beneath her sleeves, she slowed her mount. She scanned the surrounding ground on both sides. The light was dim, but she noticed an outcropping of rocks only a few feet ahead of her. She swung her leg over the saddle and slid to the ground. Pulling the reins behind her and hiking her skirts up in one hand, she ran toward the boulders.

"He's here! I found him!" Madeline cried out as she knelt beside Fingal. She brushed away the matted hair and dirt from his face. She leaned over him and pressed her lips to his cheek and whispered. "Fin."

"Ma—" Fingal croaked.

"Edward! He's alive! Hurry!" Madeline looked over Fingal's body, finding more wounds that she imagined any man could sustain and live. She tugged at the neckline of his leine and ripped it down the center. She couldn't believe her eyes when she found he'd packed the gashes along his ribs with yarrow and moss. While they looked infected, he'd kept himself alive by using what he could in nature to tend to his injuries. She looked at his shoulder, which was clearly dislocated, and grimaced. He would be in even more excruciating pain when it was set, but it couldn't wait any longer. "Fingal, can ye still hear me?"

"Maddy?" Fingal rasped.

"Simon, bring me the waterskin," Madeline ordered and reached out her hand. She slid her arm beneath his head, lifting it just enough that he wouldn't choke. She eased the container against his lips, controlling how much water slid into his mouth. When he'd had as much as she dared give him, she poured some over his face and wiped away as much grime as she could. She glanced up when Edward came to stand beside her. "We need the litter to get him out of here. He's burning with fever, and his wounds are infected."

"I canna believe he survived," Edward murmured.

"He willna much longer if his wounds go unattended," Madeline stated.

Once Fingal was on the litter, Madeline looked at the spot where she'd found her husband. She had seen no rocks in her visions, but she'd known to look there. She tilted her head back and looked at the sunlight as it peeked between the trees and cast shadows over the steep embankments. She refused to question how this miracle happened. She was only thankful that it occurred.

Fingal was certain he was dead. He'd thought that he'd died several times over the last few days as he shifted in and out of consciousness. He'd eaten berries that he prayed weren't poisonous, and even forced down a few bugs. He'd used what he could to stop his wounds from bleeding and hoped that the yarrow would slow the inevitable infection.

When he heard Madeline's voice calling to him, then felt the kiss she brushed on his cheek, he was certain he'd died. But he couldn't understand why

Madeline would be in heaven before him. He'd nearly choked when he felt the water hit the back of his throat, and it was the first sign that he was actually being rescued. When Madeline rattled off orders to get him out from the spot where he'd last collapsed, he knew Madeline was truly there.

He made no objections as she fussed over him, only asking for several kisses to prove he was alive. He'd grunted and passed out when Nichol set his shoulder, but he'd listened to Madeline's orders that he drink the willow bark tea she brewed. He'd howled when she poured whisky over his wounds. Had men not restrained him, he feared he would have injured Madeline in the process. She added a healthy portion of whisky to his next mug of willow bark, and he faded back into unconsciousness. When he woke, his skin felt tight along his ribs. Madeline's hands swatted his away when he reached to feel his stitches.

By the time night fell, nearly ten hours after Madeline found him, he felt strong enough to hold her hand. He squeezed hers as she laid beside him and told him about her dream. He'd tried to grin when she told him about yelling at Harry, but this made him wince with pain. The swelling around his eyes that he'd suffered the day of the battle had already gone down, so he was able to see Madeline's panic when he sucked in a hissing breath.

"Maddy," Fingal whispered. "Dinna fash."

"Ye're a bampot if ye think I'm nae going to worry. Ye're far worse than I was, and ye nearly worried yerself into an early grave. Dinna tell me what to do, Fingal Grant. I shall fuss over ye as much as I want," Madeline scolded, but there was no bite to her tone. She settled beside him, covering them with the plaid she'd brought with her. "Fingal, I love ye. Dinna ever scare me like this again."

"I didna mean to, wee one," Fingal's mouth twitched in a smile as he tried to lift his hand to tuck hair behind her ear. "Ye are the bonniest lass I have ever seen."

"Even in yer state, ye can tell tales," Madeline leaned forward and kissed the corner of his mouth. He took her by surprise when he turned his head and brought their mouths together. She attempted to keep the kiss light, but Fingal found the strength to cup the back of her head and deepen it. "Fin, ye are going to do yerself a mischief if ye dinna rest."

"I've been resting for the past five days," Fingal huffed then tried to wink. It appeared more like a wince, but Madeline recognized his smile. It was the one that made her melt, the one that made her want to climb into bed. He tried to reach for her cheek, but his hand brushed her chest. "Ma cross?"

"What?" Madeline asked in confusion as she pulled out the cross he'd given her.

"Ye're wearing the cross I made for ye," Fingal explained.

"Ye made it? I havenae taken it off since ye gave it to me," Madeline confessed before bringing it to her lips.

"Ye ken, wee one, ye may have a face like an angel, but ye have a body made for sin."

"Och, the whisky is working," Madeline chided. It surprised her that Fingal's drunken words didn't evoke any reaction but a laugh. No fear, guilt, or shame assailed her. She even felt brazen enough to lean over him, her breasts brushing his chest, as she whispered. "Ye better nae delay yer recovery by being foolish. I wish to do more than sleep when we return to our bed."

"Maddy," Fingal spluttered as his eyes shot open.

"Aye, Fin?" Madeline said with false innocence.

"Come closer, lass, while I tell ye just what I plan

to do when I'm healed." Fingal attempted another wink as Madeline lay down beside him. Despite his injuries and still fearing for his life, it was the first time Madeline slept through the night since before Fingal left for Braemar.

CHAPTER FIFTY

Traveling back with Fingal was slow going. Madeline insisted upon walking beside his litter until Fingal became so overwrought when he noticed her exhaustion that Simon and Nichol fastened the litter between their horses, and Madeline rode behind them to monitor Fingal. The trip to Freuchie Castle, normally a day and a half, took nearly three. Harry and Tommy awaited them as their horses stopped. Harry's stunned expression turned to horror before Madeline's eyes. As Nichol and Simon lifted down Fingal's litter, Madeline reassured Harry that her anger had evaporated the moment she found Fingal. She didn't blame him for anything, and apologized several times for being so thoughtless about his injuries.

Madeline greeted Davina with a tight hug before they made their way to Fingal and Madeline's chamber. Davina helped Madeline give Fingal a sponge bath, much to his displeasure. He'd insisted Davina leave before he agreed to Madeline unwrapping his plaid. While the rest of his body was weak and ailing, his cock wasn't. He gave Madeline a pointed look when she gasped, shocked to see Fingal's response to her leaning across him to wash his arm. He'd stealthily pinched Madeline's nipple as she worked. He went so far as to suggest there was only one way to truly ease his suffering. Madeline crossed her arms and pursed her lips before telling him that she could think of three ways, and she wouldn't do any of them until she was certain it wouldn't kill him.

Despite his good humor when he arrived home, fever overtook Fingal his first night back at Freuchie. Madeline sat beside him for more than a fortnight as he fought back from the brink of death over and over. She bathed him, fed him what she could, sang to him, and prayed over him. She didn't leave his side and nearly came to blows with Harry again when he suggested she try to get some sleep in her old chamber.

Fingal woke with clear vision and an appetite on the sixteenth day after their arrival at the castle. He discovered much of his strength had returned while he slept. Madeline squealed when he pulled her against his good side as she tried to rise from the bed. While he wasn't well enough to do much more than kiss Madeline and run his hand over her body, he promised he'd make it up to her tenfold for causing her to fear she was a widow.

It was nearly a moon before he was well enough to leave their bed to do more than bathe and use the chamber pot. He was cantankerous with everyone except for Madeline, who he listened to like a docile lamb rather than the roaring bull he was with everyone else. Most members of the clan didn't believe at first that Fingal would ever take orders from a woman. But word spread throughout the clan that Madeline wasn't to be underestimated, and it soon became known that the couple was completely devoted to one another.

During his fevers, he'd deliriously muttered about the battle. Madeline pieced together enough to tell Edward what she believed happened. It stunned her into silence when she heard of Lady Bevan's involvement. She couldn't think of the woman as Lady Farquharson. In Madeline's mind, she would always be a former rival at court. The two hadn't gotten along. The former courtier had always gloated when she bedded men Madeline flirted with. But Madeline had delighted in reminding the widow that any worthwhile prospect thought Gwendolyn was too old to remarry and that she'd likely die an old hag at court.

When Fingal remained conscious long enough to tell her in full detail what he'd learned before he killed Dougal, Madeline was livid. She prayed the rosary thrice that night to atone for the curses that spewed from her mouth when she learned the extent of Gwendolyn's involvement.

"Do ye think she kenned I was one of the women Finneas and Dougal caught?" Madeline asked.

"I imagine so. If nae before they left ye for dead, then certainly after," Fingal answered as Madeline settled back against the headboard beside him. She nestled closer as his arm wrapped around her. She closed her eyes and inhaled the fresh scent from the bath they'd just shared. She hadn't intended to get into the tub with Fingal, but he'd pulled her in. She had abandoned trying to escape and tossed her soggy chemise over the side.

"But Dougal and Finneas referred to a 'him' more than once. Could there be someone else?" Madeline wondered aloud.

"I suppose that's a possibility. But mayhap they said that to make it less conspicuous. If they said 'her,' it would have made people suspicious. People would have guessed there were only two women in positions to be involved and have influence. It was clear Lady Farquharson wasn't the one, so that would have only left Lady Bevan," Fingal reasoned.

Madeline lifted the discarded sheaf of parchment that sat in her lap. She and Fingal looked at the missive from King Robert that prompted their conversation. "I canna believe he's letting that witch remain with Clan Chattan," Madeline said with disgust.

"She's nae staying there permanently," Fingal reminded her, but Madeline snorted.

"If ye think she's going to agree to return to Wales, then ye're as daft as the king," Madeline said with a roll of her eyes.

Lady Bevan had been raised in Wales, where her father was an emissary for John Balliol, and her husband had been an emissary from one of the Welsh princes. When he died, Lady Bevan manipulated her way into staying at court. Both Gwendolyn's parents were members of Clan Hay; her mother's family lived along the border with England, while her father was a Hay from the eastern coast.

"She isnae going to her mother *or* her father's people. She will worm her way into some mon's bed, likely Laird Chattan, and find a way to stay. Ye must be daft if ye think she's going to ignore the chance to be that laird's leman when he leads a confederation of six clans. She'll consider it an improvement," Madeline snorted.

"King Robert willna stand for it," Fingal disagreed, but Madeline rolled her eyes again.

"Of course he will. Queen Elizabeth willna let the woman through the gates after Lady Bevan tried to seduce the king. She likely would have succeeded if Queen Elizabeth hadnae overheard. The queen would put her to death before the king does."

"Then we should pray she mucks it up," Fingal

sighed. "I dinna care to speak aboot her when I have ma bonnie wife in ma arms again, and I'm nay longer an invalid." Fingal waggled his brow at Madeline, who giggled and pulled loose the tie that kept her robe closed. As Madeline wrapped her hand around his length, Fingal eased a finger into Madeline's sheath. Starved for one another's touch, their kisses were passionate from the moment their lips touched. Madeline's legs dropped open as Fingal's questing fingers elicited a moan. His thumb rubbed her hidden pearl until her hips rocked with his hands.

"Fin," Madeline panted.

"I intend to bring ye pleasure all night, *mo chridhe*," Fingal pledged. They'd taken to using terms of endearment, and listening to Fingal call her "my heart" set Madeline aflame. "I shall use ma hands, ma tongue, and ma cock."

Madeline did nothing to resist as she felt her body straining for the pleasure only Fingal brought her. When the waves of her release finished coursing through her, her need to show Fingal that she desired him just as much had her scrambling onto her knees. Holding back her hair for her, Fingal watched as his wife's mouth sank down over his rod. It was a mixture of agony and ecstasy.

"Maddy, I canna hold on much longer. This isnae how I want to finish," Fingal said as he pulled Madeline away. She straddled Fingal's hips, knowing that while he was well enough to make love, it would be more enjoyable for them both in this position. Her sheath welcomed his sword to where they both wished it could always remain. They moved together as though they'd been partners for years.

While neither could explain how they'd fallen in love so quickly, considering all that had stood between them, they found they shared a deep understanding of one another. They watched each other, deriving as much pleasure from touching as being touched. As their names echoed in their chamber, Madeline sagged against Fingal with a contented sigh. Fingal kissed her shoulder and along her neck.

When they lay beside one another, slowly catching their breath, Madeline smiled as she looked at the ceiling. She imagined she could see all the way to the stars and into the heavens. She rolled onto her side and placed her hand over Fingal's heart. When he turned to look at her, her heart melted. She stretched and feathered a kiss across Fingal's lips.

"Fingal?" Madeline asked.

"Hmm," Fingal mumbled as his hand trailed along Madeline's back.

"Are ye usually a deep sleeper?"

Fingal looked at his wife in confusion. "Nay. Never."

"Then I hope ye dinna mind if the crying wakes ye a few times a night," Madeline smiled.

"Cry—" Fingal blinked as his face broke into a grin that made Madeline catch her breath. "A bairn?"

"Aye. Sleeping with ye—" Madeline grinned impishly. "Is far too pleasurable to give up. Besides, I like this chamber too much to go to another."

"Wife, ye may never leave this chamber or this bed again," Fingal growled as he rolled Madeline onto her back.

"Are ye happy then? Ye willna mind sharing a bed with ma belly or even a bairn?"

"Happy is far too mild a word, Madeline. I love ye, and I will share this bed with ye until ma last breath," Fingal whispered reverently.

"Fingal, I love ye. I dinna ever want to go back to how things started. I ken now there is nay sin in loving ma husband. I expect us to be auld with white hair long before either of us takes that last breath,"

Madeline said as she cupped Fingal's jaw and kissed him. As they settled next to each other, arms wrapped around one another, Madeline felt like her sins had been washed away, just as the prioress had once told her. In their place was an abiding love for her husband and the family they would share.

EPILOGUE

"Mama! Mama!" Madeline looked down at her five-year-old daughter Adeline tugging at her skirts. Three-year-old Sarah stood beside her, sucking her thumb. "Tell Da to leave ye alone. Ye said we would make flower crowns on our walk today."

Madeline dug an elbow into Fingal's ribs as he laughed. She fought more successfully to smother her own giggles. She whispered in Fingal's ear. "This shall have to wait until this eve. I promised Adeline and Sarah that I would take them for a walk."

"And Da, ye promised to show me how to run a dragon through with ma sword," Magnus insisted. Fingal grinned at Madeline before nodding at their seven-year-old son. He eased Madeline to the ground before running his hand over her swollen belly.

"Magnus, I shall teach ye just the trick. But ye must also learn how to be a guard who protects our clan," Fingal infused seriousness into his tone as he looked into the bright blue eyes of his tawny-haired son. Their children had all inherited his hair and Madeline's eyes.

"Does that mean we have to go flower picking

with Mama and them again?" Magnus asked in disgust.

"'Them' are yer sisters. They are younger than ye and canna protect themselves yet. As a Grant guard, it's yer duty to protect all who belong to this clan, especially those who are most likely to be hurt. If ye canna do that for yer sisters, then mayhap I gave ye that wooden sword too soon. It's nae a toy, Magnus. With it comes ma trust, along with duty and responsibility."

"Aye, Da."

Madeline thinned her lips as she fought not to grin. The hero worship in her son's eyes for Fingal warmed her heart. Fingal wrapped his arm around Madeline's waist as he scooped Sarah into his arms. Her soggy thumb brushed his neck as she wrapped her arms around him and rested her head on his shoulder. Madeline and Fingal walked behind Magnus and Adeline. They exchanged a glance as Magnus took his younger sister's hand in one of his, while his other hand held up his sword in a defensive position.

They made their way out to the meadow where Madeline and Fingal played with their children as Harry, Tommy, Simon, and Nichol stood watch. Madeline cast her gaze over her husband and children as she rubbed the spot where their bairn kicked. Each time they ventured out for an afternoon such as this, Madeline remembered the dream that foretold her of the happiness and love she and Fingal would share.

There had been trials and struggles over the past eight years, but none that diminished Fingal and Madeline's love for one another. Blizzards that caused food shortages, battles that called Fingal and Edward away, and illnesses that threatened Davina and Madeline as they tended to the ill did nothing to break their trust and faith in one another. They learned to rely on one another implicitly, and it served them well during a harrowing journey to Stirling Castle while Madeline carried Adeline. Summoned to give testimony against Lady Bevan-Farquharson for her role in not one, but two, slave auction rings, Fingal stood beside Madeline as she recounted her experiences for the first time to anyone other than Fingal and the men who'd escorted her to Freuchie Castle.

Fingal came to stand behind Madeline and wrapped his arms around her belly. She rested her hands over his as he nuzzled her neck. They stood and watched their children playing, their oldest and youngest named for Fingal's parents while Adeline was named for Madeline's mother.

"Do ye still think this one is a lass?" Fingal murmured between kisses.

"If how active Adeline and Sarah were is any indication, then it's definitely another daughter," Madeline smiled. Fingal loved all his children, and was as happy to have daughters as he was to have a son.

"Have ye thought of a name?" Fingal asked.

"Ceana," Madeline stated. "That was the Mother Abbess's name before she became a nun. If it hadnae been for her and her wisdom, we wouldnae be standing here talking aboot names." They'd received news two years after they married that the prioress passed away in her sleep. Fingal traveled with Madeline to Inchcailleoch at his suggestion, so that Madeline could attend the funeral.

"Tis a sweet name for a lass," Fingal said as he turned Madeline in his arms. "Do ye ken how much I love ye, wee one?"

"Mayhap nearly as much as I love ye," Madeline said before going onto her toes to kiss Fingal.

"Ew!" Three little voices exclaimed.

"Mama, I thought ye were going to tell Da to stop kissing ye," Adeline declared. Fingal and Madeline smiled, but didn't break their kiss until three sets of little arms wrapped around them. They rested their heads together as they basked in a love neither thought they needed.

THANK YOU FOR READING A SINNER AT THE HIGHLAND COURT

Celeste Barclay, a nom de plume, lives near the Southern California coast with her husband and sons. Growing up in the Midwest, Celeste enjoyed spending as much time in and on the water as she could. Now she lives near the beach. She's an avid swimmer, a hopeful future surfer, and a former rower. When she's not writing, she's enjoying the California sunshine with her family.

Visit Celeste's website, www.celestebarclay.com, for regular updates on works in progress, new releases, and her blog where she features posts about her experiences as an author and recommendations of her favorite reads.

Have you read *Their Highland Beginning, The Clan Sinclair Prequel?* Learn how the saga begins! This **FREE** novella is available to all new subscribers to Celeste's monthly newsletter. Subscribe on her website.

THE HIGHLAND LADIES

A Spinster at the Highland Court
BOOK 1 SNEAK PEEK

Elizabeth Fraser looked around the royal chapel within Stirling Castle. The ornate candlestick holders on the altar glistened and reflected the light from the ones in the wall sconces as the priest intoned the holy prayers of the Advent season. Elizabeth kept her head bowed as though in prayer, but her green eyes swept the congregation. She watched the other ladies-in-waiting, many of whom were doing the same thing. She caught the eye of Allyson Elliott. Elizabeth raised one eyebrow as Allyson's lips twitched. Both women had been there enough times to accept they'd be kneeling for at least the next hour as the Latin service carried on. Elizabeth understood the Mass thanks to her cousin Deirdre Fraser, or rather now Deirdre Sinclair. Elizabeth's mind flashed to the recent struggle her cousin faced as she reunited with her husband Magnus after a seven-year separation. Her aunt and uncle's choice to keep Deirdre hidden from her husband simply because they didn't think the Sinclairs were an advantageous enough match, and the resulting scandal, still humiliated the other Fraser clan members at court. She admired Deirdre's husband Magnus's pledge to remain faithful despite not knowing if he'd ever see Deirdre again.

Elizabeth suddenly snapped her attention; while everyone else intoned the twelfth—or was it thirteenth—amen of the Mass, the hairs on the back of her neck stood up. She had the strongest feeling that someone was watching her. Her eyes scanned to her right, where her parents sat further down the pew. Her mother and father had their heads bowed and eyes closed. While she was convinced her mother was in devout prayer, she wondered if her father had fallen asleep during the Mass. Again. With nothing seeming out of the ordinary and no one visibly paying attention to her, her eyes swung to the left. She took in the king and queen as they kneeled together at their prie-dieu. The queen's lips moved as she recited the liturgy in silence. The king was as still as a statue. Years of leading warriors showed, both in his stature and his ability to control his body into absolute stillness. Elizabeth peered past the royal couple and found herself looking into the astute hazel eyes of Edward Bruce, Lord of Badenoch and Lochaber. His gaze gave her the sense that he peered into her thoughts, as though he were assessing her. She tried to keep her face neutral as heat surged up her neck. She prayed her face didn't redden as much as her neck must have, but at a twenty-one, she still hadn't mastered how to control her blushing. Her nape burned like it was on fire. She canted her head slightly before looking up at the crucifix hanging over the altar. She closed her eyes and tried to invoke the image of the Lord that usually centered her when her mind wandered during Mass.

Elizabeth sensed Edward's gaze remained on her. She didn't understand how she was so sure that he was looking at her. She didn't have any special gifts of perception or sight, but her intuition screamed that he was still looking.

THE CLAN SINCLAIR

His Highland Lass **BOOK 1 SNEAK PEEK**

She entered the great hall like a strong spring storm in the northern most Highlands. Tristan Mackay felt like he had been blown hither and yon. As the storm settled, she left him with the sweet scents of heather and lavender wafting towards him as she approached. She was not a classic beauty, tall and willowy like the women at court. Her face and form were not what legends were made of. But she held a unique appeal unlike any he had seen before. He could not take his eyes off of her long chestnut hair that had strands of fire and burnt copper running through them. Unlike the waves or curls he was used to, her hair was unusually straight and fine. It looked like a waterfall cascading down her back. While she was not tall, neither was she short. She had a figure that was meant for a man to grasp and hold onto, whether from the front or from behind. She had an aura of confidence and charm, but not arrogance or conceit like many good looking women he had met. She did not seem to know her own appeal. He could tell that she was many things, but one thing she was not was his.

His Bonnie Highland Temptation **BOOK 2**
His Highland Prize **BOOK 3**
His Highland Pledge **BOOK 4**
His Highland Surprise **BOOK 5**
Their Highland Beginning **BOOK 6**

PIRATES OF THE ISLES

The Blond Devil of the Sea **BOOK 1 SNEAK PEEK**

Caragh lifted her torch into the air as she made her way down the precarious Cornish cliffside. She made out the hulking shape of a ship, but the dead of night made it impossible to see who was there. She and the fishermen of Bedruthan Steps weren't expecting any shipments that night. But her younger brother Eddie, who stood watch at the entrance to their hiding place, had spotted the ship and signaled up to the village watchman, who alerted Caragh.

As her boot slid along the dirt and sand, she cursed having to carry the torch and wished she could have sunlight to guide her. She knew these cliffs well, and it was for that reason it was better that she moved slowly than stop moving once and for all. Caragh feared the light from her torch would carry out to the boat. Despite her efforts to keep the flame small, the solitary light would be a beacon.

When Caragh came to the final twist in the path before the sand, she snuffed out her torch and started to run to the cave where the main source of the village's income lay in hiding. She heard movement along the trail above her head and knew the local fishermen would soon join her on the beach. These men, both young and old, were strong from days spent pulling in the full trawling nets and hoisting the larger catches onto their boats. However, these men weren't well-trained swordsmen, and the fear of pirate raids was ever-present. Caragh feared that was who the villagers would face that night.

The Dark Heart of the Sea **BOOK 2**
The Red Drifter of the Sea **BOOK3**
The Scarlet Blade of the Sea **BOOK 4**

VIKING GLORY

Leif **BOOK 1 SNEAK PEEK**

Leif looked around his chambers within his father's longhouse and breathed a sigh of relief. He noticed the large fur rugs spread throughout the chamber. His two favorites placed strategically before the fire and the bedside he preferred. He looked at his shield that hung on the wall near the door in a symbolic position but waiting at the ready. The chests that held his clothes and some of his finer acquisitions from voyages near and far sat beside his bed and along the far wall. And in the center was his most favorite possession. His oversized bed was one of the few that could accommodate his long and broad frame. He shook his head at his longing to climb under the pile of furs and on the stuffed mattress that beckoned him. He took in the chair placed before the fire where he longed to sit now with a cup of warm mead. It had been two months since he slept in his own bed, and he looked forward to nothing more than pulling the furs over his head and sleeping until he could no longer ignore his hunger. Alas, he would not be crawling into his bed again for several more hours. A feast awaited him to celebrate his and his crew's return from their latest expedition to explore the isle of Britannia. He bathed and wore fresh clothes, so he had no excuse for lingering other than a bone weariness that set in during the last storm at sea. He was eager to spend time at home no matter how much he loved sailing. Their last expedition had been profitable with several raids of monasteries that yielded jewels and both silver and gold, but he was ready for respite.

Leif left his chambers and knocked on the door next to his. He heard movement on the other side, but it was only moments before his sister, Freya, opened her door. She, too, looked tired but clean. A few pieces of jewelry she confiscated from the holy houses that allegedly swore to a life of poverty and deprivation adorned her trim frame.

"That armband suits you well. It compliments your muscles," Leif smirked and dodged a strike from one of those muscular arms.

Only a year younger than he, his sister was a well-known and feared shield maiden. Her lithe form was strong and agile making her a ferocious and competent opponent to any man. Freya's beauty was stunning, but Leif had taken every opportunity since they were children to tease her about her unusual strength even among the female warriors.

"At least one of us inherited our father's prowess. Such a shame it wasn't you."